"The Nauti series is one that absolutely no one should miss. The characters are brilliant, sexy, and real, while the high-octane action and soul-gripping plots have you on the edge of your seat. I loved it!"
                                                                                          —*Fresh Fiction*

"Steamy, smoking, hot, erotic, risqué. Romantic . . . Intriguing and hard [to] put down."
                                                                            —*Night Owl Reviews*

"Completely blown away by this surprising story, I could not put [it] down . . . and before I knew it, I had read this entire novel in one sitting. Lora Leigh has spun a smoldering-hot tale of secret passion and erotic deceptions."
                                                                            —*Romance Junkies*

"Wild and thrilling."
                                                                            —*The Romance Studio*

"The sex scenes are, as always with Leigh's books, absolutely sizzling."
                                                                            —*Errant Dreams Reviews*

"Heated romantic suspense."
                                                                            —*Midwest Book Review*

continued...

More praise for

Lora Leigh

and her novels

"Leigh draws readers into her stories and takes them on a sensual roller coaster."   —*Love Romances & More*

"Will have you glued to the edge of your seat."
—*Fallen Angel Reviews*

"Blistering sexuality and eroticism . . . Bursting with passion and drama . . . Enthralls and excites from beginning to end."
—*Romance Reviews Today*

"A scorcher with sex scenes that blister the pages."
—*A Romance Review*

"A perfect blend of sexual tension and suspense."
—*Sensual Romance Reviews*

"Hot sex, snappy dialogue, and kick-butt action add up to outstanding entertainment."   —*RT Book Reviews* (Top Pick)

"The writing of Lora Leigh continues to amaze me . . . Electrically charged, erotic, and just a sinfully good read!"
—*Joyfully Reviewed*

"Wow! . . . The lovemaking is scorching."
—*Just Erotic Romance Reviews*

Nauti

Enchantress

Lora Leigh

OKS, NEW YORK

THE BERKLEY PUBLISHING GROUP
Published by the Penguin Group
Penguin Group (USA) LLC
375 Hudson Street, New York, New York 10014

USA • Canada • UK • Ireland • Australia • New Zealand • India • South Africa • China

penguin.com

A Penguin Random House Company

This book is an original publication of The Berkley Publishing Group.

Library of Congress Cataloging-in-Publication Data

Leigh, Lora.
Nauti enchantress / Lora Leigh.—Berkley trade paperback edition.
      pages   cm
ISBN 978-0-425-25599-5
I. Title.
PS3612.E357N3845   2014
813'.6—dc23   2014008223

PUBLISHING HISTORY
Berkley trade paperback edition / June 2014

PRINTED IN THE UNITED STATES OF AMERICA

10   9   8   7   6   5   4   3   2   1

Cover photo by Radius/Superstock.
Cover design by Lesley Worrell.

For Sharon

I reached out to you and your fingers touched mine.
Lightning raced through me, static filled my veins.
My woman's soul cried out in joy . . .
Then betrayal sang her venomous song.
And I learned your touch wasn't mine alone.
Your kiss wasn't drawn from the depths of a hunger that
*   only a true heart can feel.*
Your passion, your need, your desperate desire, and your
*   pleasure . . . It wasn't mine to claim.*
It was for whoever lay beneath you.
It was for whoever drew your interest in that moment.
And there my heart lay bleeding . . .
There my soul lay wounded . . .
And still, the lesson was unlearned.
For my heart still sang at the sight of you.
For my soul still ached for the touch of you.
And the woman . . .
The woman is still lost in the dream of you.

LYRICA MACKAY

ONE

The blizzard raged.

A curtain of heavy white fluff poured from the skies, blanketing the ground and laying an enchanting veil of wonder over the land. The heavy, wet snow was thicker than it had been when Lyrica arrived at Kyleene Brock's house. Now, the silent icy flakes were twirling and dancing in the heavy winds, creating a wondrous ballet of nature at its most beautiful.

And at its most dangerous.

Lying on the couch, her head propped against the thick pillowed armrest, she ignored the fact that the black chiffon and embroidered silk gown fell back to her thighs and that her robe had worked open from the loose knot she'd tied it closed with.

Kye's brother, Graham, wasn't here, she reminded herself. That was how she'd ended up stuck here with Kye after they had realized how heavy the snow was falling. Her friend hated staying alone. The house was too big and too lonely when it was just her.

Kye had acted as though something was bothering her, too, something she may have wanted to talk about. Not that she'd gotten around to talking about it. The minute the electricity had gone out and the other girl had realized they were stuck there for the night, she'd become almost angry, or worried about something. Something she had refused to discuss.

Pushing aside the thought, Lyrica concentrated on the scene outside instead.

The winds howled and swirled through the naked branches of the trees, whipping the thick flakes into masses of heavy drifts. The sight of it was magnificent, majestic. Mother Nature was throwing a glittering, pure white cape over the land outside and she was doing it with style.

Had Lyrica been at her mother's inn, or the small apartment she rented in Somerset, the show wouldn't have been quite so beautiful.

So romantic.

It was a night meant to be shared with someone other than a friend. A night to be sheltered in strong arms rather than reclining alone before the fire.

Lifting one arm over her head, she pulled at the waves of her hair absently, twirling them around her finger, tugging at them as she watched the snow fall and felt the bittersweet regret she felt each time she came to the Brock home.

When she'd heard Graham had returned the summer before, she'd been certain she would have a chance to . . . what? A chance at his heart? A chance to be held in his arms, to feel his kiss?

A chance to be his next flavor of the month?

No doubt, that was all she would have had a chance at. And despite the fact that she knew it, still he held her spellbound. No matter how hard she looked, no other man measured up to him, and no other man—or woman—could steal her attention from him.

She missed him.

He seemed to be absent from home more often than not in the past months. His current little love bunny, damned if she could even remember this one's name, lived just outside Louisville. Graham drove out to see her often enough that Kye had begun worrying if Graham was more serious about her than he let on.

Lyrica did more than worry.

She often tormented herself with the fear that he was falling in love with the cool, sophisticated blonde.

She hated him for the very fact that this woman had lasted longer than the others.

She often hated him for the fascination she didn't want to have for him.

A man hadn't played into her plans for the future until she'd met Graham Brock. Until she'd stared into his golden brown eyes, like dark amber, and become trapped within a world of fantasy, hunger, and need that she had yet to escape from.

What would she do if he married the other woman?

Could she bear to see him marry?

It would break her heart.

The sound of the living room doors opening once again pulled her from her thoughts as a drowsy smile curved her lips.

"You know, Kye," she commented as she heard the doors close again before several steps were taken into the room, "maybe we should have just called the guys and told them we were scared here alone after all. I bet they would have been right here on those snowmobiles and then we could have just gone to the apartment."

Her brother and cousins had made the offer to come out for her hours before, and she knew they would have enjoyed the chance to use the snowmobiles they rarely got to ride anymore.

"That really wouldn't have worked for me."

Eyes wide, her heart suddenly racing in her chest, Lyrica found herself staring into Graham Brock's dark amber gaze as he stood behind the couch.

He had savage features with a thin, deadly looking scar bisecting his cheek and running into the closely cropped beard he wore. His brows were lowered, a scowl pulling at his expression as he glared at her.

She should have been embarrassed. She was lying there with her gown nearly showing the fact that she wore no panties beneath it; her robe gaped open; and instead of hurrying to cover herself, she just grinned up at him.

"Still the overprotective big brother with Kye?" she asked, her heart suddenly racing in excitement as she felt her thighs tighten at the ache centered between them. Sometimes she just hated her body's response to him.

"Something like that," the answer came as his gaze drifted down her body before jerking back to her eyes. Have mercy. He was staring at her the way Dawg stared at his wife, Christa.

"Little sister can't stay a virgin forever." She winked up at him. "At least, that's what I keep telling my big brother."

The look in his eyes and the expression on his face had heat suddenly flooding her body. Graham rarely looked at her with the full strength of that dark hunger that lurked in his gaze. Sometimes she caught a glimmer of it, but never had she felt the full force of all that sensual, erotic hunger.

She was feeling the full force of it now.

She licked her lips nervously, stilling as his jaw tightened and his fingers gripped the back of the couch as though to keep himself from reaching out for her.

Did she really want to be his flavor of the month?

Was there a chance she could be something more?

"What the hell are you doing here?" Moving around the couch, he strode to the fire to grab the poker and prod the burning wood viciously before grabbing more logs and tossing them to the flames.

Freed from the sensual spell that his look had wrapped around her, Lyrica moved slowly into a sitting position that ensured her gown fell down her thighs a bit and pulled the robe tighter around her.

Propping her elbow on her knee, she rested her chin on her palm and watched him.

He wasn't wearing a shirt, leaving his upper body bare. The firelight reflected off the bronzed flesh and rippling muscles beneath. He looked like a warrior, a noble savage just in from the battlefield.

The light dusting of chest hair hid the fine, spiderwebbed scarring she knew his chest held from the wounds that had sent him home the year before on a medical discharge. Though, Kye seemed to think there was more involved than just those wounds.

Snug jeans cupped a manly, sexy-as-hell ass and emphasized the hard, flat planes of his abdomen while . . . Oh, sweet mercy—

He turned to face her fully.

Those jeans did nothing to hide the heavy erection beneath as the broad shaft pressed demandingly against the denim. It rose high enough beneath the material that she wondered if she could catch a glimpse of it if he moved just right, beneath the low rise of his jeans.

Her mouth dried out, then watered quickly at the thought. Flicking her tongue over her lips to moisten them as she swallowed tightly, her gaze was suddenly caught by his again. And what she saw there had her heart threatening to strangle her it was beating so hard.

"You shouldn't be here," he growled.

"You weren't supposed to be here," she retorted breathlessly as he stood by the fire, watching her with narrowed, hungry eyes. "I didn't hear you drive in."

And she would have heard him. As heavy and deep as the snow was outside, there was no way he could have slipped in.

"I never left," he informed her, scowling. "Only a moron would have ventured out today knowing this was coming."

"Well now, doesn't that put me in my place?" she murmured, amused at the veiled insult, though she held back the fact that Kye had sworn he was gone.

His lips thinned at the comment, the dark amber of his eyes gleaming harshly between narrowed lashes.

"I'll get the snowmobile out and take you to Dawg's." He all but demanded she leave with that offer. "His place isn't far from here."

She wasn't about to go anywhere unless he physically dragged her out of the house. Not now. Not with this tension whipping through the air and the sudden, heated certainty that she had no intention of ignoring whatever it was that flared between them so often.

Lyrica Mackay as Graham Brock's new flavor of the month? Her brother, Dawg, would have a stroke when he heard that one.

"If I wanted to get out in the snow, Graham, I would have let Dawg do just that earlier. It's beautiful to watch, but I'm really not into being out in it," she informed him archly. Her gaze drifted to his bare chest again, loving the way the firelight played against the mat of hair at his chest. It looked like burnished gold, warm and inviting.

She was pathetic.

She was hopeless.

No doubt he and his latest little love bunny laughed often over the silly little Mackay and her crush on him. It was nauseating. No matter the insults she flung at herself, she couldn't keep her gaze from him, couldn't stop wanting him.

He was her fascination. Her weakness. She couldn't help it, no matter how hard she tried.

"I can't believe Dawg didn't head out here anyway," he growled, muscular arms crossing over his broad chest as he continued to glare at her.

"He might have, if he had known you were home," Lyrica pointed out with a grin. "I believe he may be under the impression that you're not exactly in residence."

His eyes widened briefly before his scowl turned to a glare so fast that she almost missed the transformation. "You're trying to get me killed," he muttered.

She would have laughed, but she couldn't get the sound past the racing beat of her heart or the breathless need tearing through her.

She hated what he did to her. Hated how he made her realize things about herself that she hated realizing. Things such as the fact that she was ready to beg him to touch her.

"Well, if Dawg killed you, Graham, then Kye wouldn't have to worry about any more of your little snuggle bunnies running around the house at all hours," she pointed out innocently, though the thought of it had the power to make her burn with jealous anger. "I think she lives in fear of seeing any more of your naked lovers traipsing down the hallway. She's convinced she's been traumatized, you know."

Several months before, she and Kye both had watched in amazement as his lover had stepped into the kitchen completely naked, then opened the fridge and gathered a variety of fruits and cheeses, along with a bottle of wine, before moving upstairs once again.

For the briefest second, amazement transformed his features.

"Kye lives in fear of it, or you do?" he growled, his voice deepening, turning darker.

A flush raced over her face. She could feel the heat of it, the anger spurring it, and narrowed her eyes back at him in response.

"I just hope you use protection. It would be a shame if that fine body of yours started wasting away from some bug you'd picked up and couldn't get rid of." She mocked his response lightly. "There's little enough eye candy in this county as it is. Losing some of it would be a crime."

"Viper," he muttered.

"Prick," she countered, a brow arching with a satirical grin. "Really, Graham. You're pretty to look at and all, but I'm sure your attitude would spoil the view eventually."

His arms dropped from his chest and he prowled closer to where she sat on the couch.

Oh, boy.

She had no idea what she'd set loose inside him, but there was no doubt something was free. His eyes glittered with it, his expression hardening as he moved closer.

"That tongue of yours is going to get you in trouble," he warned her.

Suddenly, the daring and curiosity that had filled her moments before deserted her. He wasn't hiding that hunger now. In that moment, he didn't give a damn if she saw the lust raging in his eyes and on his face.

"So Dawg tells me often," she informed him as she moved quickly to her feet. "You should discuss it with him," she suggested. "Tomorrow. Good night, Graham."

Turning, she moved to leave the living room and the hunger that flared so bright, so hot in his eyes . . .

"Like hell."

A hard band wrapped around her waist, pulling her to a hard stop as she was brought against the powerful body behind her in one smoothly executed move.

Oh god.

She hadn't expected this. She hadn't even fantasized about this. Not like this. So dark and dominant that it awoke a knee-weakening submission inside her she had never imagined she possessed.

"Graham." The soft exclamation escaped her lips as he pulled her around and brought her body against his once again, holding her to him as he stared down at her silently.

His gaze burned with lust. Narrowed and intense, it went over her face as she watched him, breathless. Her breasts rose and fell swiftly against his hard chest, her nipples pressing imperatively into the thin silk as though to reach heated flesh.

"You always have that look in your eyes," he muttered, one hand moving to cup her neck as it pushed beneath her hair. "Hungry but innocent."

She fought to breathe as she watched his lips move, not really caring what he was saying. She wanted him to kiss her. Wanted him to give her whatever it took to ease the hunger that clawed at her each time she saw him.

How unfair was it, the way she craved just the sight of him, when it was more than obvious he had no problem staying away from her?

His thumb brushed over her jaw, sending a rush of sensation racing across her flesh.

"Are you going to kiss me, Graham, or just keep spoiling the view with your attitude?" she finally whispered, desperate for that touch, that taste of him.

"Kissing you would be the biggest mistake of my life." He sighed, but he wasn't letting her go.

"Yeah, mine, too." She breathed out, curling one arm up around his neck. "So why not just make it together?"

She lifted to him.

His head lowered.

The second their lips met it was as though the hunger, carefully contained, escaped with a rush, determined to be imprisoned no longer.

His hunger was voracious. Her need was unquenchable.

Graham's lips slanted over hers as he lifted her closer, his tongue pressing between her lips, feeding on her need as he tasted every lush, sensual promise she made in return.

The lash of heat and overwhelming pleasure wasn't expected. In all her fantasies, all her heated explorations of her own body, she had never imagined pleasure like this. Hadn't guessed it could be so hot, so filled with such exquisite pleasure.

Spearing her hands into the overlong hair at the back of his head, Lyrica curled her fingers into the rough silk feel of it to hold him to her. She couldn't bear the thought of stopping. Couldn't imagine ever living without his touch, his kiss, now that she'd had it.

Heat rushed through her system as he nipped at her lower lip, licked it as he lifted her into his arms, a low, muttered groan vibrating in his chest as he lowered her back to the couch. A hard, muscled thigh pushed between hers, spreading her legs as he came over her. At the same time he loosened the knot of her robe, pushing it to the sides of her breasts as he broke the fiery kiss.

Lyrica stared up at him, dazed, drunk on the pleasure racing through her as Graham gripped her hands and lifted them to the armrest above her head, holding them securely with one hand.

"So damned pretty," he muttered, his lips moving to the line of her neck as she tilted her head back to accommodate the caress.

Every muscle in her body tightened at the sensations tearing through her as he licked, kissed, and rasped the slender column of her neck. His teeth raked over it, the sound of his harsh breathing meeting her panting breaths as he released her lips and helped her from the robe. At the same time, the slender straps of her gown were pushed down, her arms sliding from them as the material was removed and tossed aside.

A broken moan of need escaped her lips, though she fought to still it to ensure Kye didn't hear if she came to check on her. It was impossible to hold back as Graham's lips moved to the swollen curves of her breasts.

Pushing the sensitive curves together, he licked, nibbled, his lips kissing as they moved from one tight nipple to the other.

Lyrica fought just to remember how to breathe past the pleasure. She'd never known such heated, electric sensations. Had never known hunger could rise so hot, so fast through her body.

Then his lips covered one tight, beaded nipple, suckling it hungrily into his mouth as his hips moved between her thighs. The hard denim-covered wedge of his erection pressed against bare, slick flesh, ground against it, sending pleasure to mix with diabolical greed at the distended bud of her clit.

Mewls of need fell from her lips as she bit at them to hold back her cries. She couldn't let them escape. She had to hold back. If Kye heard them, she'd never forgive Lyrica. She hated it when her friends became fixated on her brother.

A low, desperate whimper escaped as Graham's hand moved from the curve of her breast to her thigh. His fingers moved up to grip the curve of her hip.

"Oh god, Lyrica," he groaned, the dark rasp of his voice sensual and filled with lust. "You'll be the death of me."

Lyrica trembled, and her eyes opened to watch as he levered his body back to stare down at the bare, glistening flesh of her sex.

Slowly, he spread her thighs farther apart and pushed the knee resting against the back cushions into the upholstery as he lifted her other leg until her calf rested over his shoulder.

"Graham." Her voice shook, hunger and the fear of the unknown, need and uncertainty, rushing through her as he drew his hand along her inner thigh.

"Shh, just for a moment," he crooned, his voice like dark velvet gliding across her senses. "I've dreamed of this, Lyrica. Let me have it, just for a moment."

His head lowered.

Lyrica's eyes widened at the first lick of his tongue across her sensitive flesh. Her hips arched, a moan slipping past her lips, her fingers sliding into his hair to grip the heavy strands.

Fiery, intense pleasure rushed through her system with furious intent, tearing through her, drowning any fear that might have been growing inside her.

There was no fear now. There was pleasure. Exquisite, heated, drugging pleasure she couldn't have resisted even if she wanted to.

He pursed his lips as he kissed the hard bud of her clit, drawing a rapturous flare of sensation from the tender flesh as her hips jerked against his lips.

"Graham. Oh god, Graham."

His tongue licked over, around the swollen bundle of nerves. Pleasure whipped and built through Lyrica as he tasted her, kissed the saturated flesh, then with a greedy tongue delved into the swollen folds to find the aching center of her body.

His tongue flicked over the narrow entrance, spreading heated, electric ecstasy with the quick, hungry licks and shallow penetrations that never seemed enough. With each touch, each taste he took, she needed more. Ached and begged for more.

"Damn you," he groaned, spreading the folds apart with the fingers of one hand to deliver another hungry kiss to her clit.

But this one lingered.

His tongue flicked over her and sensation slashed through her as she drew her hips up to meet his kiss once again.

Each touch, each lick pushed steadily increasing waves of pleasure through her system. She was lost in a blinding sea of sensation and desperate to sink deeper. Desperate for more as she felt the pad of his thumb slide against her entrance, pressing into it, spreading her flesh open as the waves began to tighten, to build.

She was so close.

Clenched, aching, her hips lifted to him, trembling, shuddering with each driving surge of sensation as she gave herself to the storm pounding at her senses.

"Graham, where the hell are you!" Strident and filled with ire, the feminine voice of Graham's current conquest filtered through the living room doors as Lyrica froze, her eyes flashing open to stare at Graham as betrayal tore through her.

Graham's head jerked up, shock and guilt reflecting in his eyes as Lyrica began struggling beneath him, desperate now to be free of him.

"Stay!" he hissed, pushing her back to the couch, leaning over her, one hand over her lips as the door opened.

The couch hid them. The fire had burned down, the weakened flames and glowing embers casting an intimate glow over the room.

"Graham, are you in here?" the irate woman called out again.

Lyrica was dying inside. She could feel the pain tearing through her, the knowledge that he had just left his lover's bed and had dared to touch her. Dared to show her everything she couldn't have—

Her heart was ripping in two. The pain was blinding, agonizing as her eyes remained locked with his.

Let him see. Let him see how it hurt, let him see that he had just destroyed something she now knew that he ached for just as much as she did. Because she would make damned sure he never had a chance to touch her again.

Because another chance would end the same way. With the

knowledge that she was no more than a stolen, forbidden moment. Something he could throw away whenever his latest lover came calling his name again.

"Dammit, I'm getting tired of this," the other woman muttered angrily, fury vibrating in each word.

A second later, the door snapped shut again.

Lyrica didn't take her eyes off his. Pain washed through her in waves, making her breathing choppy, the fight to hold back her tears iffy.

"I'm sorry," he whispered, his thumb lifting to brush back an escaping tear. "This wasn't supposed to happen."

His hand lifted from her lips.

"Get off me!" She kept her voice low, quiet, despite the need to scream, to rage.

She struggled against him again, pushing at his shoulders, ragged gasps tearing from her throat as she fought to be free of him.

"Lyrica, wait," he growled.

"Get off me before I start screaming," she demanded, her voice rough, low.

She didn't want his skanky little bunny to know about what he'd just done any more than he did.

"We need to talk—"

"Fuck you!" she cried out furiously. Her voice was still low, still quiet, but the rage tearing through her was only rising. "Get off me, Graham, or I swear to god, you'll regret it. I promise you . . ." Kicking, pushing, she fought to be free of him.

She had to be free of him.

Oh god, she hated him. She hated what he was doing to her, hated what he was making her feel. She hated this pain. Hated the need still tearing through her body, the inner anger and hunger to stay right where she was.

Suddenly, she was free.

Graham jumped from her, pushing his fingers through his hair as a brutal curse hissed from his lips.

"Stay here, dammit," he snarled, catching her before she could leave the room.

"Why? So she won't see me and fuck your little party up?" she demanded harshly.

"No," he whispered, holding her in front of him, staring down at her. The regret she saw in his face made her hate him, hate herself. "So you won't be hurt any more than I've already hurt you. Just stay here, Lyrica. Give me three minutes. Just three minutes . . ."

Releasing her, he brushed past, and the sound of him leaving the room broke the control she'd fought to hold on to. Sobs tore from her, almost as silent as the tears that whispered from her eyes.

She sank to the hearth, wrapping her arms around herself as she bent her head to her knees and fought to quiet the brutal sobs shuddering through her.

They were quiet, but still devastating to her.

And to the man on the other side of the door listening to them.

It was better this way, he thought wearily. He'd been insane to touch her to begin with. He'd known better, yet the hunger that tore at him demanded otherwise.

A hunger he had no choice but to turn and walk away from. For both their sakes.

TWO

Two months later

The snow had melted from the Kentucky moun-
tains, but that didn't mean there wouldn't be more before the
season was over. The early March weather was a little cooler than
normal—too damned bad it didn't do a thing to cool down his
body.

Pulling into the crowded parking lot, Graham gripped the steering wheel in a white-knuckled grip as a grimace tightened his jaw.

He was supposed to stay away from her. He'd sworn to himself
he would stay the hell away from her. She deserved better than a
man who couldn't trust. A man whose anger burned because of
the very fact that he couldn't stay away from her.

Glaring at the brightly lit house with music pulsing in the air
and humanity milling about it, he knew he should turn around and
just leave. Hell, she was over twenty-one. She was a woman grown
and well old enough to decide if she wanted to be here or not.

At least, that was the argument he'd given her brother, Dawg Mackay. Unfortunately, saying no to the Mackays wasn't always the easiest thing to do. Sooner or later, a man just threw his hands up in surrender, did what he had to do, and hoped it was over. Mackays were like water against stone sometimes. They just fucking eroded good common sense.

The Mackay males had decided there were certain parties that the Mackay females weren't to attend, and in Pulaski County and the counties surrounding it, everyone listened. If one of Dawg Mackay's sisters was seen at a party with certain qualities, then a call was to be made. If a Mackay couldn't be reached, then there was a list, a short list, of numbers to call. Hesitate to make the call and when the day came that you needed a favor from one of those Mackay men, good luck.

For some reason—Mercury in retrograde, bad karma, just bad fucking luck, he didn't know what—for some damned reason no one was reachable but Graham this time. And it just had to be Lyrica Mackay attempting to have a life without her brother's permission.

Hell, he felt sorry for the Mackay daughters who were rapidly approaching their teen years.

u better get here! cause dude this bitch is burnin'

Distaste pulled at his lips as he read the text. He was going to have to teach that bastard how to write, and how to describe a beautiful woman.

With the text came video.

And there just had to be video, didn't there?

Pulling up the file texted to his smartphone, Graham tapped the icon and waited the second or so it took to download.

He should have let it be, he thought, swallowing tightly as it came up. Because Lyrica was definitely burning.

So damned hot she made his fingers burn to touch her.

The music was a hard country tune, fast and rhythmic, and it played perfectly to her ability to move like the erotic fantasy she was.

And she was moving.

Laughing, her gaze centered on the redneck bastard dancing with her, she held the longneck bottle of beer comfortably in one hand as the other curled over her head. She moved with gut-clenching, erotic grace, hips swaying, the tops of her pretty breasts sheened with perspiration, her long, straight black hair flowing to the middle of her shoulder blades.

Then the son of a bitch dancing with her reached out to clasp her hips—

And she let him pull her to him. Laughing, her emerald green eyes gleamed with latent fire before she moved back to tease further with the sensual gyrations of her seductive body.

"Fuck me!" The snarl tore from his lips before he could hold it back. "I'm going to paddle her ass!"

He tried to push back the thought of what he intended to do to it after he watched it blush a pretty pink, for branding his senses. But the fantasy was still there. Just as it was every day, every night, every time he breathed.

Exiting the vehicle, he slammed the door shut, listened for the automatic door lock, then strode quickly toward the house.

She was going to make him insane—that was all there was to it. After the night of the blizzard, after tasting her, there had been no peace for him. He had a taste for her now, one he couldn't get out of his senses or make himself forget.

And that was pissing him off.

This wasn't the time. The wrong time in his life, the wrong time for his heart, the wrong time for his soul. It was simply the wrong damned time for this. He'd always known Lyrica could get under his skin, get beneath his defenses, but he'd never imagined she'd get in this deep. That she would weaken him at a time when he had no choice but to be strong.

As he entered the house and made his way purposefully to the patio, his jaw clenched with the anger that thought brought.

A chorus of boos met his appearance and he knew his reason for being there was expected. Just as they weren't for the Mackays, parties weren't his style. If he was going to get crazy with a woman, then he was going to get crazy without witnesses.

The sound of disappointed calls had the tempting motions of Lyrica's delicately rounded body stilling as she turned to him.

Immediately her eyes narrowed, and before he could reach her she lifted that damned beer to her lips and finished the drink in seconds, before he could take it from her. Not that he would have. That was her brother's prerogative, not his.

"Ready to go?" he snapped, glancing at the bottle with an air of disgust.

"Not really." Her brows arched as a mocking smile shaped her lips. "You ready to leave without me?"

He grunted at that. The question was so preposterous it didn't deserve an answer.

"You walking out or do I have to drag you out?" He sighed.

Damn, he really hoped she was walking . . .

She laughed at the question. "Where's the fun in that?"

Evidently, laughter was contagious. At least, hers was, because the curious crowd twittered with her.

Hell, he could read that look in her eyes—she was going to make damned certain this was as difficult as possible.

Breathing out in exasperation, he flicked a glance at her clothing and considered his options as everyone waited and watched.

She looked damned good, he had to say that for her.

Five feet, four inches tall, her three-inch heels pushed her to five-seven. She wore jeans that licked over every inch of skin from just below her hips until they disappeared beneath the dark brown leather boots that ended just above her knees.

Decision made.

He didn't give her time to block him or guess what he was doing. Amid the cheers of the crowd he moved forward, bent, and had her over his shoulder in a second, one arm anchoring the backs of her knees as she screamed in outrage.

Just for effect, he reached up with his free hand and slapped her shapely bottom as laughter and catcalls echoed behind them.

"You ass," she cried out, but she stilled her struggles.

Well, she stilled them for a few seconds. The feel of her hand smacking at the back of his jeans had his lips curling in amusement as he stalked out the front door.

"Hey, Graham, you have a wildcat on your hands!" Elijah Grant laughed as he moved to Graham's side.

Although the other man carried a beer for effect, he was as sober as a judge on Sunday. Dark hazel eyes watched the area carefully beneath lowered lids, and if Graham knew Elijah, there was a weapon hidden somewhere beneath the sweatshirt, jeans, and boots he wore.

Probably several.

"Elijah Grant, I'll just have Zoey kick your damned ass," Lyrica threatened him furiously.

Elijah grimaced, then a grin touched his lips as they entered the parking lot. "Tell her I like my doms in black leather instead of baggy sweats. If she dresses the part, I might let her try."

A furious snarl tore from Graham's burden as Elijah chuckled at her response.

"Why didn't a Mackay collect her?" the other man asked then. "She doesn't give her brother or cousins near that much trouble."

"Hell if I know," Graham muttered. He was still trying to figure out what the purpose of it was himself.

"So what's your count at now?" Elijah asked.

His count. After this, how many favors did he still owe the Mackays?

"Hell if I know," he repeated with an edge of anger. "I wasn't aware I had a count until recently." Until the Mackays had needed someone to follow Lyrica and her sister Zoey when they took an overnight shopping trip to Louisville just before summer ended the year before.

"Yeah, they get a man like that." Elijah sighed.

"Graham Brock, let me down this minute," Lyrica ordered. "I swear if you don't let me go I'll tell Kye how to run those damned bimbos of yours out of the house within hours. I know how to do it. Ask Declan. I swear I'll do it."

Graham glanced toward the heavens, praying for patience. If she didn't stop, he was going to end up doing something neither of them would appreciate once they came back up for air.

"Poor Declan," Elijah murmured. "Really, Lyrica, you and Zoey should leave the man alone long enough to get him some. Let him enjoy his freedom."

Declan Mackay, Natches's adopted son, had been fighting a war with his cousins almost since the day they'd arrived. It wasn't a cruel war. It wasn't one of dislike, not really. But it was an amusing one.

Reaching the Viper, Graham nodded to the door and waited as Elijah hurriedly opened it.

"Your chariot awaits, princess." Graham snickered as he bent, turned, and expertly maneuvered her into the passenger seat. He'd perfected the move during those years when he'd had to collect his baby sister from parties. Though she'd been about fifteen at the time, he thought in disgust, not twenty-four.

What the hell was Dawg Mackay thinking? Kye would shoot him with his own gun if he attempted something like this now.

At least Lyrica didn't attempt to jump from the car.

Crossing her arms over her breasts, she stared straight ahead, silent and furious.

"Think she'll consider the fact that this is Dawg's fault, not yours?" Elijah asked, the laughter waiting just below the surface more than evident in his tone.

"No." Closing the door, Graham raked his fingers through his hair in resignation, his gaze meeting the other man's. "Why do you think Dawg likes to cash in his favors this way? It's so much easier than facing the music himself."

The music being his sister's fury. Lyrica was widely known to be the one sister who had no reservations when it came to getting even with her brother. She'd spent two months living in his home when she was twenty, making his life hell with such simple teenage maneuvers that Dawg had sworn to her that he wouldn't interfere in her life as he did with her older sisters.

He didn't keep that promise when it came to certain parties though.

"Good luck, buddy." Elijah chuckled as he backed away from the car, watching as Graham opened the driver's-side door.

"I'll need it," Graham called back as he slid into the low seat and started the motor.

"Can we put the top down?" Lyrica asked, her fingers moving immediately for the radio and flipping it on as she pushed the volume up.

Way up.

He blinked over at her, completely taken aback by the cheerful smile and steady regard. He was so surprised that she was able to find and press the hardtop control before he realized what she was doing. Glancing up to see the top halfway folded back, he wondered if there was any way in hell he was going to survive the night.

As the roof settled into place, she sat back in her seat, buckled her seat belt, and threw him another smile. "I told Dawg if he sent you after me then I was staying the night with you. Did he mention that?"

God love her brother's heart. Maybe the man knew what the hell he was doing after all.

"He mentioned something about staying with Kye," he admitted.

"Hmm." Lifting one hand, she studied her nails for a second. "Did you mention Kye wasn't home this weekend?"

"Did I mention I wasn't staying after I dropped you off?" he asked. An empty threat. He'd never leave her at his home alone. He rather liked his house standing just as it was.

"Awesome!" She threw out a perfectly modulated teenage exclamation of pleasure. "The house to myself. Tell me, how hard will you spank me when you come home to find guests in your bed?"

Like hell. "Guests?" he growled.

The smile she gave him was pure intended retribution. "Guests, love. Old man Henner's bluetick hound dogs. All twelve of them. I'm certain they'll just love that big bed bimbo number six couldn't say enough about."

Training was an amazing thing. It kept him from wincing at the insulting disgust in her voice.

Vindictive little wretch.

He was damned glad he'd worn his jacket as he turned on the seat heater and amped the temperature higher to compensate for the open top.

Pulling out of the parking spot, he continued to ignore the threat next to him, gave in to the hard throb of the vehicle's motor, and accelerated quickly.

She was silent as he drove along the narrow lane, fiddling with the satellite radio stations before settling on a channel belting out R&B music. As he turned the volume down to a seductive level, he was aware of her turning in her seat so she could watch him assessingly.

"Kye should have been home by now," she stated as he pulled onto the main road.

"She'll be there sometime tonight. She didn't say when."

Kye had spent the past three weeks in California with their aunt and uncle, under duress. Her aunt pulled the guilt trip from hell to get her there. She'd flown home the second she was able to get away. Her mother's sister, as Kye called her, was a manipulating pain in the ass.

"I'll call her when she gets home. You can drop me off at my apartment instead of Dawg's tonight. I'll harass him in the morning."

The statement had him glancing at her. "What apartment? I thought you moved back in with your mother."

"My, aren't you out of the loop," she drawled in a voice that some men would mistake as a promise.

Graham knew better. He knew her well enough to detect the anger in her tone.

"It would seem so," he grunted. "Dawg didn't mention an apartment. He just said you were threatening to spend the night with Kye if he sent me after you."

"Actually, the exact wording was, 'Send him and I'll sleep with him.' Evidently he didn't take the warning to heart. Does he not know you're looking for the next flavor of the month?"

Lifting his arm to rest on the edge of the open window, Graham rubbed at the side of his face, the rasp of the short beard covering his jaw reminding him of more than the fact that he hadn't shaved.

"I probably haven't mentioned it to him," he murmured, won-

dering how fast he could get his tongue down her throat and his
fingers buried in her pussy if he pulled the car over to the side of
the road somewhere.

She'd protest at first. He knew her. Contrary little minx that
she was, she wouldn't give in easily after the way they'd been in-
terrupted during that snowstorm.

Chloe had been stuck at the house after he'd told her their affair was over. He hadn't noticed the snow piling up until she'd
mentioned it, after he'd informed her he was taking her home.

"Perhaps you should mention it to him," Lyrica suggested.
"Then he might take me seriously."

"Hmm, I'd be opposed to warning him first if that's what you
intended to do," he pointed out. The thought of tasting her again,
feeling the tight warmth, and tasting the flow of sweet heat as his
tongue rimmed the snug entrance had him a little distracted.

"You'd be opposed to warning him first?" The low, furious
tone of her voice nearly had him grinning.

"Yeah, I would be," he admitted. "He or Natches would feel
the need to hit me. They still pack a mean punch, sweetheart. I'd
at least like to experience what I'm getting my ass kicked for first."

Like hell. There were nights—hell, every night after he lay
down in bed—that he would gladly take an ass whipping for one
more taste of her. Thankfully, he was stronger before and after
those moments.

"I'm going to kick your ass for being a moron," she stated, eyes
narrowed, the emerald green almost neon as she glowered at him.

"Hmm, think that's how it'll go, do you?"

He didn't agree.

Graham flicked another glance at her. That blouse she wore
dipped low over the soft rise of her breasts before meeting to but-
tons between them. He could have it unbuttoned in a second or
two, he guessed.

He could have one of those sweet nipples in his mouth again, his tongue licking over the hard little tip, each stroke, each tug of his mouth making her burn hotter . . .

"Where are we going, Graham? Because if you're actually taking me to your house, I really will slip those dogs in on you."

She would be too damned busy lying beneath him as he slipped into her, he thought.

"Where do you want to go?" he asked, ignoring the threat.

"My apartment, Graham. Are you having trouble hearing tonight?"

He was having trouble keeping his mind out of her pants, and that was damned dangerous territory.

He didn't answer the question, but increased the pressure on the accelerator of the Viper instead. He had to get her to that damned apartment. He could remember, think, and fantasize all he wanted, but he knew the hazards of actually taking what he wanted.

"Address," he growled.

Since when did Dawg Mackay allow his sisters to move out on their own? That was damned dangerous. They were, after all, Mackays.

Lyrica gave him her address, watching him closely as she named the apartment complex the Mackay cousins had bought six months before. That explained it. She may have felt like she was on her own, but she was still beneath their eagle eye. At least, Graham was certain that was what Dawg told himself.

After giving him the address, she sat back in her seat, silent then. Graham kept waiting for another smart-ass comment or question, feeling like the anticipation of it would likely have him breaking a sweat soon.

"Why did you do that during the snowstorm?" Her voice was soft, the hint of vulnerability in it digging sharp claws into both his conscience as well as his temper.

He should have been prepared for the question.

Telling her he'd been helpless against the hunger that rose inside him wasn't the wisest course of action, and he damned sure wasn't going to take it.

"Is that why you've stopped coming to the house?" he asked rather than answering her. "Because of what happened?"

He glanced at her, aware of the steady look she had leveled on him, that quick little mind of hers working, gauging his response, his honesty.

Damn her. Damn her. She reminded him far too much of what he wanted only to forget.

"Answer me first." There was a note of hurt in her tone, one that suggested she knew he was trying to avoid the question and was coming up with her own reasons for that.

Rubbing at the back of his neck for a second, Graham kept his expression clear, with no hint of a reaction. What the hell was he supposed to say anyway?

"What does it matter?" he finally asked her. "It was regrettable. I never should have touched you."

He should have stayed in his room, because he had known she was there. He had known she would be there watching the snow. He'd sensed her in the house that evening, just as he always did.

He should have just spent the night fucking Chloe, despite the fact that their relationship, as well as his desire for her, was over. He could have done as he had been doing for months and let thoughts of touching Lyrica have their way while he fucked his "flavor of the month," as she and Kye called his lovers.

Lyrica didn't say anything more. Linking her fingers in her lap, she stared out the windshield, lips pursed, jaw tight, as the air around her seemed to hum with her anger.

Hell, he'd never seen her so pissed she was speechless.

That was almost scary.

As he drove past the city limits, Graham told himself that if he'd hurt her, he was sorry, and it was the last thing he'd wanted to do. But he was damned if he knew how to handle what she made him feel. And now was not the time to figure it out.

Pulling into the parking lot of the apartment complex, he parked the Viper in the slot marked with the apartment number she'd given him.

It was a ground-floor patio apartment. A privacy fence separated each side of her small yard from her neighbors', while leaving the front onto the parking lot clear. Which made little sense to him, he admitted.

"Call Dawg," he suggested as he put the vehicle in park and turned to look at her. "One of these days someone's going to get hurt when they have to drag you or Zoey from a party. He's been lucky so far."

She rolled her eyes. "Every house owner on the lake knows if we show up to a party to let him know. As long as the parties aren't getting wild then he lets it go."

"This one was getting wild?" The thought of Lyrica being amid some of the depraved things that went on at the lake parties had conflicting emotions tearing through him. Fury and lust, just to start with.

"It would have." She shrugged, unclipping her seat belt. "In another couple of hours the patio would have been empty and couples would have been doing the happy-happy in the shadows." She waggled her brows suggestively.

"The happy-happy?" he muttered, wondering at the phrasing.

"The happy-happy," she said, voice lowering, a sensual, hungry rasp to her voice. His entire body tensed in reaction.

His cock, already hard and throbbing in interest, gave a hard jerk, his balls tightening as she turned and gripped the dash and the back of his seat before lifting slowly toward him.

"You know, Graham," she whispered, green eyes gleaming in need, in helpless hunger, "that feeling you get when you're burning inside with the pleasure, certain the flames are going to consume you, drag you to a place where ecstasy fills every particle of your mind?" Her lips were a breath from his as he held her gaze, and he let himself sink inside the melting pleasure she described. "Tell me, did you find that place the night of the snowstorm after you left me? Did you use your bimbo to relieve the lust you teased me with?"

He was going to fuck her.

His jaw tensed, lust sweeping over him, consuming him as she knelt in the seat beside him, her upper body braced in front of him.

"Don't make this mistake, Lyrica," he warned her, one hand clenching the steering wheel, the other gripping her hip warningly. "Don't think in your anger that you can make me pay for whatever slight you perceive."

"Make you pay?" she whispered, the full curves of her breasts rising and falling temptingly. "You make us sound like enemies, Graham. I've never been your enemy."

Releasing her hip, he let his hand move to her thigh, testing the firm muscle beneath, letting himself become immersed in the thought of those lovely legs gripping his hips.

He moved his hand from the steering wheel and reached up, intending to pull her to him, the only action, the only hunger he could make sense of at the moment.

"No, you're not my enemy, sweetheart," he agreed. He'd make damned sure of it.

She caught his wrist before he could touch her hair, her head pulling back, the anger he'd sensed in her earlier suddenly flaring in her eyes.

"And I'm not one of your bimbos, your snuggle bunnies, or your damned cheap-ass tramps that tromp naked around your sister as if she wants to see their silicone-filled breasts or nasty-ass bushes. And I'll make damned sure my brother never sends you after me again."

He watched her.

Eyes narrowed, his hand returned to the steering wheel as she jerked the door open and moved to leave the car.

"Lyrica." He said her name softly, the warning in it bringing her to a stop. She turned slowly to stare at him over her shoulder. "If you ever need me, I'm here. But take this to heart, baby—tease me again, and I'm going to fuck you. Every way I know how, and I'm sure I'll think of a few new positions just for you. But I will fuck you. When it's over you'll be hurt, I'll feel bad as hell for it, and I'll make an enemy of every Mackay I know. Do us both a favor, a big favor. Stay the hell out of my bed."

Her lips curled in disgust. "Don't worry, Graham. I never was into trashy studs or used seconds, no matter how damned good they think they are. No matter how damned different I thought they were."

With that, she pushed herself from the car, closed the door all too gently behind her, then strode across the sidewalk to her patio door as though she were out for a midnight stroll. As though her body wasn't burning for him. As though her need to return to him wasn't just as high, just as imperative as his need to have her return.

In the end, it was far better she didn't, because Graham knew he would destroy them both with his lust for her. And hurting her was something he didn't want. He wanted that even less than he wanted to repeat the mistakes of the past.

THREE

June

As the elevator reached the fourth floor of the small hotel, Lyrica Mackay expelled a weary breath and wished she'd asked someone to make this trip with her.

Kye would have been the obvious choice, but Lyrica was trying desperately to stay away from the Brock house after her last confrontation with Graham. Her emotions were still too ragged, her body still too determined to remember every second of every touch he had whispered across her body.

Those memories tortured her, tormented her, and there was nothing she could do to hold them back.

The muted ping of the elevator reaching her floor sounded, forcing back her memories as the door slid open. What caused her to pause, she would never understand, couldn't explain. Why she placed her hand on the elevator door to hold it open, she never questioned.

Her body tense, she stared up the long corridor to her room.
Her gaze locked on her hotel room door, her senses heightening,
certain her door was open.

It shouldn't be open.

She remembered closing it securely when she left. She'd put out
the Do Not Disturb sign, too. There was no reason for housekeep-
ing to be there.

There was a strange sense of disbelief filling her. It sent adrenaline rushing through her system, a warning prickle of danger
burning through her mind as she tried to tell herself to move. She
should go directly to the lobby and complain.

No one had been at the registration desk when she'd arrived
though. She'd considered stopping and requesting a cup of the
coffee that smelled freshly made behind the receptionist's counter.
She'd even paused and looked around for the young man who had
been there earlier, wondering where he had gone.

As she stood there, one hand still braced on the open elevator
door out of instinct and the other tightening on her purse strap, a
figure moved in the doorway.

Disbelief held her still and silent as their eyes met across the
long distance. Dressed in black, masked, a handgun held firmly in
his hand, the man's gaze narrowed on her.

His black shirt fit snugly. He wasn't in great shape, but over-
powering her would be easy. He was taller, his legs longer. He
could outrun her.

His arm came up slowly, a smile pulling at his lips as triumph
gleamed in his eyes.

Instinct lent strength. Jumping back and hitting the door close
button of the elevator, she was suddenly thankful for whatever
urge had kept her hand on the elevator door. It closed quickly,
moving swiftly back to the lobby as she began to pray.

Seconds later she pushed through the doors as they opened and raced into the lobby, searching desperately for the still-absent receptionist.

She didn't dare wait. There wasn't time.

Running through the doors, she considered the parking garage where her Jeep was parked, but knew that would be the first place her would-be assassin would look.

Assassin.

Who would want to kill her?

Running down the sidewalk, pushing herself to move faster than she ever had, Lyrica turned up the alley and began running through the dark shadows that lay over the backstreets. She didn't know London, Kentucky, well enough. She only came there occasionally. She usually shopped in Louisville.

God, she had to find someplace to hide. She had to find a chance to call her cousin's husband, the chief of police in Somerset. Alex would send someone after her. He would call someone he knew in London and make sure she was safe.

She couldn't hear anyone behind her, but she knew how little that meant. She didn't dare pause or slow down. She didn't dare let herself believe she was safe. Turning at the next shadowed corner, she kept running, trying desperately to be quiet, grateful she'd worn sneakers rather than the low heels she'd considered.

Why was she being chased? Who would want to hurt her? Unless . . .

Someone had targeted her older sister two years before. Eve had been placed in danger because of Dawg's enemies. Had they returned?

They couldn't have. Dawg was certain they were dead.

Coming to a hard stop, she realized she'd turned into an alley with no exits. Brick walls surrounded her now, and the only way out was back the way she had come, toward the dark figure with his ever-ready gun.

A cat squalled out from beyond the alley entrance, the clatter of metal meeting cement brief, but assuring her she had only seconds. Whoever wanted to kill her was getting closer.

Looking around in terror, she moved quickly to the heavy Dumpster at her side and wedged in beside it, praying he didn't think to look there. As she all but crawled behind it, her breath escaped in a muffled sob as she realized there was a deep indent at the base of the building.

It had likely been covered once, but the bricks had been chipped away and disposed of at some point. She squeezed herself into it, huddling as close to the boarded back as possible and holding her breath as the footsteps came closer.

"I know I saw that bitch turn in here," someone hissed.

"I'm telling you, she backtracked to the garage," another snapped.

"I saw her take that last turn coming this way," the first argued furiously. "Check behind the Dumpster."

Footsteps shuffled, moving closer. There was the scrape of a shoe, of clothes against the Dumpster as someone breathed out harshly. The Dumpster shifted, but it didn't move.

"There's no one back there," the second voice retorted in disgust. "I can see behind it and it's clear. She's not here."

"Fuck!" The curse was filled with anger. "I can't believe you didn't see her come into the lobby."

"She was supposed to be in her room, dammit. You didn't see her leave it."

"Fucking moron," the other man growled. "Let's go. She has to be close. She couldn't have gotten far."

Lyrica didn't dare breathe. She couldn't breathe. Terror was like a fever, weakening her, tearing through her senses, shredding her control. Her entire body shuddered, chilled, shock and fear racing the adrenaline tearing through her body.

How long she waited she didn't know. She didn't dare move from the precarious hiding place. They were waiting for her, watching for her.

Moving slowly and reaching into the purse she clasped desperately to her chest, she pulled her cell phone free. It hadn't been working earlier. She'd tried to call her sister to let her know she'd arrived, but the automated message had told her to try again later.

Fingers shaking, she hit Alex Jansen's number again. When it didn't go through, she began calling every number in her contact list, one after the other.

None of them were going through.

"We're sorry, but this number is no longer accepting calls. Please try again later."

The message played again, the computer-generated voice completely unsympathetic to the small, barely muffled sob that escaped Lyrica's lips.

Hands trembling, she pulled the phone from her ear, closed her eyes, and huddled deeper into the small crevice she'd found in the brick building behind the stinking Dumpster.

She was too terrified to move out from behind it, the stark, mind-numbing fear rising from the depths of her soul at the very thought of it.

She couldn't make a call out. Her texts weren't going through to any of her family. Not her brother or her cousins, not her sisters or her mother or even her mother's lover, Timothy Cranston. She'd tried everyone and nothing worked. She stared at the muted display, fighting desperately to think, to figure out what to do.

Even Alex Jansen, her cousin Janey's husband and chief of police of Somerset, Kentucky, was unreachable. And she needed help. Oh god, she needed help.

She had no idea how to navigate the alleys and backstreets of downtown London. She was trapped here with no idea how to identify who was after her or why.

Why?

What had she done?

She'd just driven into town to meet some friends for dinner, then to go shopping early the next morning. The party she'd been invited to at one of her brother's friends' home in a few weeks required a new outfit. She wanted to look good. She wanted to get new shoes, something girly and pretty. Something to draw attention . . .

She'd checked into the hotel just before dark then left for dinner at a nearby restaurant where her friends were waiting for her. She could have never anticipated that someone would be waiting to kill her when she returned.

She shuddered remembering the muted pop that the gun had made as she had quickly stepped back into the elevator. The bullet had missed her by inches. She could have been killed. She would have been killed if she hadn't held that damned elevator door open.

What was she going to do now?

Dawg had taught her and her sisters how to fight. He and their cousins had taught them how to survive in the mountains. But she had no idea how to survive here, in this dark alley, without a weapon.

The vibration of her phone had her turning it in her hand, staring at it in breathless hope.

Lyrie, this is Kye. My phone is acting really wonky. Using Graham's. Where the hell are you? I've tried to call all day.

The text shocked her.

Kye? Kye had gotten through?

Graham would know what to do. He would get hold of Alex.

Someone. He would help her. He had sworn he would come if she needed him.

Desperation spurred her as she quickly typed back.

Kye. Need Graham. In trouble. Help me!

Would it go through? Oh god, please let it go through. She watched the bar, nearly crying out as the "Delivered" message showed next to the text.

What if he refused to help her? He wasn't too happy with her but, god, she needed him now.

She was dead if he didn't find a way to save her. And she really didn't think she'd like being dead.

Graham stared at the text, his senses hardening, turning to ice at the realization that Lyrica was in trouble.

"Graham," Kye whispered, her face pale.

Graham dialed Lyrica's number quickly before hitting the speaker option and hearing his call go straight to voice mail.

Inputting the secure encryption key on the stealth phone, he quickly dialed her number again.

"Kye. Kye, please help me." Terror lanced through her tear-filled voice and shoved a dull blade through his chest. Her voice came quickly across the line. "I've called everyone. No one's call is going through."

"Where are you, Lyrica?" He was moving as he spoke, watching the readout on the screen of his phone and hitting the jamming signal that would keep the call from being tracked even as the program tracked her location. "Quickly."

"Graham?" The hope, the terror in her voice ripped through his guts like a dull blade.

"Quickly, Lyrica," he snapped.

"London." Her voice was hushed, shaking. "I don't know

where. I was running, trying to get away. It's a brick building, down an alley close to the new London Suites in town. I'm behind a Dumpster. Some guys are trying to kill me! They haven't found me yet."

"I have your GPS. Turn the phone off and pull the battery now, Lyrica. And don't fucking move. If you have to run again, find a safe place, insert the battery again for three minutes, then pull it. You hear me? I'm coming for you, honey. I'm just a minute away." He tried to reassure her. "Now do as I said."

"Graham? Please hurry." The whimper of terror had his guts turning to mush as he grabbed his duffel bag from his bedroom closet and raced to the front door.

"Do as I said, now. They're tracking you and I won't be able to block it for long once I leave the house. Pull that fucking battery and stay where you are. I'm on my way."

The call disconnected.

"Graham, what's going on?" Kye was rushing behind him, fear filling her voice as well, though she spoke low, nearly whispering, as he jerked the door of his car open and threw the duffel bag in it.

"Stay here." Turning on her, he caught her shoulders in his hands and gave her a quick little shake as he spoke just loud enough for her to hear him. "Do not use your phone, Kye, it's being monitored. Do you understand me?"

Frightened gray eyes widened, dilating with shock and fear at the information.

"Why?"

"Someone's trying to track Lyrica. Stay off the phone. Do not answer it. I'll call Sam and she'll be out here to get you soon. Leave the phone here; don't take it with you."

"What if your phone is being tracked, too?" she whispered, still following him as he moved around to the driver's side.

"It's not or I wouldn't have gotten through to her. It's en-

crypted and secure. No one tracked it. But I want you to go with
Sam and stay there until I call."

"You'll call soon?" she implored, stepping back from the car
as he revved the motor of the powerful Viper.

"As soon as I can, sweetie," he promised. "Now get in the
house and lock up until Sam gets here. Now!"

Shifting quickly into gear, he tore out of the driveway, checking
the rearview mirror just long enough to see her racing into the
house.

"Call Sam." He activated the Bluetooth calling option built
into the powerful vehicle.

"Detective Bryce," responded the strong, feminine voice that
came over the line.

"Sam, could you check the house for me?" Graham kept his
tone casual, pleasant. "I'm going to be late getting back and Kye's
phone is acting up on me."

Sam would know exactly what the request meant—that Kye
might need protection and to get her out of the house.

"Sure, Graham," she answered, her own voice never changing,
though he knew she was moving, prepping. "I was heading that
way anyway to visit with a few friends."

"I appreciate it," he drawled. "On your way back, stop by the
Mackays' and ask Zoey if she'll make a reservation for you tomorrow night. She's still pissed at me for running off that hood-
lum last week who was flirting with her. But let's not let her family
know I butted in. Dawg gets cranky over that shit and he'll just
piss her off when he questions her about it."

What he said wasn't important. The fact that he said it and the
name he gave was all the detective needed. They'd worked together long enough that she was well versed in reading between
the lines.

He didn't want anyone alerted to the fact that Lyrica was in trouble until he figured out what the trouble was and the danger she was facing. The fact that Kye's phone was being monitored and jammed each time she attempted to call Lyrica was warning enough that any information going to Lyrica's phone, or her family's phones, would be overheard.

"Yeah, we try to keep Dawg calm," Sam laughed, the ease of the sound assuring him that anyone listening would be none the wiser that Graham was on his way to London. "Talk to you soon, then."

Disconnecting the call, Graham pushed the little sports car harder, taking the curves at a breakneck speed as he raced for the interstate.

London was forty-five minutes away. In the Viper, he could cut that time to less than twenty. He didn't worry about being stopped or trailed. Once his tag number was called in, law enforcement would let him go. He made certain he used the privilege often enough that he was rarely questioned over it. It shouldn't so much as blip anyone's radar. At least not until he collected Lyrica, and only then if he was seen.

Tightening his hands on the steering wheel as his teeth clenched furiously, he hoped he came face-to-face with the bastard who had the delicate, too damned fragile Lyrica hiding behind a Dumpster, terrified for her life.

They'd made a mistake. Whoever had dared to strike out at her for whatever reason had made a costly error. Because he'd make sure they paid. They should have done their homework better, should have checked closer into the fact that Kye was a friend. The very fact that Kyleene Brock kept Lyrica's number on her main contact list should have been a clue.

She was important to Graham.

He'd encouraged Kye in that particular friendship. Had gently pushed his sister in the other woman's direction to ensure Lyrica stayed on the periphery of his life, at least.

He had no intention of becoming involved with her. He wouldn't have become involved with her because of the simple fact that he hadn't wanted to hurt her.

He didn't want to break her tender heart.

Now that might not even be an option.

He'd make damned sure that he broke the bastard, ensuring the dynamics in his and Lyrica's relationship would change, though. Whoever it was, he was a dead man walking.

As he sped toward the interstate, the Viper taking the curves with a roar of power as it easily gripped the pavement, he was aware of a pickup that he passed, as well as the man most likely driving it.

The highway entrance was just ahead, and, calculating his intended speed and that of the man behind him, he quickly revised the plan he'd been considering to rescue Lyrica.

"Incoming call. Secured. Encrypted," the computerized voice announced.

"Accept," he ordered tersely.

"Need help?" Elijah Grant, formerly with the Federal Protective Service and now part of the small team Graham headed in the county, asked as the headlights in Graham's rearview mirror assured him the other man had turned around and was attempting to follow him.

With the motor Jed Booker had put in that truck, Elijah might just be able to keep up if Graham cooperated.

"I don't have time to stop," Graham stated. "If you can stay on my ass until we're close, then I could use some cover."

"You have to slow sometime," Elijah told him. "I'll be there and can slide in fast."

"I'll need the passenger seat. You'll have to be able to keep up." Hitting the interstate, Graham pushed the Viper faster. "If you can stay close, we're not going far."

"As long as we're on the interstate I can keep up," Elijah assured him as they roared up the ramp onto the all but deserted highway. "We hit more county roads and I'll fall behind."

The truck's motor was strong as hell and the speeds the vehicle had been logged at amazed even Graham. It wasn't nearly as steady on mountain curves as the low-built Viper, though, nor did it have the Viper's full speed. But Elijah could at least keep him in sight on the interstate if Graham stayed at the speed he intended.

"You'll be fine, then," Graham promised. "Just follow me and keep my ass covered when I collect my package."

"Got it," Elijah promised. "Is there any chance of compromise?"

"Not short term." The short call was safe, the security on the line still showing green rather than the yellow that would indicate possible encryption weakness. "Long term is iffy."

"I'm on your ass, then, and prepped to cover."

The line went silent, the call well within the limited parameter outside of which anyone could compromise it.

God, he hoped Lyrica was still safely tucked away at the last GPS pinpoint he had.

Glancing at the monitor, he tracked the destination and knew he was only minutes away from the exit leading to London.

She was only a few miles from the turn, on a little backstreet just behind one of the older, remodeled hotels that had been popular decades before. He knew the area and was fairly certain she'd found a way to push her slight body into one of the chimney alcoves that had mostly been boarded or bricked up once the fireplaces were removed.

She would be well hidden as long as no one managed to GPS

her phone. Though tracking it and jamming it at the same time would be difficult. And tracking would be impossible once the battery was pulled.

Unless it was bugged.

But why bug it if they already had it jammed? And if it was bugged, they would have found Lyrica before Kye contacted her.

What the hell was going on?

Silently, he went over every piece of intel from the past few months and couldn't find so much as a hint as to why Lyrica would be targeted. There were no current operations in the area. Graham and his team hadn't been called out in months to provide backup or to cover any current investigations. And the Mackays weren't even in the country . . .

The Mackays were on vacation overseas, out of reach of two of the young women who were well-known to be important to them and to Timothy Cranston. Could someone have decided to make a vengeance strike against Dawg Mackay while he was gone?

Hell, even that didn't make sense. Dawg would return the second he knew one of his sisters was hurt or in trouble. If something happened to one of them, then he and his cousins would blow back into town like a vicious wind. There would be no hiding once Dawg began tracking the perpetrators. And once they were found, Natches Mackay would make sure a bullet found their brains, if Dawg didn't beat him to it.

It didn't make sense yet, but it would, soon.

Tires screamed but held as he hit the exit and shot through it, forced to lower his speed to make the tight turns that would lead into the backstreet he was looking for.

Elijah was all but on his bumper as Graham forced himself to slow to the legal speed limit. Whoever was looking for Lyrica would still be out there. There was no reason to make anyone suspicious before he managed to find her and get her out of town.

He wanted a chance to figure out what was going on and who'd decided to come after her with a gun before they had any more information other than the fact that she'd disappeared.

"Call Eli," he ordered the computer.

"Yeah?" Elijah answered before the first ring finished.

"We're close. Give me enough room to allow me to back into the alley. There's no exit there."

"Got it." The truck immediately slowed. "I have cover ready. I'll pull in behind you. Give me a second to check the rooftops before you move."

"Got it." Disconnecting, he drew to a stop, then reversed quickly and backed to the end of the alley that the GPS had pinpointed as Lyrica's location.

She had to be here.

God help him if she wasn't.

God help whoever had her if they'd found her. If she was hurt, he'd find them, and he'd ensure they regretted that mistake in ways they could never imagine.

The sound of vehicles pulling to a stop caused Lyrica's breath to catch. She didn't dare move. The glow of lights was shining all around her, possibly compromising the shadowed little alcove she was hiding in.

Her back was killing her and her legs were cramped. It felt like she'd been there for hours, still too terrified to move, to do anything more than just breathe. Silent tears slipped from her eyes. She'd prayed silently, certain each sound was a return of the assailant.

And he had returned at least once.

She'd watched his shadow, felt fear screaming through her as he'd tried to shift the Dumpster, moving it enough to wedge himself in between the side of it and the wall, as he seemed to be attempting to look behind it.

He'd thrown the lids open instead and looked inside. He may have glanced behind it, but he'd cursed silently, moving around the alley and kicking boxes seconds later.

She'd nearly screamed in fear at the sound of glass breaking and another cat squalling seconds after he left that second time.

Now the lights would make it far easier to see her.

Moving slowly and biting her lip at the agonizing feel of her cramped muscles being forced to move, she moved into position to run. Crouched, forced to huddle on her hands and knees, tears falling from her eyes again, she promised herself if they caught her, she wouldn't beg.

A Mackay didn't beg, she reminded herself. If one did, then she would have done so by now. She would have begged Graham to explain last winter. She would have begged him to love her, perhaps. There wasn't a lot she would have begged for, but those things, at one time, she might have considered.

If only Graham had managed to get here in time to save her . . .

FOUR

"Roofs are clear," Elijah confirmed as Graham checked the clip to his handgun before pushing it back into place and chambering the first round.

"Keep your eyes open," Graham ordered.

As he stepped cautiously from the Viper, the motor still throbbed powerfully, waiting for the lightest touch to throw it into gear. Leaving his door open, he stepped around to the passenger door, opened it quickly, then moved into a protective position at the edge of the Dumpster.

"Lyrica, move it," he commanded.

For several long seconds nothing moved.

"Lyrica, baby, come on, move it. We don't have a lot of time."

What if she'd been found? What if she'd had to run again and hadn't been able to reengage the battery in her phone to contact him?

He was ready to turn to Elijah and order him to call in the team when he heard the first sob. A second later her dark head peeked around the far edge of the Dumpster and she was moving to him.

Her pale face, filled with stark fear and hope, was scratched, the shoulder-length mass of silky black hair falling mussed around her face as she struggled to get to him. Reaching out, he shoved the Dumpster a few inches out of the way and reached in and grabbed her shoulders before hauling her into his arms.

"Oh god. Graham." Sweet, warm, and far too fragile, she laid her head against his chest, her trembling fingers fisting into his T-shirt as she shuddered in his arms.

"Let's get out of here before we're seen." Moving quickly, he eased her into the passenger seat. "Get down as far as you can, and keep your head down. Let's get you out of town before anyone's the wiser."

Slamming the door closed, Graham loped around the front of the car, gave Elijah the signal to head out, then slid into the driver's seat and threw the vehicle into gear. Before accelerating he pushed her head to his lap and pulled the jacket he kept behind the passenger seat over her head and shoulders. Then he followed Elijah with a surge of power.

"We're moving slowly out of town," he told her as he felt her fingers pressing against his thigh, her cheek far too close to the erection swelling beneath his jeans. "We're going to just take it easy, draw no attention to ourselves, and once we reach the interstate we'll make sure no one's following."

"What about your tags?" Her voice was muffled, her heated breath wrapping around the heavy flesh of his shaft like a wicked, ghostly touch.

"Tags are counterfeit," he grunted. "Think James Bond."

She was silent for several long moments, but her nails were flexing against the denim covering his thigh in a sensual little caress sure to drive him crazy.

"Are you and Dawg related?" There was a heavy sigh of resignation in her voice. "The Jeep was like that before I bought it."

Graham had to grin at the thought of Dawg's Jeep Wrangler.

"Did he change the engine out before he let you have it?"

"Of course." She sighed. "Took him and Natches two weeks to get it ready for me."

Graham didn't doubt that a bit. The male Mackays were careful bastards—the females of the family, on the other hand, were far too soft, gentle, and fragile.

"We're coming up to the next alley. There are two men in the shadows up ahead. Don't move, baby."

The windows of the Viper were dark enough that he was certain she wouldn't be seen, especially with the black leather jacket covering her. The figures remained motionless where they were hidden between the two buildings, no doubt watching his and Elijah's vehicles carefully.

Theirs weren't the only vehicles on the small side street, though. Another had pulled out behind them, and a pickup waited just ahead to turn onto the street. Each of them was carrying more than one occupant, giving Graham a reasonable assurance of security as they passed.

Elijah's left turn signal blinked on; a second later Graham flipped the right signal of the Viper on. They'd converge at the entrance to the interstate a mile or so away.

Where Graham was keeping the appearance of casual boredom, Elijah on the other hand was moving a little fast, his body language nervous as he appeared to be watching everything and everybody and to be suspicious of it all.

If someone was going to follow any of these cars, it would be the pickup with the redneck acting like he had something to hide. And if anyone did follow him, Elijah would take care of it.

Keeping his speed just a mile or two above the limit, the driver's-side window down halfway, country music loud enough to assure anyone who cared to be nosy that he didn't give a damn who saw him, Graham continued toward the interstate.

The tags showing on the car were Lexington tags. The direction he would take would make it appear he was heading that way. And he'd make damned sure no one but Elijah was anywhere around when the tags flipped and he made the turn toward Pulaski County and Somerset.

"This is crazy." Lyrica shuddered as they neared the entrance ramp and Graham flipped his turn signal on again. "Why would anyone follow me like this? Why would they try to shoot me, Graham? It's been over a year since Dawg, Rowdy, and Natches helped Brogan take down the rest of that homeland terrorist group. Besides, that was Brogan's deal. Why come after me?"

Because the Mackays had far too many enemies?

"Hell if I know, baby, but we'll figure it out."

"Stop calling me 'baby,'" she snapped, her ire clear in the sharp retort. "I'm not your latest flavor of the month."

He snorted at the title. "Lucky for you. If you were, instead of snapping at me like a little brat you'd be putting that pretty mouth to a much better use. Sure you don't want to reconsider the position?"

She was still, silent. He realized he was holding his breath as he awaited her answer. Damn, her lips were so close to the throbbing, steel-hard shaft that he could barely hold back the demand that she release him, that she show him the sweet heat of her hungry little mouth.

He was crazy.

Evidently he had a death wish, because there was no doubt Dawg Mackay would kill his ass if he ever found out Graham had touched his sister. Or that he'd encouraged—hell, begged—her to touch him in such a way. And that didn't even count what Natches

Mackay, her cousin, would do. Natches's daughter, Bliss, was a Mini Me replica of Lyrica, so Lyrica gave the other man a hint of what his daughter would look like as she grew older.

Lyrica was Natches's favorite among Dawg's sisters, it was said. And it was rumored Natches had threatened to take his very elite, well-blooded sniper rifle out of retirement for any man stupid enough to hurt her.

And she would be hurt, Graham admitted. He was the wrong man for her. And this was the wrong time for him.

"Can I please sit up?" Querulous and tense, her impatient voice almost had him grinning as he sped up, the Viper cutting through the night with smooth power.

"For now," he relented. "But try to keep your head lower than the headrest, just in case."

She came up immediately, the jacket flipping from her head and pulling forward to rest on her lap.

"I need water."

From the corner of his eye he watched as she licked her lips, as much from nerves as thirst, he guessed.

"In the bag at your feet." Glancing at the rearview mirror, he watched Elijah's lights pulling closer.

"Incoming call. Secured. Encrypted," the computer announced.

Lyrica's head jerked around to him as she tore off the plastic surrounding the water bottle's lid.

"Accept," he commanded.

"Hey there, buddy." Elijah's voice was friendly, relaxed. "It's getting lonely out here."

The other man was alone with no apparent tails.

"How about pancakes?" Graham drawled.

"Sounds great. Same place as before?"

"Meet you there," Graham agreed before disconnecting the call.

Elijah would shadow their retreat and meet them back at his house. Increasing his speed, Graham drove comfortably, all too aware of every move Lyrica made beside him as she lifted the water to her lips, drank, then stared into the night silently.

She was thinking.

A writer, a thinker, Lyrica was the quiet one of the four sisters Dawg had found six years before. At twenty-four, she spread her work between her cousins' various established businesses but hadn't settled on any one vocation.

She wasn't content. Graham had seen the restlessness just beneath the surface over the years. He'd ached to help her relieve it, and though he knew better than to touch her, he couldn't seem to release the need to do just that.

"Dawg picked the wrong time to go on vacation." She sighed, lifting a still-trembling hand to brush back the long fall of heavy, inky black hair that fell over her brow.

"Or was someone just waiting for Dawg to be absent long enough to get to you?" Graham asked softly.

That thought had been bothering him since he'd headed out after her. Why would someone strike now? Was it coincidence? Like the Mackays, he didn't believe in coincidences. Someone had known that Dawg, Rowdy, Natches, and their families would be gone, and they had waited, believing that getting to Lyrica would be easy.

But they hadn't counted on Graham. They'd jammed her phone, but nothing could have jammed the secured satellite and cell encryption on the stealth phone he used.

"Why would anyone want to get to me, though?" Her voice was firm—the trembling fear that had been in it when he talked to her on the phone wasn't there now. "What would be the point?"

"That's what I have to find out," he murmured as he took the exit without warning, slowing only enough to make the turn that would take them to the lake and the house he owned there.

"We should call Dawg." Turning to look at him, the brilliant emerald green of her eyes was filled with worry and concern for her brother and cousins and their families. "He'll know what to do."

"Every number on your contact list has been compromised," he warned her. "If you even reinsert your battery into your phone, whoever tried to kill you will have your location instantly, Lyrica. Don't worry. Dawg's not stupid. And I have no doubt he's already been informed that no one has been able to reach you. By now, he's well aware that something's wrong."

But did that mean he would be there in time to help her? Graham wasn't betting on it, but he was there. He had her. And he intended to keep her for a while.

She was exhausted.

Leaning her head against the back of the seat, Lyrica breathed out a weary sigh.

Her heart was still racing, but as much from arousal now as from fear. Having her face less than an inch from that impressive bulge in his jeans wasn't exactly a calming experience.

For a second she was lying on his couch again, staring up at him, her body still trembling from the need for release as betrayal raced through her.

Hating him.

Realizing he had come from his lover and dared to touch her, to make her body burn, riot with such need that she couldn't resist it, destroyed her.

Staring through the windshield all she wanted to do was find another hole to curl up in and sleep.

"We're almost to the house," Graham promised.

The back roads he was taking were unfamiliar to her. Hell, she thought she'd traveled all the back roads into and out of Somerset and the Lake Cumberland area in the past six years. Yet Graham was showing her routes she had no idea existed.

"You'll endanger Kye," she whispered.

"Kye's not home. I've already ensured her protection."

Turning her head to look at him, she frowned, remembering a time that Kye had disappeared once before.

"This has happened before, hasn't it?" she said. "You've had to do something where you had to send Kye away."

"I have safeguards in place," he stated rather than answering her. "She's my sister. Just like Dawg has safeguards in place. Unfortunately, a man is only human. None of us foresaw you leaving the county without letting anyone know where or when you were going."

Should she feel guilty?

She didn't think so.

"I wanted to go shopping." A bitter smile crossed her lips as she held the bottle of water in a desperate grip. "Dawg didn't tell me he had a guard dog watching over me while he was gone."

But she should have known. She should have thought.

"Not a guard dog, Lyrica." Graham shook his head as he made another turn onto a more familiar road. "He left others to protect you. But I guess someone just wasn't watching when you left town, because no one called me to let me know you couldn't be reached until Kye asked to borrow my phone."

Lyrica sat up then, turning sideways in the seat, her eyes narrowing on him suspiciously. "Dawg would not have left you to watch out for me while he was out of town, Graham. That's not the same as some damned party," she informed him with amused mockery. "You're not family."

"No, I'm your last defense." His expression was hard, cold.

"I'm the only person Dawg trusts who still has the contacts and the equipment needed if the unthinkable happened. I'll get you back to the house, get you out of sight, then I'll find out why no one contacted me and if anyone has contacted Dawg, why he didn't call me. And he would have. Give me a few hours and we'll know where we stand. Then we'll know where to go from there."

Know where to go from there?

"Twilight zone," she whispered, shaking her head. "I'm in the freakin' twilight zone."

"Hell, twilight zone beats a casket any day of the week, don't you think?"

Yeah, it beat a casket, but Lyrica was wondering at the cost. She knew herself and she knew that being alone with Graham wasn't going to be a good idea.

Weary, her gaze blurry with exhaustion, she watched as he pulled the car around to the back of the house, then into the little-used garage. He stored the Viper there in the winter, but other than that, Kye had mentioned once, the garage wasn't often used.

"Here we go. Hungry?" Shutting off the motor, he turned to look at her, concern filling the golden, almost amber color of his gaze.

"I need a shower." She sighed. "I wasn't exactly sitting in a bed of roses."

"No, baby, you weren't." She didn't pull back when he reached out and tucked her hair behind her ear. "Come on, let's get you into a shower and I'll fix you a bite to eat so you can sleep."

Graham had to force himself out of the car. Moving quickly around the vehicle, he was there as she pushed the door open. He reached in and helped her easily from the low-slung little sports car, her delicacy amazing him even when it shouldn't.

He couldn't help pulling her against him as he watched her stumble just a bit. Dammit, she was exhausted, frightened, and living on sheer nervous energy at the moment.

"I'm fine," she assured him, though she didn't move, didn't attempt to push out of his arms. Instead, she leaned against him, her head pressed against his chest, her weight settling against his naturally.

He was in trouble here, he admitted. But hell, he'd admitted that six months ago when she lay beneath him, giving herself to him so sweetly.

"Come on, little bit." Swinging her into his arms, he almost grinned at the little sigh she breathed out. Her arms went around his neck, her head settling comfortably against his shoulder.

Damn her.

He was going to break her heart and he knew it. Knew it, and had no idea how to stop it.

What was worse, he'd end up breaking his own heart if he wasn't damned careful.

"What do you mean she got away?" The voice rasped across the line as hard, icy brown eyes looked down from the apartment window to the alley below.

"I mean she wasn't quite as weak as you led me to believe," he informed his employer. "She's cautious, resourceful, and damned fast. We lost her in a back alley."

Hell, she was a fucking Mackay—did this bastard think it was going to be easy? He'd done his research before he'd taken the job. Enough so that he'd initially declined, only to have to reconsider after additional intel had come through.

"One woman," his employer mused, "against a well-aimed

projectile, should not have been resourceful enough, nor fast enough, to outrun it."

"Turn the girl sideways and there's a hell of a margin for error. She's a skinny little bitch," he snorted, knowing better. The woman was sweet curves and slender muscle.

"Was her phone used?" The man asked as though he were speaking to a moron.

He let himself grin. He'd make the bastard pay for that one later. In spades.

"She made countless attempts; none went through."

"Check the report for the program I gave you. Look for encrypted numbers. Timothy Cranston, the bastard her whore mother's sleeping with, is retired Homeland Security. Make sure he didn't get through. Start running the tag numbers you should have taken of any vehicle coming into or out of the alleys you were watching. You did that, right?"

His gaze flicked over the bare windows of the deserted building across from him. "Taken care of. Nothing blipped even close to Somerset, or the names you listed."

Silence filled the line for long seconds.

"Send me the tag numbers and vehicle descriptions, as well as any surveillance you should have taken," he was ordered. "However she managed to get away, there's no doubt she's headed home, possibly back to her mother's inn and Cranston's protection. Do you have someone there?"

"There, at the lumber store, the garage, the marina, and the restaurant," he replied, naming off each business she worked at.

"Well, at least you did something right," the other man snorted.

His eyes narrowed as he stared at the reflection of his second in command behind him, listening in on the call.

"I tried," he drawled.

The answering snort was pure insult. "Try harder. Get to Somerset and find that bitch. When I arrive there, I want a pretty new toy to play with, and I won't be happy if I don't have it."

The call disconnected.

"Yeah, I'm real concerned with his pretty new toy," he growled as his second leaned back against the wall thoughtfully and waited.

"Are we ready to head to Somerset?" Pulling his weapon, he checked the clip, reinserted it, then began packing the meager supplies they'd stocked the tiny, deserted apartment with.

"The van's packed and your Vette's ready."

His brows arched. "New engine doing good?"

"Excellent." The answer was delivered with cool precision and a light shrug. "Grog says it vrooms."

He grinned, zipped up the pack, and gave a brief nod. "Let's go hear it vroom, then."

"You're not going to match that Viper." The comment had a grimace pulling at his lips as he opened the door and stepped out of the apartment.

"How the hell do you know? The fucker won't tell anyone what he did to the bitch. If Jed did as I asked and put everything in that motor I wanted, then we'll have a fighting chance," he argued.

A snort sounded behind him. No comment, no argument. But that sound of disbelief made his ass itch.

Dammit.

He was supposed to be on vacation right now, not fucking around with some damned op in Mackay territory. If they caught him there then he was dead fucking meat. They didn't like him much; he didn't like them much. It was a mutual little dislike party and he made damned certain he stayed out of their line of sight, and out of sight of Natches Mackay's rifle.

They may be getting on in age a little bit, but those men were still some mean fuckers. It didn't pay to cross them.

He appeared to be doing more than crossing them, though—he had accepted the contract on a Mackay sister's life.

Yep, he was going to have to be damned careful.

FIVE

What now?

Stepping from the shower, Lyrica gave in to a yawn as she hurriedly dried. Wrapping the towel around her body, she quickly used the blow dryer, taking the worst of the dampness from her hair before brushing the nearly straight black mass back from her face. It trailed to the middle of her shoulders, not quite as neat as she liked it but dry enough to be comfortable.

She dropped the towel and pulled a large T-shirt with a U.S. Marines emblem on the front over her head. As it fell past her thighs, she smoothed her hands down her sides, staring down at the gray material with a sense of regret. At one time, she would have been excited to be wearing one of Graham's shirts. Now she was too nervous, the fear that followed her still too fresh.

The shirt was something to sleep in, and she needed to sleep. Desperately.

She couldn't think yet. Exhaustion weighed on her mind, and

the memory of that bullet firing in her direction was still too recent.

She was safe.

Graham had told her that a dozen times since he'd locked the doors behind them. No one knew she was there; no one knew who had come for her.

She was safe.

For this moment.

But she couldn't hide at Graham's forever. And hiding wasn't going to draw out those who had decided she no longer deserved to live.

If she wasn't certain she was being used to draw Dawg out, then she would insist Graham call him. At the moment, she didn't know what to do. Anyone she called could be placed in danger, and she refused to do that to her family. She wasn't hiding behind a Dumpster anymore. She had to figure out what to do without endangering anyone else she loved.

Breathing out roughly, she stepped from the luxurious bathroom and back into Graham's bedroom.

God, how had she let him talk her into this?

Oh, yeah—he hadn't asked. He'd simply followed her up the stairs when she'd been heading to the guest room and pushed her into his room.

Now, standing just inside the bedroom with the safety of the bathroom behind her and the sensually, sexually dangerous appeal of Graham in front of her, she swore she was going to lose her breath completely.

"Your little bunny isn't going to appreciate me sleeping in your bed," she told him as he turned from the television and the news he'd been watching.

Something flared in the rich, golden brown of his eyes in that second. Quickly hidden, but not unseen.

Her heart seemed to pause for one broken second before it raced out of control. Her entire body seemed to ignite, heat pouring through her, need assailing her.

"She hasn't slept in this bed." Tight, a deep, brooding rasp, his voice darkened as his expression tensed.

She glimpsed the hunger he'd quickly hidden in his expression. The fierce, savage angles, the way his gaze seemed to lick over her, pausing at her unbound breasts, the hem of his T-shirt, then flicking up again.

"She sleeps on the floor, then?" she asked, knowing she hadn't hidden the breathlessness his look caused.

Damn him. She didn't want to need him like this. She didn't want to ache for him like this. She wanted to look over him as easily as she did other men, rather than dreaming of him, fantasizing about him, every chance she had.

"She doesn't sleep on the floor." He shrugged. "The connecting room." He gestured to a closed door but didn't finish the thought even as she watched him expectantly.

"So you don't play in your own bed?" She crossed her arms over her breasts. "I want to sleep in my regular bed. I like it fine. I'm not sleeping wherever your latest fuck sleeps."

His jaw bunched almost violently, the muscles there jumping for several long seconds as he obviously ground his teeth over whatever he found offensive in her statement. And she really didn't give a damn what he found offensive. She'd stopped caring when she'd realized how little taking her would mean to him.

"You'll sleep right here, in my bed." The snap in his voice had a surge of nervousness racing up her spine. "This is the most secure room in the house, the only one I'm one hundred percent certain can't be bugged or accessed without my knowledge. That means this is where you will stay until I can figure out what the hell is going on."

Her eyes widened.

"What about the kitchen?" He'd fixed breakfast, though they hadn't talked much, she remembered.

"I took precautions. For the short time we were there, the precautions were enough. Over time, they're not foolproof. And by god, I want foolproof," he informed her, his tone deadly now.

Moving to the bed and jerking down the blankets on the left side, he then turned back to her, his expression still tense, his gaze fierce. "Sleep on this side. It's the safest."

"Why is it the safest?" She wondered if that was a question she should have asked at the moment. "Maybe I like sleeping on the right side of the bed."

Did she really want the answer?

"Because I'm right-handed," he drawled, the lazy response spoiled by the pure anticipation that flickered in his gaze. "I keep my weapon in easy access and I don't want to be hindered by reaching for it with my left. And, baby, I've checked on you when you've stayed the night here. You sleep firmly on the left side of the bed and rarely move."

Nope, she shouldn't have asked. And she sure as hell didn't need to know he'd watched her sleep.

"Perv." She threw the accusation at him with a quick, disgusted narrowing of her eyes. "Really, Graham, I'm sure I should be surprised. But I guess I'm really not."

The look that came over his face was one that had her stomach tightening, her nipples swelling, and the sensitive flesh of her clit pulsing with heated need.

Dammit, masturbating hadn't been on her agenda before going to sleep, but at this rate . . .

"Perv?" he asked softly. "I can show you perv, sugar."

Oh, yeah, she just bet he could. She had no doubts in her mind.

"Really?" Disbelief colored the short, mocking laugh that fell from her lips, though the question was weakened by the breath-lessness that attacked her once again. "Sorry, stud, I never was much into being part of a crowd. I'm rather unique, you know."

"Definitely unique." The agreement was made with the air of a man who was most definitely considering the uniqueness of what she wasn't offering.

The key word? *Wasn't.*

But still, her knees were weak, her flesh too sensitive, the exhaustion that had been pulling at her suddenly dissipating, though a far too sensual drowsiness pulled at her as he began moving slowly toward her.

"I'm not sleeping with you, Graham. Forget it," she snapped.

"The Chinese say if you save a life, then it's forever your responsibility," he informed her softly, completely ignoring the warning in her statement.

"Since we're not in China—" she began, trying to speak over the rapid-fire beat of her heart.

"Doesn't matter." He was in front of her before she could take more than a few steps back. "I saved your life. You're mine now, Lyrica."

His chest brushed against the material of the shirt covering her breasts, exciting her already hardened nipples as she took another step away from him, her back meeting the wall.

She'd tried to ignore the fact that his chest was bare, that the light sprinkling of dark hair over its broad plane appeared far too warm. Just as she'd tried to ignore the fact that he, too, had showered. His hair was still damp, the fleece pants he wore loose. But they could never be loose enough to hide the erection rising hard and impressive beneath the material.

"Look at you," he whispered, catching her hands as she moved to push against his chest, lifting them and securing them to the wall as his fingers curled between hers. "Wearing my shirt, naked and soft beneath it, and so damned certain you can rule me with all that feminine arrogance spitting from your eyes."

Her eyes widened at the accusation. "I have no desire—"

"Don't you?" Heavy, thickly lashed, his eyelids drifted over the hunger gleaming in his gaze, his attempt to hide it a forgotten exercise. "You have desire, Lyrica, and we both know it. You've been teasing me with those pretty emerald eyes since the first day we met six years ago."

That first time. He'd been at the marina her cousin and his family owned, driving a wicked-fast ski boat, wearing nothing but cutoff jeans and dark glasses. Dawg had introduced them and Lyrica had fallen in love.

"That ended last winter." It might have sounded more convincing if she hadn't melted against him as pleasure ran through her body.

He was so warm. So strong.

His head lowered, the strong curve of his lips whispering over hers, the light rasp of the short beard, so bad boy and roguish, brushing against her flesh.

He was a rogue. A bad boy.

Dawg had been warning her about him for years and she couldn't seem to make herself stay away from him.

"Don't," she whispered as strong teeth tugged at her lower lip. "I won't be one of your women. You'll break me if you try to turn me into one."

She knew he would. She'd realized that during the blizzard, which had seemed to rage inside her soul as well as outside. A freezing, icy wasteland that had never thawed, never warmed without his touch. It was thawing now, though. Weeping, flowing from the needy depths of her body to slicken the bare flesh of her sex and her clenched thighs.

"Will I? Give me your kiss, Lyrica. Let's see if you break or just melt around me like hot sugar."

She was already melting.

Her lips parted for him, a moan whispering out as his covered them, his kiss hungry and mind-numbing.

Pleasure ricocheted through her system as languorous need built inside her. Straining toward him, her tongue met his, tasting him. She was drunk on the sensations rioting through her, becoming high on a pleasure she couldn't resist.

He could be addictive.

He *was* addictive.

She had hurt for months after he'd held her during that snowstorm. Every cell in her body had ached for him, ached for the release that had been so close, that had teased and tempted only to be taken from her so quickly.

"Graham—" She strained against him, that ache intensifying now, tearing at her senses, heating her body.

Aching.

It hurt.

She needed him that desperately, ached for him that much. How much worse would it be after he had her? After she knew what she was missing, after the pleasure consumed her, burned through her, and left nothing but ash?

Could she bear it?

"No." She couldn't bear it. She couldn't let it happen.

"No?" he whispered with wicked eroticism, his free hand gripping her hip, holding her still as the heavy length of his erection pressed into her stomach.

It was far too tempting.

The feel of it made her far too hungry for him.

"Graham," she protested breathlessly.

Hell no, she didn't really want him to stop—she simply had no choice.

"I don't hear a lot of certainty in your tone." His lips feathered from her jaw to her neck.

The feel of his mouth moving over the sensitive flesh, stroking it, sent a frisson of exquisite pleasure raking across her nerve endings, drawing a startled gasp of surprise from her at the extremity of it.

"You're just playing with me," she cried out weakly, even as her head tilted to the side to allow him free rein against the rioting nerve endings pulsing beneath the flesh of her neck. "You know you are, Graham. I won't be your toy."

A cry fell from her lips as his free hand pushed beneath the hem of the borrowed shirt, moving unerringly to the swollen curve of her breast. Immediately, one exquisitely hard nipple was caught between his thumb and forefinger, and he rolled it with wicked experience.

"Oh god . . ." Her knees weakened.

Sensation raced from the imprisoned tip to the swollen bud of her clit. Pleasure coursed through the heated nerve endings, sending flash fire strikes of clenching, painful pleasure whipping through her vagina.

It was so good. So good.

"You're such a little liar," he growled, continuing to hold her wrists to the wall above her head as his teeth raked over her collarbone. "You want this just as damned bad as I do."

Probably more, she thought, dazed, immersed in her body's rush to ecstasy.

Before she could process the move, he had the borrowed shirt lifted, his hands releasing her wrists to whip the material over her head as he turned her, pushing her face-first against the wall.

Palms flat against the barrier, her breathing short and choppy, she moaned as his hands caressed down her sides before gripping the curves of her ass firmly. Electric heat raced from where his lips pressed against her shoulder before trailing kisses to her nape, then moving slowly, with shudder-inducing sensations, down her spine.

What was he doing to her?

She'd never read about this. The romances she'd stolen from her sister Zoey had never described this. Or described how she was supposed to handle it.

"You have to stop," she whispered, closing her eyes as she rolled her forehead against the wall.

He filled his hands with the curves of her ass, parting them.

Her eyes flew open, a gasp escaping her as the damp warmth of his tongue slid down the crevice, pausing only momentarily at the tight, dark entrance between them. She went to her tiptoes, wicked pleasure shocking her.

Just as quickly her thighs were spread by broad, strong hands, wide shoulders holding them apart as he turned her, sitting between her thighs as his hands gripped her hips and his tongue speared into the drenched entrance of her vagina.

Shock no longer applied.

Disbelief was long gone.

As quickly as Graham made the move and penetrated her with licking, hungry strokes of his tongue, her senses were flung into such fiery chaos that reality no longer existed. Fighting to breathe, her fingers outspread, with the pads pressing firmly into the wall, Lyrica found her eyes opening.

Looking down the line of her body, she met the golden gaze of the man devouring her, flecks of rich, deep gold gleaming in his eyes as he stared up at her. As he let her watch, let her see his tongue as it retreated from the clenched depths of her pussy to move with languid strokes to the throbbing bud of her clit.

"You'll destroy me," she cried out, one hand moving from the wall to spear into the damp waves of his hair as he gave her clit an erotic, luxurious kiss.

His lips tightened on the bundle of nerves, suckling at it heatedly as his tongue flicked over it before licking with a deeper pressure just to the side, where the firm strokes seemed to ignite a spark that burned hotter, deeper through her sex.

She couldn't fight.

With one hand he urged her thighs farther apart, the pad of his thumb sliding against the narrow entrance before parting her flesh, stretching it slowly and slipping inside. There, the rasp of the callused pad stroked, caressed, moving inside her as more of the slick heat flowed from her and carnal need began beating at her senses.

With the stroke of his thumb, the fiery lash of his tongue at her clit, a wicked, tantalizing pleasure and decadent intensity rushed through her like a flaming wave. Heat built and spread, igniting, and in a split second exploded through her senses in fiery waves of ecstasy that she knew she'd never recover from. A pleasure that seemed never to end.

She shook, her body jerking at each slamming tide of rapture, and a distant part of her, an instinctive spark of self-preservation, warned her, screamed at her, demanded that she stop the headlong rush into her own destruction.

A destruction born of a pleasure she didn't know if she could deny herself.

"Fuck!" Graham's curse was barely heard, the knowledge that he was moving from between her thighs, barely registering.

The broad, heated crest of his cock parting the bare folds of her sex ignited the need inside her once again. A need the violence of her orgasm had only increased.

"Graham . . ." Her voice was heavy, her senses whirling between the vicious, overwhelming need and that small glimmer of self-preservation. "I'm a virgin."

A tear slipped from the corner of her eye, rolled down her cheek, and preceded the hitch of her breathing as she fought back the heavy sob fighting to be free.

Was she insane?

The thick crest of his erection was pressed against the clenched entrance of her pussy, ready to thrust inside her, to send them both spiraling out of control, and she had to open her mouth?

Was she crazy?

She knew he would break her heart. Loving him as she did, aching for him as she had, it would only be worse now. It would scar her soul. It would tear her apart from the inside out until there was nothing left of the woman she had been, and the woman she would become would be a stranger to her.

And Graham would be Graham. Too wicked, too experienced, too impossible to contain or to ever fall in love with the innocent woman who had loved him from the moment she'd met him at a sun-drenched marina six years before.

He would just be Graham.

And she would become no more than another of the little playthings whose names his sister could never remember, and whose presence in his bed would be easily forgotten.

She would be no more than the current flavor of the month . . .

"What did you say?"

He was dying.

Graham stood poised at the very entrance to rapture, at the portal of agonizing pleasure, and he couldn't push through. The head of his dick throbbed violently, blood pounding at the thick crest, and all he could hear was the whispered sob of a woman who knew only how to love. She had no idea how to just feel good. How to just take the pleasure for what it was, wring every last ounce of ecstasy from each touch, and still survive without hurting.

What he would do to her would go beyond destruction of the innocence in her eyes.

The sob that whispered from her was a sound he had never expected, despite the fact that he should have known. He did know, he amended.

She was a woman who still believed in love.

God help him, no woman could be that good an actress, could she?

"You're what?" Lowering his head to press his forehead against her trembling shoulder, he swallowed tightly, fighting with every iota of self-control he possessed to pull back, to ease his tortured flesh from the slick, heated entrance of her body.

"I'm sorry." Her voice shook. The words, so soft they were barely coherent, brought an agonized groan from his chest.

Damn her.

Damn him.

God, he was dying to have her. He couldn't force himself away from her, couldn't stand the thought of jacking off another night to the remembered taste and feel of her.

"You think this ends here?" he growled, the heightened lust and agonized need ripping at his senses. "That being a virgin is enough to keep me out of your body?"

A muffled sob sounded from her. "I'm sorry, Graham. I'm so sorry . . ."

"Six months." He nipped at her shoulder, licked over the mark. "It's been six months since I tasted you, Lyrica, and I'm so damned desperate to fuck you . . ."

He jerked back, her instinctive cry causing a grimace to tighten his expression. He pulled her around before dragging her to an easy chair and pushing her into it.

Surprise rounded her richly emerald eyes as the position placed her at the perfect height to allow him to push past her parted lips.

Gripping the base of his cock, he stared down at her, daring her to deny him. He was within seconds of *begging* her not to deny him.

He had to clench his teeth to hold back the broken growl of anticipation when she reached out, fingers trembling, to curl around the thick length, just above his own hand.

How innocent was she? he wondered. How much experience had the redneck bastards sniffing after her given her?

Was her innocence physical only?

Keeping her gaze locked with his, Graham slid his fingers into the mass of black silk at the side of her face, clenched, and held her still as he pressed forward.

Oh god. Oh god. Oh god.

What was she doing?

What was she allowing to happen?

The dark, plum-shaped crest touched her lips as they parted. The heavy veins that wrapped around the thick shaft pulsed and pounded beneath her grip.

"That's it, baby," he crooned, his voice tight, rough. "Part those pretty lips for me."

Her first taste of him was a shock to her senses. She could taste herself, a delicate, feminine taste she hadn't expected. Beneath it was a darker, male taste. Like a coming storm edging over the mountains.

Then he was filling her mouth, the clench and throb of his flesh pulsing against her tongue as she let it rub against the underside, just beneath the head.

The moan that slipped past her lips shocked her.

The hunger that rose inside her wiped away her hesitation.

This she had read about. She had watched it. It seemed a bit more familiar than what he had done to her.

She tightened her lips around the wide crest as he pressed deeper, filling her mouth with him, his hips flexing, thrusting in shallow strokes as she began to suck.

"Ah, baby, your mouth," he groaned, the heavy lust and pleasure filling his voice and sending shocking waves of pleasure racing through Lyrica. "It's so damned good . . ."

He wasn't touching her. Just his pleasure, his verbalization of it, and she could feel the rising chaos threatening to overtake her again.

"Use both hands." His voice was thicker, heavier. "Stroke the shaft for me, Lyrica. Stroke it while your hot little mouth makes me crazy."

Dazed, growing higher by the second on the knowledge that she could make him so hard, so desperate, Lyrica tightened her mouth on him. Drawing on the flesh filling her mouth, stretching her lips, a moan escaped her throat, vibrated against the heated width of his erection, and had his hand tightening in the hair at the side of her head.

"Lyrica, sweetheart . . ." The pace of his thrusts changed, lengthening, quickening as her fingers stroked around the heated flesh of his shaft.

The heavy throb of his erection against her tongue increased as the salty male taste of pre-cum spilled on her tongue.

She was dying for him.

Whimpering in desperation, her hips rocking against the seat of the chair, thighs clenching at the burning heat in her clit, Lyrica knew she was becoming lost in the pleasure again. First in hers, now in his.

She was fighting a losing battle.

"That's it. Ah hell, Lyrica. That's it, baby, suck my cock, sweetheart. Rub your tongue right there . . ." His voice thickened. "Ah hell, it's better than every dream I've had of fucking your pretty mouth. Every fantasy."

She cried out, the sound lost in his heavy groan as his thrusts increased, the thick flesh driving nearly to her throat, pulsing and throbbing . . .

"That's it," he groaned again. "Fuck. Baby. I won't last much longer. Look at me, Lyrica."

Forcing her eyes open, she stared into the savage expression above her. His eyes were even more golden than before, dark blond hair falling over his forehead, the short, bad-boy length of his beard and mustache shadowing a strong jaw and chin. Perspiration beaded his face, ran in a lazy rivulet down the side of his cheek.

"Pull back, Lyrica," he demanded roughly. "Fuck. I'm going to fill that pretty mouth if you don't pull back."

Pull back?

She hadn't come this far just to pull back.

Tightening her lips on him, sucking at him harder, deeper, another moan escaped her throat.

"Ah fuck. Hell. Lyrica. Damn you. Damn you, take it. Every fucking drop."

A hard throb of his cock and the first heated jet of his release hit the back of her throat.

Both hands were in her hair, holding her head still as short, quick strokes sent another pulse of salty male cum to follow the first. Then he was groaning her name, burying himself deep enough she nearly choked as several more quick, hot pulses of sperm shot to her throat and sent a rush of pleasure to explode in her womb.

How was that?

Crying, shuddering, her body was so tight, so racked by sensation and heat, that Lyrica felt a sob tearing from her rather than the groan she expected. She felt abraded from the inside out by the emotions rushing through her, mixing with her pleasure, excitement, adrenaline.

She was flying through space and time and nothing, no one, existed outside this moment, this man, and the pleasure he'd dragged her into.

Dressed, the dried sweat washed from his flesh, Graham sat in the easy chair next to the bed and stared at Lyrica as she slept, barely a half hour later. She'd collapsed into the chair as he'd pulled from her mouth, leaning into the upholstered back, the way her eyes drifted closed and exhaustion suddenly marked her expression breaking his heart.

She'd barely stayed awake through his careful cleaning of her face, breasts, and thighs. She'd showered, but excitement had laid a sheen of moisture over her flesh that would be extremely uncomfortable as it dried.

She needed to sleep.

He'd stolen precious reserves of energy from her. Energy she shouldn't have possessed after the hellish night she'd endured as she fought to race from a killer.

Reaching out, he brushed back the long fall of hair that shadowed her fragile face.

Delicate black brows arched perfectly over her closed eyes. The thick, lush lashes that lay against her cheeks were surprisingly long. High cheekbones, that straight, autocratic Mackay nose, and stubborn chin.

She was so damned beautiful she still took his breath just as easily as she had that first afternoon he'd seen her standing on the dock of Mackay Marina. Short, too slender, her emerald eyes haunted, her face suffused with a flush as her gaze stroked over him . . .

He'd hardened instantly and hated himself for it. She'd been fucking eighteen. Barely eighteen, and all he could think of was pulling her beneath his body and fucking them both silly.

Until he'd come up on the wrong end of her cousin's fist a few hours later.

He almost grinned as he cupped his chin and worked it at the memory of Natches's blow.

Natches had outlined briefly, but very clearly, exactly what would happen to the son of a bitch who dared to follow through on the promise Graham's eyes had been making as he'd stared at Lyrica.

Not that Graham hadn't hit back. He had.

Like a snarling bear with a smarting dick, he'd put Natches on his ass before informing him that even on his worst day he'd never taken advantage of a kid. Not that Lyrica had been a kid. She was eighteen, lush, and so damned beautiful he'd barely been able to stand it. But she'd still been far too vulnerable, far too innocent for the likes of Graham Brock.

Tonight, she'd proved it.

Too innocent.

A virgin, and he'd fucked her mouth with a desperation and total lack of consideration that shocked the hell out of him.

And what made it worse?

He knew damned good and well he was going to be between

her thighs, buried balls deep and fucking them both into a release that might end up getting him killed.

She was Natches Mackay's favorite female cousin, and he was pure hell with that sniper rifle he still kept cleaned and ready to bury a bullet in a man's head. Once he and his cousin Rowdy and Dawg Mackay—Lyrica's *brother*—returned, they'd all three come after his hide.

Damn. It would be worth it, he thought grimly. The pleasure he found in this woman's touch would be worth facing the wrath of the Mackays, their friend (and vengeful ex–government agent) Timothy Cranston, and whoever the hell was trying to kill her.

He'd take out the bastards who'd dare to terrify her. He'd fight her brother, both her cousins, and whoever Cranston wanted to send out for him.

It would be worth it.

But then what?

The question echoed through his mind, something he didn't want to think about.

What then?

He wasn't a forever man and he knew it. The option didn't even exist. His secrets went deep and they threatened to destroy him if he wasn't extremely careful. Him as well as the fragile, delicate woman he couldn't seem to stay away from, if those secrets weren't as dead as he hoped.

Added to that, someone was trying to kill her, no doubt as an act of vengeance against her brother and cousins.

The Mackays thought they'd taken care of the last of the homeland terrorists determined to destroy Somerset, Kentucky, and the world as they knew it last year. They were wrong.

Evidently they were still there.

Well hidden. Well funded. Determined to remain hidden and to destroy anyone who dared to threaten them.

But how in the hell did Lyrica Mackay threaten them? And why go after her and draw her brother's attention back to them?

There were far too many fucking questions and he didn't like the feel of any of them.

One thing was for damned sure, though—to get to Lyrica, they'd have to go through him first.

SIX

"We're clear inside and out." Elijah stepped into the kitchen, expression intent as he shifted the tool belt he wore about his hips into a more comfortable position. "Won't matter if they have a bug every half inch in this place, they're not going to broadcast through the diffusers I made." There was pure triumph gleaming in his dark eyes as he propped his hands on his hips and stared back at Graham with a grin. "You and your little Mackay are wrapped up snug as a bug in a complete blanket of privacy."

"Enough so that it would tip someone off?" Graham asked the other man.

The privacy was all well and good, but as much as he wanted it, he didn't want to become suspect simply because nothing was getting out.

Elijah shook his head, shaggy hair falling over his eyes for a moment before he brushed it back. "The diffuser perfectly mimics normal broadcast interference while occasionally allowing a series of prerecorded television and radio conversations I put together to simulate normal, everyday conversations. In this case, phone calls, sports shows, and male conversations. There are no female voices or even hints of such. Trust me, you're covered."

It wasn't the first time the man had created a device designed to completely stymie possible listeners.

"Any trace of watchers?"

The chance of anyone having identified him or suspected that Lyrica was in the vehicle with him as he drove out of London was thin to none.

"Nada," Elijah assured him with another quick shake of his head. "And I have about a dozen motion cameras set around the property sending data to my laptop. If anything even resembling a human hits the program it's running through, then I'll know about it."

Were their bases really covered so well?

"How could they know you have her?" Elijah kept his voice low, his back to the windows. "There's nothing that could have connected her to you."

Graham nodded absently before leaning against the counter behind him and crossing his arms over his chest as he considered his options.

Staring back at the other man thoughtfully, he considered the angles he could see. Elijah was doing the same, he knew. As laid-back and relaxed as Elijah appeared to be, Graham could detect the tension just beneath the surface.

"No one's contacted me yet," he murmured. "Dawg has a system set up . . ."

Elijah cleared his throat uncomfortably. "He took you off the list the night before he left." Shoving his hands in his pockets, his gaze met Graham's regretfully. "He didn't say why. Brogan called me to let me know a few hours before I passed you heading out of the county last night."

Graham straightened slowly, anger beginning to simmer inside him. "Then let them look for her. Once the bastard and his asshole cousins get home then I might let them know where the hell she's at."

"Come on, man." Elijah grimaced. "Don't put me in the middle here. Jed and Brogan find out I know shit and haven't told them, then they're going to try to hurt me."

"Try" being the operative word.

"Then duck faster than they try to hit," Graham growled. "The least he could have done was let me know he didn't fucking trust me to protect his sister anymore."

Elijah rubbed at the back of his neck as amused mockery filled his expression. "Maybe protecting her safety isn't what he's worried about, boss. Dawg has it in his mind it's her virtue he's protecting, I think."

"And why the hell would he worry about that?" There were days Graham was damned thankful for his training and his ability to lie in the face of his own guilt.

Elijah laughed as knowing surprise filled his face. "Come on, man, you two get around each other and it's like setting a fuse to dynamite. It just hasn't exploded yet." His brows lifted. "That I know of anyway."

Graham's jaw clenched. "Keep your damned mouth shut about her whereabouts," he ordered the other man again. "Let's see if any of them are smart enough to know where she's at."

He pulled her cell phone and battery from his back pocket then and tossed the two on the kitchen table. "I'll call the airfield and authorize the chopper for you. Fly out to D.C. and meet with Doogan. Give him the battery and phone and tell him to find out who the hell is tracking it and how they managed to block her entire contact list from incoming or outgoing calls. When he locates the bastard, I want to know where the hell he's at."

"Damn, I have to meet with Doogan?" Elijah asked him in disgust. "Come on, Graham. That ain't right. I'm convinced that man has bad mojo or some shit. Every time I get around him, I get my ass shot at."

Graham's boss wasn't the sanest man in the world, but he focused his insanity at the enemy rather than at any friendlies.

"You have thirty minutes to get to the airfield. I want you back this evening and I want you taking care of those cameras. You keep the outside secure; I'll work on keeping Lyrica out of sight."

And the ideas he had for that threatened to make his jeans damned uncomfortable.

"But Doogan gets me shot at," Elijah muttered, repeating the earlier accusation. "I don't like that man, Graham."

"Damn, Elijah, what makes you think I care if you like him?" Graham glared at him, amazed at the agent's cowardice in the face of the new assistant director of Homeland Security. "Tell him I said if he gets you shot, I'll shoot him. How's that?"

"Does he listen to you?" Elijah frowned back at Graham far too seriously.

"For god's sake, are you two?" Doogan wasn't that bad. The man was a little eccentric, but Graham knew he wasn't actually dangerous. He just tended to get a little overly daring when he had the right agents for the job. No doubt he would consider Elijah the right man for some job that could put him in the line of fire. But hell, that was part of the job description.

Right?

Invariably, someone did get shot if they weren't extremely careful.

Graham was always extremely careful.

It sounded as though Elijah needed to learn caution.

"I feel about two whenever I get around that bastard," Elijah muttered. "Hell, I was almost cryin' for my mommy last year when he hijacked my ass from FPS. And trust me, my momma wouldn't give a shit. That should tell you how desperate I am."

"You have twenty minutes to get to the airfield," Graham stated blandly. "Give Doogan my regards."

"Give Doogan your regards?" Elijah grumbled mutinously as he threw Graham another disgusted look. "I'll give him some- thing. My damned Glock shoved straight up his ass. That's what I'll give him." Then his dark eyes narrowed. "And you're forget- ting something. Sam Bryce knows exactly who went after her last night. You think she's not going to tell her boss?"

Sam Bryce knew better. Until he gave the word, she wouldn't say shit if Dawg himself held a gun to her head.

Elijah turned then, opened the door, and stalked from the house as Graham continued to stare at him expectantly, intently.

The fact that the agent wasn't happy with his current orders didn't worry Graham. Elijah would follow the program whether he liked it or not.

The question was whether the man would keep his former commander out of the loop. The fact that Lyrica was Brogan Campbell's future sister-in-law and that Elijah's orders were more personal than agency related threatened Graham's assurance that he would do as he was told.

Fuck it.

Knowing he'd been cut out of Lyrica's protection list without so much as a notice changed all the damned rules. He wasn't risk- ing possible exposure to call Dawg, his cousins, his buddies, or his friends. If they didn't like that then they could kiss his ass.

Lyrica's safety, and her place in his bed while she was there, was more important than Dawg's paranoia where his sister's vir- ginity was concerned.

Pushing his fingers restlessly through his hair at the thought,

Graham moved to the door Elijah had stalked through and tested the lock. He then pulled the shades down over the windows before adjusting them to allow him to glimpse anyone moving outside, while hiding the inside away from curious eyes.

Moving through the house to adjust the rest of the shades similarly, he took his cell phone from the belt holster he wore and quickly pulled up Sam's number.

"Hey there," she answered, her voice soft, her tone familiar. "How's it going?"

"As expected," he answered. "Sis still there?"

"Still sleeping." Amusement filled her voice. "She was up most of the night pacing the floors and cursing you."

Graham grinned at the knowledge that Kye had no doubt cursed him loudly.

"Sorry about that. She may be staying there a while longer."

"Not a problem. She filled the car with cases, so I think she may have suspected. Tell me, did you contact the lost puppy's owner?"

The lost puppy. No doubt Lyrica would be incensed if she knew the title she'd been given for the call.

"Naw. It's a cute little thing, though." He grinned as he spoke. "I'm thinking about keeping it for a while. It's lonely around here by myself."

Silence filled the line for long moments. "The puppy has a home, my friend. Don't forget that. And the owner might not be the sort to appreciate anyone thinking he can steal it away."

"Then I guess they should have been more careful about the care and security of the little thing," he growled. "As well as the fact that they dropped a friend from puppy-sitting duties without informing him. I might have been more inclined to give the puppy up if he had."

Sam laughed.

The muffled sound was rich, filled with amusement and wicked knowledge.

"You are in so much trouble, my friend," she continued, laughing. "And I can't wait until the fireworks. I think your sister and I will find front-row seats to the spectacle."

No doubt they would, and sell extra tickets in the process for the hell of it.

Graham snarled silently. "I used to like you."

"Sure, you did—that's why you tried to stick me with good ole Doogan when I applied for this position. I haven't forgotten that, you know."

Doogan really wasn't that bad, Graham told himself as he disconnected the call and shoved the phone back into the holster pocket. Hell, he'd never had much trouble out of Doogan himself.

Except for that little fiasco in South America.

Graham frowned as he set the alarms to the house and the fenced main yard.

There was the accident in Russia . . .

He paused and stared out at the pool.

Doogan had nearly gotten them both killed in Cuba a few years before . . .

Okay, so maybe he was that bad, but hell, Doogan had a dirty job. For as long as Graham had known the man, Chatham Doogan had carried a hell of a lot of responsibility on his shoulders. No matter how many times things had gone from sugar to shit, Doogan couldn't have done better . . .

Well, he could have refrained from sleeping with the daughter of that dictator in South America. And no doubt he could have held back just a little when he beat the shit out of that Kremlin guard for hitting his little wife . . .

Dammit.

Doogan was a damned good friend anyway.

Lyrica slept until late afternoon, awakening with a dull headache and weary resignation. She was stuck with Graham until Dawg returned home. That knowledge didn't help the pressure building in her temples in the least. The memory of the flames consuming her earlier only increased her certainty that if she didn't get away from him, and quickly, then there would be no denying him, no matter what he wanted. No matter how much it would destroy her.

Rising from his bed—his bed.

Yep, she was all but officially part of the Graham Brock fuck-me club. The one she had sworn to his sister she would never join.

Kye was going to kill her, there was no doubt. And it wouldn't be a merciful end.

Graham's sister would cut a friend out of her life so fast for becoming focused on her brother that it would make her head spin. She didn't care about letting anyone and everyone know that hooking up with her brother was a betrayal of their friendship. And she had stuck to her word every time it had happened.

Lyrica might have focused on Kye initially because of her fascination with Graham, but it was the friendship that had grown in the past year that had become more important to Lyrica. That and the knowledge that Graham went through women nearly as fast as other men went through underwear.

Graham of course didn't wear underwear. That little piece of information had been relayed by last June's bimbo, DeeDee or something. She'd been very smug, very triumphant as she informed Lyrica and Kye of that little fact after his sister made the same observation concerning his women.

Not that DeeDee seemed concerned with keeping him. She hadn't been. Evidently it had been enough to achieve the status of his flavor of the month. She hadn't lasted a month, Lyrica thought with a grimace. Kye had instantly squealed on the other woman to Graham, informing him with sisterly disillusionment that whether or not he wore underwear was information she really hadn't needed.

DeeDee had been dropped instantly.

The other woman still blamed both Kye and Lyrica for her untimely exit from the bed of the Stud of Pulaski County, as Lyrica's sister Zoey called him.

It wasn't far from the truth.

Moving quickly from Graham's bed to Kye's bedroom and slipping into the massive walk-in closet her friend had invited her to make use of whenever she needed, Lyrica hurriedly chose jeans, a violet silk top with tiny straps, and violet sandals.

There was no point in even glancing at the bras hanging in the corner; Lyrica knew they didn't fit. Kye was far more ample in her cup size. Clothes in hand, she locked herself in her friend's bathroom, showered and dressed, then dipped into Kye's vast store of makeup and hair care products.

An hour later, she stepped back into the bedroom only to come to a stop, her head lifting defiantly at the sight of Graham as he leaned casually against the bedroom doorway.

He'd changed from the light cotton pants he'd worn earlier. Jeans, a white button-down shirt, and boots covered the lean, powerful body, but nothing could hide the aura of seductive intent that filled his expression.

"You could have told me you were awake." The gleam of hungry interest in his eyes had a flush rushing through her face.

For a second the memory of what had happened in his bedroom before she'd collapsed into the bed flashed before her eyes.

Graham sitting between her spread thighs, his tongue buried

inside her. The way he'd pushed her into the chair next to the bed and buried the head of his erection between her lips.

The feel of it.

The taste of him.

The release that had torn through her each time.

"Have you contacted Dawg yet?" Pushing her hands into the front pockets of her borrowed jeans, Lyrica forced herself to break the lock he had on her gaze.

"Not yet." There was an edge to his voice that had her frowning back at him in confusion.

"Have you tried to?" That little glimmer of anger in his gaze was her first indication that if her life hadn't already gone to hell then it was well and truly on its way there now.

"Can't say that I have." An arch of his brow, a tightening of his lips, and Lyrica felt her heart begin to race furiously in excitement.

Glancing away from him, she prayed for patience for several long seconds before focusing on him once again.

"Why haven't you contacted Dawg? You have to get ahold of him." How else would he know she was in trouble? That she needed him? "He, Rowdy, and Natches need to come home. What if Zoey's in trouble, too?"

There was just one of Graham, and there were two men after her. What if he was hurt?

She felt her knees weaken at the thought. Graham could be killed . . .

But so could Dawg, Rowdy, and Natches. There was Alex, her cousin Janey's husband. And Shane Mayes, the new sheriff. His father, Zeke, and stepmother, Rogue . . .

Oh god, everyone she knew would try to help her and they could all be hurt. What had she done? By coming back to Somerset she was placing everyone she loved directly in danger.

"I think I can handle this, Lyrica," Graham assured her as her head spun with the knowledge of what could happen. "Dawg should have thought of what would happen if I learned I was taken from the list of those to be contacted if you were in trouble. Now he can guess as to who's protecting you."

"Pissing contest," she said faintly, trying desperately to keep her wits about her.

She would have to find a way to leave the house and Graham. She would have to figure out where she could go, where she could hide. She couldn't ask anyone she knew to help her. She couldn't countenance pulling anyone else into danger, even her mother's lover, Timothy, an ex–Homeland Security agent.

Timothy would never trust random agents to protect her. He would instantly contact Dawg. Then her brother and their families would fly home. Hell, Timothy would have them flown home.

She had to leave.

And she was going to have to do it quickly.

Graham watched as Lyrica's face whitened, her slight body almost swaying only seconds after she informed him that Dawg had to return. Now she wasn't arguing with him, wasn't insisting that he call—she was angry.

Terror.

He could see that deep well of fear shadowing her eyes as her mind worked through the implications and the danger to those she loved suddenly rushed through her mind. And, having realized it now, that swift, mercurial little brain of hers was searching, sorting, considering, and weighing her options.

Her escape from him.

He almost grinned. At least she was thinking of him, no matter how angry he made her.

"I'm sorry you were dragged into this. I should have thought," she finally said, shaking her head before staring back at him with such vulnerability it tightened his chest, and for the first time in his life, he felt something where his heart was supposed to be—melting.

Hell, someone besides his sister really gave a damn if he lived or died for them.

"Lyrica, sweetheart, this is a child's game as far as I'm concerned," he snorted. "Whoever had the balls to come after you hasn't been covering their tracks as well as they thought they were. I won't know just who they are but where they are, and exactly what the hell is going on, within forty-eight hours. And trust me, once I have the answers, I'll have their hides for even daring to think they could strike out at you without repercussions."

He was amused.

In the past hours he'd reached out to several underground contacts and sorted through the rumors and hints of jobs up for grabs. What he was piecing together was damned interesting. Even more interesting was the fact that if he was right, then his prey would be within striking distance even sooner than he'd imagined.

All he had to do now was wait for Elijah's return to begin making contact and making the commander of that little group sorry he'd ever dared to take such a job without talking to Graham.

"Children don't play with guns." It was obvious he wasn't convincing her.

Straightening from the door frame, he stepped back. "Come downstairs. I have the house secure, so we don't have to worry about being overheard. And I have dinner ready."

"I can move back into the room I normally use, then," she stated, instantly piecing that one together.

Graham chuckled. She had always had the most incredible ability to make him laugh. He'd always liked that about her.

"We'll discuss that," he lied, amused. "Over dinner."

Turning and moving down the hallway, Graham restrained his satisfaction when he realized she was following him.

She was still thinking, though. That wasn't a good thing. Had she pushed aside whatever plans she was making after those first few minutes, then he wouldn't have been nearly as concerned. But she was still building on whatever plots and plans were rolling through her mind.

Making his way downstairs, he listened for the pad of the leather soles of her sandals. He recognized the outfit she wore, but he'd be damned if he would let his sister ever wear it again. The way it shaped Lyrica's pretty little body would be forever branded into his mind.

The violet silk of the strappy little top did very little to hide the fact that she was braless. The slim fit of the jeans hugged her hips and thighs like a lover's caress and made him damned jealous. Hell, he wanted to touch her like that. Delicate little toes gripped the thongs of the sandals and revealed the pearly pink of the polish she'd painted them with. The whimsical color was so damned girly and flirty he couldn't help but smile at the thought of it.

"Have a seat." Gesturing to the small table sitting in front of a set of shaded windows, Graham moved to the counter and the plate of cold sandwiches he'd just finished making when she passed the silent alarm he'd set to notify his cell phone of movement.

Still silent, she moved across the room and pulled out one of the four chairs.

Damn, when had he begun actually sensing when Lyrica's Mackay genetics were kicking into overdrive and that far too intelligent brain of hers was beginning to plot world domination? Or at the very least, some scheme designed to make him totally insane.

Normally, Kye was right there with her. At those times, he actually developed heartburn. Now, though, it was worse. It wasn't heartburn—the hairs at the back of his neck were actually starting to lift in primal warning.

Snagging a bowl, he dumped a healthy portion of potato chips into it then lifted the platter and moved both to the table where Lyrica waited.

As she watched him with wide, shadowed eyes, her hands clasped nervously in her lap, he had to restrain the curse hovering on his lips.

Son of a bitch, he was going to spend all his time trying to find ways not just to keep the assailants out, but to keep Lyrica inside as well. And there was no way to be effective at both.

Placing the platter and bowl in the center of the table, Graham retrieved the plates, set them out, then filled two glasses with ice and sweet tea while he considered his options.

There were several ways he could forestall what he sensed would be an attempt by her to run, to protect everyone she loved by trying to hide, rather than dealing with this. Each would be completely effective, though all but one had several drawbacks.

Keeping her tied to his bed was his particular favorite, but if she wasn't into that, then he doubted he'd find much pleasure in it. He could lock her in the basement and seduce her there. The apartment-size lower floor was secure, all but unbreachable, and fully furnished. There were far too many pieces of furniture that she could use as weapons once she realized she was pretty much a prisoner, though.

That left one last option. Confronting her with it.

Pulling out his chair, he straddled it, placed his forearms on the table, and watched her, waiting, knowing it was coming.

That gleam of mutiny. The fiery fight that filled her, the temper that was always just out of sight, making an appearance.

"Don't you stare at me like that, Graham Brock," she ordered him, voice low, lips tightening. "No one died and made you the boss of me."

There it was.

"Keep telling yourself that," he suggested softly, hearing the deep, unconscious rasp of command in his voice. A sound he'd rarely heard since coming home. "Convince yourself of that if you have to, Lyrica. Whatever helps you sleep at night. But if you slip out, if you run, if you give even a fucking second's thought to facing this alone, then I promise you—take it to the fucking bank and cash this one, sweetheart—I will make damned sure you understand exactly how I can, and I will, ensure you never do something so stupid again." Sitting back, he placed two sandwich halves and a handful of chips on her plate, pushed it to her, then served himself.

Her eyes hadn't left his face. His expression hadn't changed.

"Wanna try me?" he finally asked.

Pounding hard and heavy already, the pulse at her neck throbbed harder, faster. Her face was flushed, her gaze edged with an arousal he'd more than anticipated.

She cleared her throat before answering him. "Not at the moment."

"And here I was hoping you would." His teeth bit into the sandwich and he was rewarded with the faintest twitch of reaction from her.

Hell no, she had no intention of trying him. At least, not anytime soon. And in this case, he'd lied—he'd prayed she wouldn't. Some lessons were best learned through pleasure rather than a need to prove exactly who was more dominant, who was the boss when it came to doing what he did best.

Protecting what he claimed as his.

SEVEN

"You're not calling Dawg out of spite," Lyrica said accusingly to Graham as he put away the remainder of the sandwiches and chips.

"You think?" Lifting his brows with heavy mockery, he pulled his cell phone from the holster at his side and placed it in the center of the table. "Bastard didn't even let me know I wasn't part of the group anymore. Damned inconsiderate if you ask me."

She wasn't certain if she should be amused by his consternation at being left out or outraged that it was the only reason he wasn't contacting her brother.

"Dawg's going to kick your ass, Graham. If Natches doesn't beat him to it." Crossing her arms on top of the table, Lyrica watched him worriedly.

The grin that tilted his lips was a little too playful. He sat back in the chair and watched her closely. Lyrica was trying damned hard not to think about the invitation she could see in his gaze.

"Natches isn't going to take a bead on me for not calling nor will he kick my ass. He'll throw his fist. Once. Dawg will get his turn and it will be over." He seemed far too calm about it.

Lyrica shook her head. "That might be true, but you're not considering one thing."

"Oh, yeah?" His grin was confident, self-assured.

"Rowdy."

Graham's eyes narrowed back at her as though considering her answer. "Rowdy's pretty laid-back. He lets Dawg and Natches get the bruises."

"It all depends on how far you push him," she informed him. "And I'm pretty certain that neglecting to let his wife know one of Dawg's sisters, who she claims as her niece, is safe, would push him to that limit. Rowdy can be dangerous."

"Rowdy also has the amazing ability to understand simple logic. Something Dawg and Natches aren't so good at," he snorted.

She couldn't argue that one.

"But we're not discussing Dawg and Natches."

"Lyrica." He leaned forward slowly, his amber eyes suspicious now. "Don't you trust me to protect you?"

It had nothing to do with trust, Lyrica knew. It was desperation. If he was determined to do this, then he might need help.

"Backup never hurt anyone when guns are involved, Graham. You should know that," she pointed out archly. "My family makes good backup."

"Your family's full of control freaks," he snorted with a laugh. "Baby, you and I both know there would be no backup. They'd rush you out of here so damned fast it would make both our heads spin. And I think that's what you're counting on. Now, I'll ask you again." His voice lowered, his expression becoming more serious. "Don't you trust me to protect you?"

She did.

Lyrica knew Graham would be a hell of a force to be reckoned with, just as she knew that if she stayed with him, she would end up being owned by him.

"I trust you to protect me, Graham." She finally nodded as she clasped her hands on the table and stared down at her nails for a long minute. "I don't doubt for a second that we'll both survive and when the smoke clears, just like Dawg and the others, you'll be victorious." Mockery edged her voice as she lifted her gaze then. "But why do I have a feeling that if it wasn't for the fact that they are my family, you would have called them the second you had a chance?"

"Of course I would have," he answered, his gaze gleaming with unabashed laughter. "There's no one I'd rather have at my back. But they're not the only game in town and they aren't even in town at the moment. Remember? I have other friends. And I have other friends just as well trained and just as adaptable as the Mackays are."

She looked around the kitchen slowly before arching a brow and meeting his gaze once again. "Are you hiding them in the closets?"

"That's as good a place as any," he informed her with a little wink before leaning forward and pulling up the recorder program on his phone. "I'll see if they want to come out and play after we go over everything that's happened."

She knew he was going to ask about that. From the second she'd seen him standing in the doorway to Kye's room, she'd known he was going to make her go over everything.

"I'd rather just forget it." She'd lived through it, wasn't that enough?

"Are you always this difficult, sweetheart?" The expression on his face became more wicked, hungry, as his voice lowered, his gaze darkening. "I have a cure for all that energy."

"Stop." She couldn't handle it. She didn't want to handle it.

Leaning her weight on her arms, she let her gaze meet his fully. "I'm not one of your damned flavors of the month, Graham. I refuse to be. And I sure as hell refuse to lose Kye's friendship so I can share your bed for a few weeks. And I really don't appreciate your insistence on making sure your sister and I are never friends again."

His gaze narrowed once again. "Kye has nothing to do with this, Lyrica. And trust me, you two are far too close for her to drop you as she has others."

"But you're just fine with taking that risk, aren't you?" Lyrica pushed back from the table and flashed him a disgusted look.

"Do you think I'm going to force you into having sex with me?" he asked her carefully.

"You don't have to force me and we both know it." Keeping her back to him, Lyrica walked to the entrance of the sunroom, taking in the closed shades and the cool, dim shadows that washed over the heavily padded furniture.

"Just as we both know Kyleene won't drop your friendship and Natches won't really put a bullet in me for it." He was closer.

That quietly, that smoothly, he'd left the table and she hadn't even known it. She hadn't heard so much as a creak of the chair or his shoes on the wood.

Turning quickly, she found herself staring at the white material covering his broad chest as his hands lifted to cup her upper arms.

"All you have to do is say no," he whispered, his head lowering until his lips were at her ear, brushing against the far too sensitive lobe erotically.

She was losing her breath.

Lips parting, Lyrica fought to take in oxygen as her hands pressed against the tight plane of his abdomen. She tried to swallow against the tightness in her throat.

Suddenly her whole body was too sensitive. Her breasts swollen, nipples aching. The skin over her stomach remembered the brush of his fingers, the dampness between her thighs reminding her far too much of his lips and tongue tasting her there, throwing her into such a rush of pleasure that the need for it was almost addictive now.

"Do you want to say no, Lyrica?" Those diabolical, far too experienced lips moved to her neck as her head tilted helplessly for him.

Fiery, electric fingers of pleasure tore across the nerve endings just beneath his lips to the swollen, aching bud of her clit as it pulsed between her legs.

She couldn't say no. Did she want to? It was for the best and she knew it. Saying no was the smartest thing she could possibly do at this point.

But she couldn't.

When his lips moved to hers, she was waiting for them. Hers parted, a moan slipping past her throat as his lips covered hers in a kiss that rocked her to her soul.

One hand gripped the back of her head; the other lifted her closer to him, wrapped around her lower back as he bent to her, then lifted her as her knees gripped his hips instinctively.

There.

A trembling cry escaped the kiss as her fingers speared into his hair to hold him to her, to immerse herself in the pleasure rushing through her senses like a tidal wave. How had she ever kept herself from begging for this? How would she keep herself from begging for it when her time was up? When the few fragile weeks he allowed his lovers came to an end?

Tightening her thighs around his hips, Graham cupped the curves of her ass and clenched erotically, sending another swift strike of sensation to her clit. The heavy length of his erection rubbed her jeans against the sensitive folds of her sex and sent damp warmth spilling out sensually. His lips plundered hers, his tongue stroked, rubbed, and tasted hers, and each caress, each flash of heat, made her weaker, pushed her deeper into the pleasure overtaking her.

She knew now what was awaiting her. She knew the lashing flames and spearing bolts of ecstasy that would consume her, and she ached for it. She hungered for it.

For him.

The thick support of one of the cushions that covered the lounge chairs met her back. Graham covered her, his hips pressing and rubbing into the vee of her thighs.

"Damn you," he growled, his lips moving from her mouth to her neck, placing stinging kisses as the short length of his beard rasped against her flesh.

The erotic abrasion had her lifting to him, needing more. Fingers tightening in his hair, she held his lips to her neck, encouraging his teeth to scrape against it. His lips and tongue drove her insane as they stimulated the oversensitive nerve endings and responsive flesh.

"Damn clothes," he snarled suddenly. Lifting his weight from her he pushed the silken top over her breasts.

Unbound, her nipples pebble hard, the swollen curves felt too tight, too sensitive as he cupped one with his palm and lifted it to his lips.

The sound of AC/DC's "Highway to Hell" sang from the kitchen, the ringtone instantly pulling Graham's attention from the needy tip of her breast.

"Fuck!" he bit out.

Jumping up from the lounge chair, his jaw tight as his gaze raked over her in hungry regret, he rushed to the kitchen.

Every cell in his body was screaming in outrage as Graham stomped to the kitchen and jerked the cell phone from the table. Activating the call, he brought the device to his ear with a sharp, "What?"

"You have friendlies entering the driveway," Elijah hissed. "And don't cuss me. I just found out myself when Cranston called Doogan. Now call Doogan and get me the hell out of here."

"And how did they know where she was, Elijah?" Graham asked carefully, anger tearing through him. "Just how loud did you squeal?"

"Hell no," Elijah retorted, the denial sharp. "I didn't tell them shit. But I'm pretty damned sure Doogan might have texted Cranston. I saw him texting. Twenty minutes later the alarm coming into your property activated an image of Campbell's truck racing past. Now get me the hell out of here."

Graham disconnected the call.

Staring back at Lyrica as she stepped into the kitchen, her expression questioning, he couldn't help but wonder if it wasn't for the best.

"You're about to be rescued," he stated as he shoved the phone into the holster he'd taken it from earlier. "Your brother-in-law and god knows who else is pulling into the drive now."

She didn't speak; she just watched him. Damned if he could read that look, either. Somber, intense, expectant. What the fuck was he supposed to say or do? He was so damned hard he could drive spikes with his dick. The need to fuck her was like a hunger that burned and raged through his senses.

"Don't leave, Lyrica." He forced the words past his lips, and dammit, that was more than he'd ever given any other woman. He'd never regretted seeing one leave before, and he'd never wanted to ask one to stay longer.

"What would staying accomplish?" she asked softly. "I'll

end up in your bed and you'll break my heart. Is that something either of us wants or needs, Graham? Do we want that between us?"

"And you think you can just walk away from it?" he asked, almost amused at the idea of it. "Son of a bitch, you really are too damned innocent for this, Lyrica. Otherwise you'd know it's simply not that fucking easy."

A frown pulled at her brow as she pushed her hands into the pockets of the jeans she wore and stared at her feet for a long moment. As her head lifted, her lips parting to speak, a hard fist landed on the front door.

"The cavalry," he said, mocking her softly. "You've been rescued, baby."

Turning, he strode from the kitchen and along the hall to the front door. Checking the security monitor at the entrance, he glimpsed Brogan Campbell's hard features as well as Chief of Police Alex Jansen. Behind them, former special agent Timothy Cranston of the Department of Homeland Security.

He could sense Lyrica behind him. Glancing over his shoulder, he saw her at the kitchen entrance, still watching him with those dark, solemn emerald eyes. She wasn't going to say a damned thing, was she? No protest, no regret. She was ready to leave, plain and simple.

Turning back, he jerked the door open and stepped back.

"There she is, safe and sound," he snarled back at the men, ignoring their surprise. "Take her the fuck home and see if you can't keep her ass out of trouble long enough to find out who the fuck is trying to kill her."

He'd be damned if he'd watch her walk out of his house. Hell, he didn't know if he could watch her walk away. He'd end up throwing her over his shoulder like a damned captive and trying to hide her away until he could get his fill of her.

Instead, he turned, moved to the stairs, and stalked up them quickly.

"Graham." The sound of her voice stopped him just before he reached the last step.

He couldn't help but turn. She stood in the foyer, staring up at him, her expression tightening his chest even though he had no idea why it should fucking hurt.

"Thank you for saving me," she said softly, her hands pushed into the front pockets of those damned jeans again. "For not hesitating."

"It's no more than I'd expect one of your family to do for my sister," he stated coldly, his hand lifting to the banister, his fingers tightening on it furiously. "It's what friends do. Right?"

Pausing, heavily lashed lids blinked over damp emerald eyes before she finally nodded. "Yeah, it's what friends do."

Graham slid his gaze to the men standing behind her.

They knew. He could see it in their eyes, in the narrow-eyed suspicion and the gleaming anger reflected in them.

"Stop glaring at me, gentlemen," he said derisively. "I promise, she's not in the running for flavor of the month. She turned me down flat. You'd be real damned proud of her."

They could see themselves out now.

Turning his back on them, he finished the final steps before striding quickly to his bedroom. Hell, he didn't have time for this bullshit anyway.

The crack of the bedroom door slamming into the frame wasn't nearly as satisfying as he thought it would be.

Lyrica flinched at the sound of wood crashing into wood as she stepped from the front door, her heart jumping into her throat at the sight of a half-dozen police officers standing at attention, rifles held ready in their hands as sharp gazes swept the area carefully.

Alex was in front of her, blocking the view of her, Brogan behind her, while Timothy and Jedediah Booker each covered a side.

"Brogan?" Pure terror crashed into her system at the sight of the security they'd left outside.

"It's just a precaution, sweetheart." Tim was suddenly there, his voice amused, affectionate. "Come on, we have to do the drama thing or Dawg would think we weren't taking this seriously. You know what a damned bitch he can be when he thinks we're not watching after his baby sisters."

He was holding her close to his side, though, the four men keeping near to her as they escorted her to the waiting black SUV with the back door open at the bottom of the rock-lined steps that led to Graham's front door.

She was shaking.

As Alex stepped aside from the open door and helped her into the SUV, his expression was far too serious and intent. This wasn't just precaution.

Timothy followed her as she slid in, pushing her to the passenger side of the seat as Jed and Brogan moved into the front seats and Alex slid into the back row, directly behind her. She should have stayed in Graham's house, she thought. If she had, then her sisters' men and her mother's lover wouldn't be here protecting her and risking their safety.

"Did Graham call?" she asked Timothy, rubbing at the finger-nails of one hand.

"No, Graham didn't call." Tim couldn't hide the steely anger in his voice as he spoke. "He should have."

She swallowed tightly. "Someone messed with my phone. And Kye couldn't call me from hers. She used Graham's because hers was acting so weird when she tried to call last night. He was afraid the numbers on my contact list might be compromised."

Immediately phones were pulled. Brogan tossed Jed his phone and Lyrica watched silently as the back of each phone was opened, batteries were pulled, and the phones inspected carefully. Finally, they were put together again, turned on, and rechecked.

"Phones are clear, Lyrica," Tim promised her, turning to watch her somberly.

"Mine wasn't, Tim," she informed him. "Graham wouldn't lie to me and he wouldn't lie to Kye."

"I never imagined he would." Running his hand over the top of his head, Tim blew out a hard breath. "Graham's partner checked in with their boss and the boss notified us of your whereabouts. We've been trying to get hold of you since last night. We've had damned near every cop in four counties looking for you as well as countless DHS agents in the area. We were about to call Dawg when I received the text informing me of your whereabouts."

"Graham's boss?" Lyrica frowned back at him now. "Graham joined DHS?"

Kye had been certain over the past few months that something was up with her brother, that he was acting far too secretive. Evidently, she was right.

"No, he hasn't joined DHS." Tim sighed, glancing away from her momentarily. "I spoke rather loosely perhaps. Graham doesn't work for DHS, but sometimes, he reports any anomalies he sees. He reports this to another agent who then reports to D.C."

"I hate it when you lie to me." And he was lying; she knew all the signs. Her mother had laughingly relayed those signs to all her daughters to ensure that, in his efforts to protect them, Tim didn't keep needed information from them. "And I'm telling Mom as soon as I see her. Maybe you'll tell her the truth."

Tim grimaced before wiping his hand over his face in irritation. "Dammit, Lyrica. I swear to god, the Mackays are going to drive me to an early grave and that's the damned truth." He cursed under his breath.

"Graham's not officially an agent, Lyrica, and his work with whatever agency he's with can't be mentioned. Especially to his sister, Kye." Brogan met her gaze in the rearview mirror then. "Give us time to get you back to your mother's place and we'll explain everything."

She rather doubted they would explain anything more than they absolutely had to. She knew these men, and she knew their protectiveness and determination to keep the true extent of their work from those they loved. How much her sister Eve knew of Brogan's work, she wasn't certain. But Piper laughingly claimed that as far as she could tell, Jed was no more, no less than the contractor he claimed to be, even though she knew he and Tim locked themselves in Tim's office far too often to "discuss" things.

Tim only did that when he was gathering information on things that were going on in the county that he needed to report back to DHS.

Retired, her ass.

Her mother as well as her sisters all knew Tim wasn't nearly as retired as he pretended to be.

"Your mother's beside herself with worry," Tim told her softly as he reached over and patted her shoulder gently. "We've all been damned worried."

"I know. I'm sorry, Tim. I tried to call."

"I guess Graham has the phone?" Brogan growled then. "I'll head back and pick it up later. We'll need it."

Lyrica lifted her head, turned, and stared through the darkened window of the SUV rather than answering.

Yes, Graham had her phone, but she'd left more than that at his house. She could feel everything inside her longing to return, to assure him she didn't want to leave. That she didn't care which flavor he wanted her to be that month, as long as he tasted her again.

How pitiful was she? How desperate?

Just as she had always known she would be.

If Tim and the males of her extended family hadn't shown up, she would be in his bed now. She didn't have the strength to deny him again. Nor did she have the strength to shock him into stopping as she had that morning.

She'd known it had simply been a reprieve. Staring into his eyes after he'd pulled back from fucking her mouth, the taste of him still lingering on her tongue, she'd been shocked by her own response, by the acts she'd already shared with him. Rocked by the pleasure and hungers she hadn't known she could share with any man, she'd needed time to come to terms with it. Or a chance to deny herself what she wanted most.

As she'd lain beneath him on the lounge chair in his sunroom, she'd known there was no running, no denying. There was no way she could walk away from him.

Until Tim had arrived with a protection detail to rival the president's.

Seeing the police officers stationed to cover her exit from the house, the way she was escorted to the SUV, and how she was blocked by large male bodies now, she knew every iota of freedom she'd wrested from Dawg over the past few years was over. Once he found out about this, she'd probably be locked up so tight and so deep that she wouldn't taste sunlight for days on end.

Dawg was too protective.

But, she admitted at the moment, she was terrified, too.

And all she wanted was to run and hide in Graham's arms again.

EIGHT

Two weeks later

Lyrica stared back at Tim as he read the investigation report her brother-in-law, Brogan Campbell, and her future brother-in-law, Jedediah Booker, had brought into Tim's office earlier. Dawg, Natches, and Rowdy had helped, he'd stated, and they'd verified everything through the Kentucky State Police as well as the Department of Homeland Security.

The contact list on her phone had been jammed by a high-tech device that affected only the numbers on that list when they were attempting to call Lyrica. The device was new technology, and detection for it hadn't been perfected yet.

"Fourteen hours after you were shot at, a young woman perfectly matching your description was found two blocks over," Tim continued, watching her somberly. "She was an informant for the state police on a drug gang moving into the area. Everything points to a case of mistaken identity."

Were they crazy? Did they really believe something so preposterous?

"Mistaken identity?" Tilting her head, she stared back at him in disbelief, certain she must have misheard him.

"Lyrica, I've had this investigated on three different fronts." Tim leaned forward, his somber expression and fierce hazel eyes piercing. "We've covered it ourselves. We've followed every lead, every shadow that could be found. The state police have covered it on their end and the Department of Homeland Security sent a team out to look into it as well. We've all come to the same conclusion. The assailants thought they'd found the informant they were looking for when you checked into the hotel. You should be safe now."

She should be safe now? She'd gone through all this because they were searching for someone else? Someone had died, even though Lyrica had been mistaken for her?

And why did she have such a hard time believing this?

"This can't be real," she whispered painfully, staring around the room at the men that filled it. "It's just wrong."

It didn't feel right. Nothing had felt right since the night she had stepped out of that elevator and realized someone was in her hotel room.

Her brother grimaced, his pale green eyes filled with regret and concern. "Sometimes the realization that there are no monsters in the shadows is the greatest battle, sweetheart."

And how very skewed was that one?

"Great." Rising quickly to her feet, she ran her hands down the sides of her hips, straightened the hem of her cotton shirt, then faced her family with that same sense of unreality. As though she wasn't fully there, yet wasn't really dreaming either.

The odd sensation had her off balance, and it refused to allow the fear that had filled her for the past weeks to recede.

"I'm going back to my apartment, then," she announced, ignoring Dawg's objection.

It was instinctive, she thought. Two weeks of believing she was in danger, only to be told there was really no danger, left her sick to her stomach with the knowledge that she seemed to be the only one that found this mistaken identity supposition to be so very convenient.

No one should have died. But someone had to throw her family off the fact that she was going to die. Or was she simply so paranoid now that she couldn't see the truth?

"Lyrica, wait another day or so." Tim came slowly to his feet, the white shirt he wore folded back at the sleeves, his slacks still appearing freshly ironed.

Sometimes it was very hard to associate the man she had known for the past few years with the man her brother and cousins knew before he met her mother, Mercedes.

"I'm not waiting, Tim. I've waited two weeks just to learn that someone else was murdered that night despite the fact that I nearly died as well." Shaking her head, she ignored the fact that Dawg stood silently, his pale gaze far too intense and knowing. "I want to be alone for a while. I want to be home."

In the short time she had lived there, her apartment had become home. It had become a haven away from the craziness that her family could sometimes be. That their lives never failed to be.

It wasn't Dawg's fault. It was just that he had a past, one that had already threatened her older sister Eve. He was terrified it would affect her and Zoey now. But he didn't stop there. No, Dawg worried over every phase of their lives, even their non-existent-because-he-fucked-it-up love lives.

Of course, he knew where Alex and Brogan had found her before he'd been told what had happened. They wouldn't have hid it from him. And if Brogan and Jed hadn't told Dawg, then gossip would have reached him quickly. There had been no fewer than twelve police officers with the chief of police when Alex rode with Brogan and Jed to collect her.

Some boss at DHS had found out about it, called Timothy, and informed him of everything he knew. From there, as she heard it, it had taken less than ten minutes to have a full squad of officers as well as Natches's brother-in-law and chief of police and his former partner Jed, a DHS agent still working in Somerset on a case no one dared to talk about for some reason, heading her way.

Two days later Dawg was back a week early from the Caribbean and her life had changed so irrevocably that she had no idea how to get it back.

"Lyrie." Dawg breathed out roughly, his still far-too-handsome face appearing more lined than it had been when he'd left three weeks before. "Take a few days here with Mom. Christa and I will head home tonight . . ."

"You think I want to leave because of you, Dawg?" she asked as she shoved her hands into the pockets of her jeans. "I'm not Eve, Piper, or Zoey. Your interference doesn't make me want to run from you, remember? I just move in and make you crazy."

He grinned, as she knew he would. They could look back at the four months she had lived with him just after they'd come to Somerset and laugh now. Then, they'd lived in a state of constant warfare with Christa, who was always either amused with both of them or furious with both of them, caught in the middle.

Finally, out of sheer desperation Dawg had sworn, on his marriage license even, that he would never interfere in her life again. To her knowledge, of all four of his sisters, Lyrica was the only one he kept that vow to.

He'd sworn it on his marriage license and she'd made him do it. Because there was nothing Dawg loved more than his wife and child.

"I'd love to have you move in with me again, Lyrie," he said with a sigh, using the nickname he'd given her in the first days after he'd found his sisters. "You know I would."

"We'd kill each other." She sighed, too.

Dawg shook his head, his gaze still heavy. "No, I don't think we would now."

Maybe they wouldn't, but still, it wouldn't work.

"I just need some time to think, Dawg."

"Or some time to give that damned hound dog Graham Brock a chance to get to you?" Natches made the accusation as he rose slowly from his chair across the room.

She'd known it was coming, and she had known it was coming from him. It had been in his eyes as he watched her, silent, thoughtful.

"If it hadn't been for Graham, she would have died, Natches," Dawg snapped, surprising more than one of the men in the room. "He did the same thing I would have done if his sister were in danger. Waited and ascertained the level of danger before contacting anyone. The fact that Timothy's contact in Washington learned of it was a lucky break for all of us."

Lyrica hid her smile. He was trying so hard to convince himself that Graham wasn't a threat to whatever virtue she may possess. He did that with her all the time. If he didn't acknowledge the reasons for something, then he didn't have to stress about something he was sworn not to interfere in.

"Come on, Dawg, you know better than that," Natches laughed. "And you know damned good and well if he ends up seducing her then he's just going to break her heart."

"Then I can just kill him." Dawg shrugged as though the thought of killing a man he considered a friend was everyday business, and he stared back at Lyrica with no change of expression.

Somber, worried. "Grant knows how it works, Natches. He has a sister himself."

She almost rolled her eyes. "Sorry, can't see any of you seducing her," she stated with amused indulgence.

"Not us," Natches agreed, his expression easy, his laughter natural as he leaned against the wall and watched her with that damned knowing expression. "But, you know, one day, we might know when some hound dog is out to break her heart rather than cherishing her as he should. We might not step up and beat the shit out of him before Graham can figure out what's going on."

Did he really think she didn't know each one of them so much better than to believe that?

She did laugh now. "Natches, you're such a liar. You actually like Kye and interfere in her life just as often as you do anyone else's."

"True." He nodded, crossing his arms over his chest. "Just remember one thing, sweetheart: It was Dawg that swore not to mess with the Romeos that come sniffing after you. Not the rest of us." His gaze encompassed the other men who were watching the byplay with interest.

"Natches, perhaps you should remember," she answered sweetly with wide-eyed innocence, "mess in my life too far, and Lexington will be seeing me on a regular basis, because I will move. Then you can deal with Dawg."

"Shut up, Natches," Dawg growled under his breath. "Just shut up."

Natches's eyes narrowed, his lips pursing thoughtfully at the reminder. She'd almost done just that when he'd sucker punched one of the bouncers at a friend's bar a few years before because Natches had been told the man was kissing her outside before she left one night.

Actually, the bouncer had kissed her cheek and thanked her for helping him with his girlfriend as he walked her to her car.

"I'm heading home." The weariness that had engulfed her for the past weeks settled over her shoulders once again. "Do what you have to do, but remember, I'm a Mackay, too." She included each man in her look then. "And trust me, I can be just as damned stubborn as any of you."

Moving to Dawg, she hugged him tightly for a minute. "Thanks for watching out for me."

His arms tightened around her briefly before releasing her. Tim was waiting at the door as she reached it and she gave him a hug as well. Behind her, she could feel the eyes watching her, the testosterone-driven assurance that they could guide her life better than she could piercing her back.

"Tell your mother good-bye," Tim told her softly as he released her. "You girls hurt her feelings when you just leave."

She knew that. She'd always known that. But sometimes, her mother was just as controlling as her brother and cousins were. They just did it in different ways.

"I will," she promised, moving back to smile at him chidingly. "It's not like I won't be back at some point, Tim."

"Better be," he grunted. "We like seeing your smile around here."

He told all Mercedes Mackay's girls that. He told Mercedes he couldn't live without her smile.

Leaving the office, Lyrica went to her old room, hurriedly grabbed the few clothes she'd had Zoey pack for her two weeks before, and headed downstairs.

Placing her luggage next to the door, Lyrica stepped into the television room, where a guest had just risen from one of the easy chairs and was moving to the doorway.

"Lyrica dear." Her voice charming, lilting, the South American beauty Carmina Lucient spoke with a cheerful smile and warm dark brown eyes.

Long and straight, her dark brown hair fell to the middle of her back and framed a delicate, almost aristocratic face. With her naturally arched brows and thickly lashed eyes, she could have been a model rather than an interior designer and fiancée to a soldier whose return home she was awaiting in the next few weeks.

Dressed in light gray capris and a sleeveless silk blouse, the woman looked classy and cool. A far cry from Lyrica's own jeans and white T-shirt that proclaimed *Despite the Look on My Face You're Still Talking*, along with a pair of ragged leather sneakers.

She was comfortable, she excused herself. Comfort meant everything at the moment.

"Hey, Carmina," Lyrica returned in greeting. "Have you seen Mom?"

"I believe she stepped into the kitchen," the other woman informed her, her gaze going to the luggage sitting in the foyer as a light frown flitted across her face. "You are leaving us, then?"

"It's time to go home," Lyrica agreed. "I'm sure the smell of bug killer has evaporated by now."

The story that she was staying with her mother again because of the smell of the insecticide in her new apartment hadn't roused anyone's suspicions, she didn't think.

"We'll no longer have our evening chats, then." Carmina pouted gently. "I have greatly enjoyed them."

"So have I," Lyrica promised. "I'm going to find Mom and tell her good-bye. Enjoy your stay."

Her mother was worried. Her dark eyes filled with tears when she saw Lyrica standing next to her luggage a few minutes later.

"Don't cry, Mom," Lyrica groaned, feeling the surge of guilt her mother could always give her. "I promise, I'll still visit."

Mercedes acted as though her children were moving to another world when they moved out of her house. Because all her children had moved out now, she always seemed heartbroken.

Tim so needed to take her on a cruise or something.

"All my babies think they have to leave me." Mercedes sighed sadly as she wrapped her arms around Lyrica and held her close. "This isn't fair. My nest is far too empty." Leaning back, she smiled back at Lyrica beatifically now. "You should convince Eve to have grandbabies soon."

"Yikes!" Lyrica jumped back. "Grandbabies? Really, Mom? Let them enjoy the honeymoon first or something."

Amused disgust pulled at her mother's expression. "If I cannot have my babies home then I should have grandbabies."

This was evidently a new idea her mother had come up with.

"Discuss it with Eve." Lyrica was not going to get into this conversation.

Her mother shook her head before her expression tightened once more into worry. Pulling Lyrica back into her embrace, she held her tightly for several long moments.

"Be careful, my soulful heart," she whispered at Lyrica's ear. The words reminded her of her childhood and the personal farewells she and her sisters had gotten each morning before they went to school.

"I will, Momma," Lyrica answered, kissing her mother's cheek as emotion welled in her throat. "I'll call soon. I promise."

She had to escape before her mother had her crying.

Grabbing her bags, she rushed from the house, refusing to look back in case her mother was crying. Because if she was, there would be no choice but to return right back to the house and stay another night, or week, or the rest of her life so her momma wouldn't shed tears over her again.

Her mother had shed far too many tears over the years, Lyrica had always thought.

Stowing her luggage in the Jeep, she was in the vehicle and driving back to town within minutes. Thankfully, the inn wasn't far from the apartment she'd rented just off Somerset's main thoroughfare.

It wasn't as busy and rushed or as loud as Main Street. She had a postage-stamp-size plot of grass in front of her patio doors with a privacy fence on each side and two parking spots right in front of it. The apartments, owned by Mackay Enterprises, the company her brother and cousins had created to combine all their business interests and oversee their children's futures, were safe, roomy, and quiet.

The best part about living there was the fact that she knew they were secure. A Somerset detective, Samantha Bryce, lived on one side of her, while the girlfriend of an officer lived on the other. That put two law enforcement personnel on the premises for the better part of any given day.

Pulling into her parking spot, Lyrica breathed her first true sigh of relief since she'd stepped from the elevator and nearly died. Pulling her luggage from the Jeep, she lugged it to her patio door and was preparing to unlock it when Samantha stepped outside.

"It's about time you got home." Samantha grinned from beneath the bill of her low-profile baseball cap.

Dressed in men's shorts and a T-shirt, the woman should have seemed oddly dressed, or far too male, yet neither was the case. Lyrica had decided that Samantha was so comfortable in her own skin that the confidence that came from it simply didn't allow her to appear as anything but self-assured.

Her long, curling waves of multihued brown hair were gathered at the back of her head in a ponytail and pulled through the cap. The trailing waves and curls were then confined with several more elastic bands to keep them under control.

Dark sunglasses were perched over the cap on her head and white leather sneakers covered her sockless feet.

"Yeah, Dawg gets kind of territorial when someone shoots at his sisters." Lyrica sighed theatrically, well aware that Samantha had been working the investigation for the Somerset Police Department at Lyrica's cousin-in-law's request. Alex Jansen had assigned the case to Samantha before he'd even arrived with Brogan and Jed to pick her up at Graham's.

Samantha grinned at the comment. "I went through your apartment when Dawg called and said you were coming home. Everything's fine, no unwanted visitors." Her hazel eyes gleamed at the last comment.

"I'll be sure to thank Dawg." Lyrica rolled her eyes. "Like I said, territorial."

"Door's still unlocked for you," Samantha laughed as Lyrica moved to push the keys into the lock.

"Sam, I'm hating you today." Lyrica sighed.

"Most people have those days," Sam retorted as she stood next to the building and waited.

Waited for her to enter the apartment?

Lyrica wasn't certain what she was waiting on.

Opening the door, she picked up her luggage and stepped inside. Only to come to a stop once again.

"Are you totally mad at me, too?" Kye jumped up from her couch, her fingers lacing together as she watched Lyrica with painful intensity.

Placing her luggage to the side of the room, Lyrica shook her head uncertainly. "No. I thought you would be mad at me, though."

Turning, she pulled the patio door closed before turning back to Graham's sister.

Kye grimaced, her gray eyes darker than normal, her expression filled with mutiny. "Look, I knew when you first accepted my invitations to the afternoon pool parties and girls' days out that you were hoping to see Graham." She propped one hand on her denim-covered hip and brushed her long bangs back with the other. "But I thought we had things in common other than him. We're good friends, aren't we, Lyrica?"

There was a shadow of uncertainty in her gaze.

"We are good friends, Kye," Lyrica agreed as she stepped to the other girl and gave her a quick, firm hug. "Despite the fact that you're Graham's sister. But Kye, if I have to hear about one more VS bra from those other dimwits you run around with, then I'm going to scream."

"You and me both," Kye agreed.

Well, at least she hadn't lost her friend. And she hadn't lost Graham, she reminded herself. He had never been hers to begin with.

For the next hour, the conversation centered on the investigation and resulting death of the other young woman. Lyrica was still torn, uncertain, and though she didn't admit it to Kye, she was still scared.

When Kye rose to leave, Lyrica stepped outside to her patio, noticing her friend's sudden nervousness as she glanced to the spare parking spot, where Graham's tan pickup had just pulled in.

Nothing else existed as Lyrica's eyes met his across the short distance.

Adrenaline.

There it was.

It was racing through her system, pounding through her heart and flushing her entire system with heated hunger. Her nipples hardened; her clitoris swelled and reminded her of the sweet release it now craved like a drug addict craved the next fix.

Graham felt trapped by the memories. The feel of her saturated intimate flesh parting at the touch of his tongue. The slick essence of her sweet juices spilling to his lips as he sat beneath her and feasted on her need for him.

It had been two lousy, miserable weeks since she'd been taken from him. Since he'd felt a sweet fire he'd never experienced with any other woman.

Why was that?

Why hadn't he ever felt the hunger and need for another as he did for Lyrica? She wasn't experienced. She was far too innocent, far too delicate. His women were usually more statuesque, better able to meet and participate in the sexual games he preferred.

Games that would no doubt shock the hell out of her. He'd already shocked her. He'd sent her running from him. She could use whatever excuse she needed to, but it was fear that had her pulling back from him.

It had to be.

Love couldn't exist for him. Lyrica was letting herself be fooled by it. Sexual intensity, uncertainty, and fear combined, creating a response she was inventing excuses to avoid until she could handle it.

So what was his excuse?

He couldn't stop thinking about her. He couldn't stop hungering for her. The hunger was like an addiction, one he couldn't get a fix for without Lyrica.

The door opened and Kye climbed into the truck, closing the door behind her slowly.

Graham had to force himself to slide the truck into reverse. He didn't tear his gaze from Lyrica until he had no other choice, until he couldn't do anything but check to ensure he wasn't hitting anything.

Or anyone.

Mistaken identity.

He couldn't get the results of the investigation out of his mind. The details of the file were burned into his brain. He couldn't forget it, not a detail of it.

That was not a case of mistaken identity. Professionals that well prepared with the advanced electronics they used did not make those kinds of mistakes. And no doubt the Mackays were well aware of it, because Lyrica had a shadow watching her.

The mistaken identity conclusion could be made plausible. If Graham had been any other man, he might have suspected it could be true. But he wasn't any other man. He was damned suspicious. He didn't believe in coincidences. And he sure as hell didn't believe in fairy tales.

That fucking "mistaken identity" claptrap was a fairy tale and nothing more.

"She's scared," Kye said softly as he turned the corner and headed to the end of the street.

Of course she was scared. Lyrica wasn't a moron, and neither was Dawg or his cousins. But in the absence of an answer, or even a solid shadow of a threat, after two weeks, they couldn't keep her hidden any longer.

"I know she is," he answered.

He'd seen it in her eyes, in her face. In the way she couldn't break his gaze and held on to him until he'd forced himself to look away.

She hadn't been that scared at the house while she had been in his care. Her expression hadn't been drawn, her eyes hadn't been shadowed with that same fear.

"Graham, what are you going to do?" Turning in her seat, Kye faced him demandingly now. "You can't just leave her there."

He shot her an amazed glance before focusing on the road once again.

"She has a brother, two cousins, a brother-in-law, a future brother-in-law, and myriad friends and other relatives, Kye. They showed me the fucking door and politely asked me to keep my nose the fuck out of it."

"And you started listening to morons when?" she demanded loudly, her expression belligerent. "That's my best friend, Graham. You have to do something."

"Like what, Kye?" he demanded as the truck came to a hard stop at the light.

Turning his head he glared back at her, furious with her as well as himself, the Mackays, and Lyrica.

"What do you want me to do, Kyleene?" he asked her again, the hard rasp of his voice causing her shoulders to tighten in reaction as she stared away from him.

"I don't have the answers either, dammit. So stop yelling at me."

The light turned green. Graham accelerated through the intersection.

Kye remained quiet, her very silence a warning that she was thinking too damned hard. All he could do was wait. With Kye, there was no rushing her.

They were nearly at the edge of town before she shifted around once again to stare at him. And he didn't like the look. His one brief glance at it assured him that his sister really was thinking too damned hard.

"I have an idea," she stated serenely.

"Kye, look, let the Mackays handle this for now. If I think she needs my help then I'll step in and take care of it. Agreed?"

"No, that isn't agreed."

Fuck.

He glanced at her again.

One knee was bent and resting on the seat as she turned toward him. She'd propped her elbow against the seat back while pushing her fingers through the side of her hair.

Classic devil child pose, he thought fondly even as he braced himself for what was coming.

"Hurry and get it the hell over with," he growled. "I can see the wheels turning, Kye, but I don't know how the hell you can come up with an answer that I haven't."

"But you have, Graham," she said softly.

He frowned, not just at the tone of her voice but at the statement she'd made.

"Did I?" His hands tightened on the steering wheel. "And when did I do that?"

"Last winter when bimbo number eight nearly caught you making out with Lyrica in the living room during the blizzard. Take Lyrica as a lover and she'll be with you safe and sound until you and Elijah can figure out what's going on."

He blinked.

Damn, was that sweat he could feel popping out on his brow?

And why didn't it completely offend him that his sister had suggested he do such a thing just to protect her best friend?

"Uh, Kye?" And how the hell had she known what had nearly happened on that couch?

"I actually made it into the room without either of you realizing I was there. Except I turned around and left as soon as I realized it was you and Lyrica." Her expression was far too serious now, far too intent. "Don't tell me you don't want her. And I know she wants you. She always has."

"And if I hurt her when it's over, Kye?" he asked. "She's your friend. Her brother and cousins are well able to protect her. If I step in, when it's all over with, her heart will be broken and you know it."

"If her heart gets broken and she's still alive, then I'll forgive you, Graham," she promised. "Even if it breaks our friendship, I'll forgive you. I wouldn't have forgiven you for just playing with her. But I'll forgive you for saving her. And if the Mackays are so damned capable, what the hell is she doing back at her apartment alone?"

Graham swallowed tightly.

"She's already kindly turned down the offer of my protection," he admitted softly, giving her another short look.

"Of course she did," Kye laughed, amusement filling her face as she watched him. "She's not stupid. She knows what a tomcat you are, brother dear. And your bimbos aren't exactly complimented by your friends. But Lyrica's different. No one will think badly of her. And she's scared, Graham. If you approach her the right way . . ."

"Enough." A hard shake of his head and he bit the word out with a hard rasp.

He couldn't handle this. He was not going to discuss seducing her best friend with her.

It wasn't going to happen.

Kye just smiled serenely. "Very well." She shrugged, turning to face forward once again. "But if you change your mind, I'm here. Lyrica's not every other woman you've taken to your bed. She won't be easy. But she would be safe."

"What the hell do you know about the women I've taken to bed?"

Her lips parted as though to actually answer him.

"Forget it." He jerked his hand from the wheel to hold it up in a gesture of silence. "I don't want to know. Just forget I asked."

Another of those little shrugs. "If you change your mind," she offered again. "Like I said . . ."

"You're here," he snapped. "I know, Kye. I know. You're here."

NINE

Her brother and cousins were going to make her crazy, Lyrica told herself several days later as she moved through the crowded rooms that housed the weekend's largest lake party. Usually, Kye would have already shown up, but so far, Lyrica hadn't found her. Perhaps, she thought, she should have called to make certain her friend was going to be there.

Unfortunately, damned near everyone there knew her, too, which meant it wouldn't be much longer before someone called Dawg.

The live band was pounding out a country tune with a hard, fast rhythm. The crowd was milling around the house and the main grounds, and some were already slipping into the private areas of the yard. It was growing late, and intoxicated couples were finding the shadows while some weren't even bothering with shadows.

The rumors that the Collier parties sometimes slipped into sexual free-for-alls just might be true. And here she was, alone amid the escalating carnality that could be glimpsed and laughed at.

What had seemed like a good idea when she'd heard of the party, while she was fighting nightmares and memories, didn't seem nearly as smart now.

It was Saturday night, and the summer partying season was just kicking off. The lake was crazy this time of year. These beginning-of-the-season parties and the desperate, winter-weary revelries never failed to end up with the sheriff being called and usually an ambulance or two as well.

If Dawg caught her here, he'd chew a strip of hide off Lyrica's ass a mile long. Not to mention what her sisters would have to say. Her mother, Mercedes, would give her that look of disappointment that would make Lyrica want to shrink inside, while Timothy would just chuckle, pat her on the head, and tell her it was just those Mackay genetics running roughshod over her good sense.

She hated the Timothy part the most. His amusement and assumption that she probably couldn't help herself.

Still, she eyed the crowd that seemed packed into the structure as she entered it. She hadn't been to many of the lake house parties, mostly because her brother and cousins knew far too many people. It wasn't uncommon for her to be stopped at the door and escorted to a quiet room while her brother was called.

She'd gotten tired of that years ago.

She made out much better at the bars outside of town, or even in Louisville or Lexington instead. Places where Dawg Mackay wasn't so well-known.

Stepping back into the entryway, Lyrica surveyed the large entry and living area, wondering how many guests were calling her brother as she stood there.

She should have stayed home. Or gone to a bar, Lyrica thought in disgust as she pushed her way through the crowd, hoping to find an empty corner where she could hide for a while.

As she passed the bar she snagged a cold beer that the bartender set out for another guest who'd made the mistake of turning his back. She always managed to get carded at private parties. She'd never heard of such a thing until coming to Kentucky. She'd never been carded in Texas, even when she'd slipped into the bars.

But then, she hadn't had a brother like Dawg Mackay overseeing every breath she took, either.

Sipping at the beer, she spied what appeared to be an empty corner behind several large, thickly growing potted plants on the other side of the room. Perfect for observing while hiding, she thought in relief.

Until she began to slip around it and came to a shocked stop.

"Fuck yeah, baby. Fuck that dick," the male groaned, eyes closed as he held the thick hips of his partner and pounded into her from behind.

The slick length of his erection was a blur of movement as he found a few more explicit phrases to throw out to her. His fingers held her hips so tight, the hem of her dress bunched above them, that Lyrica was certain the other woman would carry bruises.

But Lyrica would forever carry the memory of seeing her former schoolteacher's cock shuttling between the thighs of the prissy, pursed-lipped mayor's sister, who ran city hall like an iron-fisted prude.

A second later she was being pulled from the sight, as completely unbelievable as it was, by her neighbor Sam, who was laughing her ass off at Lyrica's shock.

"Sam, that was gross," she hissed as the other woman continued to grip her wrist and drag her from the room into a long hallway that had yet to fill with guests.

"The look on your face was priceless." Sam was still laughing, her hazel eyes filled with mirth beneath the ever-present bill of the black, low-profile ball cap she wore.

The long ponytail was pulled through the adjustable band behind her head as usual. Dressed in men's loose shorts, a sleeveless white T-shirt, and sneakers, Sam had a masculine aura that never failed to fascinate or shock most people.

She didn't make excuses for herself and she damned sure didn't apologize for who she was.

Not that she had to make excuses or apologize for anything. The new criminal investigator for the city of Somerset had enough clout with not just the city, but also the state, that she could afford to carry a little arrogance.

She was nice, though, and kind, Lyrica thought, if a little harder than most thirty-year-old women she knew.

Tanned, toned, and edging toward muscular, that male-aura thing just reached out and grabbed a person. Men were both fascinated by her and fearful of her power over them. Most women were just fascinated by her. Lyrica was equally amused and damned envious of how well Sam carried herself.

"Come on, this part of the house hasn't filled up yet, but don't count on it staying that way for long. You could be shocked again before the night's out." Sam was still far too amused to suit Lyrica.

"Come on, we've called her Miss Priss since we met her," Lyrica groaned. "And that was my senior year history teacher. That was just wrong."

Sam snorted. "What are you doing here, Miss Innocent? You should be home, tucked nice and safe in bed, dreaming of sugarplums."

"Don't piss me off, Sam," Lyrica warned good-naturedly. "I could make a bad enemy."

"So can newborns," Sam assured her as she glanced over at

Lyrica with amused flirtatiousness as they found a quiet corner, shadowed and relatively secluded, with a half-dozen couples lingering there to drink and chat.

"That was low, Sam," Lyrica said. "Really low."

Tipping the beer to her lips, Lyrica took a long drink, wishing there weren't too many of Dawg's friends here to allow her to go to the bar for a real drink.

"Really, what are you doing here, Lyrica?" Sam asked then, leaning forward, her arms propped on her spread thighs.

It was such a male position that once again Lyrica was reminded of the woman's strength.

No excuses and no apologies.

"The hell if I know." Lyrica sighed as she glanced around the shadowed room again. "Boredom, maybe. And I was hoping Kye would be here. She usually stops by the lake parties on the weekends."

"Kyleene Brock? Graham's sister? Girl, you're going to get in trouble if you keep running with her."

"Kye?" Lyrica laughed. "No way, Sam. You know better than that."

"She's trouble waiting to happen is what I know," Sam assured her with a laughing little roll of her eyes.

"Kye?" Surprise had Lyrica watching the detective closely then. "What's Kye doing? She never gets into trouble."

Perfectly plucked, slender brows arched at the retort.

"Really?" Sam drawled. "Hmm, maybe that was someone else who looks exactly like Kye Brock running around and hitting damned near every party I've been to since arriving in Pulaski County and wreaking such havoc that we actually look forward to her brief visits just for the entertainment."

Kye? Wreaking havoc? That so did not sound like her friend.

She shook her head. "Graham wouldn't allow it."

"Unlike you, sweetie, no one calls and tells on little Kye. Evidently, she doesn't mind using all the juicy little trysts she's seen to keep everyone's mouth shut."

Kye Brock? Threatening to tell secrets?

Lyrica took another long drink of the beer, shocked.

"She's a firecracker," Sam observed then, the lack of amusement in her voice pulling Lyrica's attention back to her.

"That just does not sound like Kye." She shook her head, confused. "I'd have to see that one to believe it."

"You obviously don't know her so well." Sam shrugged.

Lyrica had already suspected that one but she'd never suspected the extent of it.

"Evidently not," Lyrica agreed.

"You and your sisters just confuse the hell out of me." Sam shook her head then, a grin edging at her lips. "You're definitely Mackays, but nothing like your brother and his cousins. They were wild as the wind."

"They were deviants when they were younger." Lyrica laughed at the tactful way of describing Dawg's, Rowdy's, and Natches's sexual exploits.

"They were at that," Sam agreed, her gaze leveled on Lyrica then, the look in her hazel eyes interested and a little amused. "Yet Dawg's sisters are kept perfectly protected?"

That was a question, not an observation.

Leaning back in her chair, Lyrica watched the other woman for a long moment, wishing she had another drink.

"Perfectly protected, huh?" She gave her head a little shake. "I believe we're only as protected as we want to be. Dawg worries."

"He loves you." She nodded. "Everyone knows that. Hell of a burden, though."

"Blessing," Lyrica corrected her. "One we curse, berate, and rail at, but at the end of the day, a blessing."

Sam chuckled at that before lifting her glass and sipping the liquor she was drinking.

As she lowered her glass, the detective directed her a frank, assessing, more-than-interested look.

"And what of you?" she asked then. "Are you as innocent as everyone thinks, or just as wild as your best friend?"

"Personal interest, Sam? Or just curiosity?" Lyrica tipped her head to the side as she met the other woman's gaze directly.

Sam snorted at that. "Honey, everyone knows you have your heart and sights set already. We're just not certain whose heart you're set on yet. I was just curious as to whether or not you wanted to play a little until you decide what you're going to do."

Lyrica laughed at that, crossing one knee over the other as she leaned forward to rest her elbow against her leg. "That's proprietary information. Besides Sam, I didn't take you for the playing type. You'd never accept not being first choice."

"Hmm," Sam murmured. "An interesting observation." Then she shrugged. "Well, if you ever decide your first choice is a wasted cause, give me a call," she suggested.

Hell, Lyrica couldn't help but like this woman. Perfectly plucked brows on strong, well-defined features. If she wasn't mistaken, those shapely fingers were well manicured as well. The men's clothes should have hung on her, but she was so comfortable in them that she wore them as though they were made for her. Beneath the man's shirt, shapely breasts were neither hidden nor emphasized.

Samantha Bryce was just Samantha Bryce, and Lyrica wished she could be more like her.

"You know, Sam, I just might be tempted to do that," she stated, smiling back at her.

"Uh-oh." Sam made the little sound as Lyrica felt a presence she hadn't expected.

"Tempted, are you?" Graham growled as he moved around her chair, his fingers curling around her wrist as he pulled her from the chair. "You better be tempted to get your ass out of here because I just heard the bartender call Dawg. You have about . . ."

"Half an hour." She sighed in resignation before glancing back at Sam. "Night, Sam."

"Night, Lyrica," Sam called back to her, definitely amused, probably ready to laugh at her again. "See you soon, honey."

Hell, Somerset's most eligible lesbian had just called her "honey." She felt privileged.

Sam wasn't known for her endearments.

Following in Graham's wake, she stared at the black material covering the powerful muscles of his back and thought of the white shirt she'd managed to steal while at the Brock estate. She really liked that black shirt, too. She wondered if she could get him out of it and add it to her collection.

"Where are you taking me?" she finally asked curiously as he began dragging her upstairs.

"The second level has an exit by the main road." He didn't sound as though he were pleased. "If we're lucky, we might get you past whichever Mackay comes looking for you."

"Why bother?" She rolled her eyes as she made him work at dragging her up the stairs. "He knows I'm here. If he asks me about it, I won't lie to him."

"You make things far too interesting sometimes." He didn't sound as though he approved.

She approved of the way part of his hair was pulled back from the sides of his face and banded with a leather tie at the back of his head. He looked tough. Dangerous and tough. The bad boy personified.

"Don't worry, I won't tell him you dragged me out for him. He might wonder why you cared. Hell, I wonder why you care."

At that, he came to an abrupt stop.

He turned to stare back at her and she watched a battle rage in his eyes and wondered just what the hell it was he was fighting himself over. She'd seen that look in her brother's eyes before. Watched him as he confronted his sisters and fought to try to protect them while still maintaining their love for him.

Like Dawg, Graham was an incredibly strong man with a sense of decency and a code of honor that likely only he understood, but that everyone else could definitely depend upon.

Whatever the battle was about, she watched as he finally made up his mind. Turning along another hall, he dragged her to the nearest room, opened the door, and pushed her inside ahead of him.

Shadows surrounded her, but there was enough light falling through the floor-to-ceiling windows to identify the room as a sort of living area. A television, couch, sofa, and two recliners took up the center of the room, while antiques appeared to occupy the space along the walls.

"What the hell are you doing here, Lyrica? I can't believe you'd actually show up at a party like this," he growled, following as she crossed the room to one of the huge, uncovered windows that looked out on the lake.

She watched his expression in the glass, her heart tripping at the hunger in his face, in his dark gaze. He was watching her as though he was dying for her.

"And what kind of party is it?" she asked. Barely admitted anger that he hadn't visited, hadn't checked up on her, ignited inside her.

She was crazy. She should have never allowed him to drag her up here.

"A free-for-all fuck night," he threw back to her. "You know what kind of parties Collier has."

"He's as much of a head case as you are." She curled her lips angrily. "Tell me, do you share your bimbos or just your taste for bimbos?"

"Don't push me, Lyrica. You should remember what happens when I get too damned hungry for you," he reminded her, his voice harsh. "Why are you here?"

She turned to him slowly, aware that his arms bracketed her, his palms flat against the windows as she stared up at him.

"I'm here for my free-for-all fuck night," she said sweetly. "I wanted to try the bimbo role out before I actually accepted the position."

Something flared in his eyes. Heat and hunger, anger, and male demand. And for a second, she wondered exactly what she'd managed to free inside the man whose control always seemed so tightly held, so intent.

Graham was being pushed too far, too close to the limit of his control. The hunger that raged through him was wearing at the determination to keep his hands off her. Watching her sitting there with Sam Bryce, the other woman watching Lyrica with the same interest and hunger men watched her with, had been too much for him.

Sam was a friend, a damned good friend, but if she touched Lyrica then she'd become an enemy he could never forgive, just as any man would.

Lyrica was his.

That thought shocked him. She was stronger than he was. Strong enough to say no, to stay away. And even knowing he should do the same, still he couldn't quite shake the hunger raging through him.

The need for her only grew daily, dreams of her haunted his nights, and he swore his cock had been hard since the day he met her. Definitely harder since her far too short stay at his home.

"Lyrica, you shouldn't be out like this, honey." He sighed, try-ing like hell to keep from actually touching her. "You should be more careful right now and you know it."

Shadows haunted her eyes at his statement, raged in the emer-ald depths, along with a vulnerable need that sank tender claws inside his chest.

She shook her head once. "They weren't after me. The investi-gation . . ."

"Lyrica, don't," he whispered. "You know there was more to that, just as I do."

"No. If there was, Dawg would have—"

"Put a tail on you just like he did?" He sighed. "Even I've seen your bodyguard, sweetheart. Dawg knows better. He simply can't prove it."

"Or maybe you just can't accept the truth," she said accusingly as she lifted her hands from her sides to push against his chest. Not that he moved, despite the strength she put behind her insis-tence that he do just that. "Sorry, Graham, I'm not so interested in being bimbo number twelve. Try me next time, why don't ya?"

"Damn you! You're so stubborn you'd walk into a bullet be-fore you'd give in, wouldn't you, Lyrica?"

Jerking her against him, one hand at her hip, the other in her hair, tugging her head back, he glared down at her, knowing he was destroying himself just as he'd destroy her innocence.

"I'm stubborn? Oh hell no, you have me so beat. At least I can admit when I want something. Just because it's the worst thing I could want doesn't mean I'm not honest enough to admit to want-ing it." She just couldn't let it go. She couldn't stop, couldn't un-derstand how ragged his control was. "Damn you, Graham. Damn you for making me want what we both know I can't have."

The pain that filled her emerald eyes struck at his chest, at the guilt he couldn't seem to shed, no matter how he tried.

"Do you really believe I think you're anything like any other woman I've had in my bed?" he rasped, the sound of his own voice almost shocking him. "You know better than that. Damn you, Lyrica, I've never led you to believe such a thing."

"I think you'd cut your own dick off before you'd ever let any woman mean anything to you, Graham," she retorted angrily. "Especially me."

The sound of the explicit words falling from her lips had that organ swelling impossibly harder, throbbing furiously.

Lowering his head slowly he watched the slumberous arousal that began to transform her face, erasing the anger as her lips parted. But god, he didn't dare take what she offered. If he kissed her, the battle would be lost.

Only sheer, desperate will kept him from taking those pretty, parted lips. Moving to her ear instead, he nuzzled the sensitive flesh just beneath the lobe, inhaling the scent of her as his body tightened further.

"So innocent," he whispered, his free hand gripping her hip and pulling her closer to the fiercely engorged length of his arousal as it throbbed behind the zipper of his jeans. "Too innocent."

Sharp little nails dug into the thin cotton of his shirt to prick at the flesh of his sides as she drew in a hard, desperate breath.

"You don't know that," she said roughly.

"I've had my tongue up that sweet pussy, baby. I know you're a virgin." As he spoke, Graham turned her quickly, moving her until he was pressing her against the wall.

The shadows of the room he'd pulled her into surrounded them, locking them into an intimate swirl of heat, hunger, and music pulsing from the rooms below them.

"I told you I was a virgin, asshole," she snapped, though the hunger raging through her made her voice far too soft, too needy.

"You didn't have to tell me," he admitted softly. "I knew. It was what was in your voice when you told me, Lyrica. All the dreams of happily ever after and prince charming. I'm no prince charming and happily ever after doesn't happen, baby. But that doesn't mean we can't mean something to each other. That we can't steal at least the edge of the fairy tale."

The edge of the fairy tale?

She wanted it all. The handsome prince, the castle in the air . . .

No, she wanted the fairy tale where Graham loved her just as deeply, just as fiercely as she loved him.

Her voice was dazed, her body melting against him, melting for him.

How much was she melting? he wondered, the craven demands sweeping through his senses as lust, barely controlled, raged through his body in waves of desperation.

"Dawg will kill me." He nipped at her lobe, lifting her against him until he could push one heavy thigh between hers.

The thin material of her panties beneath the light chiffon of her dress and the denim of his jeans were no barrier between him and the sweet heat of her intimate flesh.

"Graham." The soft exclamation of need filled the air around him and clawed at the fragile threads holding his hunger under control.

Barely in control.

"I could eat you up right here." He flexed his knee against the sensitive pad of her sex, grinding gently, working against the tender bundle of nerve endings hiding there. "I could spread you out and make you scream for me, Lyrica. Until you realize how hungry I am. Until you realize nothing can prepare you for an animal. One far too hungry and far too desperate for every perverted desire one man could have for a woman."

He knew himself too well. Knew too well the fantasies that he jacked off to where this woman was concerned.

She shivered in his grip, a little moan leaving her lips as they pressed to the hard flesh between the opened edges of his shirt.

The little straps of her dress gave way to his lips as they moved along her shoulder. They slid aside, fell down the rounded slope of her upper arm, and left all that lush flesh completely free of obstacles.

"What you want isn't what scares me. I'm not a child." It was the fact that it was all he wanted from her that broke her heart.

Her fingers were pulling at the shirt, dragging it from where he'd tucked it beneath the band of his jeans, anyway. The need to touch him, to feel the heat of his body, an impulse she couldn't deny herself.

"You're a baby," he groaned. "I should be shot."

But that didn't keep him from caressing the smooth, exposed flesh of her upper back with one hand or from gripping the curve of her ass as he moved her against his thigh.

"Oh god, Graham, please," she whispered as she breathed out, the plea that filled the sound nearly breaking the chains holding his determination not to take her in this damned place.

He knew what she ached for.

He knew what she hungered for.

What he was dying for.

First.

The kiss their lips ached for.

Those pretty lips beneath his parted, surprise tightening her against him, perhaps a hint of shock . . .

Because he wouldn't be able to take her kiss any more easily than he'd be able to take her innocence.

"Get away from me, Lyrica," he groaned even as he lifted her, parted her thighs, and drove the hard wedge of his cock into the vee. "God, get away from me before I destroy us both."

Guiding her knees up to grip his hips, he slid his palms up her thighs to cup each curve of her rounded ass and hold her in place as he thrust against her.

"Get away from you?" she gasped as his lips moved along her neck to the rise of her breasts as they lifted above the rounded cups of her dress. "I've tried. I swear, I tried so hard . . . And all I've wanted is to be right here again."

Every muscle in his body tightened at the admission. His hips jerked, grinding against the intimate flesh between her thighs. He was so desperate for her now that he couldn't imagine not having her, not taking her.

Now.

Dawg would kill him. He'd already sent Graham the message that fooling with his little sister was a dangerous endeavor when he'd learned Graham was still looking into the attack on her.

And Graham tried, not because of the threat, but because of Lyrica. Because she was too sweet, too innocent for him.

But he'd already tasted her, more than once. He had the hunger for more buried so deep in his senses that he couldn't rid himself of it.

He had to taste her again.

Tangling the fingers of one hand in the back of her long black hair, he dragged her head back again as her fingers gripped his biceps. Nails dug into his flesh as her lips parted, the emerald fire of her gaze gleaming back at him.

His favorite color.

Lyrica emeralds. Staring into her eyes, he swore he could feel something in his chest tightening, burning as though trying to dig its way out. Some feeling, some emotion tied so closely to the hunger he felt for her that he knew he should be pushing it back . . . Then the door to the living area opened slowly.

Graham froze.

The silhouette standing in the entrance, the broad, tense power and aura of determined male protectiveness, was all too familiar.

"Graham." His voice low, harsh with disapproval, Natches remained at the doorway. For the moment. "Let her go."

"Natches, don't . . ." The desperation, the pain in Lyrica's voice tore at Graham's heart.

"Shush, Lyrica," Graham commanded her, his voice firm. "I knew better. We both know I did. This should have never happened."

Her gaze swung back to him, anger filling her eyes as outrage flashed across her face.

"Damn you, Graham," she spat out furiously. "Damn all of you."

Before he could guess her intent, her fingers were clenched in his hair, her lips on his, the heat, hunger, and fury in the press of her lips doing nothing to hide her innocence, or her pain.

It did nothing to aid his self-control.

The taste of cherry heat . . .

A hint of beer . . .

A fiery arousal burning out of control, desperate, filled with fantasies, with uncontrolled need and a woman's fury.

And he wanted more.

He wanted all of her.

His tongue parted his lips as he tasted her, felt hers meeting it, dueling with it as he wrapped both arms around her, no longer caring who the hell watched.

"Lyrica, Dawg will be here in about two minutes flat," Natches snapped. "Do you really want him to have to see this?"

The cry that tore from her lips shattered Graham.

"When Dawg shows up, I won't let her run, Graham. She can watch the two of you argue over her presence at a fucking orgy with a man he calls a friend."

Graham jerked his head back, broke the possession of her lips, and quickly released her as he forced himself to step back.

He almost reached for her again as she swayed before him, her gaze filled with betrayal gleaming in those emerald eyes.

The first tear fell as she stiffened, pushed past him, and all but ran from the room. Moving past her cousin, she disappeared from sight, her fury the last sight he had of her.

Natches stepped into the room and closed the door behind him.

"Rowdy's waiting in the hall for her," he told Graham, amusement edging his voice.

Graham watched as Natches advanced into the shadows of the room until he was standing no more than five feet from him. Tense, prepared for a possible fight ahead, Graham watched the other man carefully.

"I don't want the warning or the fight," Graham growled. "But I won't back down from it, either."

Natches grinned as his deep green eyes, so like Lyrica's, gleamed with mockery.

"There are easier ways to die, Graham," Natches informed him. "You're too hard for her. Too damaged. She deserves a man without the baggage you carry."

But what if Lyrica eased that hardness? What if she stilled the nightmares when nothing or no one had been able to?

That thought had disgust filling him. Easing the horror of his life, of his past, wasn't her responsibility. It was his nightmare to carry, not hers to ease.

Natches pushed his fingers wearily through his hair as Graham continued to glare back at him.

"What if that were your sister, Graham, with me?"

"I'd kill you," Graham assured him. "You're married and old enough to be her father."

"Graham . . ." The mocking chastisement was obvious as Natches crossed his arms over his chest in an obvious effort to contain his fists.

"Do you think I haven't already considered all this?" Graham snapped out, running his fingers through his hair and turning away to pace to the wide bank of windows along the wall.

Looking down, he stared out at the darkened lake, his mind in turmoil as he fought against the need to follow after Lyrica rather than remain there with her asshole cousin.

"You'll break her, Graham," Natches stated then. "She doesn't deserve it and it will only add to your nightmares."

He knew that, too.

"I have no desire to hurt her." He turned slowly to face one of the most dangerous men he knew. "But I won't see her hurt, either. We both know that report is bullshit. By god, I was there for her when no one else was. I saved her ass, and I'll be damned if I'll stand by while some son of a bitch finishes the job."

Before he could anticipate the move, Natches's fist flew out with what felt like a cement two-by-four plowing into the side of his face. Graham stumbled back, only barely managing to keep from landing flat on his ass.

"Just a taste of what's coming," Natches snapped. "Because Dawg hits a hell of a lot harder. And don't doubt we have her ass covered. Well enough to know how often you follow her, how long you hang around outside her apartment, and just how many questions you're asking. Back the fuck off. She doesn't need you."

Graham narrowed his eyes on the other man, fury pumping hot and strong through his system as he felt ice begin to spread through him. Natches had been a hell of a sniper, but he wasn't the only hunter the Marines had created. And he wasn't nearly as desperate as Graham was becoming.

"That one was free, Mackay," he rasped, his voice harsh, the need to hit back swirling through him. "For Lyrica, only because I know she likes that pretty face of yours." Her most handsome cousin, she called the other man fondly. "The next time that fist goes rabid on me, though, I hope you know how to duck. Fast."

Natches chuckled. "I guess we'll see, won't we? Because if you don't stay the hell away from her then you're going to get the chance to try for it."

The other man turned and strolled casually back to the door, pulled it open, and stepped into the hall before closing the door behind him and leaving Graham in the dark. Leaving him with the memory of that brief moment when her taste had burned through his senses like nothing he'd known before.

Maybe he just needed to get laid, he thought as the music from the party below intruded on his thoughts. But not here, not tonight. Not until he could escape the memory of her kiss, of her touch, and the hunger for more that was only burning brighter than ever.

Reaching up, he probed at the rapidly swelling flesh of the left side of his face. Fucker! Natches couldn't just hit the eye or just pop him in the mouth. Hell no, the bastard had to take out the whole side of his face. He'd remember that if the chance ever came around to return the favor.

He couldn't blame the other man, though. If it were Kye that some bastard resembling Graham was sniffing after, then he knew he'd do the same.

Or worse.

Maybe, if he was lucky, the blow had knocked some sense into his head.

Hell, he just wasn't that lucky.

Son of a bitch. He just hadn't needed this.

TEN

The next morning, Lyrica pulled into the parking lot of Mackay's Bed-and-Breakfast Inn, incensed.

She was furious. She couldn't believe the gall of her cousin Natches. It wasn't bad enough that she had to listen to the gossip for two hours straight at the spa. Hell no—when she called Kye to confirm the rumors, her best friend wouldn't even speak to her. In fact, she'd informed Lyrica that she wouldn't speak to her again until Graham's face had healed from Natches's blow.

"Really, Lyrica." Kye sniffed tearfully. "Graham wouldn't even tell me who hit him. I had to find out myself from some little twit who was actually at the party."

"You act as though I can control Graham or Natches," Lyrica protested. "For god's sake, Kye, you know better than that."

"I know I can't stand to see how horrible his face has been bruised." Kye had been furious. "I refuse to even speak to a Mackay until it's healed, and that includes you."

"Kye . . ."

"Not until it's healed," Kye snapped angrily. "Every time I see his face I just get more furious."

She hung up the phone. Lyrica was still staring at the device a moment later when a text with an incriminating photo popped up: Graham, glaring at his sister as she snapped the picture. And the left side of his face was bruised so horribly she gasped.

The second she left the spa she headed straight to her mother's inn. God knew she loved her cousins and her brother, but this was going too far.

Stomping up the steps, she pushed into the foyer, eyes narrowed, searching for Tim. There were very few people who could even attempt to talk any sense into a Mackay. The only one she knew of was Tim.

The sound of voices in the common living room, a shared space for the guests and family, had her turning and stepping into the large room.

Her mother, Mercedes, sat at the round café table next to an open window and sipped coffee as her guest and new friend Carmina spoke in soft, sweet tones.

Mercedes's head turned as Lyrica came into the room, her eyes widening as she hurriedly set down the coffee.

"Excuse me," she told Carmina distractedly. "I'll be right back."

Anger was churning so hard, so hot inside Lyrica that it was all she could do to hold it back as her mother gripped her arm and steered her quickly from the common room and across the foyer to the dining room, then into the kitchen.

"What in the world is wrong?" Mercedes demanded, her voice low as her gaze swept over her daughter. "Are you okay? Is Zoey well?"

"Oh, I'm fine," she bit out roughly. "But Natches Mackay is another story, Momma, because I'm going to brain him."

Mercedes stepped back, staring at her daughter in shock. One hand propped on a still-shapely hip, she lifted the other to her face, her fingers covering her lips and chin thoughtfully for a few long seconds.

"Oh, dear," she murmured. "What has Natches done now?"

"What has he done?" Lyrica all but snarled. "Not only can I not attend any party that goes on in this stupid county without being carded, having my brother called, or being asked politely to leave, but I guess whenever one of their know-it-all friends decides to pull me out of one, instead of waiting on permission, Natches thinks it's perfectly acceptable to plow his fist into the man's face. My best friend's brother's face, actually, and now Kyleene isn't speaking to me at all." Fists clenched, she lifted her hands and pressed them to her temples as a vicious groan rasped from her throat. "He's insane."

Mercedes was still staring at her in shock. Her mother evidently couldn't believe Natches would stoop so low, either.

"Oh, dear." She breathed out softly. "So Kye is angry with you?"

Lyrica breathed out roughly, shaking her head at the futility of what she seemed to be facing before answering. "Kye's furious. And I can't even blame her."

"How can she blame you for what transpired between her brother and your cousin?" Her mother sounded confused now. "Dear, it wasn't your fault. It seems a misunderstanding, nothing more. You know how they get when they believe the wrong sort of man is paying attention to you and your sisters. He likely simply misconstrued the situation . . ."

Lyrica flushed heatedly. She couldn't help it.

The moment her mother even hinted that Graham was attempting to seduce her, she flushed so brilliantly there was no hiding the truth from her too-perceptive mother.

"Oh." Her mother drew out the word slowly. "So, exactly what did Natches see, Lyrica, that made him so irate that his fist and Graham's face became so well acquainted?"

Oh, didn't her mother have a way with words? And tones. She was speaking to Lyrica as though her daughter was five and had been caught attempting to distract attention from her own actions.

"Momma, whatever Natches may have seen, he saw because he invaded the privacy of a room that was off limits. I am over twenty-one. I am not mentally deficient, and neither am I in any way unable to decide for myself who to take for a lover," Lyrica stated, calmer now, but no less furious. "And I won't lose my friendship with Kye because Natches got a little pissy over the fact that I kissed Graham. Not the other way around."

Mercedes breathed in deeply, a frown forming at her brow as she slowly straightened the hem of her blouse over her jeans. "Lyrica, you know how very protective he and the others can be. Perhaps Natches didn't see you initiate the kiss . . ."

Lyrica gave her head a hard shake as she turned from her mother and paced to the window looking out on the backyard. "He knew. He knew and it didn't matter to him, Momma."

Of course, there had been the way Graham had been holding her, his hips so obviously wedged between her thighs. The scene her cousin walked in on had been incredibly intimate. Incriminating.

"It's not as though either of us is married or breaking any sort of rule." She turned back and glared at her mother. "I'm a grown woman, not a teenager with no understanding of the word 'sex.'"

Her mother winced. She couldn't imagine any of her daughters having sex yet, Lyrica knew. As far as her mother was concerned, they were all still virgins.

"Lyrica, you know how the Mackay men can be. If Kye is truly your friend, then she will forgive you. She will understand the ways of men such as these."

"Momma, that is not good enough." Lyrica dismissed the idea that this could be fixed by simply understanding how her brother and cousins worked. "I won't live like this. I warned Dawg I won't. I want Natches to stop this now."

"Lyrica, you cannot control Natches . . ."

"Where's Tim?" She was tired of discussing it.

"How is Tim supposed to fix this?" Mercedes asked, surprised.

How the hell was Lyrica supposed to know?

"He can threaten him," she snapped, incensed, "say man things the moron understands—I don't care, but he better fix it before I fix it myself." She glared at her mother. "They won't like how I fix it, Momma. None of them will."

"I'll speak to him, I promise," Mercedes swore. "You know how the boys are, though, with such men, Lyrica. At the moment, Tim and Rowdy are trying to—"

"Rowdy's here?" Her eyes narrowed dangerously. "Wonderful, because I have something to say to him as well."

"Lyrica, wait." Her mother followed after her in concern. "This is not Rowdy's fault any more than it is Tim's."

"Really?" Gripping the stair rail as she took the first step, she turned and threw her mother a glare. "He was there, too. Who do you think made sure I went to my car while Natches threw that punch? Surely you didn't think he was alone. They're never alone. When it comes to me and Zoey now, they're like coyotes. They harass us in pairs."

Turning back, she climbed quickly up the stairs before moving along the main hall until she came to her mother's private suite of rooms and Tim's office.

The door was open, and when she stepped inside the roomy office, she found Tim sitting behind his desk while Rowdy stood at the far side of the room, watching her expectantly.

She focused on Rowdy first. "That rabid cousin of ours hit Graham," she told him furiously. "He had no right, Rowdy."

"He had every right, Lyrica." Rowdy was patient, his voice bringing her to a hard stop as she stared at him in shock. "Graham knows the score here—don't think he doesn't. And Natches warned you the other day he wasn't going to back off."

"Knows the score?" she ground out in disbelief, moving behind the nearest chair to give her hands something to grip besides his neck. "Are you crazy? What score is there to know? If one of Dawg's sisters kisses you, then you're going to get punched? Natches didn't punch Charlie Miller when he caught me kissing him last year."

"Charlie Miller hasn't left a string of mistresses behind him, the last eleven of which were given bimbo numbers by the gossips in this town." Rowdy argued patiently as his arms went across his chest in a classic Mackay stubborn pose. "His opinion of marriage is extremely low and his sexual exploits extremely high. Natches was just letting him know that he's risking more than losing a damned good woman if he breaks your heart. If he—or any other man—thinks he can just play with your heart and get away with it, then we're going to break body parts. The message was delivered and understood."

Lyrica stared at him in disbelief for a long, silent moment before turning to Tim.

"Is he serious?" she asked, astounded.

A heavy sigh as Tim's hand passed over his face was her answer. When he stared back at her, she could see it in his eyes.

Lips parted, she could only stare between the two men in outrage.

"The thought of being called bimbo number twelve is almost overshadowed by the fear that the brother and cousins I love so dearly will swallow me whole into some black, blank void where nothing or no one can touch me," she finally whispered, painfully. "Realizing the lengths the three of you will go to in ensuring everyone abides by your rules and by your arrogant determination of the life I will or will not live hurts more than realizing exactly how little I meant to the father who should have loved me."

"Lyrica, that's uncalled for." Tim rose abruptly from his chair as Rowdy's arms fell slowly from his chest, his gaze becoming heavy as he stared at her.

"Is it uncalled for, Tim?" she whispered. "The Mackay cousins entertained this whole county, probably the entire state, with their sexual exploits when they were younger, but Dawg Mackay's sisters have to hide their lovers or deny them to ensure they're not attacked." She shook her head, her chest tight with the knowledge that was staring her in the face. "Do you think it would matter, Rowdy, that I already know Graham's past, and I've stayed as far away from him as long as possible despite the fact that I can't bear the thought of another man touching me? Did it even count that the second he knew I was in trouble, he was there? No questions. He just found me and made sure I was safe until the decision was made that he wasn't good enough to keep me safe."

"Lyrica, it's not like that." Rowdy grimaced with a heavy breath. "Trust me. I know it's hard to understand. I know you don't like it. None of you have liked it or understood it. But there are certain rules men obey only when their brains get rattled a bit. I've been there. Dawg and Natches were there. Graham is cut from the same cloth."

A pain-filled facsimile of a laugh left her lips as she slid her hands slowly from the back of the chair and turned to Tim. "I'm sorry I disturbed you," she forced herself to say. "I'll leave now."

"Lyrica, dammit, wait," Timothy called, moving out from behind the desk as she turned to the door.

Lyrica shook her head and kept going. There was nothing left to say. Natches, Rowdy, and Dawg weren't going to relent, and they weren't going to let this go.

She had laughed at Eve when she'd learned how she'd fought against Brogan. Everyone had known Brogan was crazy for her. The same with Piper and Jed. The two men weren't even liked by the Mackay cousins at the time. They were distrusted and watched with suspicion. Lyrica had thought it so amusing at the time. Both of her sisters had refused to talk to Dawg, refused to try to make him understand what they needed.

If Rowdy and Tim knew what Natches had done, then there was no reason to go to Dawg—he would know as well. And, like Tim, he no doubt agreed with his actions. Dawg was usually more determined to protect his sisters than even his cousins were.

They were always in agreement in these matters.

Moving quickly down the stairs, she pushed through the front doors and hurried down the front steps to the Jeep. She didn't even stop to say good-bye to her mother. She couldn't.

It hurt too bad, and tears weren't something she did well.

Tears were something she'd sworn years before she would never shed again.

"Better call Dawg." Rowdy breathed heavily as he stood next to Timothy and watched the Jeep accelerate away from the house. "He's not going to be happy."

Timothy breathed out roughly before rubbing at the side of his nose and grimacing heavily. "That damned deal he made with her," he snorted as he dropped his hand and shoved it into the pocket of his slacks. "I warned him he was making a mistake."

Rowdy stared down at the shorter man again, still amazed by the transformation Mercedes Mackay had wrought in him. He was no longer the dark, miserable special agent on a fast track to a stroke. He was actually pleasant most of the time now. And he smiled.

Rowdy still found that really weird, too.

"Stop staring at me, Mackay," Timothy growled. "It's unsettling. Now, which of us gets to call Dawg?"

"I should let you," Rowdy said in disgust. "But no doubt you'd blame it all on Natches."

Timothy looked up at him, highly offended. "Seems to me it was his fault. If he hadn't hit so hard then Lyrica wouldn't be so hurt. Hell, I saw Graham's face this morning, Rowdy. Natches damned near broke it."

"He didn't even knock the bastard off his feet," Rowdy snapped in disgust. "He's stronger than he looks."

"His sister was still crying. She almost didn't let me in the house until Graham stepped out from the kitchen and sent her upstairs."

Rowdy stared outside thoughtfully as Timothy moved back to his chair and sat down.

"How's Graham taking it?" Rowdy asked, turning in time to catch Timothy's quick grin.

"He's damned disgusted by Kye's reaction and the fact that anyone even learned the identity of who hit him to begin with." Timothy chuckled in amusement. "He's a good man, Rowdy. And as much as I don't like what Natches walked in on myself, it doesn't change the fact that I don't believe Graham would play with her. I think he cares about her."

Rowdy was prone to believe it as well, but if Graham didn't start using his head instead of his dick, then he'd break Lyrica's heart anyway.

"Graham likes his bimbos, Timothy." He breathed out heavily. "Lyrica's no man's toy or his bimbo. He needs to establish that, not just to Lyrica, but to everyone who might believe otherwise before they realize there's anything between them. Otherwise, Lyrica's going to be hurt whether he cares for her or not."

Timothy just stared back at him silently.

"You don't believe me?" he asked as Timothy sat back in the chair, his arms resting comfortably on the armrests.

"I actually think he deserved to have his face busted if he really was all but fucking her against the window of that lake house," Timothy stated. "But, gauging by Lyrica's fury, I'm going to assume Natches might have overreacted to whatever he saw. I know him and I know Lyrica, and I know she's Natches's favorite. Just as I know he and Graham have had a disagreement for years over something. Something deep, Rowdy. And that resentment just may end up being what breaks her heart."

Rowdy frowned in confusion. "Natches doesn't have anything against Graham."

"Yeah, he does, Rowdy," Timothy stated somberly. "He's kept it to himself and that was a good thing. I had hoped it wouldn't end up affecting Lyrica, though. I could have been wrong."

If Natches was pissed at Graham over something, especially something he'd carried alone for a number of years, then the chances of him overreacting rose considerably. Natches wasn't a man who dealt well with resentment.

The very fact that he'd kept whatever it was hidden concerned Rowdy.

"Get the details we need from the surveillance cameras across from that apartment, and let's see if we've missed anything," Rowdy told the former special agent. "I want this threat against Lyrica erased immediately. I'll talk to Natches. Better yet, call everyone together, we'll just meet at his place."

If Lyrica ended up hurt because of his cousin's stupidity, then Dawg just might end up breaking Natches's face next.

ELEVEN

Natches's home sat on the banks of Lake Cumberland, a few miles from Dawg's farm. Whereas Dawg's two-story farmhouse with its wraparound porch and old-time charm surrounded by flowering bushes and myriad blooms soothed the senses, Natches's place had a feeling of hidden beauty.

The sprawling single-story home with its dark wood siding was nestled among a variety of evergreen trees and brush—mostly holly and laurel that grew naturally in the area. One would have to look closely if one didn't know the house sat there.

It wasn't hidden so much as it was very cleverly disguised, and Natches and his wife, Chaya, preferred it that way.

Lyrica pulled into the driveway beneath a canopy of dense growth and shook her head. She would have smiled, not for the first time, over her cousin's idiosyncrasies if she wasn't so upset. Over the years the family had been certain Natches would grow out of his penchant for plants and landscape design that made his home seem to be more a part of the land itself than the building it actually was. He hadn't grown out of it yet, though.

Stepping from the car and moving along a moss-covered stone path to the backyard, she noticed the blooms that now grew around the wood supports of the back porch.

"Lyrie!" Bliss, Natches and Chaya's twelve-year-old daughter, bounced out through the kitchen door, her long, ribbon-straight black hair and emerald eyes a perfect match for Natches's.

Bliss had the dark Mackay looks but the softer turn of her cheek, her eye shape, and the arch of her brows were her mother's. Still, the girl looked enough like Lyrica that she was often mistaken for her daughter by strangers.

"Hey there." Bliss threw her arms around Lyrica and gave her a firm hug before the girl jumped back with a wide smile. "Where's your dad?"

"He's in the house making Mom give him that look that means he's about to go hide in his work shed and say bad words again." Bliss laughed. "He's so funny."

"What's he doing to your mom?" Lyrica smiled as the girl tugged at her hand and drew her inside.

Chaya chose that moment to step into the kitchen, her brown eyes sparkling menacingly as she stalked into the room.

"He's being himself of course," Chaya bit out before turning to her daughter. "Your aunts are on their way to pick you up for a while. They're taking you shopping with them."

"Uh-oh." Bliss's gaze flicked to the doorway her mother had just stepped from. "Dad's about to get in trouble, huh?"

"Oh, baby, your daddy already crossed that little line." Her mother smiled tightly as Bliss giggled at the mocking threat in her mother's voice.

She turned back to Lyrica. "They'll kiss and make up before I get home. Bet me."

Lyrica shook her head. "Do I look that easy, kid?"

Bliss shrugged innocently. "Well, since he's in trouble because he hit some guy over you, I thought I'd give it a try."

Bliss laughed in delight at the surprise on Lyrica's face before rushing from the room and calling out to her father in glee.

"Lord, she's just like her father," Chaya moaned. "She scares me."

"When's she going to go boy crazy so Natches will stop stressing over his cousins' love lives and stress over his daughter's upcoming one instead?" Lyrica asked.

Chaya grimaced at the thought of that. "Come on, Lyrica," she protested. "Let's not rush the divorce I can feel coming when he completely loses touch with reality. Let him focus on you a while longer."

"Divorce?" Natches strode into the room, a smile of genuine warmth and playful charm filling his expression as he caught his wife in strong arms and pulled her to him. "Never. I was thinking a deserted island instead. There would be no boys there for Bliss to get crazy over."

Dressed in jeans and a dark T-shirt, Natches was a mature man. That maturity had placed a few lines and creases along his eyes, a hint of gray at his temples, but other than that, he was still a powerful force.

Chaya grimaced and shook her head as her husband placed a loving kiss at her neck. "Natches, sweetheart, are you still trying to fool yourself?"

Wearing loose cotton pants and a white T-shirt, her shoulder-length golden brown hair pulled to the crown of her head in a clip, with wisps falling around her face, Chaya appeared far younger than her husband though Lyrica knew the difference in their ages wasn't that vast.

Chaya had once confided to Lyrica that Natches had been

there the day her first child had died in a fiery blast that terrorists had instigated in the Middle East. If it hadn't been for him, she would have died that day, too, she had admitted.

In the six years since Lyrica had been a part of their lives, the love and sense of bonding between this couple had never ceased to amaze her. Just as with Dawg and Christa, and Rowdy and Kelly, their commitment to each other had only increased over the years.

They were both nearing fifty, but they hadn't seemed to age much at all since Lyrica and her sisters had arrived in the county. It was as though their love kept them young, kept them seeing the innocence and beauty in the world.

"Talk to your cousin." Chaya moved from his arms after giving him a quick, forgiving kiss. "Kelly and Janey are coming to take Bliss shopping with the other girls. Then you and I will talk."

Natches's brows lifted and cunning sensuality filled his eyes as he watched his wife leave the room. It was a look he probably had no idea others could see. The look of a man who knew joy, never-ending surprise, and pleasure in the woman he loved.

"For a man who loves his wife so dearly, you have an amazing ability to believe other men have no capacity for the same feelings, Natches." Crossing her arms over her breasts, Lyrica watched her cousin suspiciously as that cunning sensuality morphed and she caught the slightest glint of calculation before it was quickly hidden.

"I have never said I don't believe in it," he retorted as he adopted an expression of such innocence it was almost believable.

Lyrica knew him better than that.

"That look might fool your daughter, but it doesn't fool me, cuz," she informed him.

Still, it remained.

"Lyrica, you're so suspicious." He sighed.

"Natches," she drawled with tight mockery, "you're so full of bullshit."

He merely grunted at the accusation.

"Why were you and Chaya arguing over me to the point that Chaya's sending Bliss shopping with Janey and Kelly?" she tried again.

The look he shot her was classic Natches. Playful, charming, with a barely there glint of cunning that locked onto any weakness and used it instinctively. He was a master manipulator, a man with instinctive perception, and a sharp-eyed, merciless sniper. A man who in the past had taken aim between a cousin's eyes and pulled the trigger.

"Sometimes Bliss only hears part of a conversation . . ."

"Stay away from Graham, Natches." She didn't beat around the bush.

She could do that with Rowdy and Dawg, laugh and playfully tease and still get her point across. She knew better than to even attempt it with Natches.

"Then you stay away from him." Natches dropped the pretense instantly, his emerald green eyes narrowing on her as he hooked his thumbs in the front pockets of his jeans.

Lyrica stared at him in disbelief. "You're kidding me."

"No, I'm not kidding you." At least he wasn't lying to her. He'd been known to do that.

"Why are you doing this, Natches? Why take a stand like this over something that's none of your business?" she asked him, confused now.

"Who says it's none of my business?" A dark frown flitted at his brow. "You're my business, Lyrica. And Graham Brock's bad news for you."

She would have laughed at him if the disbelief hadn't run so deep.

Her lips thinned. There were very few ways to convince Natches to let something go. He was worse than Dawg. Her threat to move away and let him deal with Dawg's anger had obviously not worked.

"Natches, stay out of this," she warned him softly.

"Why should I?" He seemed to be laughing at her, albeit silently.

"Because if you don't, then I'll be too concerned you'll hurt him, and I'll give up on the one man I can't seem to stay away from." It was the truth. Stark. Simple.

"So why would I bother to back off if it's working?"

He wasn't a stupid man, though. Tension filled his shoulders, his expression veiled as he watched her carefully.

"Because then I'll have given up not because the man isn't in my best interests or because it's my choice; I'll have done it because it's your choice. I'll never stop resenting you for it and once I've accepted that's how it will end, then I have to accept that it doesn't matter who I love, because you'll always stand between us. Why should I bother to love then? Why should I bother to care that whoever I sleep with cares for me in turn?"

"Stop trying to snow me, Lyrie. You might say that, you might mean it right now, but you're too damned stubborn to actually do it."

"Natches, at this point, I'm struggling to decide for myself if Graham Brock is something I want or merely something I've been fascinated with for years. Don't turn the question into a quest to prove to myself and to you that you have no control over me, or a lesson in the fact that you can control me by hurting someone I care about. You wouldn't like either outcome, and neither would I."

Unlike her sisters, she believed in facing Dawg, Natches, and Rowdy in ways they understood rather than from a stance of pure stubbornness. She loved them, very much respected them, but she knew that if given the chance, they would wrap her and her sisters in cotton batting and do whatever they thought necessary to avoid ever seeing them hurt. And they'd never realize how the total sterility of such a life would destroy them.

"How much do you expect me to let him destroy you?" he growled, anger beating just beneath the surface. "I know things about him that you don't, Lyrica. Things that would hurt you if you ever learned the truth of it."

"You'll tell me that, but I know you—you will never tell me what those things are, will you, Natches?"

His expression was the only answer she needed.

"Until you can tell me, then let's drop all the dark hints as to the man he is, was, or could be." She sighed wearily. "He saved my life. And I know he tries to be a good man. No matter what kind of man he may be, he's a good man."

"He's a dangerous man!" he snapped. "He may have saved your life, but he could also end up getting you killed."

"And how many times was Kelly warned of that where the Mackays were concerned?" she argued bitterly. "Or Christa? You forget, Natches, I know your pasts, I know the men you were before you fell in love, and I know how dangerous the three of you were. What if Chaya had walked away from you because of Johnny?"

He'd killed Johnny Grace. The cousin he'd been raised with, the one who had attempted to kill Christa and would have killed Dawg. Natches had put his rifle sights between the man's eyes and he'd felt no remorse pulling the trigger.

"Look at your past, at Dawg's and Rowdy's, and tell me that you didn't deserve to be loved."

"Hell no, we didn't deserve it. Not then we didn't," he growled back at her. "And what we have wasn't handed to us, either, Lyrica. We had to change to be able to have the hearts we share, and if Graham Brock thinks he can have you without facing one of us, then he can think again." He moved to her quickly, gripped her shoulders, and stared down at her with the merciless lack of remorse she imagined was in his eyes when he killed his cousin. "I love you, girl. I see you and I see the child that owns every beat of my heart. The one I'd go into hell fighting for, and I'll be damned if I'll betray my instincts on this. If I do, I may as well tell every man who ever meets her that would hurt her to go ahead and do just that. Graham knows the score, and I have no doubt if I beat the hell out of him, you'll hate me. For a while. But at least you'll by god hate me with a whole, beating heart rather than half a one or, god forbid, from a casket. Remember that one."

With that he turned and moved quickly from the room, his footsteps heavy, his warning ringing in her head.

"No one said a Mackay was easy to talk to."

Lyrica swung around to face Rowdy as he stepped through the back door, his handsome face creased in concern as he stared at her quietly.

Rubbing at the chill that raced over her arms, she stared back at the cousin they always said was the logical one. The one who could be reasoned with. Today, none of them knew the meaning of the word "reason."

"He's irrational," she whispered, shaking her head. "All of you are."

His lips quirked into a gentle, understanding smile.

"Not irrational, simply determined to protect family." Moving to the counter, he poured a cup of coffee from the heated coffeepot and sipped at it before leaning against the counter and watching her with the solemn concern he seemed to approach every problem with.

"How can you agree with this, Rowdy? It's wrong."

He turned to face her slowly.

Sunlight slanted through the window at his back, striking at his black hair and his forest green eyes, warming the white short-sleeved shirt he wore tucked into belted jeans.

"Whether or not I agree with him is beside the point." He shrugged. "I understand how he feels, though."

"Am I wrong, Rowdy?" The logical one, Rowdy rarely let his own personal opinion of someone cloud his actions. "Do I see a good man where something else exists?"

"I believe Graham's a good man, Lyrica," he finally said. "I believe he's an honorable man. But a man's lust is rarely driven by his honor. And a man like Graham has buried the kind of vulnerability that would let him love a good woman, so deep he doesn't even believe it exists anymore. The question then becomes, does he want you enough to revive it? Because that's the only way he'll have you without all three of us coming down on him like a nuclear explosion the first time someone calls you one of his bimbos."

She flinched at the reminder that she and Kye weren't the only ones who noticed the women, or the type of women, Graham went through so casually.

Maybe she did need to move just far enough away that the Mackays couldn't oversee every move she made or every man she became interested in.

"You know, if you were like your sisters, dating regularly, doing all the crazy shit they've gotten into over the years, maybe Natches wouldn't be so extreme," he told her gently. "But you don't. You sneak in a party here and there, knowing you're going to be dragged out, but that's about it. It's never serious for you. And Graham Brock is the only man you've ever focused on. That scares us. Because we know Graham, and we know that even good men are capable of bad things."

"And all three of you evidently lost touch with reality a long damned time ago," she told him roughly. "My life or who I sleep with is nobody's damned business."

His face hardened. "And that's where you're wrong. You're a Mackay, Lyrica. Whether you like it or not you'll always be a Mackay. And trust me, trouble and Mackays go hand in hand, to the point that we'll never, at any time, turn our backs if you're getting involved with a man who has the same ability to find danger as we've always had. If you want to have a nice, quiet, sane affair then find a nice, quiet, sane man to have it with and I promise you, I'll stand in front of Dawg and Natches myself to make certain you can have it in peace."

An instant, instinctive response came over her. Her lips thinned; her eyes narrowed.

"Why, Rowdy," she drawled, "where would the fun be in that?"

Turning on her heel, she pulled the back door open and stalked from the house, outrage trembling through her body. Her cousin watched her with thoughtful focus until she disappeared.

Rowdy listened, heard her Jeep start and, seconds later, pull from the drive.

He snagged another coffee cup from the cabinet and poured it full before lifting it and carrying it with his own to the breakfast table that sat on the other end of the kitchen.

Natches didn't disappoint him. He was there within seconds of Rowdy taking his seat, from where he watched nature at its finest just outside the window as a doe and her spotted fawn bounded through the forest.

"She's too damned stubborn," Natches growled as he jerked a chair out and straddled it furiously. "If we're not careful, she could end up devastated."

Rowdy turned and gave his cousin a firm look. "Keep Trudy retired."

Trudy was Natches's modified rifle, the same one he'd used to kill the cousin who'd threatened them all. With the additional threat Lyrica was facing, Natches may not keep his promise to keep his first instincts in check.

"I'll let Trudy sleep," Natches assured him with a grin. "For now."

Rowdy breathed out at the statement, relieved, then turned at the sound of the door opening again.

Dawg stepped inside, a scowl on his face as he tromped over to the coffeepot and poured his own mug.

None of them mentioned the fact that no one knocked before entering the house. They did that at one another's homes, just as their wives did. They were home, no matter which house they sat in, and that was how they liked it. Sometimes, it was as though they were triplets rather than first cousins.

Rowdy watched both of them with narrowed eyes. "I'm going to assume Graham Brock made the same visit to you two that he made to me this morning?"

Dawg made a sound somewhere between a growl and a snarl.

Natches crossed his arms over his chest and grunted in irritation.

Rowdy breathed out heavily. Lyrica had missed Graham by only moments when she'd arrived at Timothy's office earlier.

"Suggestions?" he asked when neither of them commented.

"Shoot him!" Natches and Dawg spoke at once.

"We have a plan, remember?" Rowdy growled, then he glanced at them both thoughtfully. "How long would she grieve for him, do you think?" Rowdy asked as though he were actually considering the prospect.

"Would the three of you really like a suggestion or are you just considering it for appearance's sake?" Chaya asked as she, Christa, and Kelly stepped into the room.

Rowdy bit back his grin as the other two gave him a long-suffering look.

"A suggestion we could live with would be nice." Dawg was the one who answered, his voice morose as he lifted his coffee to his lips.

"Do what you always do," his wife said softly as she bent to kiss the top of his head lovingly. "Track the danger, keep a close eye on it, intercede if you have to, torture the hell out of Graham, and keep to the original plan. Just make sure he realizes the future discomfort he'll face if he breaks her heart. But let Lyrica make the choice, and if the fall hurts, then let her hurt, Dawg. Let her live."

"Or she'll hate all three of you." Mercedes Mackay stepped into the room then, with Timothy close behind her.

"Geez, Timothy, we didn't invite your ass," Natches snarled, though with a lack of heat that actually indicated his respect for the other man.

"Nice to see you, too, Natches," the other man said with a grunt. "And as always, your hospitality overwhelms me."

Moving to Christa and Chaya, Mercedes hugged them briefly, thankfully, then gave each man a hard, firm look. "She's your sister—cousins or not, I count each of you her brother, not just Dawg. But she is my daughter. If I can bear her broken heart, then so can you."

"Who called them?" Natches muttered, despite the affection in his gaze as he glanced at the dark-haired beauty Timothy Cranston had managed to fall in love with.

"Rowdy invited me before he left the office," Timothy answered. "It seems Graham's made a point to come to each of us to protest his lack of involvement in the investigation concerning the attack on Lyrica." Timothy's face held no evil smile, no wicked anticipation. He was far too somber. "Which, coincidentally, gave me an idea."

"Oh Lord."

"God save us."

"What did we do to deserve this?" Natches groaned as though in pain.

Timothy grunted humorlessly.

"Tell us and get it the hell over with." Dawg sighed.

"Why, we let him become part of the investigation," Timothy replied instantly. "A very intricate part. The attack on her doesn't sit well with any of us, especially considering that we all suspect the poor girl who actually died was no more than an attempt to allay our suspicions."

Rowdy watched him speculatively now, as did Dawg and Natches.

"The attempt was too professional," Timothy explained. "Especially for such sloppy execution. Either we're being played with, or, according to the call I received just after Rowdy left, Graham is the least of our worries. We're looking at something potentially more dangerous to her than we first imagined."

"What's happened?" Rowdy beat the others to the question.

"Just after you left the office, Tracker contacted me. He says he accepted the contract on Lyrica some months ago with the express purpose of learning who offered the contract. The hit was attempted and deliberately botched. He's certain he can flush the backer out, but once again, he's been pressed to make another attempt or the backer will rescind the agreement and put the contract out for bids once again."

The muttered, explicit curse that slipped past Dawg's lips didn't surprise any of them. Rowdy plowed his fingers through his hair with restless concern. Natches's gaze iced over, its cold emerald depths stone hard.

Tracker.

No one knew his real name, where he came from, or his true

loyalties. All they knew was his apparent disinterest in getting in Natches Mackay's crosshairs. There was a strange sense of loyalty from the other man toward the Mackays, though a confusing one considering the fact that the Mackays hadn't even known of him until long after they'd gotten as far out of DHS as possible.

"Son of a bitch," Dawg whispered as the women who stood behind the men held on to them as though to steady themselves.

Rowdy could feel the trembling fear in Kelly's grip and reached up to hold her hand in assurance.

"Send the girls to Texas." Natches looked around the room, the hard-eyed assassin he had once been clearly apparent now. "Bliss, Laken, Erica, and the others. Send them to Cade and Marly. Cade, Brock, Sam, and their boys will make damned sure they're safe. They'll take care of them. See if we can get Zoey to go with them. They've been begging to visit again since last year."

"I'll have John Senior dispatch his plane immediately for the trip," Timothy said quietly. "We get the girls as far away as possible until we know what the hell is going on and who's behind the contract."

"I'll contact Alex and the others," Dawg said. "We'll meet with them this afternoon. They're not going to send their kids with ours without an explanation."

Dawg wasn't just a brother now; he was a weapon honed by years in the Marines and having to make choices that required he set his emotions and his fears aside.

"I'll contact Tracker and set up a meeting, then call Graham once we have a time and a place," Timothy injected, eyeing them all steadily. "Keep him in the loop this time. Lyrica's life is more important at this point than anything else."

"And we're supposed to let Graham help us, how?" Dawg growled as he rubbed at the back of his neck. "Dammit, my stomach is burning. I'm getting too damned old for this shit."

"I told you days ago to get her out of sight and none of you wanted to listen," Natches snapped. "Your indigestion and my acid reflux acting up at the same time? No way in hell. We listen to our guts, Dawg, like we used to, before we lose her."

"Graham will do what no one would ever believe we'd allow him to do." Timothy's gaze hardened, causing each of them to watch him in narrow-eyed suspicion. "Place Lyrica back with him for protection. If, as Tracker and I suspect, the backer is someone in Somerset, then they'd never expect us to deliberately place her there. They won't suspect we're searching for them."

"What do we tell Lyrica?" Natches was the one to ask the question they were all avoiding.

"The truth," Mercedes declared, her tone commanding, the strength her daughters had inherited echoing in her voice. "You will tell her the truth."

Tracker was six feet, five inches of hard, merciless power. Rumor had it he'd been a Navy SEAL before arriving on the soldier of fortune scene eight years before, though no one could confirm the rumor.

He'd been approached by damned near every security firm in the world, offers had been made to back a security company led by him, and the leaders of several different countries had met with him, willing to pay any price to have him head their emerging forces.

He'd turned down every offer, as had the six-member team he led.

Whoever he was, wherever he came from, no one could deny he was a force to be reckoned with.

Stepping into the darkened offices across from Lyrica's apartment to face the man, Graham couldn't help but feel a familiarity when he looked into the striking blue eyes of the man leaning casually against the wall, facing not just the Mackays, but also their extended male family members as well.

Among them were Alex Jansen, chief of Somerset Police and husband to Natches's sister, Janey; Brogan Campbell, the FPS agent who recently married Dawg's sister Eve; Jed Booker, Brogan's partner and the fiancé of another of Dawg's sisters Piper; and Zeke Mayes, a close friend and the former Pulaski County sheriff, who had turned over the reins to his son, Shane, in the last election and now ran an electronic security firm headquartered outside Somerset with his wife, Rogue. Shane Mayes was there as well. Though unmarried and unrelated, the younger man, who was closer in age to Graham than to the Mackays, stood sure and confident at his father's side. John Walker Jr., Zeke's brother-in-law and one of Timothy Cranston's unofficial agents, was there as well, along with Timothy himself.

Cranston was the man they all had in common. He'd first commanded the group the Mackays were a part of through DHS about twelve years before. He'd manipulated and tricked the Mackays and their friends in various ops that eventually built them all into an intelligent, unbeatable force. Then he'd met Dawg's sisters and fell in love with the woman who had given them life. He was now bringing men into the Mackay females' lives as though he were born to direct their destinies.

What part Tracker would play in the schemes that filled Timothy's head, Graham wasn't certain. What plans the former agent had for Lyrica, Graham intended to learn. What he did know now, though, was that Tracker was a man of many talents, and though his reputation suggested he could be convinced, for the right price, of course, to kill a man, that wasn't exactly the truth.

"Graham." Tracker nodded his shaggy dark head as Graham

locked the door behind him and stepped fully into the room. "Good to see you again."

Stepping forward, Graham accepted the mercenary's handshake with a nod.

"You, too, Track. And I'm damned glad you're the one we're facing rather than another party."

Tracker gave a mocking snort at the comment. "I turned it down at first," he admitted. "But I was too curious, I guess, because the mark was from Somerset. Once I learned it was one of Dawg Mackay's sisters, I reconsidered."

"Took you long enough to come forward," Alex Jansen commented coolly. "One might say a little too long."

"One might," Tracker agreed, his lips kicking up at one corner wryly. "But one might be unaware of the fact that trust isn't my first inclination and that having my reputation as a merciless killer smeared by a shadow of compassion isn't exactly the compromise I'm looking for here."

"We're not here to snipe at his background, Alex," Timothy stated from where he sat behind the bar on the other side of the room. "Let's hear what he has to say, then we can plan accordingly."

As though agreement had been voiced, Tracker moved from the wall to step behind the bar with Timothy as the rest of them converged on the bar stools in front of the wide teak counter.

"Two million dollars," Tracker stated as Timothy passed out a file folder to each of them. "The hit has to appear to be either an accident or a case of mistaken identity. When that girl the drug cartel killed showed up, I decided to use it to try to flush out whoever's backing the contract. So far, it hasn't worked. At last contact I was given one more chance before the down payment has to be returned and a new offer will go out."

Graham opened the file to find pictures of Lyrica, notes on her various jobs, schedule, friends, and family. Along with it was the Mackay itinerary for the weeks they were on vacation.

"In checking out her background I learned that Graham Brock's sister was a close friend and that her number was on Ms. Mackay's contact list. They talked daily, so I took a chance that if she couldn't contact her friend and her phone appeared to be malfunctioning then she would turn to her brother. Thankfully, the plan worked."

Graham glanced up from the file. "You could have just called."

"Not until I learned exactly whose phones were compromised." Tracker shook his head before leaning back against the empty shelves of the former bar. "When she disappeared, my employer demanded the records of a tracking and jamming program he provided that would ensure no one accessed her phone. I sent it and waited. The only encrypted number he couldn't pinpoint on the report was Graham's." He nodded in Graham's direction. "For the rest of you, I was sent call logs, though text and discussion logs weren't tracked, it appears."

"Son of a bitch," Timothy exclaimed. "How was the encryption cracked?"

"From what I can understand about the program, it's usually hidden in a download of some sort," Tracker answered. "A picture, website, whatever. Backtracking, I was able to identify a URL common to the unencrypted numbers of those on Lyrica's contact list. How it got into the encrypted numbers, I haven't ascertained just yet."

"A lot of work," Alex muttered. "A hell of a lot of money. The question is, why? What does Lyrica know that has her marked?"

"My question as well," Tracker answered. "And one of the questions I initially asked upon taking the job. I'm known to be the nosy sort." A mocking smile tugged at his lips, though his gaze remained stone cold. "The answer I received was that the contract was a vendetta, not a personal strike."

"Fuck!" Natches hissed, his voice low, vibrating with menace. "Our old enemies perhaps?"

The homeland terrorist group had been silent for years.

"My sources say no." Once again, Tracker answered the question. "I'll be honest, gentlemen, I've spent more time trying to track who, what, and why on this contract than I've spent on any other. There are no answers, though I have managed to cross out every Mackay enemy I could identify."

"What about my enemies?" Timothy asked.

"That one I can't answer," Tracker informed him. "You have far too many, Timothy, and even more than even I can identify."

"It's not Timothy," Natches stated.

"Then who?" The question came from Rowdy, who was sitting at Timothy's right, every line of his body tense and filled with fury.

"I don't know." A quick shake of his head was the only indication of Natches's confusion. "But it's not Timothy. There's something familiar to this program, though; I just can't identify what. It's as though I've seen it somewhere else, heard of it, or something." He tapped one particular page. "Lyrica's phone went offline here." He pointed to the included graph as he turned to Graham. "Is that where you had her pull the battery?"

Graham checked the graph then.

"That was it." He confirmed the time. "I kept the call brief, just long enough for my GPS to pinpoint her, before I had her disconnect and pull the battery from the phone."

Natches frowned again, shaking his head. "That shouldn't have worked." He sighed. "Not with the program I'm thinking of."

"Good luck tracing it," Tracker retorted. "My second in command has been working on it nonstop for the past three months since we were given the contract, and even her sources haven't been able to identify it or its creator."

"Angel?" Graham asked him, remembering the tiny bundle of dynamite that had fought viciously with the mercenary. "She's still putting up with you?"

Tracker flicked him an irritated glance. "Stay the hell away from her, Graham. Angel's no flavor and I won't have her become one."

What the fuck? He blinked back at Tracker as the Mackays and their friends glared over at him.

"The 'flavor' comments are starting to piss me off," he told them all. "And I never had any intention of inviting Angel into my bed. That woman knows her way around a knife far too well."

"If the comments bother you, then stop sleeping with those rich, spoiled little heiresses with too much money and too little brains," Natches snorted.

"Really?" Graham grunted at the comment. "Are we going to go there, Natches?"

The other man looked up and the calculated menace in his gaze had an answering expression that tightened Graham's own expression.

"Enough," Rowdy warned them both.

"Angel has been in the apartment next to Lyrica's since we accepted the contract," Tracker informed them then. "She's also been shadowing her wherever she goes when she leaves the apartment. And I should tell you all, she just left again." He glanced at the watch he was wearing. "That woman doesn't sleep a lot, does she?" He glanced at Graham as he made the comment.

Graham gave him a level stare in return until the other man gave another of those crooked, mocking little grins.

"Angel couldn't have been shadowing her or I would have

known about it," Dawg stated, his voice hard as one finger tapped soundlessly against his open file. "I've had someone following her since she moved back to her apartment . . ."

Tracker stared back at him knowingly. "Jim Bailey. A hell of an investigator and bodyguard, but he has nothing on Angel. Hell, she even rode with him a few nights after convincing him he was the best thing since sliced bread. He's not taking the job seriously and spends more time on his cell phone than he does watching for tails. His belief is that only a fool would go after a Mackay and risk their wrath."

"Fucker!" Natches breathed out, fury lending a dark roughness to his tone that had his cousins flinching. "I'll take care of him."

"Leave him in place," Tracker suggested. "Whoever the contract's backer may have in place to follow Lyrica won't be watching for anyone else, though Angel hasn't detected anyone yet. When this is over, discuss your bill with him maybe. Until then, use him."

That was what he would have done, Graham admitted.

"What information is coming to you from your backer?" Timothy asked.

"It's in the back of the file," Tracker informed him. "I convinced him I had to complete another job after my first attempt on Lyrica fell through. As far as he knows, I'm not due back for another week. I had hoped my time here would reveal the backer's identity, but that hasn't happened yet. That's why I came to Timothy. I have two weeks after my supposed return to complete the job and give this man Lyrica's lifeless body. If I don't, he'll find another team. If that happens, there won't be a warning. She'll just be dead."

Like hell.

Graham could feel his fury burning chaotically. He wouldn't allow all the vibrant, sensual energy that filled her to be silenced.

She was too much a part of his life, too important to him to allow her to be threatened.

He closed the file slowly.

"Contact Angel," he growled. "I want to know where the hell she's headed."

Tracker arched his brow at the demand. "She'll contact me when Lyrica stops."

"What role do you intend to play in this, Tracker?" Graham hoped like hell the man didn't think he was just going to sit back and watch while the rest of them fought to protect her. He'd help, or he'd wish he had.

"Getting involved, Graham?" Tracker asked softly, the question causing Graham to tense. "I didn't expect that, despite the appearance of interest. She doesn't appear to be a 'flavor' to me." His gaze flicked to Dawg.

The smile he gave the other man was hard and filled with warning. "And it's not exactly any of your business," Graham assured him softly.

Tracker grinned at that. "I don't know, she's pretty as a little speckled pup. I might want to take her home with me."

The comment drew a reaction, despite Graham's best intentions.

The conversation between him and Sam where Graham had identified Lyrica as a pup popped into his mind. The knowing look on Tracker's face assured him that was the intent. There was no way in hell the other man had tapped his phone or bugged his house, and that left only one other person he could have compromised.

Sam Bryce.

"I'll take care of that one, Tracker," he promised the other man, knowing the mercenary would be well aware that Graham knew how he'd managed to come by the information.

"I'm sure you will," Tracker answered softly. "But be certain you know the means by which it was acquired before you destroy a friendship, Graham. I'd hate to put you on the dark side of the acquaintance list. Know what I mean?"

"I don't," Dawg snapped, obviously tired of the oblique conversation. "Want to clue us the fuck in or shut the hell up?"

Tracker's grin was one Graham had seen on the Mackays' lips more than once. Equal amounts of mocking amusement and irritation.

Though, there was a hint of respect there, too, Graham thought.

Rather than making one of his infamous smart remarks, Tracker inclined his head in agreement. "Point taken," he murmured. "Graham and I perhaps know each other a little too well."

"And that perhaps bothers me a little too much," Dawg said as he shot Graham a glare.

Hell, he was getting damned sick of the glares, glowers, and silent promises of retribution being shot his way.

"How do you intend to proceed with this?" he asked the mercenary rather than adding to whatever fuel the Mackays were gathering against him.

"That's my call," Dawg inserted, his voice soft, challenging, as Graham met his glare.

"Would you like to enlighten us, maybe?" Graham asked. "Or was my invitation here a mistake?"

"Probably." Natches spoke before his cousin could, a tight smile pulling at his lips as the icy emerald green of his gaze locked on Graham.

"Natches," Timothy said, his tone chiding, "let's not antagonize him. Graham's a very important part of the plan and you know it."

Those words sent a chill racing down Graham's spine as he centered his gaze on the former agent and began to see why the Mackays had become such a force to be reckoned with after they'd aligned with this soft-spoken, often far-too-amused little bastard.

"And what part is that, Timothy? Sacrificial lamb, maybe?" Graham was barely holding his own anger in check now.

Timothy smiled. A deliberately wide smile as his hazel eyes gleamed with hard purpose. "Sacrificial lamb always seemed a waste of a good agent to me, Graham," he stated. "No, you'll not be the lamb being led to slaughter, nor will Lyrica." His voice hardened. "We all have our strengths here, just as Lyrica has her weaknesses. One of those weaknesses being her inability to live with any of her cousins for more than a few days at a time without sparks flying. That will only distract all of us."

Graham felt his gut tighten at the information.

"Then she won't be staying with one of them?" Shock and dread began to fill him. "Bullshit. You can't leave her in that damned apartment alone." He turned to Dawg, noticing the other man was staring at the file lying in front of him as though he could set it aflame with his gaze alone.

"We have no intention of leaving her there alone," Timothy assured him, pulling his gaze back.

Still smiling, the former agent slid his hands into the pockets of his slacks and watched Graham too closely, with far too much amusement.

"Then what is your intention?" Graham snarled.

"She'll be staying with you," Timothy answered, and shock tore through Graham's mind. "The rest of us will be watching, maneuvering, and flushing the backer out into the open. Your only job is keeping her alive—"

"Unless it's too late." Tracker was suddenly moving. "She's been hit. The Jeep was plowed into from a side road and she's in a ravine. Angel can't get her to answer and hasn't gotten into the vehicle yet. Location's being texted to you."

Graham was moving behind him before the others could process their shock, racing from the side entrance of the abandoned business to the Viper he'd parked next to the black Corvette.

They tore out of their respective parking places almost simultaneously, but it was the Viper that hit the street first.

All Graham could hear as he loaded the location's coordinates into the computer verbally were the words that Lyrica had been hit and the terror that began shredding his guts at the thought.

She'd been hit.

God help him if she hadn't survived.

TWELVE

She was shaking.

Lyrica could feel the shudders. They originated inside her body and reverberated outward, trembling through muscle and bone until it was all she could do to keep her teeth from chattering.

Her Jeep was surprisingly intact. Whatever the hell kind of tank Dawg had turned it into during the years he'd driven it had saved her life.

"Ms. Mackay? Are you sure you're okay?" The young woman who had helped Lyrica out of the Jeep and up the ravine to her own car stared back at her with the wildest damned green eyes. "I called for help. They'll be here soon."

Lyrica had never seen eyes quite like hers. They were aqua green, vivid and bright, and filled with concern as she ran her hands over Lyrica's arms and legs and up her rib cage.

If she hadn't recognized the experienced search for broken

bones and internal bleeding, she would wonder if the other woman was copping a feel.

Lyrica focused on the woman's face again, realizing she'd seen her before.

"You . . . you're my neighbor." She felt disoriented, her thoughts scattering easily.

"Yeah, I moved in about three months ago." Sitting on her haunches, the other woman frowned back at her. "Are you certain you're okay?" She held up fingers. "How many?"

Lyrica blinked back at her. "Really?"

"Give me a number, girlie," she demanded with a quick grin and firm voice. "We don't have all night here."

"Two." A tickle at the side of her head had her lifting her hand. She came away with a vivid swipe of scarlet against her fingers.

Blood.

Hell, she was bleeding.

"Is it bad?" she asked the woman. "If you called an ambulance, my family will probably beat them here. They don't handle the sight of blood really well."

At least, not the blood of those they cared for.

"It's not bad," she was assured.

The woman whisked her shirt off, revealing a minuscule white undershirt, the lace bra beneath it apparent as she took the black T-shirt and dabbed at the blood.

"You were lucky. Damned lucky, girlie. That van should have crumpled your Jeep instead of just throwing you into that ravine."

Thankfully, Lyrica had been hit from the passenger side instead of the driver's. Otherwise, the force of the blow would have probably killed her.

"His lights were off," she whispered, her heart beating so fast it was hard to speak.

The gleam of the full moon against chrome had been her only warning, giving her a fraction of a second to lessen the impact. Still, she'd been unable to avoid it. That, along with the sharp twisting of the wheel, had unbalanced the Jeep and sent it careening into the ravine.

"I saw that." Her rescuer nodded, watching her in concern. "Are you sure you're okay? No double vision or anything?"

She felt her lips tremble.

"I'm alive, right?" For a moment, she couldn't understand why she was alive.

"Amazingly." Eyes somber, the aqua green of her gaze staring down at Lyrica in concern, the woman brushed back her dark bangs and nodded. "I was sure you weren't for a few minutes there, though."

The sound of a powerful motor accelerating toward them, tearing along the blacktop, had her sighing in resignation.

A Mackay hadn't arrived first, it seemed.

The young woman crouched in front of her was suddenly on her feet, one hand reaching behind her back as she moved to the front of the car. Tires screamed behind the little sedan and Lyrica watched the woman's gaze narrow for a moment before she seemed to relax.

Black as death, the top down, the Viper came to a rocking stop, seeming to shudder in the sedan's headlights.

Graham jumped from the open car as the sound of another powerful motor came screaming around the curve. Just as the Viper had, the Corvette's tires screeched in protest as the engine suddenly began powering down, finally coming to a stop just ahead of the Viper.

"Lyrica." Graham was in front of her, kneeling in the dirt next to the sedan, his hands going over her much as the woman's had done.

"It wasn't mistaken identity," she whispered, staring into the golden hue of his eyes. His eyes went gold only when he was pissed. Or when he was aroused. She rather doubted it was arousal at the moment.

"Are you hurt?" He didn't answer her.

His hands cupped her cheeks, his gaze holding hers with an intensity that seemed to mesmerize her.

"I'm scared." Her voice trembled, shocking her with the weak, horrified sound of it. "Someone really wants me dead, Graham."

"Come on, baby, we have to get you out of this car. Angel has to go." Reaching down, he lifted her gently from her seat as her hands gripped his shoulders, her head falling against his shoulder.

She'd known it the moment she'd realized the van was going to plow into her Jeep—the attempt on her life in London hadn't been a mistake at all. It had been deliberate.

"Get the hell out of here before the ambulance arrives." Graham snapped out the order as he lowered her into the passenger side of the Viper.

She was aware of the woman getting into the sedan, the driver of the Vette jumping back into it. Just that fast, the two were pulling quickly away and racing from the scene of the wreck.

As the other vehicles sped into the night, Graham hurriedly closed her door before running to the driver's side and jumping in.

"Call Dawg," he ordered crisply.

The order didn't make sense until Dawg's voice crackled through the car's stereo system.

"I have her," Graham snapped, the Viper continuing to accelerate as he raced away from the wreck. "You know where we'll be."

"Status?" Dawg seemed to be snarling.

"Quick exam shows no broken bones or internal injuries," he reported. "I'll know more once we reach the safe house."

"Contact immediately if that changes," Dawg ordered him.

"I'm with Alex, coming on the scene now. We'll contact you once we're finished."

The call disengaged as the Viper flew around the curves of the road leading away from her mother's inn, where she'd been heading.

They were heading toward the lake, she realized.

The top was still down, though the lights of the dash were dark and she realized the car's headlights weren't on, either. She couldn't see the road well enough to know if they were driving along the mountainous road or racing into hell.

Looking over at Graham, Lyrica realized he was wearing glasses. Sunglasses? They were dark, wrapping around his face with the faintest hint of color at the very edges.

She had to have died, she thought.

None of this could be real.

None of it made sense.

Just as she was certain they were going to go tearing off the road and flying into oblivion, the car's lights were suddenly back on and Graham was tearing the glasses off, dropping them onto the console next to him. The headlights revealed a mile marker placed about a half mile before the turn leading to his home.

The Viper slowed enough to take the turn comfortably, without the scream or whine of the tires' protest.

"We're almost there, baby." Broad, powerful fingers covered hers where they rested on her lap and gave them a gentle squeeze.

She stared down at his hand. His fingers laced between hers, dark and broad, safe. Once again, he'd saved her. Once again, it was Graham who'd reached her first, who'd raced to her rescue as though he had no other purpose in life.

There was no escaping him, no escaping the heat and the hunger that shadowed her every waking and sleeping moment, she realized.

She belonged to him, and not just because he had saved her life. She had belonged to him since the moment she had met him.

Whatever he wanted.

However he wanted her.

For as long as she had, she was his.

Graham pulled the Viper into the garage, aware of the door closing securely behind him as he turned off the ignition and pushed open the door. Moving quickly, he strode around the vehicle, jerked Lyrica's door open, and reached in for her.

She was staring at him as though she'd never seen him before. Those emerald eyes, dark with shock, filled with terror, stared back at him with such heavy fear and confusion that he felt his chest clenching in fury.

As he'd raced to the scene of the wreck earlier, he'd realized how very close the present was coming to the past. Except this woman belonged to him. For whatever reason, he couldn't walk away from her, couldn't get her out of his head.

Long ago and far away, he thought. That night seemed a life-time ago. The explosions, the gunfire ripping around them, and the woman in his arms, with her bright green eyes and black silk curtain of hair that, despite the short length, he had imagined more than once was Lyrica's.

As she died in his arms, her lover, the man he had once called a friend, stood over him with a hard, cold smile, his weapon aimed at Graham's head, his finger tightening on the trigger.

"House is secure," Elijah called from the kitchen as Graham snapped back to the present and stepped into the house, Lyrica cradled in his arms. Elijah's expression was tight, savage as Graham passed him.

"No word on the van that hit her," Elijah reported as Graham strode quickly through the kitchen and took the stairway at the back of the house that led upstairs to his room. "Angel's mounted video camera recorded it all, though. Angel was coming around the curve behind Lyrica just as the van raced toward her from the side road. Timothy will have it within the hour and begin breaking it into frames for evidence."

He was going to kill the bastard, Graham promised himself as he moved quickly into his suite.

"Pull up the advanced security protocols," he ordered Elijah as he strode through the small sitting room and into the large bedroom.

There, he laid a still, silent Lyrica on his bed, the uncomfortable feeling that he had no idea what the fuck to do now almost overwhelming him.

She did that to him sometimes, he thought. Made him feel as though he were touching a woman for the first time, feeling things he hadn't felt before.

"Everything's in place." Elijah entered the bedroom, carrying the medic bag he kept with him whenever possible.

"I'm okay," Lyrica assured Graham, her voice still trembling as she glanced at the bag.

"I have to be sure, baby." He touched her cheek with the tips of his fingers because he couldn't help himself. Because he had to touch her, to feel her warmth, to be certain she was alive.

She was silent as he moved back, her gaze following him, holding his gaze, as Elijah began his own examination.

Elijah was gentle, his expression, his actions showing no hesitation, no personal emotion as he touched her. His hands went over her arms and legs, his fingers pressing into her belly, her sides. His voice was quiet as he questioned her. Checking her temple, he then ran his hands over her head and through her hair before sitting back.

"I'd still prefer she be x-rayed and checked over by a physician," Elijah finally announced as he rose from the side of the bed and packed the blood pressure cuff and stethoscope back into the bag. "So far, though, she appears fine."

"Dawg's Jeep is built like a tank," she stated, her voice still weak. Too weak to suit Graham. "I had enough warning to twist the wheel before they hit, though. The moon was shining on the chrome. They had their lights out." It would seem Tracker's backer had taken matters into his own hands without giving the mercenary a chance to complete the contract after all.

"They made a mistake," he assured her.

It shouldn't have happened this time.

His fists clenched at his sides as guilt struck at his chest. If he'd heeded his own instincts, then it wouldn't have happened. If he hadn't trusted her brother's precautions and instead done as everything inside him had demanded and kept her with him, then no one would have had a second chance to attempt to take her from him.

She looked away from him before turning on her side and drawing her knees up slightly. She looked lost, forlorn. As though this attempt on her life had somehow drained the hope that the first one hadn't touched.

Waving Elijah from the room, Graham locked the door before turning back to her, his eyes tracking over her slender figure.

She was dressed in white shorts and a sleeveless shirt. White leather sneakers covered her feet, though her clothes and the shoes were dirt streaked now. Her fragile arms and legs were scratched and heavily bruised, the sight of them striking a match to the rage already simmering inside him.

"Dawg and the others will be here soon," he told her, striding across the room to stand beside the bed. "Are you leaving with them, Lyrica, or are you staying here?"

He didn't expect her family to demand she leave, but with Natches, anything could happen.

She looked up at him, vulnerability darkening the emerald depths of her eyes as her lips trembled momentarily.

"Answer me," he growled, his fingers curling into fists at his sides at the thought of her being taken from him again. "If they demand you leave, Lyrica, what will you do?"

She licked her lips nervously, the resigned fear that filled her eyes slowly evaporating as that sparkle of determined will began to return.

"What do you care?" she demanded mutinously, color beginning to return to her pale face as she pushed herself into a sitting position.

Before he could answer, a determined knock at his door sounded.

"Graham, let me in!" Kye cried out. "I know she's in there. Let me in."

Grimacing at his sister's demand, he turned away from Lyrica's question and moved to the door instead. As soon as he unlocked it and pulled it open, he was all but run over by his sister in her haste to get to her friend.

"Oh my god." Coming to a stop in front of Lyrica, Kye rocked back on her feet, staring at her friend in shock. "Lyrica, sweetie, you have to stop getting into trouble," she demanded, her voice thick with tears. "I don't know if my nerves can take much more."

His sentiments exactly, Graham thought with a spurt of affection for his sister.

"Yeah, I'll get right on that—promise," Lyrica said with heavy irony. "Why don't you be a real friend, Kye, and get me some clothes or something? I really need a shower."

Kye glanced back at him in question.

Nodding, Graham let his gaze move over Lyrica one more

time. She wasn't shaking now, and the terror that had held her in its grip seemed to be relaxing marginally. Not that he could blame her for any of it, but he needed her fighting.

"In a minute, I'll do just that," Kye promised as she turned and dragged the chair Graham kept by the bed into place where she could face Lyrica.

Graham watched in resignation as his sister sat down, crossed her jean-clad legs, and stared at her friend like a prosecutor prepared to drag a statement free.

"Ah, Kye," Lyrica groaned, her head hanging as she braced her hands on the mattress beneath her. "Don't look at me like that. I don't have any answers for you. I swear I don't."

Graham leaned against the door frame, almost grinning at the mutiny in Lyrica's voice. His sister could be a demanding little wretch when she wanted answers, and that look on her face was well-known.

"I haven't asked any questions yet," Kye snorted. "I was more concerned with how you're feeling." Concern filled her face as she reached out to push back Lyrica's hair and check the scratch on her face. "Lyrica, I told you not to be out driving at night, didn't I?"

"You did." Lyrica sighed.

"You didn't listen to me, though, did you?" Kye demanded almost angrily.

"Kye, regardless of what you think, I don't obey your every whim." Amusement mixed with the exasperation in Lyrica's voice. "Come on, I'm okay, right? Let's just focus on that. And once you get me some clothes, I can get a shower and face my brother and cousins and god only knows who else before they arrive here soon."

Kye's head lifted, her eyes narrowing as she turned on Graham then.

"I'm not leaving again," she stated stubbornly.

Graham frowned back at her. "You know the rules, Kye," he reminded her. "You can stay with Sam, or I'll have you flown out to California. It's your choice."

He didn't leave room for argument.

"I hate this," she snapped. "Lyrica's my friend, Graham. She shouldn't be stuck here alone."

His eyes widened at the outburst as a deliberate chuckle left his lips. "What am I? She's not alone, Kye. I'll be here and god only knows who Dawg Mackay will try to force me into allowing to stay. I won't have you endangered by this, and besides, how am I supposed to seduce her if you're here to run interference? Think about that one, since it was your damned idea."

Whatever argument was brewing in her sharp mind was thrown into reverse as Lyrica suddenly swung her head around to look at him, her eyes narrowing as he turned and stalked from the room.

He might as well put it out in the open now, he thought. He'd be damned if he'd let Kye's little rule about being her friend affect his chances of keeping her in his bed any more than he'd let her brother's objections.

She was his. He'd already made his mind up, and by god everyone else could step the fuck back or else he'd just push them aside. As of tonight, her objections could go to hell. She wanted him just as damned much as he was aching for her, and he was damned well about to do something about it.

Lyrica turned and stared back at Kye, who seemed to look at everything in the room but her.

"What have you done?" she asked her friend wearily. "Kye, dammit, I thought we agreed that sleeping with your brother was against the friendship rules or something."

Kye's gaze swung back to her then, the militant light gleaming there making Lyrica's neck itch in warning.

"Well now, that was just before someone decided to try to kill you, right?" Kye burst out, her hands gripping the arms of the chair so tight her fingers paled. "This is one of those exceptions to the rules. I told him if he had to seduce you to protect you, then I'd rather you be his lover than see you dead."

Lyrica blinked back at her, her stomach tightening at the reminder that dead had become a possibility earlier.

"How do you get this stuff into your head?" she groaned. "First I'm part of a power play by your brother to take the Mackay throne or some crap; now you're throwing me in your brother's bed because you think it's the only way to save me." She shook her head at Kye's machinations. "Really, you need to find a hobby, because you drive the rest of the world crazy."

Kye gave a disgusted little snort at the thought. "Hobbies are for people without purpose. I have a purpose—"

"Directing the lives of those around you?" Lyrica charged as she gripped the blankets beneath her in desperate fingers rather than trying to strangle her friend. "Kye, I love you like a sister, but I don't need any help where your brother is concerned."

"Ain't that the truth," Kye drawled in amusement. "He's been so hot for you for years that it's all he could do to keep from jumping your bones at any given time. Why do you think he started the bimbo squad? He had to find someone to take the edge off all that lust until he could figure out how to keep your brother and cousins from killing him once he got you into his bed."

Lyrica stared at her friend in disbelief for several long seconds.

Finally, she forced herself to her feet, keeping a wary eye on the other girl, and walked stiffly to Graham's closet.

"I need a shower," she finally muttered. "Maybe I need to clean the dirt out of my ears from that wreck or something. Because I can't be hearing you right."

"Leave Graham's clothes alone," Kye suddenly hissed, moving so fast she was blocking her way before Lyrica could open the door to the huge walk-in closet. "It's only going to make him think you're willing to give in to him easily. Bad mistake. Stay right here; I'll go get you something."

Kye moved from the bedroom before Lyrica could protest or agree. Lyrica could only shake her head.

Moving into the closet, she chose a soft, long-sleeved button-up shirt in dark gray. She'd seen him wear that one before. The incredible softness of the material had skimmed over the powerful muscles of his upper body and made her mouth water.

Taking it from the hanger, she stepped from the closet and closed the door behind her before making her way to the shower.

Déjà vu struck her with frightening awareness as she stepped beneath the heated water a moment later.

The sense that fate was determined to replay the danger against her until she realized she couldn't escape wasn't lost on her.

As hot water sluiced over her bruised flesh, a heavy sigh left her lips. Terror was just a thought away; that bleak, overwhelming certainty that she would never be free of the threat facing her tightened at her chest.

Why?

What had she done?

The same questions were going through her mind that had played through it before, and the same lack of answers faced her.

Perhaps this time, though, the answers would be found. There was no way to convince anyone, let alone her, that this was an accident.

As she showered, she replayed the night in her mind. The call to her mother and the overwhelming sense that something was wrong. Her mother had sounded nervous, frightened perhaps, but had refused to talk to her about it. Eve and Piper were there with Mercedes, but they had seemed hesitant to talk to her as well.

Between the guests of the inn and her sisters, she hadn't felt her mother was in danger, but she had felt as though her mother, as well as her sisters, was hiding something from her. That feeling had convinced her to make the drive to the inn.

Once she'd left her apartment she'd called again, frowning as the voice mail picked up. She'd left a message that she was on her way, but no one had called her back.

God, had anyone even told her mother what had happened?

Graham had talked to Dawg in the car, she remembered. The shock and fear were slowly easing and allowing her to remember the accident with more clarity.

Dawg would have called Timothy, if Alex hadn't. The woman who had helped her from the Jeep had said she'd called an ambulance. The report of the hit-and-run would have gone through Alex's office. But how had Graham learned of it so quickly?

And who had arrived in the Corvette just behind him?

As she washed her hair and carefully soaped her body, the confusing details began to mount. As Graham's car had raced around the curve, the young woman who had stopped to help her had moved to the front of the car. And though she hadn't realized it then, Lyrica now clearly remembered the hardened expression on the woman's face as she stood as though braced for danger. Just as she remembered the brief glimpse of the weapon emerging from behind the woman's back until familiarity had flickered in her expression.

Lyrica hadn't had a chance to get to know the young woman who had moved into the apartment beside hers just before life had exploded. And she sure as hell hadn't known the man who had arrived behind Graham, though her neighbor seemed to know him well, just as Graham had known the woman—Angel, he'd called her.

Oh, someone had so many questions to answer. And this time, she wasn't going to allow anger, arousal, or loyalties to hold her back. And if she didn't get her answers, then everyone she suspected of withholding them would regret it. She wasn't a Mackay for nothing.

THIRTEEN

She wanted answers, did she?

Lyrica had forgotten that demanding answers from the men in her family was like trying to force nature to reverse course.

And it was just as effective.

Definitely more confusing.

And boy, did those answers have the power to kick her ass once they were forced out into the open.

Lyrica sat silently, furiously, in Graham's living room just before dawn, glaring at the men who were watching her warily.

Sometimes, she thought, a person was just better off not asking, because a Mackay and his schemes were way too confusing at the best of times.

This wasn't the best of times. And that meant life was beginning to border on the ridiculous.

"So, the man who shot at me in London wasn't really trying to shoot me, he just wanted the person who hired him to think he was trying to shoot me." She really needed to get it all in perspective. "And he knew all along where I was hiding behind the Dumpster, just as he knew Kye would be trying to call me and would eventually tell Graham the problems her phone was having when she dialed my number. He also knew Graham would head out after me, and that same hired assassin was meeting with you tonight across from my apartment when I left for the inn, and my so-called neighbor is actually a member of his team. Have I gotten all this straight so far? Tell me, Dawg, have any of you wondered yet if that enterprising would-be assassin is possibly related to the rest of you game-playing, calculating, manipulating, overdramatic Mackays?" Her voice rose as incredulous disbelief overwhelmed her.

She wanted to get the facts out in the open before she exploded. That way, there were no mistakes or misunderstandings as to why she was furious with every one of them, excluding Graham, who had been just as much in the dark as she was.

After all, that was an important part of understanding exactly how insane her life was becoming, and the toll it was taking on her and her sisters when it came to dealing with their brother and his related sidekicks.

"Your perception is amazingly accurate." Graham spoke up for them with a hint of mockery from where he stood with his shoulder braced at the side of the fireplace. "And your self-control is astounding under the circumstances."

Shooting him a silencing glare, she turned to her brother again. "And you knew all along that the whole 'mistaken identity' thing was bullshit. So much so that you had a bodyguard who was supposed to be following me? Except he wasn't following me tonight as I left home because whatever floozy he'd picked up knocked him out and left him unconscious by the side of the road. How am I doing so far?"

"Your sarcasm excels, as always," Natches pointed out as

Dawg wiped his hands over his face and blew out a weary breath. "It even rivals your exceptional memory skills, it seems."

"Natches, stop," Rowdy hissed.

"And you. I thought better of you." She flicked Rowdy a scornful look. "I never imagined you would allow yourself to become mired in the schemes those two manage to get themselves stuck in." She flicked her fingers at Dawg and Natches as she leaned forward, anger burning hot inside her as understanding hit her like a slap in the face and seriously undermined her trust in her family. "All three of you were hiding the fact that you didn't believe that bullshit mistaken identity story any more than Graham did, yet you still let me skip along as though I were as safe as ever."

"Oh hell no, that's not how it worked," Dawg protested instantly, his expression creasing in angry defense. "Instinct and evidence are two different things, little sister. And if you recall, I tried to get you to either move in with me or stay with your mother and Timothy. You insisted on returning to your apartment."

"Did you tell me you didn't believe it?" she demanded, glaring back at him fiercely. "Did you even warn me?"

"And terrify you on the off chance I was wrong?" he argued, the strong, determined lines of his face tightening in conviction. "It's been a lot of years since my gut has had to guide my life, little girl, and I'm getting older. How was I to know it wasn't indigestion?"

She blinked back at him in disbelief.

"Indigestion?" She was amazed that he'd even come up with such a far-fetched excuse.

"It could have been," he growled in defense. "You remember Natches had that acid reflux thing year before last? He was convinced it was his gut warning him something was wrong and he all but boarded up the house until Chaya and Bliss threatened to shoot him with his own rifle."

"That wasn't acid reflux," she snapped, shooting Natches a disgusted smirk. "That was because he found that hunters' stand in his woods and he was convinced everyone in the known world knew better than to hunt on his property, so of course it had to be a sniper instead. His own paranoia was his damned problem."

Her cousin straightened in his chair in outrage, emerald eyes gleaming like hard, cold gems between lashes so thick and lush most men would be embarrassed by them. Instead, Natches used them shamelessly, whether he was charming his wife or issuing one of his icy promises.

"The acid reflux thing is the reason I was out in the woods to begin with," Natches pointed out—and she so knew better than to trust that innocent expression on his face. "I felt the need to check out the property just in case it was a warning of danger. I've made a few enemies, you know."

"Deliberately," she charged sharply.

"Deliberately?" Those thick lashes surrounded eyes that widened in supposed outrage. "Come on, Lyrica, I've been a good boy for a lot of years now. Chaya's a damned good keeper, I'll have you know. I can even move about in society without too much trouble," he informed her with deliberately insulting amusement.

"You're a fucking menace to society, Natches," she retorted furiously. "Don't pull that with me."

"Hey, that was a lot of years ago." Natches glared back at her. "I haven't been a menace to anyone but my wife and child since Bliss was born, I'll have you know."

"What do you call torturing me and my sisters?"

"My god-given right as Dawg's cousin," he said with a heavy frown, his expression filled with conviction. "And don't think he wouldn't do the same if you were my sister. You and your sisters belong to us, just like our kids do. We can torture you all we like. That doesn't mean we'll allow anyone else that privilege."

He was making her crazy. Dawg and Rowdy just sat with their heads lowered, the expression on their faces one of long-suffering patience as Natches demanded attention. Brogan Campbell was watching with narrow-eyed curiosity, while Graham watched with simple, astounded disbelief.

Evidently, he'd just not had enough experience dealing with the three Mackays at once. This was an education for him. And no doubt the death of any chance she might have had at a relationship with him.

"I might as well be your daughter for all the peace I get," she pointed out, almost shaking in anger now. "Your poor child will likely join a convent just to find some peace."

Natches's eyes narrowed on her, the emerald gleaming between his heavy lashes in venomous contempt.

"Oh hell, come on, Lyrica," he drawled bitterly. "Stop fucking teasing me here. You and I both know I'll never get that damned lucky."

The F-bomb? He dared to use a word he knew would have his wife chewing his ass for hours, just to distract her from the situation?

Oh, classic Natches, and she so wasn't fooled.

"Whoa! Time out here, kids." Chaya jumped in at that point, her husband's use of the F-bomb clearly concerning her, just as Natches had anticipated.

"She started it." Natches turned on his wife, his arm flying out as he pointed a finger at Lyrica as though he were five years old.

Chaya rolled her eyes. "No doubt, sweetheart," she agreed with placating patience. "Could you put aside the inner child now and let the man out to play again?"

His lips twisted into a little snarl, but his arm lowered as he settled back in his chair with a glare in Lyrica's direction.

God, could this get any more incredible?

"You know, the three of you are going to cause me to move to Lexington just to get some peace," she informed them all as she rose from her chair. "I think I've had enough Mackay explanations for the night. You've exhausted me more than both attempts on my life have managed to do so far."

It was no more than the truth.

"Well, look on the bright side—I promised not to hit Graham again, even knowing you're going to be sharing his bed here," Natches stated sarcastically as she turned to leave. "You have a free pass to be bad for letting him protect you for us."

She froze.

She heard Graham's muttered curse and Chaya's groan clearly, and she tried counting to ten before turning back to Natches.

She made it to five.

"Letting him protect me for you?" She swung around on him furiously. "No, cousin of mine, I don't have a free pass to any damned thing. Both of us know exactly where it's going to end, just as we know you'll wait until all this is over then think you can hit him again just because the danger is gone, then stick your nose right back into my life again. And don't even bother thinking that I believe this magnanimous gesture toward Graham is anything more than it is. It's just your own inability to force him out of the situation and your knowledge that I'll probably only end up doing what both Eve and Piper did and try to hide the fact that I'm sleeping with him from the three of you once it happens."

Natches just rolled his eyes at her. "You think you know us all so well." He flicked his fingers at Dawg and Rowdy, and the other two men covered their faces with their hands in defeat as he ignored their hushed orders to just "shut the fuck up, Natches."

"I know you well enough." She laughed bitterly. "I know all of you far too well at the moment, that's for damned sure." She flicked Chaya a pitying look. "And I can't say just how much we all appreciate the fact that you at least keep him distracted sometimes, Chaya. You deserve sainthood."

With that, she turned and stalked from the room, ignoring Natches's amusement as he laughed at his wife and thanked her for "keeping him distracted."

Lyrica couldn't believe their nerve any more than she could believe that they'd refused to share their suspicions with her. Though it shouldn't have surprised her, she admitted.

Hell, she should have suspected . . .

Perhaps she had suspected, because she hadn't felt entirely safe since the day she'd left Graham's home and returned to her apartment. Except for those few times she had been with Graham.

Stalking to his suite, she realized just how close panic was to the surface, and just how very unprepared she was for the danger facing her. And that only increased the risk for everyone involved.

Damn.

It took every ounce of self-control Graham possessed to keep the unruly flesh between his thighs from becoming painfully engorged as Lyrica tore into her family. With her eyes gleaming like green fire, that flush mounting in her cheeks, and mutinous fury stamping her expression, all he could think about was replacing all that defiance with hungry arousal.

She was a tempting mix of spice and sweetness and he realized he couldn't wait to slide into his bed with her.

"I hate you!" Natches's sudden declaration in his direction had Graham arching his brow in surprise.

"I'm brokenhearted," he replied drolly, amused at the childish display of temper. "Am I still allowed on the playground?"

At Lyrica's outburst, Chaya had plopped into the chair beside her husband, hung her head, and covered her face with her hands until it was over.

She was obviously well versed in Mackay dramatics.

Now she lifted her head and glared at Graham as though warning him to silence. But he wasn't a Mackay—he didn't have to put up with the bastard daily.

Yet.

Until he did, he could be just as damned snide as he wanted to be.

He wasn't worried until Natches's lashes lowered to stare back at him with cunning calculation, his smile full of icy disdain. Because until that moment, he'd forgotten Natches knew the very secret Graham had been hiding for far too long.

"You think you're safe, don't you, Graham?" Natches asked softly as everyone in the room seemed to hold their breath in anticipation.

Natches pissed was never a good thing, Graham knew, but he'd be damned if he'd kiss the man's ass at this point.

Secret or no secret.

"I think I'm damned tired of playing into your game of Mackay machinations." Graham grunted as he straightened from his slouched position against the fireplace. "Safe or not, Natches, I'm no puppet, and I refuse to play one now."

The expression never changed.

"You're cold inside," the other man murmured then, disgust touching his voice. "Calculating and so absorbed with the mistake you made that you'll make everyone in your life pay for it until the last breath you take."

Graham glared back at him, wishing he could deny the claim. Unfortunately, they both knew he couldn't.

"I learned my lesson," Graham informed him. "There's a difference."

"Is there?" Natches smirked. "You want Lyrica so damned bad it's about to eat you alive. But instead of paying attention to your own instincts, you'll end up finding a reason, a transgression you'll convince yourself she made, or you'll make up your own just to ensure you never have to resurrect that dead little heart of yours. And then she'll begin to realize that all she has of you is whatever pleasure you give her . . ."

"Enough, Natches. You think I want to hear this shit?" Dawg snapped in disgust as he rose from his chair and paced behind it to stare at his cousin furiously. "Let it the hell go for now."

Natches jerked to his feet, facing Graham as Chaya followed and laid her hand on her husband's arm warningly.

"Oh, I'm not going to hit him again." Natches chuckled, the sound icy, filled with distaste. "I'm going to wait. And when Lyrica walks away from him, her little heart shattered in her chest, then I'll remind every damned one of you of how you made me keep my rifle locked away instead of putting my fucking crosshairs right between his eyes."

With that, he gripped his wife's hand, gave it a little tug, and stalked from the living room.

The slamming of the door leading into the garage moments later had Graham scratching at his jaw in confusion before turning back to find all eyes on him once again.

"This happen often?" he asked the men, whose expressions ranged from resignation to contemplation.

"'Bout once a month or so." Rowdy shrugged. "He gets bored sometimes when Chaya's too busy to entertain him."

"Good thing she seems to enjoy entertaining him," Graham remarked caustically before moving to the bar for another drink.

Dealing with Mackays would end up driving him into AA at this point.

"You'll be entertaining him if you hurt her." The warning didn't come from a Mackay this time. This time, it came from the one man Graham least expected—Brogan Campbell.

He had short dark red hair and the shadow of a darker beard, intense blue eyes, and savage features. He was a man Graham respected for his strength, but rarely agreed with.

"My days of entertaining the Mackays or their relations ended with that fist Natches planted in my face. As I told him then, that one was free. Another one will cost all of you. Now, if this little meeting is finished, dawn is nearly here and I'm damned tired. Get the hell out of my house or find a bedroom and leave me the hell alone. I really don't care which."

They were all tired. Tempers were beginning to fray and patience was wearing thin. Especially with him.

"Yeah, time to go." Dawg wasn't moving, though.

His hands gripped the back of the chair a little too tightly as the others rose and began filing out of the room toward the garage, where two SUVs were parked. Once the room was empty of everyone but him and Graham, Dawg stared at Graham with implacable determination.

In that moment, Graham realized he'd been wrong. Natches wasn't the one to watch out for any longer, unless the threat he represented had the potential to be fatal. In this case, Dawg was the one to keep an eye on.

"Lyrica and I have an agreement," Dawg said softly, the pale green of his eyes almost colorless now as his gaze met Graham's. "I stay out of her life and she doesn't move to Lexington. That's worked for us so far, because she's not really one to poke at things, ya know?"

Graham didn't answer him. Instead, he watched the other man closely, hearing more than what Dawg was saying.

"I looked into your past myself," Dawg stated then. "Whatever Natches knows, he's not sharing yet, but I'll warn you, he's close to telling me, Rowdy, and Timothy. Once he's convinced whatever happened will hurt Lyrica, your secret's out. But he forgets, I'm not one to wait when I want to know something. I've known how interested Lyrica was in you from the moment you two met. When you returned to Somerset, I knew something wasn't right, so I made some calls."

Graham stared back at him, forcing back the emotion, the searing regret and humiliation.

Dawg's expression was heavy with compassion and understanding, and that only made things worse.

"You're a good man, Graham," Dawg said softly then, releasing the cushioned back of the chair and straightening slowly. "You're a damned good man, and I don't want to hate you." He shook his head wearily. "But that's my sister, and I guess I love her near as much as I love my own kid. And I'm an overprotective bastard," he admitted with resigned regret. "So knowing she'll be sleeping with you doesn't sit well with me. Not because she doesn't deserve someone to hold her, but because she chose someone that just doesn't have it in him to hold her as long and as tight as her sweet heart deserves. And that, my friend, will ensure I hate you, because you're too fucking stupid to realize how much she does love you, and too damned selfish to just walk the fuck away from her."

Dawg didn't wait for an argument, a protest, or an explanation. He turned and moved for the doorway as he rubbed at the back of his neck with the air of a man fighting his first instinct. The instinct that demanded he protect the sister he loved.

"Dawg." Graham stopped him just before he left the room.

"Yeah, Graham?" He turned back, but he wasn't expecting Graham to have anything to say that would change his mind about the outcome he could see coming for his sister.

"It's not selfishness." Graham had to force the words from his lips.

The doubt on Dawg's expression had fury lashing at him. A self-fury, one he knew there was no escape from.

"Okay, Graham." Dawg sighed. "Just remember what I said . . ."

"Goddammit, Dawg," he snarled as he slapped the liquor glass he'd never filled to the bar. "It's not fucking selfishness. She's like a drug I can't kick. Since the first time I saw her. I didn't touch her when she was younger, I swear to god I didn't."

Dawg looked away momentarily, proving he'd always suspected Graham had dared to touch her during those earlier years.

"She was just eighteen when I met her." He shook his head as he paced to the wide windows at the side of the room and stared into the summer dawn. "Eighteen." Shoving his hands into his back pockets, he could see her as she had been that day. "So fucking innocent and filled with such hopes and dreams. I would have shot myself before destroying that. But that was six years ago." He turned back to Dawg then, knowing there was just no way to explain fully what she did to him. "Six years, Dawg, and I can't stay away from her anymore. And that's not selfishness, but I'll be damned if I know what to call it. And I'll be damned if I'm going to let her face some fucking assassin without me there to make damned sure she comes away from this without being hurt."

Uncomfortable now, resigned to the fact that Lyrica's brother had every reason in the world to hate him, Graham waited for the legendary Mackay fury to erupt.

Dawg wasn't known as the least temperamental of the Mackays. When he was younger he was the one who fought the fights Natches often instigated. Right after Rowdy would try to defuse them.

Graham figured he was about to get intimate with another Mackay fist any second now.

Instead, the other man shocked him more than he wanted to admit. Saddened, heavy with regret, Dawg's gaze flickered with momentary anger before even that died away and he nodded heavily.

"When you figure out why you can't stay away from her, Graham, maybe you'll let her, or someone who cares for her, know," he said softly. "Otherwise, trust me, your soul will know the minute she gives up on your heart. And once she gives up, it will be over for her. Forever. Then it will be too damned late to realize what you've lost."

Dawg turned away from the younger man, fighting to hide the satisfaction he was feeling, the knowledge that the other man's admission had given him.

Damn.

Sometimes it felt like that boy could have been his own son instead of that damned Garrett Brock's. He was so damned much like a fucking Mackay that Dawg had, at one point, even had the DNA report the DHS had on Graham pulled to compare to Mackay DNA. A man could never be too careful when it came to the depravity his and Natches's fathers had been capable of.

Graham wasn't related to them, but it hadn't changed the similarity Dawg often saw in him. A similarity Rowdy and Natches had laughed over a time or two themselves.

Moving into the garage, he stepped into the waiting SUV and closed the door behind him. The other vehicle had already left, and the one waiting for him was filled with Rowdy, Natches, Chaya, Timothy, and Brogan Campbell.

"What the hell took you so long?" Natches grumped from the backseat where he slouched with deliberate laziness. "Did you do Lyrie a favor and kill the son of a bitch?"

Natches was always their ace in the hole. He could play the bad cop while pulling out the best of a man, or woman, without even seeming to try. Although he could be a calculating, manipulating bastard, he always did it with dedication and all those warm, fuzzy feelings he swore he didn't have for anyone. Well, except his wife, his daughter, his cousins, his best friends . . . Dawg almost laughed at the thought.

He grinned instead. "Why would I do that, cuz? I'd never forgive myself for having to bury the man who loves her enough he's determined to take a bullet for her if need be."

Natches snorted at that. "Lust ain't love, man. I thought you figured that out when you met Christa."

"Exactly," Dawg stated softly as Timothy pulled from the garage. "Just like Graham began realizing the day he met Lyrica. It took me eight years to get it right, though. I think this boy might have me beat. He's already figuring it out."

Dawg glanced back in time to meet the triumph in the emerald depths of Natches's gaze and, behind him, in the forest green of their cousin Rowdy's.

"Plan's working, then?" Timothy was all but chuckling as he drove from the Brock property.

"Plan's working." Dawg breathed out in satisfaction as he turned back in his seat and stared at the road ahead of them. "Ahead of schedule, due, I imagine, to this interference in Lyrica's life. But it's working damned good."

Silence filled the van-size SUV for a few long moments before a voice could be heard from the back of the van.

"Guess I was left out of the plan," Brogan muttered in resigned acceptance. "Damned good thing I'm not just smart but observant. I told Eve last year that the three of you had this in mind, and she told me I was crazy."

Rowdy chuckled at that as Dawg felt a grin curve his lips.

"So, Brogan," Natches drawled, "did you figure it out when we chose you for Eve?"

All of them turned to stare back at Brogan, except Timothy. No doubt he was watching through the rearview mirror.

"You're lying." But the suspicion, the fear was there.

"Think Jed figured it out?" Rowdy asked with quiet humor.

That was the moment Brogan knew just how effectively the Mackays had maneuvered him.

"Fuckers!" He tried to snarl, but there was no true heat there. The poor son of a bitch was just too damned happy with his little Mackay honey. Just as Jed was. "You three are fucking dangerous."

"Three?" Timothy said. "You got that all wrong, Campbell— try seven. Me, Alex, Zeke, and John Junior, too. Every now and then, John Senior likes to put his two cents in as well."

"All I can say is that it's a damned shame that the seven of you are that fucking bored in your old age," Brogan said.

"Bored?" Natches questioned the supposed rationale for the maneuvering. "Hell no—it's not boredom, it's exhaustion. We're getting old, man. It's time to start enjoying ourselves more. The future is yours, Brogan. Yours, Jed's, Graham's, and whoever we give Zoey and Kye to for safekeeping. We've kept this little piece of Kentucky clean for a lot of years. It's time to hand it over to the next generation and just pray we chose wisely."

"I have one question," Brogan stated then, the sudden dangerous softness in his voice showing that he'd suddenly thought of something that perhaps didn't please him so well. "The threat against her, by god, I hope you didn't instigate that."

Dawg turned back to him, along with Natches and Chaya, while Rowdy turned his head slowly to his side. Timothy made damned sure Brogan glimpsed his look in the rearview mirror.

Five of the most dangerous people Brogan was sure he had ever met, and they were staring at him with such icy, certain death in their eyes that he didn't think before nodding.

"I was just making sure," he drawled as though those looks hadn't given him a moment's worry.

"And trust me, once we find the bastard that did, he won't live to see a jail, a trial, or a sentence," Dawg said. "He won't get a second chance, Brogan. All he'll get is a very quiet, very brief burial."

No one fucked with his family, especially his sisters, and got away with it if he could help it. And should he become too weak or too old or, god forbid, should he be taken out before he could stop it, then he and his cousins had done their best to make damned sure they had backup.

A man had to have backup, he'd always thought. It was the way he planned.

He had backup for those he loved, just in case . . .

And he prayed daily that it was never needed.

FOURTEEN

Moving into his bedroom, Graham fully expected to find Lyrica stretched out in his bed. Furious, but in his bed where she belonged. Instead, he found her in the sitting room, the lights extinguished as she stood at the window and stared out into the early morning fog blanketing the land.

"You know you're not protected just because the room's dark," he reminded her as he moved slowly to the window.

Turning, she watched silently as he closed the heavy curtains before staring back at her.

"How long will this take?" she asked, pulling the robe Kye had brought to the room earlier tighter around her body. "How long will I be here, Graham?"

The thin silk did nothing to hide the tempting curves it covered or the matching violet silk gown she wore beneath.

"In a hurry to leave?" he asked, feeling a hint of anger at the thought.

"In a hurry to no longer feel as though I'm a danger to every-one I care for," she retorted rather than answering his question.

The fear that she would be the reason someone she loved was hurt, or killed, weighed on her. It tormented her and left her filled with a searing guilt she couldn't rid herself of.

"You're no danger. The danger is to you. Those you love, those who love you, won't see you hurt by this, Lyrica." God, he couldn't keep his hands off her.

Before thought and action coincided, his arm slid around her waist. He pulled her to him, flush against his body, the little gasp that fell from her lips causing his to quirk in amusement.

"You knew this was going to happen." His voice sounded too dark, too rough. "We've both known for years that you were going to end up in my bed."

"I knew," she whispered, the pulse beating heavily at the side of her neck, drawing his gaze before it slid back to hers.

"Are you sure this is what you want?" he asked, determined to let her go if it wasn't. "If it isn't, now is the time to tell me."

Her soft, pink little tongue swiped over her lips, reminding him far too well of how it had licked over his cock that first night she had spent in his room.

"If it wasn't what I wanted, then I wouldn't be here, Graham," she assured him.

"Then god help both of us." Because he was too damned hard, too damned wild for her to do anything but give in to him.

She shouldn't have been surprised by the immedi-ate pleasure that suffused her body, Lyrica thought distantly. She should have expected it—it happened every time he touched her.

His lips touched hers, rubbed against them, and her breathing became hard, her heartbeat racing out of control as his hand slid beneath her hair to cup the back of her head. To hold her to him as he parted her lips and began sipping from the hunger that raged through her.

She didn't just want him, she realized, she needed him. Her body came to life as it never had before, her flesh tingled in anticipation, the swollen bud between her thighs aching as her moan whispered between their kiss each time he touched her.

She didn't know what to expect. She had no idea what to do. Until the spiraling storm of sensation began to rage inside her. Only then did instinct overcome shyness and hunger overcome trepidation.

Sliding her hands up the powerful breadth of his chest to his wide shoulders, she held them with desperate hunger as Graham's head tilted, his lips slanting over hers with a groan.

The feel of his hands sliding down her back to cup her rear and lift her into the cradle of his thighs stole her breath. His hands guided her knees to his hips as she found herself pressed against the wall, the hard wedge of his cock pressing firmly between her thighs.

His kisses were hungry, deep, his tongue flicking over hers, tasting her as she tasted him, a haze of heat and need enveloping them as his kisses became harder, hungrier.

Even that first night it hadn't been like this, this powerful, the pleasure rising so fast she felt herself teetering on the edge of mindless desperation.

The silk of her robe fell around her hips and thighs as she felt him tugging at the shoulders of it, sliding it against her skin. Terrified of losing his kiss, she lowered her arms long enough for him to jerk it from her, the silk forgotten as it fell away from her body.

His groan vibrated against her lips as her fingers slid into his hair, feeling the heavy warmth against her flesh. As though in retaliation, his hand slipped beneath her gown, cupping the bare curves of her ass before slowly, destructively, parting the globes and sending a flash of forbidden fire to attack the hidden entrance they protected.

Lyrica cried out as his head jerked back, his lips pulling from hers as he palmed her rear again and repeated the caress. That heated, swift spike of sensation at her anus had her juices spilling from her vagina, saturating her pussy and sensitizing the swollen folds.

He moved as his lips covered hers again. Holding her to him, he strode from the sitting room to the bedroom, the journey barely registering until she felt her back against the bed and his lips sliding along her jaw to her neck.

The rasp of his short beard and mustache created a prickle of heat that sent a shuddering hunger for more echoing through each inch of flesh he touched as he kissed his way to her shoulder. There, he nipped at her skin, rubbed his lips against it, then delivered a sharp, heated kiss.

He was marking her, she thought, dazed. Marking her flesh for anyone to see. But no one could see the mark he'd already left on her heart.

"Get this off." The growl in his voice had flames licking at her breasts as he pulled back and hurriedly tore the gown over her head.

Staring up at him as he tossed the material away from her, Lyrica shuddered at the look on his face. It was pure lust, hunger at its sharpest, but in his eyes flecks of gold gleamed with something that had her heart clenching in response.

"God, you're beautiful," he groaned as his hands cupped the weight of her breasts, his thumbs brushing over the hardened tips of her painfully sensitive nipples.

A whimpering cry fell from her lips at the touch of his callused thumbs, the ache radiating in the tight tips and echoing in the tingling bud of her clit.

"Here." Reaching out he gripped her hand, pulling it to the outside curve of one breast. "Hold them for me, Lyrica. Give them to me."

Oh god.

He was serious.

Lifting the opposite hand he cupped her fingers around the other mound, his expression tightening as she cupped her own flesh, seeming to offer her nipples up to his hunger.

And he took clear advantage of it.

His head lowered, his eyes locked on hers, his lips covering the nearest tip and suckling it into the heat of his mouth. The rasp of his tongue licking, stroking the violently sensitive nub had a fiery wave of exquisite pleasure shredding her control.

Heat suffused her entire body. It was burning through her thighs, pulsing in her pussy, and throbbing around her clit. Her hips moved against the hard wedge of his cock as it pressed against her, his lips drawing on her nipple, his tongue stroking and rubbing it until her fingers tangled in his hair to hold him closer to her.

Each lick, each draw sensitized the tender tip further until the raking sensations shuddering from her nipple to her clit had her gasping with each surge. Only then did he move to the opposite breast, his lips covering it, sucking it inside, and devouring her there as he had its mate.

Arching to him, whimpering cries fell from her lips, need becoming a fiery demand, a racing imperative she couldn't fight. His teeth raked against her nipple as he moved back, his lips moving down her torso, his tongue licking at the sheen of perspiration that covered her body. He tasted her flesh, each stroke of his tongue a lash of sensation that radiated along her nerve endings to tighten around her clit demandingly.

Then his lips were there.

Her eyes flared open, her gaze moving down her body, focusing on the movement of his tongue against the swollen, sensitive folds of her sex. Long, slow licks swiped through the narrow slit, circled the aching bud above, then he sucked it in slowly between his lips.

"Graham," she whispered, the broken cry torn from her as pleasure sang through her body.

Her hips jerked against his hold and she writhed beneath the caress as he pushed her thighs farther apart. His hands slid beneath her knees, lifting her thighs, parting her farther as his tongue moved wickedly lower.

Lyrica's hands fell from his shoulders, her fingers clenching in the blankets beneath her as the licking strokes rimmed the clenched entrance of her pussy. His mouth flickered over the entrance, licking around it, laying heated, suckling kisses to it as she gasped at the pleasure.

"So sweet," he groaned against the swollen folds. "So incredibly sweet, Lyrica."

His tongue speared inside the trembling tissue of her vagina, licking and thrusting inside her as she cried out at the sensations. Pleasure raged through her. It tore through her senses, stronger, brighter than it had been before. Her thighs tightened against his hold, the internal muscles tightening as well, as his tongue pushed inside, licked and separated, her body growing more desperate as ripples of response began to spread outward.

"Graham, please . . ." she cried out desperately as the suckling heat of his mouth returned to her clit.

The need for release was burning inside her, a fiery, maddening ache that was impossible to control.

Hips lifting, pressing tighter to the hungry draw of his mouth, she pulled at the blankets beneath her, her head grinding into the mattress, hard, brutal pulses of incredible sensation building, clenching in her womb until the resulting explosion whipped through her senses like a blinding, overwhelming cataclysm.

The orgasm imploded inside her, jerking her into the possession of his lips and mouth, around the shuddering bud of her clitoris as he held her hips in place with powerful hands.

Groaning, he pulled back, his lips moving up her body as he came over her, one hand tearing at his jeans as he fought to undress without releasing her.

"Lyrica, sweetheart." His voice was tortured as she lifted closer to him, the need building higher rather than easing at her release.

"Graham, please." Gasping breathlessly, she was willing to beg. "Oh god, I can't stand it."

"I can't wait," he muttered, burying his lips in her neck as the crest of his cock pressing at her entrance had her breath catching.

Easing back, he caught her gaze with his, the brilliant gleam of golden flecks holding her mesmerized as she felt the press of his shaft parting her flesh, working against it until the head lodged inside her, throbbing within the tightened clench of her flesh.

Pleasure-pain racked her body as she cried out with the sensations.

"You're so fucking tight, Lyrica," he groaned, the slow movements of his hips working him against the stretched, sensitive inner flesh.

Withdrawing partway, he then eased inside again as his lips lowered to hers, their breath mingling, panting and rough as she felt him tense above her.

"Hold on to me, baby," he whispered against her lips, drawing one of her arms to his shoulders as she lifted the other. "Just hold on to me."

She could feel the rasp of his jeans against her inner thighs, the throb of his cock as it lodged just inside her. Pulling back again, his lips covered hers, his tongue pressing inside, tasting her, distracting her . . .

She screamed into his kiss.

The sudden, striking blaze of fiery sensation tearing through her vagina should have been pain. The feel of him thrusting past her virginity, only to draw back then push deeper inside her, should have dampened her response.

But she could only feel her flesh growing slicker, wetter, her response raining down on the slow, deliberate strokes that burrowed his flesh deeper inside hers. Each slight withdrawal and deeper penetration had her crying out his name, arching to him, and begging for more.

The feel of his hips working against her, his flesh shafting inside her, tore through her senses as each stroke raked over nerve endings never before caressed, never before subjected to such a brutal, fiery caress as the one invading her now.

Pulling back, Graham's lips stroked over hers once again before he leaned back, kneeling between her spread thighs, his gaze going to the point where his flesh impaled hers. Following the look she whimpered at the sight of his erection pulling back, impossibly wide, slick with her juices, heavy veins throbbing and pulsing with the flow of blood racing through them.

A hard thrust of his hips and he buried himself to the hilt inside her.

"Ah fuck," he snarled as brutal pleasure slammed into her senses. "That's it, baby. Clench on my dick. Milk it with that tight little pussy."

The explicit demands had her womb clenching in response, her vagina tightening, flexing around the hard flesh as he began moving inside her again.

As he leaned over her once again, Lyrica felt the tight rein he'd kept on his lust until now break. Growling against her neck, with one hand he gripped her hip, the other burying itself in her hair as he moved against her.

Long, deliberate strokes stoked the burning pleasure building in the tissue rippling around his shuttling cock. He kept his pace even, deliberately rhythmic, without speeding into the crashing race for release. And it was killing her.

Tightening her knees at his hips, she sobbed beneath him. The hard rake of sensation at her clit combined with the powerful thrusts inside her was throwing her headlong into a storm she didn't know if she would survive. Who and what she was would be changed, she thought desperately, her fingers clenching on his shoulders now.

She couldn't survive a pleasure this brutal and still be the person she was before it began.

She arched desperately against him as the waves of sensation began growing, burning hotter, higher. The sensitive muscles of her pussy rippled and shuddered around his cock with each stroke, his erection burying deep, each thrust moving faster, harder, filling her, stretching her with such a calamity of sensations that it pushed her headlong over a precipice she hadn't seen coming.

She was thrown into the maelstrom.

Everything around her, inside her, her very senses exploded with such a fiery release of ecstasy that it jerked her taut beneath him, stealing her breath and her ability to scream. All she could do was shudder beneath him as spasms of violent response rippled through her cunt, exploded in her clit, and sent pulse after pounding pulse of rapture to dissolve her senses.

"Ah god, that's it, baby," he groaned as he buried deep, held still, and let them both feel the rippling response stroking over his cock. "That's it, just come all over me, Lyrica. Give it all to me, baby."

She collapsed beneath him, fighting just to breathe, to find some semblance of sanity as she felt him slowly pull free of her.

"We're not finished yet," he growled as she began to relax. "Not yet."

Forcing her eyes open, her lips parted in shock to see him working a condom over the dark plum-colored, mushroom-shaped crest of his cock. He was still impossibly hard, incredibly thick, and ready to take her again.

Graham felt as though a vise were tightening around his balls, the tortured need to spill inside her, naked, without the latex between them, making him crazed. He'd never wanted to take a woman bare, but forcing himself to roll the condom over his flesh was like a bitter dreg of resentment.

The thought of spilling inside her, of watching her body bloom with his child, suddenly filled his head, sliced at his chest until he was forced to push it away.

Now was no time for the ever-deepening need for this woman, and it certainly wasn't the time for a child.

With the condom firmly in place he let his fingers slide through the swollen folds of her pussy, gathering the slick excess of her juices to assure himself she was still ready for him.

Her release had milked his dick until holding back his own release had been next to impossible. Feeling her flesh milking his cock, rippling over the sensitive head, sucking at the cum building in his balls, had been the most pleasure he'd ever known in his life.

"Turn over for me." Lifting her he moved her until he had her breasts pressed into the mattress, her hips lifted for him, the clenched, snug little entrance of her pussy waiting for him. "That's it, baby," he groaned. "Give me that sweet pussy just like this."

Holding her hips with one hand, he used the other to guide the broad flesh into place. He watched as his flesh parted the flushed, slick flesh and began pressing inside. Watched as she stretched around him, her cries filling his senses as the snug muscles began to grip him, milk him inside her, lashing his flesh with heated ripples despite the covering of the condom.

God, he wanted to go slow. He wanted to ease in. Wanted to relish every sensation.

The hard, desperate thrust inside her tightly clenched cunt shocked him. He was buried to the hilt, her flesh tight around him, stroking his cock, tearing past his control.

"That's it," he groaned as her hips rolled beneath him, causing her inner muscles to stroke him tighter, to ripple exquisitely around him. "That's it, baby, fuck me back. Give it to me, Lyrica."

The sharp clench of her tissue nearly had his cum shooting past his control.

She liked the raw, sexual words, he realized. Or was it the sound of tortured pleasure in his voice that had her pussy clenching so tightly on him?

Whatever it was, he couldn't fight the lust pounding through him, the imperative need to pound inside her until he drew her release from her again. Until he could give her his.

Holding her hips, he watched his flesh shuttling fast and furious, penetrating and retreating, fucking into her with desperate strokes as her cries began to fill the air around him. She strained beneath him, her hips rocking back to him, her fingers clenched desperately in the blankets beneath her.

He was too fucking close.

Fighting for breath, for control, he slid his thumb into the narrow crevice of her rear, found the incredibly sensitive entrance there, already slick from her juices as they spilled from her pussy.

"Graham," she cried out in shock as he pressed his thumb into her, feeling the flesh part, the burning grip on his thumb transferring to his cock as her pussy clenched and spasmed, her body tightening as a wail of ecstasy escaped her lips.

The milking heat of her inner walls tightening around his cock triggered his own release. Her anus clenched at his thumb, sucking at it as her pussy sucked at his dick, her release raining over the latex-covered flesh.

Burying himself deep, he clamped his teeth over the low growl that escaped him, electricity racing up his spine before tearing back down it and striking at the depths of his balls.

The first agonizingly rapturous jerk of his cock shredded his senses. His seed spilled from his body as he pumped inside her, jetting harshly in response to the heated slide of her juices spilling along his latex-covered flesh, the gripping muscles rippling around his cock.

Burying himself deep inside her, he let the steady, hard pulse of his cum spill from him. Each lash of pleasure burned at his senses until he collapsed against her. His breathing was rough, agonized. Sensation still coursed through his senses, rasped over his flesh. Beneath him, the shudders of her own release still trembling through her body, Lyrica's little sobs of pleasure dug sharp talons of another, unfamiliar need inside his chest.

Never in his sexual history had he known anything so brutally hot, so exquisitely pleasurable as fucking this small, too innocent young woman through the near-violent orgasms that had gripped her.

Nothing had ever affected him more, either.

Drawing from her, his knees still weak, Graham grimaced at the tangle of denim around his legs. Hell, he hadn't even taken his jeans off, and working them free of his body now was almost impossible.

Long moments later, fully naked, he forced himself to the bathroom, where he disposed of the condom before running warm water over a hand towel and wringing it tightly into the sink.

He didn't pause to consider what he was doing. He didn't even think about it until he'd eased Lyrica to her back and gently wiped the perspiration from her body. He was parting her legs, the cloth cleaning the smear of blood from her inner thighs before he realized he was doing something he'd never done before for any other woman.

He was taking care of her. Easing her. Claiming her.

Son of a bitch, he'd had no intention of claiming her when this began.

He had no right to claim her.

Hell, this wasn't supposed to happen.

FIFTEEN

Something had changed, Lyrica thought two days later as she awoke. Lying in Graham's bed, awaking alone, was beginning to bother her. No matter how long she lay there, he didn't check to see if she was awake. When she went to bed at night, he did join her. But the only proof she had that he slept in the bed was the indent in the pillow each morning and the mussed blankets.

His day was filled with meetings with Elijah, calls to contacts, and hours spent on his laptop searching down "leads." She was starting to think the leads were no more than an excuse to ensure he didn't have time to touch her.

If it weren't for the way he watched her, she'd believe she'd imagined the hours she'd spent with him buried inside her. Because he sure as hell wasn't doing anything to touch her now.

Whatever the shadow she'd sometimes glimpsed in his gaze over the past year was, it seemed to have grown in the past two days. His expression was remote, his mood dark, and only his eyes betrayed the lust that still lingered between them.

Confused and uncertain, she forced herself from the bed and into the shower, the change in Graham still plaguing her even as she dressed for another day behind closed curtains, hiding from whatever threat existed outside.

She was getting tired of hiding.

She'd known she would. If she had known what was going on to begin with, she would have demanded her brother and cousins come up with a plan that would draw the threat out into the open rather than piecing everything together the way they were now.

Had she been given a chance to consider it the other night, she might have demanded it then. One thing was for certain, she couldn't continue like this. She was already going stir-crazy.

Her life wasn't one of idle days and lazy nights. She worked three jobs in any given week: Dawg's lumber store, the marina, and the restaurant Natches and his sister ran in Somerset, simply named Mackay's.

She worked wherever she was needed most at the time or wherever her interest drew her on any given day. She didn't just sit around, unless it was in front of her laptop writing. And writing wasn't a vocation for her. It was an outlet for the hopes, dreams, and pains that she often found herself too sensitive to.

Freshly showered, her long black hair blow-dried to ribbon straightness and falling to the middle of her shoulders, Lyrica hurriedly dressed.

A white lace bra and matching panties, a fluttery chiffon skirt in soft pastel waves of color, and a white cotton camisole tank that fit over her breasts with snug appreciation for her curves before skimming over her stomach and disappearing into the thin band of the skirt. Pushing her feet into a pair of tan brown leather sandals, she left Graham's bedroom and headed to the kitchen.

They had twenty-four more hours, she decided, to at least come up with a reasonable lead. After that, they were going to have to revise their plans just a little bit, because living like this . . . there was no way she could continue to do it for long.

Her heart wouldn't survive it.

Stepping into the kitchen, she was surprised to see Graham sitting at the small breakfast table with his laptop, a steaming coffee sitting at his elbow.

His head lifted as she stepped into the kitchen, his golden brown eyes narrowing on her, the flecks of gold firing instantly as she paused at the doorway.

"You're not in the office," she observed as she moved to the coffeepot.

"Don't appear to be, do I?" His tone was carefully modulated. Not a hint of mockery or sarcasm was to be found in his voice or his expression.

But she still felt it.

Tensing, she poured the coffee before cradling the cup in her hands and turning back to him.

"Do you have a problem with me being here all of a sudden?" she asked curiously, hiding the flash of pain that struck her at the thought.

"Did I say I had a problem with you being here?" A dark blond brow arched questioningly, and still there was no sign of the dark anger she could feel just beneath the surface.

"You wouldn't say, whether you had one or not," she felt the need to point out. "Other than sleeping with me, you'd take care of me the same way you'd expect my family to take care of Kye. I know you that well at least."

Something flickered in his gaze then. An acknowledgment of her point, perhaps?

Lifting the cup to her lips to ensure she gave away as little of the pain the thought caused her as possible, Lyrica sipped at the coffee slowly.

"If I had a problem with you being here, then trust me, you wouldn't be here," he promised, his expression tightening as he turned his attention back to the laptop.

"You have me for twenty-four more hours," she stated, her resolve hardening. "Then I'm calling Dawg."

With that, she set the coffee cup on the counter and turned and walked from the room.

"Like hell." He caught up with her before she cleared the kitchen doorway. Catching her arm in a firm grip, he had her swung around before she realized he'd even moved from the table. "What the fuck do you mean by that?" The gleam of gold in his gaze seemed to intensify as he pulled her to him, his powerful body tense, tight, and hard against her.

"Stop with the he-man bullshit, Graham," she snapped, pulling away from his touch as quickly as possible. Even angry and hurt, she felt nothing but pleasure when his skin touched hers. "I don't have time for it, and I don't want to deal with it. Dawg has twenty-four hours to figure out what the hell is going on and how to fix it, or I'm leaving."

His expression became so tight, so fierce, it bordered on savage. Lips thinning, the muscles at his jaw clenched tight, he glowered down at her with such dominant force that she almost backed down. It was as though some preprogrammed female part of her DNA instinctively reacted to the demand for submission.

"The hell you are. Do you think I'm busting my ass to figure this out so you can give me a deadline before waltzing out of here and making yourself a target? I don't think so, sweetheart."

She smiled back at him, making damned certain her smirk was identical to the one Natches was known for.

His eyes narrowed.

"Twenty-four hours," she said again, calmly. "Then I'm leaving."

"I'll lock you in the fucking basement." It was a promise.

"You could have been a Mackay," she stated, her voice heavy with derision. "How long do you think it will take before Dawg finds out?"

"As long as it takes me to call him and tell him you're trying to leave. About five minutes after I lock the door."

She had to laugh. "You have to come back in at some point, Graham. Do you think I'll actually let you leave alive?"

A frown jerked between his brows, outrage glittered in his eyes, and he was so tense, so prepared to lock her in that damned basement, that the power pumping into his muscles actually seemed to make his biceps appear larger.

"I'll send Elijah in first," he said.

The back door opened at that moment and Elijah stepped in, a questioning grin tugging at his handsome lips as he arched a dark brow over humor-filled blue eyes. "Send me where?"

In the same instant, he seemed to sense the tension filling the room as it whipped from both of them.

The door closed slowly behind him. "Should I leave?" His throat cleared uncomfortably as he remained by the door.

"Of course not, Elijah." Lyrica grinned, stepping away from Graham and moving to the coffeepot. "I was just getting ready to make some fresh coffee before going upstairs and working on a new sales program I promised Dawg. Would you like a cup?"

Elijah's gaze moved to Graham as the other man stomped back to the table and the open laptop.

"Is it safe?" he asked, the barest hint of mockery tugging at his lips.

"Unless she throws it at you," Graham stated, his voice low as he threw another glare her way.

"She wouldn't throw it at me." Elijah gave a confident laugh. "She likes me. Don'tcha, Lyrica?"

"All the girls like you, Elijah," she laughed as she threw him a smile over her shoulder. "Some much better than others."

He winked. The charmer. "Yeah, they like my redneck charm," he drawled. "Works every time."

Lyrica only snorted before starting on making fresh coffee. Rinsing out her cup, she set it beside the coffeepot before turning back to the two men. Both were watching her closely.

Propping her hands on the counter behind her, she tilted her head inquiringly. "Is something wrong?"

"No," Graham murmured. "Not for a good twenty-four hours at least."

"Not on my end." Elijah grinned. "I just stepped in to let the boss know about his cows since he couldn't get out there today. He's particular about bovines, ya know?" He turned to Graham then. "What happens in twenty-four hours?"

"I guess we'll just have to wait and see, won't we?" Graham answered tightly. "Now, tell me about my damned bovines."

Bovine his ass, Graham thought in irritation. The cows were fine; he'd checked on them himself no more than two hours before. Elijah's only job was monitoring those cameras and tracking anyone who came too close to the lake house.

Graham owned over five hundred acres, with the western corner butting against the lake and no neighbors for several miles. If anyone was out there, then it was Elijah's job to identify and track them.

"You had a few strays." Turning to Graham, Elijah's gaze hardened while his voice remained easy, almost teasing. "This one little shit slipped away from me on the upper end of the lake, though. I'll go out later and see if I can't pick its trail up again."

As he spoke he tapped an icon on his phone and pulled up a picture.

There was no way to tell much about the watcher, except the fact that it sure as hell wasn't a poacher, hunter, or lone fisherman. The figure was dressed in black, with a black military face hood in place and dark glasses. Male or female, who the hell knew?

"Was it off the farm when you caught sight of it?" Graham asked.

"Naw, I saw the little critter just ahead of that outcropping of boulders up the ways a bit." Elijah tapped the phone again to point out the fifth of a dozen cameras spread around the house. Five was just above the back of the house, the same side Graham's bedroom was on.

"I'm confident you'll track it down," he murmured, glancing over at Lyrica.

Leaning against the counter, she watched them in amused interest, though the expression on her face was frankly skeptical. The last gurgle of the coffeemaker indicated the brew's completion, prompting her to turn, fill three cups, then slide the pot back into place.

"Here, you two drink your coffee and talk about your 'bovines' in peace," she said. "I figure they're kind of like Dawg's 'cows' when he doesn't want Christa to know he and Natches are out checking for trespassers. The two-legged variety."

"Huh?" Elijah turned back to her, frowning as though confused.

Lyrica only laughed. "Natches uses a similar expression whenever he's lying through those disgustingly healthy teeth of his, Eli. Save it."

"Those are his teeth?" Poor Elijah, she distracted him so easily, Graham thought in disgust. "He's too old for teeth like that."

"He's forty-three, not fifty-three," Lyrica laughed. "Now, Rowdy just hit forty-five. And those are indeed his natural teeth as well."

Graham frowned. Elijah's gaze flicked to those pretty, sun-kissed legs as she set the two cups on the table.

"Hell, none of them look forty," Elijah said with a grunt as she moved back. "They're aging well at least."

"Let's see if I let them live to see their next birthdays," Lyrica suggested, her smile tight as she turned away from them, collected her own coffee, and moved for the doorway.

"Lyrica." Graham watched as she tensed at the doorway before turning back to him.

"Yes, Graham?" The saccharine sweetness of her smile didn't fool him in the least.

"We'll finish our discussion, soon."

"Of course we will." She shrugged as though not in the least concerned. "Until then, you have twenty-three hours." Then she flashed Elijah a bright smile. "See you later, Eli. Tell Timothy and Dawg I said hey when you see them later."

She left the room, the little skirt flirting just below her thighs as she turned the corner and headed back through the house.

As Elijah turned, his arched brows and the grin on his lips assured Graham that the other man found the situation immensely funny.

"Poor Graham," he murmured.

Bracing his elbows on the table, Graham directed a focused, narrow-eyed look on the younger man. "You have something to say?"

"An observation, perhaps," Elijah murmured.

"And that would be?" Graham doubted he really wanted to hear it.

"You obviously have twenty-three hours to fix the situation or she's leaving." Leaning back in his chair and crossing his arms over his chest, Elijah watched him knowingly.

"So?"

He shook his head pityingly. "Or twenty-three hours to give her a reason to hope it takes her brother a while to figure this mess out." Dropping his arms, he rose to his feet, his gaze flashing with something more than pity as the amusement dropped away. "If you don't want her, Graham, let her go—give someone else a chance to make her happy. Or finish what you started and see what you'll be throwing away when it's over. If you let her go now, she might have a chance of finding happiness later. That would be the humane way to handle this."

Graham rose slowly to his feet. "Interested, Elijah?" he asked softly, his fingers curling into fists at his sides at the very thought of the bastard touching her.

"Not me." His smile was hard, cold then. "I like living too much. But I'm sure there's a nice, safe accountant, manager, or, hell, landscaper who could be. Give one of them a chance."

Pulling the door open with a jerk, Elijah left the kitchen, the door closing just a little too loudly behind him.

Graham cursed.

The bastard.

Elijah had worked undercover in all three areas before coming to Somerset. Accountant, manager, or landscaper his ass. Graham would shoot him first.

But he had a point. Maybe the deadline wasn't a deadline for her brother, but one for him.

Lyrica Mackay wasn't nearly as maneuverable as she let her brother and cousins believe she was, he thought with a heavy sigh. Nor was she willing to give him time to find the self-control he needed to make sure her heart wasn't shattered when this was over.

She was nothing like Betts.

The thought caught him so completely off guard that for a moment he was back there. The sun beating down on his desert helmet, attacking the dark sunglasses he wore as the military convoy dropped into base.

The four-man unit he was scheduled to take into the mountains above Kabul was in that convoy, he knew. His men were assembled, their gear ready for a week-long trek into territory sure to test the luck they'd held on to for months when it came to serious wounds or fatalities.

Then his third man turned and reached into the vehicle, and a second later Graham had kissed that lucky streak good-bye as the soldier helped a lone female from the truck.

Betts Laren. Delicate and black haired, though the shining cap was cut to frame her pixieish face rather than falling down her back. Her lashes weren't as thick and lush as Lyrica's, her slender body more compact than fragile, her eyes a softer green. But she'd relieved the lust he couldn't seem to get a handle on where thoughts of the third Mackay sister were concerned.

The army intelligence officer was fearless and charming, and she'd fooled him in ways he'd never believed a woman could fool him.

Shaking his head, he stalked to the door and opened it, stepping out to the shaded porch to draw in the scent of Kentucky warmth as the memory of the smell of death began to fill his head.

He'd kept from touching Lyrica for two fucking days. Hellish days. He was so damned hard, so ready to fuck, it was all he could do to keep from throwing her over the table when Elijah flirted with her outrageously.

He'd known he wasn't going to last much longer when he'd forced himself from the bed that morning. But he'd managed to get a handle on it, to push back the extremity of his lust. If he could detach himself from his need just a little more, then he could take her again and trust his ability to still think straight.

He would be able to still the hunger just a little while; keeping her heart from becoming more involved, perhaps. He didn't want to hurt Lyrica.

There was no doubt he already trusted her. Lyrica didn't balk at telling him exactly what was on her mind at any given time. And when she did, he always sensed it.

But he wasn't a safe bet for her. He wasn't a safe bet for any woman. His secrets were dangerous, and the chances of their resurrection far too probable. The only question was when.

He frowned, wondering . . .

Not possible; he shook the thought away. That particular secret still lay in a coma in a French hospital. He knew. He checked daily. And he lived with the knowledge that he'd jeopardized his own future when he hadn't killed the man when he had the chance.

Breathing out a sigh of relief that Graham had left the kitchen, Lyrica stepped back inside to refresh her coffee and snag one of the prepared sandwiches Graham and Kye usually kept in the fridge for lunch.

Neither of them was big on cooking, Kye had laughed as she'd looked over the selection of sandwiches. So twice a week, one of them would put together the sandwiches, wrap them, and place them in the crisper.

They were always damned good, too.

Not too big, no condiments or additions. Just thick hoagie

rolls and a variety of thinly sliced meats. Who needed tomato and lettuce, she thought as she bit into one of the meaty selections.

Finishing the sandwich and her coffee, she wandered into the sunroom, the memory of lying on that nearest chaise lounge with Graham between her thighs sending a flush racing over her body.

Damn him. Threaten to lock her in the basement, would he? Oh, just let him try. She'd make damned sure he regretted it.

And of course, threatening to lock her away was far better than touching her, wasn't it?

God, had she really wasted the past six years of her life? Because if he thought for one damned minute that he'd made up for six years of tortured arousal, then he'd best think again.

Yeah, she had wasted those years.

She was wasting her time now, she thought as she heard the back door open. She would have let him know she was there if she'd had a chance—she was turning to head back into the kitchen when Elijah's comment stopped her in her tracks.

"She's not Betts, Graham." Elijah's voice was heavy, filled with regret.

"I didn't say she was," Graham answered and Lyrica heard the sound of the fridge opening and closing.

"You should have stayed the hell away from her," Elijah growled then, his voice harder, colder than she could have imagined possible. "Let her love—"

"An accountant, manager, or landscaper?" Graham gave a short, mocking bark of laughter. "Fuck you, Elijah. I told you this subject was finished. Now let it go."

"Let Lyrica go, then," the other man snapped back at him. "Stop hanging around her like some dark, tortured warrior. You've done just enough to keep that girl hanging on without giving her any part of yourself. Where's the fairness in that?"

"Drop it, Elijah." Graham's voice was dangerously soft now.

"She's . . . no more than a stand-in for her . . ." Elijah's accusation sent a wave of agony ripping through Lyrica's heart as she heard something heavy thump into the wall.

Probably Elijah.

Stepping to the doorway silently, she saw Elijah shoved into the wall, Graham's forearm braced against his throat, his back tense, every muscle defined as he held the younger man firmly in place.

"You don't know what the fuck you're talking about." Grating, rasping with fury, Graham's voice carried clearly to her.

"Don't I?" Elijah bit out fiercely, doing nothing to fight back. "I might not know what happened or how it happened, but what I do know is that she and Lyrica resemble each other enough that it'd be damned easy for you to pretend—"

"Don't make me kill you, Elijah. You don't know what the hell you're talking about and repeating that crap will only hurt Lyrica."

"Why do you care?" Elijah's lips drew back furiously, though still he did nothing to fight back. "You don't intend to keep her. You just intend to fuck a little pain out of your system before you send her back home to her brother. Tell me, Graham, did you call her name when you were—"

"No!" Lyrica jumped forward as Graham's fist drew back, the power bunching in his shoulder and arm a clear indication that Elijah was about to be on the receiving end of something Graham would never be able to take back.

"Let him go," she whispered as the two men froze.

Elijah's gaze was filled with regret, but purpose. Jerking his head around, Graham's gaze was so razor sharp it sliced into her soul as it locked onto hers.

Endless, bitter fury seemed to reflect in his eyes now. For the first time she was seeing the soul of the man, and the bleak misery there had her flinching at the pain of it.

His pain.

And now hers. Because now she knew she truly was no more than his latest "flavor," and she couldn't even hate him for it, because she'd known. She'd known all along that she would never be more than that.

Slowly, Graham moved back, his fingers flexing as the muscles at his jaw clenched violently.

"Get out!" He snarled, turning on Elijah with the promise of certain violence. "Now!"

Elijah gave a hard, disgusted twist of his lips before turning, gripping the door, and slamming out of the kitchen and onto the back porch.

Graham swung back around, the gold in his eyes brilliant now as he watched her for several long, tense moments.

"Eavesdropping doesn't become you, Lyrica," he stated furiously.

"Yeah, and it's true what they say, eavesdroppers hear nothing good of themselves, right?"

"Fuck!" A hard grimace tightened his face as he raked his fingers furiously through his hair. "I would have never let you hear that bullshit." He glared back at her as his arms dropped to his sides once again. "And that's what it was, fucking bullshit."

It was more. She could see it in his eyes, in the furious pain burning in the golden depths.

"I didn't mean to overhear." She swallowed tightly. "It all happened so fast."

Lifting her hand, she dropped it to her side again helplessly.

If it was bullshit, he would explain, right?

She waited, watching him, knowing with every shuddering beat of her heart that he wasn't going to explain a damned thing. Because to explain it would mean admitting it wasn't bullshit, she thought painfully. Admitting that she was no more than a stand-in for another woman.

What was she supposed to do now? What was she supposed to say?

She looked away for a long moment, the shadows that filled the room from the tightly closed windows and the curtains pulled over them sinking into her heart.

When she turned back to him, she couldn't help the trembling of her lips or the pain that lashed at her heart.

"Did you think of her when you were with me?" she whispered, unable to stop the words before they escaped. "Oh my god, I can't believe I asked that." She tried to laugh, but the sound was bitter and filled with self-disgust as she held up a hand in a staying motion as he started to speak. "I don't even want to know. I don't even think I can bear to know either fucking way."

He shook his head, breathing out roughly, but he refused to say anything, refused to explain a damned thing.

"Does Kye know?" she asked painfully, her heart racing so hard, pounding in agony at her chest.

"There's nothing to fucking know, Lyrica," he bit out, his voice rough. "For god's sake, what you heard was Elijah's perception of one fucking comment made long before this summer. He doesn't know what he's talking about and he has no idea how close he is to getting his fucking ass kicked for hurting you like this."

Hurt? This wasn't hurt. It was agony. Because what he was saying felt true, but she could also feel the lie.

"Who is Betts?"

He flinched as though she'd struck him.

That was all the truth she needed to see.

She rushed past him, unable to stand there any longer, unable to face him or the tears she could feel burning in her chest.

Even as she ran, she expected him to stop her. She expected to feel his arms coming around her and pulling her back into the heat of his hard body. She didn't. As she rushed out the door, she paused long enough to glance back at him. He stood where he had been before she moved, appearing to stare at the spot where she'd stood. Still, silent, and just as alone as he wanted to be.

SIXTEEN

"This is Natches. Leave me a message if you have to."

Natches's voice message usually managed to make her smile, but this time, she couldn't seem to make the effort.

"It's Lyrica." She swallowed tightly. "Hell, you have my number . . ." Her voice broke as she fought back a sob. "Can you call me back, Natches? I really need to talk to you."

She disconnected the call.

She couldn't call Dawg. If she did, she would start crying the second he heard the pain in her voice and softly asked, "Hey there, baby sister, tell me what hurts."

Dropping the phone into her bag, she stared around the bedroom. She had to pack her clothes. She'd just recently unpacked them when Graham had suggested there was plenty of room in his closet and dresser. Her hands had actually trembled as she'd put her things away, thinking of his claim that no other woman had shared this space with him.

Gathering her strength when all she wanted to do was rage, to run from the house and escape Graham and the pain building inside her, she bent and dragged her suitcase from beneath the bed where he'd stored it.

A shadow of something attached to the bed frame had her frowning and lifting the white dust ruffle to investigate further. The handgun attached to the metal rail surprised her. There was another on the other side of the bed.

Pulling back slowly, she straightened, then lifted the leather bag to the mattress and opened it quickly. She was turning for the closet when Graham stepped into the room.

His gaze went instantly to the luggage, the anger in his gaze darkening as he snapped the door closed behind him.

"You promised me twenty-four hours," he reminded her, the low rasp of his voice sending a surge of awareness, of sensual trepidation up her spine.

Not fear. He'd never hurt her. But this was a part of Graham she had no experience with. A side of him she had never seen before. The dark, wicked eroticism on his face, the sexual knowledge that gleamed in his eyes and her own awareness that he wouldn't hesitate to use it to hold her there.

And when everything was over, when she was no longer his preferred flavor, what then?

"A promise based on the assumption that staying here would hurt less than walking out," she informed him as that thought slashed through her heart.

"Staying here would hurt less than being dead?" A sharp bark of laughter escaped his lips. "Excuse me for disagreeing, sweetheart, but I think the process of getting dead might hurt worse."

Would it really? Graham could destroy the part of her that loved, that believed in love. Would death hurt more than losing what she sensed could have been between them? Or would have been between them if he had been willing to share his own heart.

"Natches or Dawg will be more than happy to pick me up. Once I'm with them, I'll be safe. They'll make certain of it," she informed him, stalking to the dresser to remove the items there despite the prickling of her skin as he watched her.

"Take a single item out of that dresser, Lyrica, and the considerate lover I'm really trying to be will evaporate. Is that what you really want?"

Considerate lover? Well, by god, wouldn't he have to be a lover first? Evidently, they'd just had sex, nothing more. That wasn't her definition of a lover.

"What I want isn't an option," she snapped, turning and bracing her hands on her hips as she faced him again. "And staying here is no longer an option, either."

His lips tightened further, the muscles at his jaw clenching as he folded his arms in a move that only increased the appearance of width in his already broad chest.

"Because you learned I had a past lover?" he said mockingly. "I've had many."

No kidding. So many in the past year that she had nearly lost count herself. But it wasn't the quantity that hurt as damned much as the knowledge of the one she hadn't known about.

"A lover that mattered," she cried out furiously, painfully. "One that you regret so desperately that you're taking me to your bed because I look like her?"

It was killing her. The thought of it was so demoralizing, so painful she could barely breathe for it.

"Go to hell, Graham. The least you could have done was told

me. You could have let me know you'd lost the woman you loved . . ."

He was on her before she could attempt to evade him. Pulling her to him, lifting her from the floor, and tossing her to the bed with the utmost gentleness and the utmost dominance.

Rolling to her back, she sat up quickly, one hand braced on the mattress, the other brushing her hair back from her face as she stared back at him.

"You think I'm taking you to my bed because you look like Betts?" he snarled, already jerking his boots off. "Oh, hell no, baby. I took her to my bed because *she* looked like *you*. Because I couldn't think for the need to fuck you, couldn't sleep for dreaming about it or get through the day without fantasizing about it. Because the hunger tearing me apart blinded me to such an extent that I didn't even know when I was being betrayed."

Fury whipped over his expression and in his eyes, filled his voice, and left Lyrica staring back at him in shock.

Whipping the T-shirt over his head, his hands went instantly to his belt and the metal button securing the band of his jeans. In only a few seconds he was shedding the denim, the heavy, engorged length of his cock standing out from his body fiercely. The fingers of one hand wrapped around the shaft, stroking it slowly as his eyes narrowed on her.

"Spread your legs," he ordered, his voice a deep, lust-filled rasp that sent weakening need flooding her further.

She shook her head, though not in denial of the order, more in denial of the revelation that she'd torn from him.

"We need to talk . . ."

"Oh, baby, we've talked enough. Now spread your legs."

She shook her head again.

"Want to test me, pretty girl?" he whispered, stepping closer to the bed. "Spread your legs. I'm going to eat my fill of that sweet pussy and see just how crazy I can make both of us while I'm doing it. And you're going to just lay that pretty little body right back there and enjoy every minute of it. And maybe, just maybe, by the time I'm finished fucking us both into oblivion I'll have a handle on whatever the hell it is that you do to me."

What she did to him? What did she do to him that made him so angry?

"This won't solve anything," she argued desperately, though even she was aware of the fact that she wasn't trying to escape him. "You know it won't."

"Sure it will." One knee rested on the edge of the mattress. "You'll be so fucking tired when your deadline rolls around that you won't be able to consider leaving, let alone actually packing or walking out my door. Now, spread your legs, or I'm going to spread them for you. And when I do, I'm ripping any panties you're wearing right off your body, and before I finish, I'll spank that pretty bare pussy of yours until you know better than to lie on that bed and argue with me."

A spasm of clenching pleasure gripped her womb, sending a rush of heated, slick warmth to spill from her sex. It was all she could do to keep from moaning at the very thought of it.

"Oh, you like the thought of that." Satisfaction and lust gleamed in his eyes and darkened the savage lines of his face. "Let's see how much you like the application of it."

"Oh." A gasp of surprise parted her lips as he reached out, gripping her legs and pushing them back before spreading them wide enough to make room for his body.

As he slid between her knees, he gripped her wrists, pulling them from the bed and pressing her torso back.

Just that quick, just that easy, he had her spread out before him, and before she could process the thought, he ripped her panties from her hips.

"Damn you, Graham," she exclaimed in outrage, managing to angle her upper body upright. "That was a matching set."

The fine material of the skirt was pushed back to her hips, the folds between her thighs bare but for the heavy layer of slick, glistening moisture that coated the inner seam of her intimate lips.

Her face flamed at the sight of her juices welling from her and preparing her so quickly for his possession.

Pulling her hips toward him and lifting them slightly, Lyrica found herself on her back once again as Graham's broad hand cupped the dew-rich folds. Parting the swollen lips, his fingers found the trapped, slick heat, groaning in appreciation at the excess.

Lifting his hand, his gaze locked with hers, he lowered it again, patting the tender flesh with a quick little flick of his fingers.

Prickling heat raced over the folds of her pussy. Her clit pulsed in shocking pleasure and throbbed in hunger.

"You like that," he growled, the sound low, harsh as his expression tightened further in lust. "Let's see how you like this."

His hand lowered again, the light tap sending heat racing across her flesh as her hips jerked at the sensation.

She couldn't bear this. Her clit was throbbing so hard, was so swollen, she swore she could feel air brush against it.

Another tap of his fingers and she cried out, her legs falling open farther, the need for more, for the rising clash of sensations, overwhelming her.

"Do you like it, baby?" he demanded relentlessly. "Tell me to stop."

"No!" The whimpering denial fell from her lips unbidden. "Oh god, Graham, please . . ."

Her hips lifted again as though pleading for more.

The next tap was heavier, sending a flush of licking flames to surround her clit and tighten around it in impending climax.

Graham's low, harsh chuckle had her breath catching as she forced her eyes to open, forced herself to stare back at him, anticipation clawing at her senses.

"Oh, I'm not letting you off that easy," he promised her. "You're not coming yet, sweetheart. As much as I'd love to watch your orgasm consume you. Not quite yet."

Panting for breath, Lyrica could see the determination in his eyes, in the hard lines of his face.

"Making me wait to come won't change anything," she retorted, though weakly.

It might have had more effect if it hadn't sounded like a moaning plea.

"We'll just have to see about that," he stated, too confident, too dominant. "Want to make a bet on it, baby?"

She wasn't betting on anything at the moment. She stared back at him silently instead, licking her dry lips nervously as his eyes narrowed on the action.

Cupping her pussy once again, one finger eased between the folds as her hips lifted to him once again. His touch slid through the heavy slickness there until it found the entrance to her vagina.

"Pull your top up." The order came as his finger found and rubbed at the clenched entrance of her pussy. "Show me your breasts or I'll rip the bra off next."

A deep, heavy spasm of pleasure rippled through her womb at the threat.

Hands shaking, she pulled the snug cotton up her torso, revealing the lace-covered curves he wanted to see before pulling it over her head and tossing the material away. Her breathing grew heavier, her heart beating faster as she released the front catch of her bra, almost panting as she struggled to pull the straps over her arms and remove it as well.

Her breasts were swollen, her nipples so hard, so aroused, they ached. After tossing the bra from the bed, her hands moved to the sensitive mounds, cupping them, moaning at the heavy flush that mounted his cheeks as he watched her.

"That's it, baby. Let me see you touch your pretty breasts. Show me what you like. What you want."

Drowsy, wicked sensuality flared inside her. She should be ashamed, but it was a distant thought. So distant that the flush that heated her breasts was one of arousal rather than shame. She would consider the other emotion later, she decided. Much later, after she'd followed the sensations racing through her to their ultimate conclusion.

"Show me, Lyrica. Now." The order was reinforced by a surge of pleasure she couldn't have anticipated.

"Oh god! Graham!" Swift, brutal pleasure struck at her as she was suddenly impaled by the hard thrust of his finger. Using the pad of his palm to press against her clit, he nearly sent her tumbling into her release.

"Show me," he growled, lifting himself closer as that wicked, experienced finger rubbed with destructive sensual strokes deep inside her pussy.

Touch herself. That, she was experienced in.

She'd masturbated enough to thoughts of him that she knew well how to caress her own body, knew the pressure to use, where she was most sensitive.

Finding her nipples with her thumb and forefingers, she didn't bother with slow, gentle strokes. The hard flares of nearly painful need striking at her senses would pay little attention to gentle anything. She gripped the sensitive buds, rolling them firmly, pulling at the exquisitely heated flesh and whimpering as the slightly rough touch sent lightning forks of painful pleasure to strike at her pussy.

Now, this she hadn't known. Just how much better that pinching pleasure at her nipples could make the penetration of her vagina.

Twisting beneath the rubbing caress inside the clenching tissue as she worked her nipples with quick little tugs and rolls of her fingers, she thought she'd go crazy from the sensations. Rapture nudged at her clit, the need to orgasm burning through her senses even as the need to prolong the deepening pleasure battled side by side with it.

"That's it, darlin'," he crooned, the dark sexuality of his voice spurring her pleasure. "Work those pretty nipples. Show me how you want them pleasured while they're in my mouth."

Her hips jerked again, twisting in desperation as his finger withdrew. A second later, two returned, broader, hotter, penetrating her with such striking sensations that her body bowed as the rippling spasms of near orgasm shuddered through her.

"Ah, like that, do you, sweetheart? Do you like this?" His fingers twisted, scissored inside her, creating a friction and a pressure that had her fighting to breathe as the fiery lashes of impending ecstasy tore through her.

She twisted, her hips thrusting against him, her head pressing into the mattress, grinding into it as she fought for that one just-right sensation that would trigger her release. Her need for it was a pulsing, burning blaze, growing out of control as it washed through her senses.

"That's good, baby." His voice was rougher now, darker. "Let's see if you like this."

She was only barely aware of him moving until the rubbing strokes inside her pussy eased.

"Don't stop." She couldn't bear it. "Oh god, Graham, please don't stop."

Slowly, the pressure returned, stroking, rubbing, barely moving inside her yet creating a firestorm that blazed through her senses.

It was so good.

It was electric. The pleasure was so intense it bordered pain and she only craved more.

She was begging for more. Thighs spread, her feet dug into the mattress as her fingers roughened her nipples with desperate need. She could feel the perspiration dewing her flesh, feel the slick juices ease past his fingers to spill from the clenched depths of her sex, as fiery sensation erupted over and over again within the sensitive tissue, yet the striking overload of pleasure was never enough to send her into release.

"That's it, lift that sweet pussy to me," he crooned as her hips lifted again.

His fingers withdrew.

A desperate cry was tearing from her lips as his fingers impaled her once again just as his lips surrounded the pounding, engorged bud of her clit.

"Graham, it's so good. So good." She was panting, fighting for breath as the sensation whipping through her body increased. If it was a firestorm before, it was a conflagration now. Burning, melting through her, building with rapacious intensity.

Flickering strokes of his tongue tormented her clit as it caressed around it, over it. Then it would pause, and *rub*, just rub, as the fingers buried inside her were rubbing, at the side of the painfully sensitive flesh before resuming the torturous flickering strokes once again.

She felt suspended within a cloud of purely sensual flames. The licking heat burned around her, inside her. It pulsed and throbbed as fingers of electric static struck over her flesh, clenched at her pussy.

When he'd pushed her to the brink of sanity, when the need for release was like sensual talons raking through her senses and her orgasm was like a wave cresting within her, he stopped once again.

"Damn you!" she cried out as his fingers eased back, the callused tips releasing that highly responsive spot they'd found inside her feminine flesh.

Then he kissed her.

His lips settled against her intimate folds and delivered a series of heated kisses. Fierce and heated, his tongue took quick, intimate swipes against the saturated flesh, her juices lying thick and slick upon her flesh.

Greedy, hungry kisses. Suckling, a heavy male groan rasped from his throat as his tongue swiped against her entrance.

Caressing hands stroked her inner thighs, then behind her knees. Lifting her legs, pushing them back, he opened her further to him, revealing the feminine flesh hidden between the folds and allowing his lips and tongue free rein.

In one hard, striking thrust his tongue sank inside the snug muscles of her cunt, flickering there, licking, drawing more of her moisture free to his carnal kiss.

Wild, wicked waves of pleasure crashed over her senses. Drowning, immersed in the electric pleasure whipping over her, Lyrica fought for something to hold on to. Her fists clenched in the blankets. Straining against the pleasure, desperate to fly over the sharp edge, she felt suspended upon the ecstasy building just beyond.

"Graham. Please. Oh god, please, I can't bear it." She was whimpering, desperation clawing at her body, tightening it as his caresses moved back to her clit.

His tongue circled with lashing tastes, preparing it for his lips to surround it, to suckle it inside the moist, fiery heat of his mouth.

Two fingers impaled the tightly clenched tissue of her pussy, pushing in, assaulting the tender flesh with waves of burning pleasure. Waves that rolled across, traveled through, and seared the sensitive nerve endings there before surging over her body with increasing heat.

His tongue lashed at her clit, and his mouth suckled the tender bud as his fingers found that place again.

"There!" Her strangled scream came as her feet pressed into the mattress again, her hips lifting to him then stilling, locked into place where the extremity of the sensations was at its height. "There. Oh god. Graham. Let me come. Please, please let me come."

The caresses inside her shifted, the pressure increasing, the rubbing strokes moving faster, sensation massing, tightening, whipping around her with blinding force as the feeling of electric static intensified. It shot through her body, centered in her womb, infused the sucking heat at her clit, and threw her suddenly, powerfully, into a supernova.

As her release was tearing through her body, she was aware of him moving, quickly positioning himself between her thighs and thrusting, working the heavy width of his erection inside intimate muscles clenched tight, flexing and spasming in rapture.

The impalement pushed the pleasure higher.

The first rush of release rocked through her, then began tossing her higher, each wave of incredible pleasure throwing her from peak to peak in tumbling rolls, giving her no respite from the intensity of it.

His lips surrounded one tightened nipple with hungry demand. His hips moved, the hard length of his cock powering into her with fierce, driving strokes.

Her orgasm exploded around her again, with devastating results. Her senses disintegrated with waves of blinding ecstasy that tore past any shield she may have had against the man who caused it. Tore past, filled her, warmed her where she'd been unaware she was cold, and became a part of her.

A part of her Lyrica knew she would never be free of.

When it was over, she found herself collapsed on the bed, Graham breathing heavily as he lay over her, his heart racing against her breasts. His lips were at her neck, his muscled body as damp with perspiration as hers.

Pleasure like that should never exist, she thought with sudden, blinding knowledge. No woman should ever have her heart, body, and mind so ensnared by a man that walking away from him meant walking away from a pleasure she feared part of her would wither away without.

The whisper of his voice at her ear was nearly drowned out by the racing beat of her heart as it echoed in her ears. She felt his lips moving against her neck, felt the raging regret that filled his voice.

"I'm so sorry." The words were a brush of sound, barely heard, so quiet that at first she thought she must have imagined the words.

"I'm so sorry." He whispered them again as his hard body settled and relaxed against hers.

Sorry.

He was so sorry.

Because he knew he was going to break her heart?

Why else would he be sorry, but to sense, to know, that in those moments when the pleasure had been at its height that her soul had opened to him as well.

He owned all of her, and he knew it.

And he regretted it.

Because he knew when it was all over, she would just be one of his past flavors. One he'd grown tired of.

SEVENTEEN

Natches and Dawg Mackay were waiting on him when he entered the kitchen a short time later. Sitting at the kitchen table with Elijah, steaming cups of coffee in front of them, they looked as comfortable as they would in their own homes.

Damned Mackays.

Territorial bastards in their own space, they could be just as arrogant in another's, he knew.

"Elijah, when did you start allowing the riffraff in without permission?" He glowered at the agent who was hanging his head in resignation where he sat at the side of the table.

"Hell if I know." Elijah sighed. "Probably about the same time I realized they could be more dangerous than Doogan. He just gets me shot at. Mackays would actually shoot me."

"So will I." Graham poured coffee for himself, lifted the cup to his lips, and sipped while staring back at the Mackays coolly. "What's happened that you felt the need to visit?"

No alert had come through and his security hadn't picked anything up. They were probably there simply to aggravate the crap out of him.

"Lyrica called earlier," Natches told him quietly, the color of his eyes identical to Lyrica's. "She sounded upset and asked me to call her back. She even said please."

"She always says please. She's polite like that," Graham pointed out while inwardly cursing.

Dammit, he should have anticipated that she would call her family and ask one of them to come for her.

"So why did she call?" Natches asked, strangely less confrontational than Graham expected him to be.

"I guess you'll have to ask her." He wasn't about to get into explanations where that mess was concerned.

"She found out about Betts Laren, didn't she?" It was Dawg who broached the subject as he sat back in his chair, his pale green eyes narrowed on Graham. "You can't take solid advice, can you, boy?"

Evidently, Natches had finally broken and told Dawg what he knew about that final mission Graham had taken in Afghanistan.

Graham set the coffee cup on the counter carefully before turning back and facing the two Mackays warily.

"That's a subject Lyrica and I will discuss when I find the time and place I deem appropriate," he informed them both. "Until then, I'd prefer not to talk about it. That way she can't walk into a conversation that will only confuse and hurt her without explanations. Explanations I'd like to make in my own time." He cast Elijah a pointed look as the other man's expression tightened in regret.

Natches grinned.

Damn, Graham hated the smirk that curled that man's lips.

"How old are you, Dawg?" Natches asked.

"Forty-four," Dawg answered instantly. "You, Natches?"

"Forty-three," Natches stated good-naturedly. "Tell me, Dawg, what have we learned about secrets that those so-called intelligence agencies demand we keep?"

"Always have backup," Dawg stated instantly, his gaze becoming mockingly questioning as he continued to watch Graham. "Do you have backup, Graham?"

Exactly how much did they fucking know? His gaze slid to Elijah's, and he read the same question in the other man's eyes.

"Why would I need backup?" he asked, knowing that even Natches shouldn't know the full story behind that mission.

"Just in case." Dawg shrugged.

"Just in case someone comes looking for five million in stolen diamonds," Natches answered, his expression triumphant as he sat back in his chair and waited for Graham's response.

"Are you accusing me of stealing from the army, Mackay?" Graham growled as though highly offended.

A crack of laughter escaped the other man as he shook his dark head knowingly.

"Come on, Graham, I spent too many years over there and I know people who won't even talk to Cranston. I know what happened after Agent Laren was killed and the insurgents escaped. Army intelligence was in there within an hour. Her partner's body was absent for a week and unidentifiable except for DNA when it was found." He chuckled at the thought. "Did you actually buy that one? If that was the truth, then what happened to the missing bag of diamonds? There were two bags; one was missing. Where is it?"

Graham shrugged. "Perhaps the insurgents found it."

Dawg grunted at that.

"Strange." Natches clucked his tongue. "They were meant as payment to Afghani and Iraqi security forces for information on troop movements and deployments, yet those payments never made it. I knew they hadn't, because quite a few of those forces were double agents, weren't they?"

Fuck. Where the hell had the bastard gotten his information?

"That's a hell of an imagination your contacts have, Natches," he stated, holding back the anger brewing inside him. "Imaginations like that could get men killed."

Or women.

Natches leaned forward then, his expression hardening, his gaze becoming brighter. "Dawg and I, we're the men you want to trust to cover your ass, Graham," he stated savagely. "Now, you can tell us what the fuck's going on, or we're collecting Lyrica before we leave. And I think we both know she'll probably go."

Graham wanted to believe she wouldn't leave with her brother and cousin, but he knew how hurt, how uncertain she had been.

How angry she had been before he'd overwhelmed her with pleasure.

His gaze slipped to Elijah, watching as the other man gave an imperceptible nod of his head in agreement. Graham might be pissed as hell at the other agent, but Elijah had been chosen as his second-in-command for a reason. Because he knew what the hell he was doing, and he was loyal. Breathing out in weary resignation, Graham picked up his coffee cup before moving to the table and taking the remaining seat.

"I don't have the diamonds," he told the other men. "You're right, there were two bags, each holding two million, five hundred thousand apiece in perfectly cut and polished diamonds. Only one bag remained between the two locations where they were hidden."

"And the partner's body?" Dawg asked quietly, leaning forward to rest his weight on his forearms as he placed them on the table.

"We're not certain." Graham shook his head. "AI had his DNA on file, but a virus was detected in the file manager and a change placed in his file several days before the body reported to be his was recovered. He was, at one time, a damned good hacker before signing on with the independent security agency being used to back up the mission. Army intelligence suspects he's still alive, but we've found zero hint of it, let alone confirmation."

"So you were working on the assumption he was still alive?" Natches asked. "My source in Afghanistan believes you actually have the diamonds."

"One bag is actually missing. The other is locked in a secure vault at CIA headquarters in Langley," Elijah said. "The suspicion that Graham stole the diamonds came from outside the agency. We're trying to track it down at present and maintain the idea that army intelligence believes in his innocence, while allowing the rumor to continue circulating among certain groups. I need to know your source."

Graham had known that was coming. It was one of the reasons he hadn't faced the knowledge Natches had seemed to have since returning. They were tracking the security agent's contacts, looking for a hint as to where it may have come from, although he was only one of the sources from which intelligence was attempting to unravel the flow of information.

Natches turned his head slowly and stared back at Elijah.

"Natches, kill me if you have to." Elijah sighed as though the thought of it really didn't impress him. "But this information is too damned important. If Betts's partner isn't dead then we need to capture him. If he is, then we need to know who in army intelligence is still leaking information that Graham has those diamonds."

"And you dragged my sister into this bullshit?" Dawg snarled then, turning on Graham. "You dared to mess with her—"

"Whoever's after those diamonds dragged her in," Graham snapped softly, glaring at both men. "That, or the partner, Betts's lover, isn't dead and he's after revenge as well as the cache. That's the only explanation that makes sense."

"And her lover, partner, whatever the fuck he was to her, or anyone else would know Lyrica's a weakness to you how?" Dawg's voice was quieter now, more dangerous than ever before.

"Did you ever see Betts Laren?" Elijah said. "She's almost Lyrica's double, except for the shorter hair. I accused Graham earlier of being interested in Lyrica because he couldn't get over Betts, but maybe he was sleeping with Betts because of Lyrica."

Graham shot the man a silencing look. Son of a bitch, he was going to have to teach Elijah, at the end of his fist, to keep his damned mouth shut when the Mackays got nosy.

"Mackays don't play second fiddle to anyone," Dawg grunted with dangerous emphasis. "Especially my sisters." His pale, furious gaze moved back to Graham then. "How would anyone involved in that shit know my sister is your weakness?"

"Fuck if I know." Plowing his fingers through his hair in restless anger, Graham fought to find the answer to that one. "That's the only reason I've pushed this suspicion away a thousand times, Dawg. But we had an attempted intrusion this morning. Dressed fully in black, with a military-style black mask covering his face. At first, there was nothing to identify him from the clothes or the figure, until I looked at how he wore them. The security team covering Betts wore the same uniform all the agents at that security agency wore. But they distinguished themselves in the way they wore them. Every other soldier in that agency tucks in any clothing edge possible. Shirts in pants. Pant legs in boots. Masks tucked beneath shirts. Ammo vests secured and snug in the vicinity of their waistbands."

"And that team changed this how?" Dawg asked.

"Black bands at the wrists covering from the edges of their shirts to several inches above that. Black covers of similar fabric over the laces of their boots. Elijah has an image of the intruder taken with his phone."

Both Mackays turned to Elijah as he pulled the picture up.

"It took me a while to realize why the image bothered me," Graham said, grimacing. "Whoever that is, if it's not Betts's partner, then it's someone from his team or someone very, very close to it."

"I started tracking the other two men who were part of his team," Elijah stated. "One is currently on assignment in Africa: Whit Chaney, an explosives expert. I spoke to a contact of mine there and he sent satellite proof of his presence. We haven't located the second member yet, though. Bradley Connor."

"Bradley has some computer hacking experience." Graham frowned. "Our intelligence didn't indicate that it was enough to plant that virus, though. But anything's possible at this point," he admitted.

"I want to know how they knew to use Lyrica against you," Dawg repeated, evidently determined to get answers Graham didn't have.

"Dawg, if I had that answer to give you, then all of this would make a hell of a lot more sense than it does." Graham stared back at him levelly. "I never mentioned Lyrica, the Mackays, or home. Betts was even unaware of the fact that I had a sister, and she died before I could question her."

In his arms. Betts had died in his arms, her green eyes filled with regret and pain as she'd haltingly revealed the plan she and the man she'd loved had hatched.

"I knew I could get in your bed." She smiled sadly, blood easing past her lips to trail down her cheek. *"I knew your weakness, Graham."* Her gaze flickered, her breathing rattling. *"It hurts, Graham . . . it hurts . . ."*

Wiping his hands over his face, he shook his head, at a loss as to how to get the answers he needed.

"What makes you believe this has anything to do with what happened there?" Natches asked him then. "I need more than suspicion."

"The Freedom League's last attempt at vengeance against the Mackays was made two years ago," Graham said. "With the judge's cooperation, DHS has managed since then to round up the last of the aging politicians who were part of that militia. They're gone. The men and women who conspired with Chandler and Dayle Mackay are dead, dying, or suffering from Alzheimer's in several rest homes. There's no reason to strike out at Lyrica unless it's in retaliation or to use her against someone who knows her well."

"Or loves her well," Natches suggested. "What would make your ex-lover believe you loved Lyrica?"

Graham shot Elijah a warning look. One that promised him that the Mackays were treading on his last patient nerve.

"Natches," Elijah said, "we've been trying to draw out whoever escaped with half of those diamonds for two years now. Every conversation, every moment spent together between Graham and Betts Laren has been gone over with a fine-tooth comb. He's had several polygraph tests as well as being debriefed by CIA interrogators. If Lyrica's name had been mentioned, trust me, it would have come up by now."

Natches ignored this point, turning his head to Graham instead. "What about memory enhancement protocols?"

Memory enhancement protocols? Graham sat back in his chair and stared at Natches in disgust. "I'm not a lab rat, Mackay. I'm a fully trained intelligence officer with the Marines and known for my ability to overcome or identify every drug they tried on me during training. The MCIA put a lot of effort into training me for several years before sending me to Afghanistan."

"Marine Corps Intelligence Activity," Dawg grunted. "Come on, Graham . . ."

"Since Secure Sector, the security group that went in with us, began taking contracts for the military, the percentage of lost, missing, or simply stolen money, jewels, and equipment out of the

Middle East has risen. Secure Sector has a contract with the Marines to provide cover for them as needed, which left the ball in MCIA's court to apprehend those responsible. I don't need memory enhancement protocols because I would have known if I'd been drugged or if any attempts to take me in any other way were used."

"Then we're missing something." Dawg sighed, shaking his head. "There has to be an answer."

For a situation where there had to be an answer, Graham couldn't come up with anything.

"I still have some things to go over," Graham admitted. "I've only recently connected a few of the dots." While he was lying against Lyrica, his body vibrating from a release that had damned near blown his mind, a thought had slammed into his brain.

What would he do if anything happened to her? If he lost her, the way Betts's lover had lost her. The suspicion that the lover had survived had only grown in past months. Contacts the agent had used in the past were missing or dead. Lines of communication he was known to employ had been used several times.

Of course, it could have been someone else. There was room for doubt, but if there was one thing Garrett Brock, his father, had taught him, it was never to trust coincidence.

"I want her away from you," Dawg stated then.

Graham bit down on the instinctive protest that rose to his lips. Letting her go would be for the best; he knew that. If this was because of him, then the danger to her rose every day that she was with him.

"That's not your decision to make, brother of mine."

All eyes turned to Lyrica as she stepped into the kitchen.

"She moves through this house quieter than a frickin' brush of air," Elijah complained as he slowly moved his hand back from the weapon tucked beneath his shirt and glared at Graham. "What the hell did you do? Give her lessons or something?"

"I'll take credit for that, if you don't mind," Dawg grumped as he rose to his feet and opened his arms for the tiny, delicate young woman he'd accepted into his heart, along with her sisters, the first second he'd realized who they were.

Lyrica moved into his embrace, her arms wrapping around his waist as Dawg placed a gentle kiss at the top of her head before she moved back.

"You called Natches earlier," he stated, staring down at her, though Graham couldn't see the man's expression. "You okay?"

"I'm okay." Her voice was soft, but even Graham heard the hesitation in it before she added, "But I'm not leaving."

He couldn't stop the flare of satisfaction that rose inside him at her words and her refusal to leave him.

"Even if you were targeted because of him?" Natches asked softly.

Graham knew what they were doing now. Attempting to break her trust in him, to break her desire to stay, and he was damned if he could blame them. If it were Kye in this position, then he'd do the same thing.

Lyrica's gaze met his then. "What are they talking about?"

The time for explanations had come, far sooner than he'd ever imagined. Hell, he'd hoped never to have to reveal exactly what had happened to him. That part of his life had nearly been over. They were growing closer to whoever had been tracking the diamonds and when they found him, or her, then the threats from that particular direction would cease. Graham's part in the investigation into Secure Sector would be finished.

It hadn't waited, though.

Briefly, keeping details to as much of a minimum as possible, he told her their suspicions. As each of her questions was answered, he watched her grow quieter, her gaze become cooler. Sitting beside him in the chair Dawg had vacated, her hands linked in her lap, she was silent, wary, as the last of the explanations were given.

"I actually suggested an answer to the question of how they learned about you," Natches drawled in irritation. "Memory enhancement protocols are a series of drugs that, with the subject's cooperation, have actually been known to draw out details the person was unaware existed. And in some cases with agents who have agreed to it, they've actually learned they are susceptible to some truth serum drugs."

Lyrica was shaking her head slowly.

"It's an option," Natches growled, his anger finally showing. "And by god, I want answers."

Her head jerked up at the sharp demand and, for the first time, Graham saw the fear in her eyes.

"Lyrica?"

She swallowed tightly. "You've never mentioned the one letter I sent you two years ago, just after you were home for that short leave."

He stared at her, watching as her gaze dropped to her fingers once again, a flush mounting her cheeks.

God, he remembered that summer. He'd found her in the gardens beyond the swimming pool, stepping along the cool, shaded stones in nothing but that damned emerald bikini. He'd joined her beneath the arbor, watching as she settled in the thick, heavy cushions of the swing before joining her.

"I didn't get a letter, Lyrica," he finally told her, feeling the certainty that somehow Betts or Dorne, her lover, had found that letter first.

She nodded then. "I thought perhaps it had been lost in the mail." A bitter smile shaped her lips. "When you came back last winter, though, it seemed that perhaps you might have read it." A little shrug lifted her shoulders as she reminded him of the blizzard and how close he had come to taking her as another woman lay upstairs awaiting him.

"What was in the letter?" Natches asked, his voice silky soft. A second later he shot Graham a glare as a flush broke over her face.

"It wasn't what I said that was important," she whispered. "I sent a picture, though. One I thought he might keep."

Lyrica could feel the chill of guilt racing over her as she lifted her gaze to Graham's, seeing the heavy regret in his eyes and hearing his voice as once again he whispered how sorry he was.

If his enemies had found the picture of her, in the green bikini, that Kye had taken by the pool earlier that day, and they'd read her letter, then they could have assumed she was the weakness they needed.

She would have been the weakness they needed.

The one woman he didn't think he could have because of her family and her innocence, and added to that, her deliberate flirtation and teasing. He could have returned to battle distracted, only to come face-to-face with a woman who resembled her. A woman he thought he could have without ties, in ways he couldn't have Lyrica.

"You're coming back with us." Natches's tone brooked no refusal.

"No matter the reason, it's me they're after," she told her cousin softly. "Whether because they believe Graham has the diamonds or to make him pay for another woman's death, I'm still the bait."

"You're no fucking bait." Natches came to his feet furiously, his emerald gaze burning with anger now. "You'll not stay here."

"I'm over twenty-one, Natches—"

"Then act like it, by god. Start thinking with your head instead of your damned hormones," he told her roughly as he shot Graham a killing look. "Does he love you, Lyrica? When this is over, will he have been worth risking your life for?"

"Enough!" Graham straightened from his chair then, his voice a lash of fury as he and Natches faced off. "I'll be damned if you'll stand here and insult her for something she has no fault in, Mackay. Stop acting like a damned prick for five seconds—"

"So you don't have to lose your flavor for this month?" Natches snarled then.

"God. Stop." Lyrica pushed her way from the table and jumped from the chair, avoiding Dawg's attempt to pull her to him as she faced all four men now. "You two fight over me like I'm some trophy to be won," she cried out. "No one can make this choice but me. It was my fault they found something to use against him. It's me some bastard wants to see dead, not the two of you," she informed her brother and her cousin harshly as she crossed her arms over her breasts, fighting back the icy chill of terror that threatened to grip her. "It's my fight, too."

"Because of him." Natches threw his hand in Graham's direction. "If he hadn't been lusting after you like a buck in rut then you wouldn't be in danger."

"If I hadn't been teasing him every chance I had, then maybe he wouldn't have been like a buck in rut," she yelled back at her cousin, furious with the accusations flying from his lips. "For god's sake, Natches, you've not exactly lived a safe and peaceful life from what I've heard."

"Maybe that's what I wanted for you and your sisters," he snapped back at her. "I didn't want you facing the danger the women we love have had to face."

"And who are you to dictate the life I was meant to live?" she retorted fiercely. "If something happens to Graham, I'll never forgive myself. It will be my fault."

"Like hell," Graham snapped, glaring back at her. "This is no one's fault, Lyrica, but the one who began it."

"That won't change how I feel," she argued back, silently daring him to attempt to send her away. "Don't you understand that, Graham? If I hadn't sent that letter then the chances of them guessing at a weakness would have been nil. I put the ammunition in their hands, and the fact that I didn't mean to do it doesn't count. If I leave, they'll still follow me." She pressed her hand to her chest in emphasis. "It's me they're after to make you pay for attempting to stop them from committing a crime. If they can't find me, then they'll just wait, because I can't stay hidden forever." She shook her head at the thought, at the sheer desperate loneliness that would fill her. "I can't live like that. I'll face what happens here, with you. At least when it's over, I'll know some bastard didn't make me cower."

Son of a bitch, how was he supposed to protect her when she stood in front of him like that, her eyes blazing with courage and a certainty that this was her fight, even though it wasn't.

And she had no intention of leaving. He could see it in her eyes, in her expression. She wouldn't walk away, and if they made her, she wouldn't stay away.

"They're right, baby," he said softly. "If you go with them, just for a little while . . ."

"While you set yourself up as a target instead?" Tears glittered in her eyes as she seemed to tighten her arms around herself. "And that's what you'll do, isn't it, Graham?"

"It's what I'm trained to do," he admitted, wishing he knew why his chest was so tight, why he wanted nothing more than just to hold her.

"It won't matter what you're trained to do." She shook her head. "They're after me, not you." Her gaze moved to her brother and cousin then. "I suggest we figure out exactly how to use the fact that they probably have no idea that we know what's going on or why they're targeting me. You know what Graham's facing now. Help him fix it. And I'm not leaving here until it is fixed."

She turned and walked slowly to the doorway, then turned back to stare at Graham for long, silent seconds.

"I'll be upstairs." Turning to her brother, then to Natches, she gave them a small smile, one filled with love and regret. "Let me know when the two of you have a plan. Leave me out of the loop, and I promise you, I won't forget it."

She left the room then, catching Natches's grimace and knowing that had been exactly what was on his mind. His first inclination was to wrap those he loved in cotton and surround them with bubble wrap to keep them safe.

He may as well get used to the fact that she had no intention of being a spectator to her own life.

It would be good practice for him, she decided. Several months before, his daughter, Bliss, had confided to Lyrica her dream of joining Homeland Security or the FBI when she was older. She wanted to bring men such as the ones who'd attacked her aunt Eve to justice.

She hadn't told her father yet.

Lyrica sighed as she headed back to Graham's suite. Maybe Bliss should wait awhile, a long while, before informing her father of those plans.

EIGHTEEN

"Hit me again, Natches, and I promise, I'll hit back," Graham informed the other man mildly as he watched Natches's fist clench atop the table. "And I'm twenty years younger than you are. I promise, I do hit harder."

Natches's hand jerked, one hard finger pointing back at Graham as he snarled. "You are becoming a pain in the fucking ass!"

"I thought you weren't supposed to drop the F-bomb." Graham arched his brow in query at the memory of Chaya's disapproval whenever Natches used the word. "And that pain you're feeling is probably hemorrhoids. I hear stress from screwing with everyone's lives can actually cause those."

Natches turned to Dawg with a fierce glare. "I don't like him anymore. Get Lyrica. We're leaving."

Dawg breathed out as though tired and shook his head, exasperation marking his expression and filling the pale green of his eyes.

"Lyrica's not leaving." Rising from the table and carrying his cup to the sink, Graham felt certain that the danger revolving around Lyrica had begun in Afghanistan.

"Graham." Dawg sighed heavily again, and Graham could hear the objection rising from him.

"Removing her from sight isn't going to help," Elijah said, choosing that moment to weigh in. "Just as Lyrica said, the focus is on her. Besides, trust me, once Doogan learns the specifics of this, he won't allow it."

"Chatham Doogan can kiss my ass!" Natches enunciated savagely, his lips pulling back from his teeth in a primal snarl. "That fucker gives me acid reflux for real."

"And I may agree with that wholeheartedly"—Elijah's tone turned to ice, a rare occurrence for the laid-back former Texan—"but be that as it may, I'm still a duly sworn agent and I will be reporting this. Lyrica's a friend, Natches, and this group has killed highly trained, skilled soldiers. She doesn't have a hope of surviving if we don't end this here."

Natches moved suddenly from his chair, throwing it back with savage disregard for the wood as he stalked across the room, his expression enraged. When he swung around on Elijah, Graham's brows lifted in surprise.

"That loyal to the agency, are you? Well, you can just pack the fuck up and get the hell out of town, boy," Natches ordered the younger man. "Your services sure as hell won't be needed once this is finished."

Sharp and mocking, Elijah's grunt of amusement had Graham watching the scene in interest rather than putting a stop to it.

"That's it, Mackay," Elijah stated silkily. "Throw your weight around and see where it gets you with me. Or with Doogan. He's not Cranston, and I'm not Harley—remember that."

The air seemed to grow thick with nearing violence now. Coming to his feet, Elijah sauntered to the back door, his expression harder, colder than Graham remembered ever seeing it.

"You don't know what the hell you're talking about," Natches growled, the sound dangerous, a warning that had Graham and Dawg both tensing now at the impending Mackay eruption.

"Don't I?" Elijah asked softly, opening the door as he stared back at the older man, his gaze filled with a flinty lack of mercy as it flicked over the youngest Mackay cousin. "Did you even wonder where he went when he disappeared after that beating you arranged for him?" He laughed, the sound sending a chill racing down Graham's back. "Tell me, has Zoey forgiven you for it?"

The door closed sharply behind Elijah, the silence he left behind him thick and heavy.

The second the other man left the room, Natches turned to Dawg slowly, watching as his cousin came out of his chair, the older man's expression heavy.

"Let's find Rowdy," Dawg announced then. "We'll take care of this little problem Graham brought home with him, make sure Lyrica's safe, then we're going to have a little talk, cuz."

It was evident Dawg was unaware of Harley or the beating Natches had evidently arranged.

Without waiting for an answer, Dawg moved from the kitchen and headed for the front door. Moments later, the sound of the door closing with deliberate patience sent a small flinch through the muscles at Natches's jaw.

"You don't seem the type to arrange a beating, Natches," Graham remarked, actually feeling an ounce or two of compassion at the heavy look on Natches's face.

"Well," Natches murmured as he propped his hands on his hips, hung his head, and shook it slowly, "I'll be damned. That's what I thought, too. That would have been a waste of my time, don't you think?"

Leaning back against the counter, arms folded over his chest as he crossed his ankles, Graham contemplated the other man's expression thoughtfully.

"Don't remember it, huh?" he asked.

It really wasn't Natches's style. He liked exercising his own fists whenever the opportunity arose.

"I don't," Natches murmured, frowning. "But you know what?"

"Hmm?" Graham watched him closely.

"Whatever the hell he's talking about, he's right about one thing. Zoey hasn't forgiven any of us."

A hard shake of his head and Natches straightened, his arms dropping as he headed for the kitchen door, following Dawg's departure. "Keep her safe." Deadly menace filled the Mackay's tone. "I'm sure we'll be back."

Graham remained silent as the other man stalked from the house, the door closing a bit louder that time. Natches wasn't known for his temperance. His temper, yes.

With their departure the heaviness in the atmosphere of the house dissipated, and Graham found himself finally able to draw a deep breath.

No one said dealing with Mackays was easy. Doogan had once sworn that working with them was like facing demented zombies whose main aim was the destruction of a person's sanity rather than his life.

"Dawg was spinning his tires as he pulled out, which usually means he's pissed off with Natches," Lyrica said as she reentered the kitchen, that flirty little skirt caressing the flesh of her silky thighs.

The little white cotton tank was tucked into the low waistband, the strappy sandals making her feet look more delicate than normal.

Restraining a sigh, Graham felt his cock swelling behind the zipper of his jeans and the arousal beginning to tighten his body again.

"Who's Harley?" he asked.

She knew who he was talking about, at least. For a second, Lyrica's eyes flickered with sadness as her expression became more somber, with a hint of pain.

"Someone Zoey cared very much about." A bittersweet smile tipped her lips. "Someone who left before she ever knew what she felt for him. Why?"

He shook his head. Zoey's life and issues with her brother and cousins would have to wait until later. "The name just came up." Pushing away from the counter, he motioned for her to follow him. "Come to the office with me. I want to show you some pictures, see if you've seen any of these men."

"The men you suspect were involved in the theft?" She moved beside him, the somber look on her face as she glanced up at him clenching at his chest.

"If one of them has made contact with you, it will narrow the field down to figuring out who, if anyone, was working with Betts. The faster we capture them, the faster you'll be safe."

The faster she would be out of his life, Lyrica thought painfully as she moved into the office across the foyer, the door closing behind them.

Leading the way to the wide desk on the other side of the room, Graham seemed more distant, harder than normal, as though he were deliberately drawing away from her. And he was, she thought. Flavors weren't lifetime commitments, she reminded herself. They were a moment out of his time—intense, a relief from whatever hunger plagued him.

She could live with that for now.

For now.

"Here." Sitting down at the desk, he pulled a thick folder from the file drawer at the side and slapped it to the top of the table before sitting back in his chair and patting his lap with a rakish grin that erased that distance with a suddenness she found completely shocking. "You can sit here."

On his lap?

They would not be looking at that file long, but the experience promised to be more than the frightening venture she'd imagined.

"Think that's safe, do you?"

"I didn't say it was safe," he assured her with another of those crooked, far too sexy grins he used against her at the oddest times. "I said you could sit."

"What if I can't concentrate while I'm sitting there?" she asked then, her voice lowering. "It looks far too . . . pleasurable a seat."

He was hard. The outline of his erection beneath his jeans had her heart pounding, need heating her thighs and the sensitive flesh between.

"Just turn around there, sweetheart, and sit," he invited. "Let's see if I can't make it even more pleasurable than you imagined."

Turning her back to him slowly, a knowing grin tugged at her lips and she sat slowly, her legs resting outside his as he pulled her back against him and arranged her position to suit him.

"Comfortable?" he asked, her back snug against his chest, the hard wedge of his shaft pressing between the cheeks of her rear and rising along her lower back.

"Or something," she murmured.

Trying to control her breathing was all but impossible, and there was no lowering the rate of her heartbeat. It was thumping like a drum being used with a heavy hand.

"You feel good against me, Lyrica." Lifting her hands, he placed them on the arms of the leather chair as his legs spread, parting hers farther as he leaned forward. "Now, let's see if you know anyone here."

As he flipped the file open, the first picture stared out at her.

Commander Jimmy Dorne. A ruffian, she thought.

A bully.

"I'm pretty certain Dorne was her lover," Graham revealed. "He was enraged when she died."

Barrel-chested, his blond hair thinning, the man wore an expression that was faintly cruel. And the woman who had betrayed Graham preferred *that* over the man currently running his fingertips along the edge of the skirt Lyrica wore?

That was not a mistake she would have made.

There were several more pictures of him, in combat gear as well as in street clothes. In each one, the cruelty she could see in his hard eyes and unsmiling expression was apparent.

"I've not seen him." She shook her head. "And if I had, I would have remembered him simply to ensure I avoided him."

His fingers paused in their caresses before slipping beneath the edge of her skirt and to the inside of her thigh. Evidently he liked the answer, she thought as her heart rate began to pick up quickly.

Several dozen pictures of other men, all soldiers, eyes hard, a few bitter, followed. Staring at each closely, Lyrica made certain they weren't men she had come in contact with at any time.

Not that they were men she would have been attracted to at any rate. They weren't Graham.

The next pictures were not of soldiers. Soft green eyes stared out from the photos, framed by heavy, thick black hair cut short to frame the delicate features of the woman whose pouty lips and sensual expression seemed to shout "experience."

She didn't look cruel, petty, or mean. She looked a little lost amid the sensual knowledge in her eyes, though, as if happiness wasn't something she had ever attained.

This was Betts Laren.

She stared into the camera as though to seduce the photographer in each photo, always aware, Lyrica thought. This was a woman who always seemed to be aware that she was never alone.

Lyrica's resemblance to her was unmistakable. She could have been a distant Mackay relative, it was so close.

"I do look like her." Lyrica breathed in slowly, deeply, to hold back the flash of pain that he could have loved this woman, even unknowingly.

"No." He sighed. "She looked like you, Lyrica. I took one look at her and all I saw was her resemblance to you." Graham brushed her hair from her shoulder, his lips moving over the bared flesh there with a light, destructive caress. "I left here that summer with the scent of you in my head, the hunger for you eating me alive, and a month later she walked into my tent with that same secretive little smile you have, without the innocence I was so damned afraid of breaking in you. I wanted you so damned bad it was eating me away from the inside out."

"I wasn't running from you," she reminded him, her head lowering, eyes closing as his lips moved to the back of her neck.

"Maybe I was the one running, Lyrica," he stated softly. "I never even thought to question the dozen similarities she displayed to your expressions, your mannerisms. I should have."

"I sent the letter the week you left for Afghanistan." Her lashes fluttered as his fingertips trailed up the insides of both thighs, his short nails rasping the sensitive flesh. "I wanted you to know . . . I missed you."

That wasn't exactly what the letter had said.

"A real letter?" The scrape of his beard against her shoulder sent a shiver racing up her spine.

"Written in real ink with my real hand," she drawled a second before her breath caught at the little nip he delivered to the shoulder he'd been caressing.

"I wish I could have read the letter," he whispered as the hands caressing her thighs moved higher, to the edge of her panties.

His fingers were a whisper stroke of pleasure against the damp material of her panties. Her inner muscles clenched at the sweeping sensation of static heat and aching want. Even her nerve endings felt restless and far too close to the surface of her flesh.

Gripping the arms of the chair, Lyrica surrendered to him, to whatever he wanted, to one more memory to hold for the day when he no longer wanted her.

While his fingertips played above the silk of her panties, tormenting the flesh beneath and drawing more of the slick, wet heat from her body, his other hand moved to her side, tugging at the material of the shirt and pulling it over her breasts.

"That's it, baby," he whispered at her ear. "Just lie back and enjoy it. Do you know how many nights I've jacked off imagining you just lying back, taking the pleasure I have to give you?"

"You didn't have to imagine," she whispered. "I was here."

"And so sweet, so innocent." He breathed against her ear a second before nipping it erotically, then placing a gentle kiss to the heated flesh. "I didn't want to hurt you. I didn't want to lose you in my life, Lyrica. I couldn't imagine that."

Lyrica closed her eyes, fighting back hope, pain, everything but the pleasure.

"Sweet Lyrica." His lips trailed down her neck, his hand cupping the sensitive weight of her breast.

The feel of his finger and thumb gripping the nipple through the thin material of her bra with a firm, erotic pressure brought a cry from her lips. Arching into him, her hands clenched on the arms of the chair as pleasure suffused her. Her body tightened further when the hand caressing her thigh tugged at her panties until she helped him rid her of the material.

Dropping it to the floor, his fingers returned, parting the folds, stroking them before gently rimming the clenched entrance.

"Please . . ." she whispered, moving against the probing caressing. "Oh god, Graham. It feels so good."

More of her heated dampness spilled to the fingers stroking the sensitive entrance to her inner depths.

"That's my baby," he groaned, two fingers spearing immediately inside the wet depths of her vagina as she arched back, crying hoarsely at the pleasure suddenly tearing through her. "Show me how wet and hot that pretty pussy gets for me."

Scandalizing, wicked, the words sent a pulse of pleasure to clench at the inner muscles and the swollen bud of her clit. Her juices spilled from her, rushing over his fingers to saturate them with slick heat.

Each stroke worked inside her, used the natural lubrication to press deeper, to stretch her with his caresses. The pleasure-pain of each impalement had her body stretching, tightening around his incredibly satisfying stroking fingers.

His fingers pulled back, nearly releasing from her intimate depths and pulling a mewling cry of protest from her. He couldn't stop yet. Waves of a nearing climax were building in her, pounding at her clit, making her crazy for the addictive pleasure of the release he could give her.

His lips settled at the bend of her neck and shoulder, the rasp of his short beard pulling a moan from her lips. His lips kissed the flesh there gently, taking a lazy, sensual taste of her as her breath caught in her chest.

Then a harsh, desperate cry tore from her lips.

His fingers thrust inside her, stretching her with wicked pleasure as his teeth gripped the surprisingly sensitive tendon beneath
his lips and bit her with hungry demand.

She came.

That fast, wailing with the pleasure as her body tightened,
jerked, then dissolved around his fingers in a rush of fiery heat.

Prolonging the excruciating pleasure with each fierce thrust
inside the gripping tissue, he gave little mercy, holding her on the
peak of release until she was shuddering with it. Ecstasy pum-
meled her in remorseless waves as sensual shudders clenched her
muscles, locking her in place against him until he allowed the
tremors to ease, allowed her to find her breath.

She was only barely aware of his movements. The release of his
jeans, her awareness that he was quickly rolling a condom over
the length of his cock.

Oh god, she couldn't come again. She was wasted, her pussy
weak from the spasms still echoing through it.

But as soon as the clenching, ecstatic pulses of release eased
moments later, she was suddenly thrown into a catastrophic race
back into the flames.

Lifting her, Graham impaled her on the iron-hard length of the
erection he'd released from his jeans. The heavy, fiery penetration
was a shock to the senses, a pleasure bordering on agony as the
chaotic, sensual storm began swirling through her again.

"Oh god, Graham." The inner flesh shuddered around the girth
impaling her.

Her heated, slick response spilled around his flesh, easing his
way as he pushed inside her in that one hard, fierce thrust.

Resting her head back on his shoulders, she dug the tips of her
feet into the carpet beneath them and moved against him. Shifting,
lifting, falling, following the hard grip of his hands, she rode him
with sensual demand. With the feel of each throbbing inch burying

itself inside her, stroking sensitive, greedy flesh, stretching her with a blaze of heat as she met each inward stroke, Lyrica knew this erotic dance would be one she would never forget.

"Open your eyes, baby," he whispered as she felt the chair moving, turning to the side. "Look at me."

Drowsy, heavy with pleasure, her lashes lifted, her gaze focusing on the mirror she hadn't realized hung on the wall across from them.

A whimper escaped her parted lips as she watched.

The sight of herself sprawled back against him, her thighs parted over his, her body all but bare, was shocking. Her expression was unfamiliar. Flushed, drowsy, and sensual. She looked like a sacrifice to his hunger, lost in it, overwhelmed by the pleasure.

Graham lifted the edge of the skirt that had fallen over her thighs, pulling it to her hips with one hand as the other tugged one leg farther out, revealing more to the reflection across from them.

"Graham." She didn't know if she was turned on or too shocked to know what to feel.

With her skirt out of the way, he lowered both hands to her thighs and tugged, pulling her legs farther apart to reveal the sight of her impalement.

Stretched, the folds of her intimate lips parted, his dark flesh penetrated her as her juices clung to the base with a loving caress.

"Watch, baby," he whispered at her ear again as his hands moved to her hips once again.

He lifted her slowly, so slowly. Lyrica's eyes widened as he began pulling free of her, watching as slick moisture coated his cock, watching as it pulled from her body even as her pussy clenched, tightening around the departure.

Graham pulled back until only the very tip of his cock lingered at her entrance and she could see the dark crest throbbing, the heavy veins pounding with the fierce beat of his heart. He looked too large, the bulging crest throbbing and dark, almost angry-looking as it remained tucked against her entrance.

Then he was lowering her and Lyrica couldn't help but watch the intimate invasion. Watch as her flesh flowed around him, stretching for him, taking him as a whimpering cry fell from her lips and she felt herself spilling around him again. Exploding around his cock, the pleasure pulsing through her with such force that her body jerked with every internal explosion. Moisture eased from her as he thrust in and out of her, the hard flesh gleaming thicker, richer until she was forced to close her eyes against the rocking pleasure.

"That's it," he groaned. "That's it, baby. Suck my dick with that pretty little pussy. Fuck. Yes. Ah hell, Lyrica . . ."

His hips were moving beneath her, thrusting hard, spearing inside her with desperate lunges as his fingers found her clit and sent her rolling into another explosive orgasm.

She felt him coming as her clit exploded beneath his fingers. He erupted with a hard flex of the shaft buried inside her, heat suddenly jetting against the too sensitive tissue, moist and so sensual, so erotic, that her womb clenched and spasmed again, throwing her relentlessly into another explosion that tightened her vagina around the already pulsing length of his cock.

She shouldn't feel it like that, she thought distantly. Not with the condom she'd glimpsed between his flesh and hers. She shouldn't feel his release like fiery caresses filling her.

She shouldn't . . . but it was so good. The pleasure was so exacting, so deep that the fluttering response of her vagina clenched at his flesh again, holding him and rippling around him until the fiercely engorged flesh finally stilled.

Exhausted, completely unraveled and boneless, she wanted nothing more than to sleep. Nothing else mattered, to the point that she closed her eyes. Just for a minute, she promised herself.

Just a little nap until she caught her breath. Darkness whispered over her and stole her into a warm, sheltering place of utter peace and dreamless rest.

Lifting her, Graham turned her in his arms, sheltering her against his chest as he managed to restore his clothes enough to get her to the bedroom. Lifting her in his arms, he carried her upstairs, wondering if his knees had the strength to make it to the bedroom.

He laid her on the bed, pulled the remnants of the pretty skirt from her hips, and for the second time that day collected a damp cloth to dry the perspiration from her body. Between her thighs he cleaned the mix of her silky response and his semen from her, feeling none of the overwhelming panic he would have felt with any other woman.

He knew the moment the condom burst. Hell, he'd felt the release boiling in his balls, had known despite the release he'd had that morning, he was going to explode inside her so damned hard it would steal his mind.

And he'd been right.

His senses had completely overloaded as he watched himself fuck her, watched his cock stretch her until he was certain he had to be hurting her. Instead she'd cried out for more, coming around him with such snug inner spasms it had stolen his control completely.

Finishing cleaning her off, he shed his clothes and removed the ruined condom before pulling a pair of cotton pants on and returning to the office.

He'd left the file on the desk and the office open. Instead of storing it in the drawer now, though, he gathered it together and left the office with it. Locking the door behind him, Graham pulled the phone from the pocket of his pants at the vibration of a call coming through.

Checking the caller ID, he answered it quickly.

"Everything okay?" he asked Elijah as he moved up the stairs.

"Everything's clear." There was still a thread of anger in the other man's voice. "I wanted to check before returning Doogan's call, though. He's demanding a report."

Of course he was, Graham thought with a heavy sigh. "This isn't something I want to hide from him, Elijah," he answered. "She's too important to risk simply because her family and Doogan clash."

"Natches has his moments. They're either dumb ones or smart ones, no in between, and the dumb ones seem more prevalent," the other man stated harshly. "He hasn't changed much over the years, from what I understand."

"Not a whole lot," Graham admitted. "The dumb moments aren't nearly as numerous as they were before Rowdy and Kelly married, though, from what Dad said before he died. Rowdy and his cousins used to be some hell-raisers."

"Yeah, now they're just hell to be around," the agent grunted.

"There is that." Graham almost chuckled at the thought. "By the way, when reporting to Doogan, don't give him the name of the contact that brought the information in." He refrained from mentioning Tracker's name. "Doogan doesn't need to worry himself over some things. That contact is one of those things."

"No kidding." Graham could almost see Elijah pushing his fingers through his hair and rubbing at his neck. "Okay, I'll call the bastard back. I put a few more cameras up while I was out and tied the entire program into this number. If you hear it ping, check it. Your number's secondary and it might mean I've somehow been compromised and you're in deep shit."

Reentering his bedroom, Graham moved into the huge walk-in closet just inside the doorway, where he'd installed the monitors and controls to his own hidden camera system.

"Got it," he murmured. "Check in on schedule and keep your eyes open."

"Always," Elijah promised.

Disconnecting the call, Graham closed the closet door, moved to the wall behind it, and depressed the hidden release there. The wall slid down soundlessly, revealing a large security monitor and a dozen different views of the property surrounding the house.

Elijah was stationed on the hill across from the house, looking down on an angle that afforded him a view of the back gardens and pool area as well as the side of the house and front drive. The other views were clear of human intrusion, and that was all that mattered at the moment.

He depressed the control once again and the wall slid back into place but the restless feeling inside him still plagued him.

Something wasn't right. It was nagging at him, refusing to come together. Something he couldn't quite put his finger on.

Something he had a feeling could very well end up tipping the scales out of his favor and into his enemy's if he didn't figure it out quickly. If he didn't figure it out before he lost Lyrica forever.

NINETEEN

Emerging from the bathroom several mornings later, her only covering the lacy black panties with a tiny, vividly pink bow just above the cleft of her rear and a matching bra sporting a bow between her breasts, Lyrica came to a stop at the sight of Graham stepping into the bedroom wearing nothing but loose black cotton pajama bottoms. Carrying a large tray in his hands with several covered dishes, he was obviously surprised to see her awake and showered.

"Breakfast?" A flush washed through her at the gleam of interest reflected in the glitter of gold in his eyes.

"Breakfast works." Clearing her throat, she moved for the silky robe she'd left lying on the bottom of the bed.

"Please don't." The rasp of command that filled his tone was tempered only by the hunger that filled his gaze. "You look perfect the way you are."

Perfect the way she was? Oh Lord, she was barely dressed. The lacy lingerie was no more than a tease, covering only what it had to.

Moving to the bed, Graham set the large tray in the middle of it before carefully removing the covers he'd placed over the food.

Fluffy scrambled eggs, perfectly fried bacon, diced fresh tomatoes, and golden brown toast.

"Come on." Motioning to the bed with a jerk of his head, he climbed into the center and waited.

She didn't make him wait long.

This was another memory for her to tuck away and take out when it was over and she was forced to return to reality once again.

"No sandwiches this morning?" She grinned, secretly hoping she'd never see another sandwich in her life.

"Kye and I eat out a lot." He chuckled as she tasted the eggs and bacon and almost moaned at the taste of home-cooked food.

She could see why, she admitted, as the taste of the fresh tomato exploded against her tongue. For something so simple, the meal was exquisite.

For the next few minutes they were silent, the food consuming their attention until finally Lyrica sat back, replete, and eyed the amount still left on the plates.

He must have scrambled a whole carton of eggs, she thought in amusement.

Lifting the coffee cup nearest her to her lips, she sipped and hummed a sound of appreciation. Just the way she liked it. A little coffee with her cream and sugar.

"How do you drink it like that?" He chuckled, lifting his own and bringing it to his lips.

No sugar, no cream, just straight, rich coffee.

Lyrica suppressed a shudder, but not the doubtful look she gave him. "It's a little strong for me," she admitted, holding back what she was sure would have been an embarrassing giggle.

Setting the cup on the bedside table, Graham moved the tray to the dresser before returning to the bed, propping himself against the headboard as he retrieved the coffee and watched her closely.

"You surprise me," he said then. "I expected you to become bored while you were here. I didn't expect you'd find so many ways to entertain yourself while we were trying to track down whoever's responsible for the attempts against you."

The night before, she had finished a spreadsheet she'd been trying to find time to complete for Dawg's lumber store. The night before that, she'd finished the new menu layout for the restaurant Natches and Janey owned. A detailed supply list was still awaiting her attention for Natches's garage in town as well as an advertising plan for the marina Rowdy and his father, her uncle Ray, owned.

"I keep a lot of little projects for downtime," she admitted, curling her legs to her side as she leaned on the pillows propped against the headboard and faced him. "Between the four main businesses Mackay Enterprises began with, and the two apartment buildings Dawg, Natches, and Rowdy bought, a pawn shop Janey had to have, and a convenience store Eve and Brogan just added, there's always a new program needed, a shopping cart to set up, or an inventory system to improve."

Tilting his head, the dark blond and light brown strands of hair falling over his forehead, he watched her curiously now. The short length of his beard and mustache, his bare chest.

He was the image of a rakish pirate, scars and all.

Reaching out, she touched a circular scar at his shoulder, a whisper-caress over flesh that seemed not long healed. Below it was a long, thin scar that the light mat of curls covering his chest didn't hide near as well as one might think they would.

"That one was a long time ago." Remaining still, one broad palm resting on her ankle, the other resting over his bent knee, he watched her with a faint smile. "Dad and I were hiking above the house. I was fourteen, bouncing around, showing the old man up." Fondness touched his expression for a moment. "I tripped on something, damned if I remember what it was, and went head over heels back down the damned incline. When I came to a stop, my shirt was sliced open and my chest along with it. The first time I ever saw Dad scared."

There was a warmth to his voice as he spoke of his father.

"Kye rarely mentions your parents," she said softly. "And there are no pictures in the house of them except the one in the living room."

A single five-by-seven that sat next to the formal couch on a cherry side table.

"Kye's still angry, I think." He sighed. "She was only fourteen when they died. I was still in the Marines with several more years to go on an additional tour I'd taken. She was home alone when Zeke, Rogue, and Shane had to come out and tell her they were gone."

"She seems very bitter," Lyrica observed. "I mentioned them once, and she completely shut down. It's one of the few subjects she refuses to discuss with me."

"She doesn't discuss them with anyone," he admitted as his thumb stroked against her ankle almost absently, his gaze seeming to settle on the past rather than the present. "She and Mom were incredibly close. Girlish secrets, shopping trips." He breathed out heavily. "She was here when they left that night. She heard them arguing about the trip. Mom hadn't wanted to leave because Kye

had a dance that weekend and she didn't want to chance returning home late. She's still very angry at Dad, for convincing Mom
to go."

His head settled back against the wood of the headboard as he
focused on Lyrica then. "It was a hard time for her, for both of us."

"You were close to your father then? And your mother was
close to Kye?"

He laughed at that. "That wasn't what I said," he pointed out.
"Kye was their baby; I was their son. She was the surprise they
were certain they'd never have another chance for, and she was a
delicate, fragile little girly girl." He shook his head as he smiled.
"Dad, though, he was a very distant person emotionally, but he
loved us. It just wasn't a love he was able to show. He kept me
with him for the most part while he worked on the farm, so I guess
I didn't get to know Mom nearly as well."

A shadow touched his gaze then, as though some thought had
spoiled the memories he was allowing himself to touch.

"My mother always spoiled us with love. She still does," Lyrica
said softly. "We didn't have much, but we never missed it. Mom
made so many things an adventure and tried so hard to ease the
nightmare that Chandler's visits made in our lives."

She looked down at the hand covering her ankle, the broad,
strong fingers, the way his thumb brushed against the skin covering her anklebone.

"You have very gentle hands," she said softly. "Chandler didn't.
He was very harsh and always so very angry."

Thankfully, the man who'd fathered her and her sisters hadn't
been around much.

"Elijah said Brogan mentioned that he had you and your sisters taken from your mother at one time?" he asked her gently.

Lyrica inhaled slowly, deeply. "It was horrible," she admitted,
shaking her head at that memory. "We were placed in foster care

with Kenny and Lucy Tannley." She almost shuddered at the thought of them. "Kenny was a drunk that leered at Eve and Piper like an animal stares at meat. Lucy thought foster children were no more than her personal servants and maids."

They had slept in the basement on a few thin blankets. Eve and Piper had kept Lyrica and tiny little Zoey between them and the three of them listened to Zoey as she cried most of the night for their momma.

"I'm sorry." The apology had her lifting her head to stare back at him.

"It's over." She shrugged as she pushed the past behind her once again. "There were a few bad experiences, but we survived. And we survived intact."

"Dawg raged for weeks after Timothy brought you home with your mother. I was home that week. I was actually at the bar when Natches, Rowdy, Alex, and Zeke were called to collect his drunk ass."

She winced at that. "It's the one and only time Dawg got drunk after his marriage to Christa. I felt so bad for that."

"He loves the four of you, probably about as much as he loves his daughter," he told her. "It broke his heart that he hadn't known about you or your mother."

"We had no idea Chandler had another family. That we had a brother or cousins. Though I guess we should have. Momma said the marriage the village priest performed was never made official though. Timothy checked. It didn't surprise her, or us."

He was petting her.

His hand stroked her ankle, brushed over her calf, caressing, just gentle touches meant to ease memories that might hurt.

"Dawg's our hero." She grinned up at him. "Him, Natches and Rowdy, Uncle Ray. When Timothy first put us on that plane and told us he was taking us to our brother, we were terrified. We'd found out about him weeks before when Eve went searching for Chandler. We had no idea he was dead. And Momma was so sick." That was a bad memory. There had been days, nights, when they were certain she would suffocate, it had been so hard for her to breathe. "But, from the moment we arrived, we were family."

"Everyone who knows him and Natches agrees the four of you were put on this earth to prepare those two for their daughters' adulthood." He chuckled.

"Oh god, don't go there." She hung her head and groaned in amused horror. "We're not practice; we're their training in how to torture their daughters fully once they realize there's life out there that doesn't include Daddy. They should have had more kids."

"Why didn't they?" Graham was amused, almost chuckling at the thought.

"I think they might have, if it hadn't been for our arrival." She did laugh then. "Right off the bat Eve and Piper were slipping out at night, testing their wings, testing their freedom. I think they terrified Dawg and Natches, though Rowdy has always found it highly amusing. So I imagine they decided one daughter was enough and they'd probably be exhausted by the time they managed to force the girls into convents that no boys could possibly breach. We exhausted them."

He smiled with genuine warmth. "I can't imagine that." He cupped her cheek, his thumb brushing against her lips. "Natches can see the beauty his daughter is going to be in you. Do you know how many rednecks around here are terrified to even look your way?"

"You weren't," she pointed out, leaning closer, wanting a taste of his kiss again. Wanting his touch, his warmth and strength.

"I was terrified," he admitted, though his eyes told another story. "Natches threatened to cut my dick off if he caught me around you."

Disbelief shot through her, causing her to pause as she drew closer to him. "He did not!"

"Oh, yes, he did." He didn't wait for her to complete the journey. He pulled her to him, grinning down at her as she ended up against his chest. "I decided the risk was worth it. He's not as good as he once was, I'm sure. And I can't see Rowdy helping him, so I figured my man parts might be reasonably safe."

"I would have protected your man parts." Nodding, she stared up at him with all seriousness as laughter tried to tug at her lips. "Trust me. I would have never let him get anywhere near them."

"Had plans for them, did you?" Hunger gleamed in his eyes, filled his expression.

"Well, I definitely intended to put them to use," she admitted, her breath becoming hard, uneven at the feel of him releasing the catch of her bra.

"Put them to use now," he whispered, one hand cupping the back of her head and holding her in place as his lips lowered to hers. "You just go ahead and put them to hard use, baby. I promise not to object in the slightest."

His lips took hers, moving against them with a slow, heated hunger that had a whispery moan falling from her lips as she lifted to him.

The feel of him smoothing the bra straps over her arms and pulling the material from her body didn't make much of an impression. But when he pulled her closer, her nipples brushing against the soft rasp of his chest hair, the pleasure went so deep, so fast, her stomach clenched with it.

Parting her lips with his tongue, Graham tasted her kiss, drawing the hunger and need that were lying still but aware inside her fully free. Within seconds he had her burning, her clit swelling, the tender flesh between her thighs growing slick and wet as one hand smoothed to the lace-covered curve of her rear to cup it erotically.

His hand slid to her thigh and lifted her leg over him until her thighs straddled his, the sensitive, lace-covered folds of her pussy pressing against the engorged length of his cock as it rose below the thin material of the cotton pants he wore.

Pulling back, breaking the incredibly heated kiss, his lips moved to her jaw, to her neck.

"You burn me alive," he growled a second before his teeth raked against the sensitive skin beneath her jaw. "Like the sexiest fire in the world."

"I can't think when you touch me." She was breathless, pleasure racing through her system and overtaking her again. Holding out against the exquisite sensations was impossible.

She was greedy, Lyrica admitted.

Greedy and so hungry for more of him that the need was almost painful.

Sliding her hands along his shoulders, her nails rasping against the tough flesh, Lyrica tilted her head back, giving him free rein to the tender flesh of her neck. A gasp escaped as he cupped her breasts at the same time, his thumbs and fingers finding the hard points of her nipples and tugging at them firmly.

A burning, erotic fire attacked the tender points, ricocheting through her system to strike at the swollen knot of nerve endings between her thighs.

"Like that, pretty baby?" he groaned against her neck.

"Love that," she whimpered, her nails digging into his shoulders, her hips moving helplessly against the hard flesh of his cock grinding between her thighs.

She loved him.

She was lost to him, and Lyrica knew it.

Every part of her was lost to him.

Then his lips moved until they covered one nipple, drawing

strongly on the swollen tip as he sucked at her erotically. As he swirled his tongue around the nerve-laden tip of her breast, his gaze held hers, staring up at her as he sucked at her with increasing heat and hunger.

"Graham." She whispered his name, couldn't help herself.

Drawing back and releasing her flesh from the tortured pleasure, his hands moved to her hips and the elastic lace of her panties. Before he could remove them, or tear them from her, she let her nails rake down his chest, her own head lowering.

It was her hunger now. Her need to bring him the same riotous pleasure he was giving her. The same sense of erotic chaos building through her senses.

Finding the hard, muscular contours of his chest, she moved lower, easing back along his thighs as his hands speared into the hair at the back of her head. Hardened, flat male nipples drew her attention first. As she lashed at one tight disc with her hungry tongue, his groan sent a surging increase of need racing through her senses.

She loved the pleasure he gave her. Loved it, ached for it. She was becoming addicted to it and determined he would never forget her particular flavor once she was gone.

Moving lower, her senses becoming drugged with searing hunger, her heart began racing with sensual power. Beneath her touch Graham tightened. His hard body lifted to her lips as they moved to the powerful planes of his abdomen.

He couldn't take his eyes off her.

For years, as shameful as he'd known it was, he'd lain back beneath his lovers when they'd touched him like this and imagined it was Lyrica. Imagined her lips touched him. Imagined her nails were rasping over his flesh as she lowered the waistband of the thin pants he wore over the pounding length of his cock.

"Fuck!" The groan was torn from his lips as her hair, like warm, living silk, brushed over his sensitive length.

"Ah hell, Lyrica, baby . . ." His body tightened to a breaking point as her hot little tongue moved lovingly over the crest of his cock.

Licking, tasting him, she drew the bead of pre-cum from the slit at the tip as her emerald gaze darkened in rising hunger. A heated flush covered her face, and drowsy, sensual, sexual pleasure suffused her expression.

When her swollen lips parted and sucked the engorged, darkened head of his cock into her mouth, he nearly lost his control over the semen pounding in his balls. She was loving it. He could see it in her eyes. Loving the pleasure she was giving him. Loving the tension and rising hunger building inside him that was impossible to hide.

The lashing pleasure enclosing the sensitive, too tight crown drew a hard, agonized grimace of pleasure to his face. Jaw tight, his thighs bunching, he felt the electric heat surrounding him, searing into his cock as she sucked him deep. Her tongue stroked as her mouth worked over the heavy width. Drawing him in, drawing back, taking him until he knew the full depths of her mouth with an intimate eroticism he wouldn't have expected.

"That's it," he groaned, the sound resembling a rasp of erotic torture. "Suck it deep, baby. Give me that pretty mouth."

Those pretty, pouty lips stretched around the width of his flesh, consuming the crown and working it with such pleasure that holding back was becoming next to impossible. His hips moved to her suckling, her caressing, the moist heat of her mouth causing his cock to throb, his balls aching to release.

Tightening his grip on her hair as he leaned back into the pillows behind him, his hips lifted, thrusting shallowly as the innocence in her eyes combined with the carnal act sent his blood pressure rocketing.

Son of a bitch. She was killing him.

"Fuck. That's it, Lyrica . . . baby . . ." Groaning at the whiplash sensations racing to his balls and gathering at the base of his spine, he knew holding back had become a second-by-second triumph.

"Ah hell." His fingers clenched in her hair again, hips rising and falling as he held her to him, fucking her lips with tenuous control. "Baby. This isn't going to last much . . . ah fuck!"

Delicate, silken fingers encased his balls, playing with them, her fingertips rubbing and stroking, sending erratic, electric currents wrapping around his scrotum, tightening . . . The sweet, hot suckling flames surrounding the crest of his dick tightened, drew him deeper. Her tongue licked and stroked and Graham lost his mind.

He felt it rupture. Felt his control snap, pleasure exploding through him with tidal waves of force as his body jerked tight and his semen blasted into the snug depths of her mouth.

And she took him.

Pulse after pulse of his seed spilling to her throat and he felt her shuddering, felt her vibrating around his cock as he swore something far more important than his release rocked from his senses and flowed from him to her.

What the fuck was he doing?

What was he allowing to happen with this woman? What was he losing to her when he'd sworn he'd never lose another part of himself to anyone?

And he was helpless against it. He was helpless against her, arched in a pleasure he knew he'd never before touched as he spilled his release to the suckling depths of her mouth. But she was the one marking him, he knew. She was marking his soul, destroying him, and he was helping her.

Pulling back, watching her lips release him, seeing the sweet, soft innocence in her eyes, he knew it didn't matter how hard he tried to tell himself no woman could be so innocent. He'd been telling himself that for six years now, and it did him as much good now as it had that first day he'd met her.

Because he wasn't pulling away from her.

His senses were so immersed in her, so rocked by the pleasure and the sensations overtaking him, that his cock was just as hard now as it had been before he spilled his release to those tempting lips.

God help him.

Quickly rolling a condom on, he couldn't think of anything but having her again. Feeling the warmth of her, the sweet innocence that still softened her gaze.

Pulling her to him, over him, he tucked the head of his cock at the saturated entrance of her vagina and, holding her hips with one hand, began easing her onto his erection.

Breathing harshly, air sawing from his lungs, he tried, oh god, he tried to go easy. Tried to take her gently. He wanted to take her gently. But the lust raging through him had other ideas.

His hips pushed upward, separating swollen muscles, becoming enclosed in a slick, so-fucking-hot, rippling vise of pure ecstasy.

"Ride me, Lyrica," he groaned, finally seating himself fully, her fist-tight grip surrounding his sensitive flesh and throwing him straight back into that swirling vortex of inevitable destruction.

Straightening above him she began moving, her hands lifting to her breasts, watching him, drowsy, dazed green eyes glittering between heavy lashes. Lashes that flickered in growing ecstasy as her thumbs and fingers plucked firmly at her little nipples.

Gripping her hips in desperate hands, he moved under her, giving her a rhythm to follow as her panting breaths became whimpering moans that drove him crazy with lust. The sounds of her pleasure sounded drawn from her soul. Low, resonating with a pleasure neither of them had a hope of controlling.

"Fuck me," he growled, watching her, moving harder beneath her, rocking her against him as his balls began to throb with the need to spill his release again. "That's it. Ride me harder."

He was dying with the need to come. It was burning through his cock, pounding at the crest, racing through his bloodstream.

Holding her to him, he reversed their positions quickly. Coming over her and lifting her hips to his penetration, Graham felt his senses overloading with the pleasure he'd only found with this woman.

His lips covered hers, drinking in her cries, her pleasure as he began driving into her, fucking her with a hunger, a need he'd never experienced in his life.

Her cries echoed around him.

When her orgasm gripped her, the muscles of her snug little pussy tightened with almost painful intensity around his cock, triggering his release along with hers. Flames rocked up his spine, shot back to his balls, and exploded through his senses.

He was coming, filling the condom with a release that he wanted nothing more than to feel surging into the unprotected depths of her flesh, marking her as his.

His.

God help him, if he wasn't careful, he would belong to her.

TWENTY

Time was running out.

Two weeks after Lyrica had returned to his house, he could feel the advance of each day like a noose tightening around his neck.

Graham could feel it like a bomb, silently ticking off the time, but he was unaware of the number remaining on the countdown.

Watching the cameras Elijah had installed on one monitor, he also watched the cameras his father had installed and hidden on the laptop sitting beside it.

Lying on the desk directly in front of him was the file he'd shown Lyrica several days before. Several reports were spread out around it, the pictures lying off to the side, unneeded once she'd confirmed she'd seen none of the men involved with the group.

"There are no anomalies in the cameras, no sign of the intruder's return, and no one showing any curiosity at all in the fact that Lyrica seems to have disappeared." Elijah paced the office slowly as he spoke, head lowered, staring at the floor thoughtfully.

"It's been two weeks. The waiting game isn't on our side if we can't flush out whoever's behind this."

"Angel's hit a dead end as well," Tracker stated from where he rested at the edge of the bureau on the other side of the room. "The wait-and-see game is on their side."

Behind him, Graham could feel Lyrica tense, the slender hand resting on his shoulder slowly fisting. Reaching for her and drawing her to him, he pulled her into his lap, wrapping his arms around her and resting his chin on her shoulder as his gaze moved around the room.

Elijah, watching the act, reached up and rubbed at the back of his neck, blowing out a hard breath. "I don't know what to do."

"Tracker?" Graham asked quietly.

"No contact yet." Arms crossed, his gaze hooded as he glanced to Lyrica, he gave a quick shake of his dark head. "I sent the message night before last that I'd completed the previous mission and was en route to Somerset. There's been no reply. I have the rest of my team lying low and waiting. As soon as contact's made, they'll move."

Lyrica was rifling through the pictures again, her graceful fingers trembling as she shuffled through them slowly.

The sight of those slender digits trembling with fear enraged him.

Lifting his head from where his chin rested against her, Graham turned to Elijah again. "Has Doogan managed to find anything?" he asked the agent.

"Doogan went and got himself shot again two nights ago on another op," Elijah snorted in disgust. "Out of a six-man team, only one escaped unscathed. Two are in critical, one recovering, one limping, and Doogan's out of commission with a concussion and a bullet hole in his shoulder."

Graham winced at the information.

"If that boy keeps looking to die, fate's going to hand him his wish on a silver platter," Tracker grunted. "He's a fatality waiting to happen."

Lyrica stilled against Graham again, tensing further.

Damn, Tracker, it wasn't enough that there was somebody out there trying to kill her, he had to mention fatalities, too?

Shooting the mercenary a scowl, Graham watched as the man gave an apologetic shrug before uncrossing his arms and bracing his hands on the top of the bureau where he rested.

The look in his eye reminded Graham of the warning he'd given before Lyrica had entered the office earlier.

He was hiding her. He kept her in the house behind closed doors and carefully darkened windows. There hadn't been so much as a sighting of her since the night of the wreck.

Weariness and worry had lined Dawg's and Natches's faces as they'd pointed out the same thing that morning while Lyrica slept.

He was keeping her hidden. Whoever had the contract up for her was waiting to see where she was, evidently in no hurry at all. That meant it was someone close. Someone who wouldn't seem out of place over a long period of time.

"We need a plan now," Tracker growled. "It concerns me that the contract hasn't been rescinded, yet he hasn't replied to my message, either. It's time, Graham."

"Like hell . . ."

"I know him."

"I agree with Tracker," Elijah said as Lyrica's soft statement had Graham looking back at her as she turned to him.

Lifting his hand in a gesture of silence, he glimpsed Lyrica's pale face and wide emerald green eyes.

"What did you say?" His gaze went to the picture she was holding, the photograph shuddering from her trembling grip.

"I know him," she said again, her voice soft, fear shadowing it. "I didn't see this picture the other day. Why didn't I see it then?"

Tracker and Elijah moved to the desk as Graham took it from her, frowning down at it.

"Because I wasn't aware this one was in there," he muttered.

Frowning, he flipped the picture over, checking the identification number on the back quickly before he began shuffling through the reports.

"That was a late arrival from Doogan." Elijah stared at the picture of the soldier standing with Betts Laren. "Check the back of the file for the report. I don't recognize him."

"I do." The statement had them stilling, staring back at Lyrica in surprise as her voice sharpened. "I do know him. He's been at the inn several times. I've fixed his breakfast. I even told him about my favorite places to shop when he asked so he could tell his fiancée the best places to go."

"Who is he?" Graham had never seen him. He hadn't been part of Betts's group in Afghanistan, nor part of Betts's team.

"Kevin Davis," she said softly. "He's engaged to one of Mom's long-term guests, Carmina Lucient. He was there for a few days last month before returning to Iraq for the end of his tour. He's not supposed to be back until sometime next month."

"Here's the report." Graham narrowed his eyes on the official information that had accompanied the picture. "Kevin Davis, he was actually assigned to Betts's team and should have been with her on that last mission. There's nothing here that states he wasn't there. He was assumed killed in action when he didn't return. He hasn't been seen since."

"Bingo," Elijah growled.

"Trained in tactical warfare, a Ranger. Laren had him pulled the year before she was killed for the team she put together. He also has ties to the commander, Jimmy Dorne, if I remember that file myself," Tracker murmured. "A distant blood relation, if I'm not mistaken."

"Third cousin." Graham read the information from the file. "Dorne's parents raised him, though, after his own were killed."

"Do you think Carmina's involved?" Lyrica whispered then, suddenly terrified. "She's there with Mom, Graham. They've been best friends since Carmina arrived."

"I'll call Timothy and Dawg," Elijah stated, flipping his phone out and heading for the far corner of the room.

"I'll head out, apprise the team, and get back with you tonight. We'll see what kind of plan we can come up with to draw him out then." Tracker headed for the door as well.

Lyrica moved quickly to her feet, turning to Graham. He could see the demand in her eyes.

"No!" He cut her off before she could speak. "Elijah will contact Timothy and Dawg. They'll get your mother out of the house and somewhere safe while they watch Ms. Lucient. You're not going."

"He's waiting for me to show myself," she retorted, rubbing at her arms as though to warm them. "Get Mom out of the house and I'll go in. If Carmina is in on it, then you can catch her in the act of calling him."

"It's too damned dangerous." His guts were clenching, cramping with awareness of the danger she would face.

"It's too dangerous not to," she argued, that militant Mackay gleam of stubbornness brightening her gaze as her hands went to her hips in determination. "We can't go on like this, Graham. At least I can't. I want this finished."

His teeth snapped together furiously. "Are you in that big of a hurry to leave me, Lyrica?"

She flinched as though the question were a lash laid to bare skin.

"Is it a requirement that I leave once this is over, Graham?"

Her hands slid from her hips and moved instead to clasp in front of her. "I wasn't aware there was a deadline."

He stilled then.

Was there a deadline?

What the fuck was he going to do once it was over?

He could see the questions raging in her eyes as he stared at her, but he couldn't make himself answer the question.

Lyrica swallowed tightly.

She'd known, she reminded herself. She'd known flavors didn't last long in Graham's life. She'd just so hoped he'd become fond of her particular taste, perhaps.

"I see." She forced herself to say it softly, her chest clenching painfully as her eyes suddenly felt raw, the pressure behind them actually hurting as she forced herself to hold back the tears that would have filled them. "Well then, at least I know now."

"Dammit, Lyrica," he snarled then, anger tightening his features. "I didn't say any of that."

"No, you didn't," she agreed. "This has gone on long enough, Graham. I won't hide any longer. I told you I couldn't go on like this. Now it's over. Get Mom out of there and I'm going in. I'm not hiding anymore."

"And just what made you come to this harebrained conclusion?" he bit out furiously.

Oh, that was it.

"Harebrained?" Keeping her voice soft, well aware that Elijah was still on the other side of the room, still on the phone, she went on. "Well, excuse me for being harebrained, Graham, but it's my life that's on the line and on hold here, not yours."

And it wasn't his heart breaking in two at the knowledge that she'd never had a chance at having her love returned.

No, that was hers.

Stupid little Lyrica, always looking for rainbows where none existed.

He stepped closer, his expression tight, the gold in his eyes more subtle, like chips of gold ice. "No." He repeated the word succinctly, pure arrogance filling every line of his face. "I will not risk you so needlessly. And don't test me on this, sweetheart, because I can and I will lock your ass in a room somewhere until this is all over."

Would he?

Drawing herself stiffly upright, her hands curling into fists at her sides as she shot him a disgusted look, Lyrica turned and stalked furiously from the room.

She'd be damned if she would let him order her about. That was the second time he'd threatened to lock her in a room somewhere, and she wouldn't give him the chance to do so.

Slipping quickly to the kitchen doorway, she slid the keys to Graham's pickup from the peg on the wall, praying he was more involved with something other than the surveillance screens on the computer monitors. If she was lucky, he wouldn't have a clue that she'd stolen them until she was gone.

She knew the doors and windows were all electronically keyed to alert him if they were opened. But what he didn't know was that Kye had found a way to bypass the one on her window. For Kye, slipping out of the house had been the same as slipping out from Dawg's eagle eye had been for Lyrica. Just to see if they could get out and back in, without getting caught.

Unlike Lyrica, Kye bragged she had never been caught.

She had described to Lyrica exactly how she'd rigged the window to hold the alarm at bay and how she reconnected it once she returned.

Lyrica had no intention of returning.

She'd been aware that he'd made the resolution of the danger the deadline for their affair. And here she'd thought she had a chance—

No, she'd known better, she thought as she slid into Kye's room and closed the door quickly behind her.

Her friend's room sat directly over the garage, and thankfully, Graham had pulled the pickup from the garage to make room for the vehicles that needed to be hidden whenever Natches and Dawg drove to the house rather than slipping over from Dawg's farm through the woods.

Had the pickup been in the garage, the chances of being stopped before she ever started would have been much higher.

Knowing the truck was outside the garage had determined which keys she'd taken. She should have taken the keys to his precious Viper, she thought furiously as she moved to Kye's vanity table, stole a bobby pin, and moved quickly to the window.

Seconds later, the bobby pin, rather than the metal strip attached to the window beneath it, was completing the circuit with the electronic box. Sliding the window up, Lyrica crawled through the opening, slid to the garage roof, and within moments was shimmying down the drainpipe with the same ease she moved down the wood support posts of the inn's wraparound porch.

She was in the truck and accelerating from the driveway in no time, racing from Graham's house, and his life, as tears whispered down her cheeks.

It wasn't supposed to be like this, she thought painfully. It wasn't supposed to end when the danger to her life was over. That was supposed to be the beginning.

Tracker stepped from behind the garage, his eyes narrowed as the truck pulled around the corner. A heartbeat later it was speeding away from the house toward the main road and, he knew, back to the girl's mother's.

Pulling the phone from his vest pocket and flipping it open, he hit the contact number. He didn't have to wait long.

"I'm in place," Angel said in answer. "I have the nest in my sights but nothing's moving."

That was odd enough.

"There will be soon," he promised her. "The bird just flew and I suspect that's where she's headed."

"Is this a good thing or a bad thing?" she asked curiously.

Tracker chuckled at the question. "A good thing, I hope. Perhaps seeing the prey will cause the wolf to make a move. Keep an eye on things and keep me apprised."

The phone flipped closed as Graham raced from the back door, filled with panic, fear, and a man's knowledge that something too precious to be lost had just escaped his life.

Poor dumb fucker, Tracker thought. He should have taken better care of her.

A second later Tracker was flying backward, to land on his ass with a surprised curse and a thud. Jumping to his feet, he faced Graham's furious wrath coolly.

"Bad move, Brock," he growled. "I don't take kindly to that shit."

"Fuck you!" Graham snarled in his face. "Why the fuck didn't you stop her?"

Rage was like a living, burning entity searing his insides as he faced the mercenary, using every ounce of self-control he possessed to keep from killing the bastard.

"It's not my place to stop her." Tracker stood still, his stance one of precaution as he watched Graham carefully now. "It's my job to keep her alive."

"And you think—" Snapping his lips closed, he turned and hit the garage remote, bending and moving beneath the door when it was no more than halfway raised to rush to the Viper.

He'd catch up with her quickly enough.

Dawg's place was just up the road and she would head there first. Elijah had just gotten off the phone with him and her brother knew to be waiting for her.

As the garage door lifted enough for the Viper to clear it, Graham hit the gas, throwing the vehicle into gear and racing from the interior with a scream of the tires. He rounded the curve that led to the front of the house even as he shifted gears, pushing for more speed.

Seeing his pickup race from its parking space had sent his mind exploding. Everything inside him was screaming about the danger she was facing by leaving the house. Every second she'd been with him, his body had clenched at the thought of her so much as sticking her head out the door and giving anyone a chance even to glimpse her.

It was imperative that no one see her. To keep her alive, he had to keep her hidden.

And now, she wasn't hidden.

Taking the turn onto the main road, he was racing toward Dawg's in less than a minute. The Viper ate up the miles, taking the curves with a smooth, easy performance he didn't even pay attention to.

All he could think about was the danger Lyrica would face if she reached the inn. All he could consider was life without Lyrica in it, and the knowledge that if he weren't such a stubborn bastard, she would have never slipped away on him.

The turn to Dawg's farm was just ahead, and still he hadn't caught up with her.

That fucking pickup wasn't that fast, he thought, a premonition suddenly racing up his spine.

No, she wouldn't have gone to the inn, he tried to tell himself. She wouldn't have considered something so foolhardy without him or her brother at her side.

As he reached the turn, the sight of Natches's modified ruby red Charger coming at him, moving so fast it was nearly on two wheels, had him stomping the brakes as he swung the Viper into a turn the second the car passed; the sight of both Dawg and Natches in the front had that premonition cementing to stark knowledge.

"Incoming call. Secured. Encrypted." The computer announced the call.

"Accept." The growl was torn from his throat, fear filling his senses, sharp and acrid on his tongue.

"What the fuck did you do?" Dawg yelled into the connection. "Lyrica wasn't on her way here. She's on her way to the inn. She passed Rowdy less than five minutes ago, tearing the roads up in that fucking truck of yours."

He was sweating.

As he shifted gears quickly, the Viper tore around the Charger, taking the lead as Graham cursed furiously.

"Graham, I'll take your head off if she gets hurt." Natches wasn't screaming. He was icy cold, calm.

"You have that friend of yours with you?" Graham bit out, referring to the sniper rifle Natches always kept close at hand.

"Why?" the other man asked with cool, biting fury.

"Don't bother with the house; get in place with it once you arrive," he ordered, the Charger still in his rearview mirror despite the pure power Graham was pouring into the modified engine beneath the hood of the Viper.

Dawg was cursing furiously.

"There's an angel in the trees," Natches informed him. "Why me?"

"Fuck if I know," Graham snarled. "Just do it."

Flicking the disconnect button on the steering wheel, he pushed the Viper harder, hearing the tires scream as he took the curves now. Rather than risk the more heavily traveled route to the inn, Graham took the dirt road ahead instead.

Turning onto it with a spray of dirt and gravel, he was forced to fight the steering wheel for a precious second before the Viper was racing toward its location once more.

The direct route to the inn would alert Davis and his fiancée, if she was involved, that he was coming. The back road that ended just behind the tree line behind the house would hide his arrival. Something warned him that slipping into the house might be all that saved Lyrica.

Some inborn sense of danger, a warning he didn't dare ignore, tightened in his gut. This was why a move hadn't been made. Someone had known she would make her own move.

Davis couldn't have known her that well. But the fiancée had been at the inn for months. Long enough to have gotten to know Lyrica. Long enough to know how close each girl was to her mother.

Damn, he should have seen this coming. Lyrica had called her mother just after leaving her apartment that night. She'd told Mercedes she was coming, that she'd just left. Carmina would have known Lyrica was on her way. If Davis was just waiting for a chance to get to her, then he could have easily been in place to force the Jeep off the road.

If Lyrica's vehicle hadn't been so well reinforced, she would have been dead. Whoever had driven that van—Davis, he was guessing—hadn't been expecting the steel reinforcements Dawg had welded into the frame just in case something like that had happened during the years he'd driven it.

It would have taken far more than a van ramming the passenger side to hurt the driver. If he'd rammed the driver's side, then he'd have accomplished his goal. The sheer force of the blow would have killed her.

But he'd hit the passenger side, expecting the Jeep to crumple and fly over the edge into the depths of the ravine.

He hadn't been wrong about Lyrica making an appearance on her own sooner or later, though. But was he expecting it this soon?

He couldn't know Graham knew he was alive. He was suspected to be dead, and there was no way anyone could know Graham had even tied this to Betts Laren.

Unless Carmina Lucient's presence at the inn had enabled her to learn far more than even Graham feared.

TWENTY-ONE

Lyrica remembered the years in Texas, before Timothy had found them and saved them. Before he had brought them to Kentucky and given Dawg the chance to show them what family really meant. She remembered the fear whenever Chandler had arrived, his strict, icy presence filling the house with a heavy, fearful tension.

And she remembered those few times she and her sisters had been separated from their mother.

Mercedes hadn't sat at home worrying or pacing. She had searched for her children while they were in foster care. She had fought Chandler. She had even risked her own safety by threatening to report her daughters as missing. She had put her own life, her security, and her need to provide her daughters with a better life on the back burner to ensure their safety.

And Graham expected Lyrica to wait, knowing her mother could be in danger soon? Knowing her mother was worrying for her? She hadn't even been able to talk to her mother or Zoey in the time Graham had kept her hidden. She had only seen her two older sisters because their fiancés were working with Graham on the investigation.

Pulling the pickup into the driveway of the inn, she was relieved to see that Carmina's car wasn't in the driveway. Timothy's pickup was there, as well as her mother's sedan and Zoey's beat-up, too-fast, older-model Mustang.

Guests were normally absent through the middle of the day. Sightseeing, shopping, and other activities kept them busy, which left the inn reasonably quiet.

She was already throwing open the door to the pickup as it rocked to a stop. Running the short distance to the steps leading to the wraparound porch, she was certain she would hear the Viper racing behind her at any second.

Pulling open the door and rushing into the foyer, she quickly moved through the dining room to the kitchen.

It was empty, and that was unusual. Her mother was normally in the kitchen in the afternoons with whichever daughter was helping her that day, going over the next morning's menu and preparing a light dinner for guests returning that evening.

The realization that she wasn't there had fear sending Lyrica quickly to the other end of the kitchen, where Timothy kept a handgun holstered beneath the wide lip of a prep counter. Reaching beneath the counter, she found the holster empty.

Ice formed in her veins.

Secondary.

He'd placed a secondary in the kitchen after the trouble her sisters had faced the year before. Her mother was usually in the kitchen and Timothy wanted a backup that no one was aware of. Lyrica had been there when he'd placed it, but her mother hadn't been. He'd warned her not to tell her mother because Mercedes tended to be very nervous in the areas where the weapons were hidden.

Moving silently, her gaze returning often to the dining room entrance, she went to her knees, quickly opened the lower cabinet doors hidden behind the prep area, reached up, and found the smaller-size Glock holstered there.

Extra clip, god love Tim's over-prepared heart. Still kneeling, she pulled the weapon and ammo clips free and shoved the extra clip into her back pocket. Watching the entrance from between the boxes of dry supplies stacked beneath the prep counter, she chambered the first round as quietly as possible before rising to her knees and pushing the weapon into the band of her jeans.

Smoothing her T-shirt over the gun, she fought back the fear as she had when she was younger. She buried it beneath the knowledge that if she didn't act, if she didn't do what had to be done, then the consequences could be more than she could bear.

Before she could begin straightening, a scraping at the back door caused her to freeze. She eased back to retrieve the weapon she'd tucked into the band of her pants. Holding it in a two-handed grip, the barrel pointing to the floor, she peeped around the counter, her heart thundering in her chest as she watched the door slowly ease open. Mouth dry, her throat tight with the knowledge that whoever was coming in was coming in way too slow assailed her.

The house was too quiet. A heavy sense of impending danger seemed to slide through the air like a bad smell. Even the slight breeze that slid through the door as it swung slowly open couldn't dispel the heaviness in the air.

No one stood in the doorway, though. For a moment, it looked as though a ghost had opened it.

"Lyrica, shoot us and I'll crack your ass." It was all she could do to hold back her sob at the sound of Dawg's voice.

Dawg wasn't the only one who stepped quietly into the kitchen. He came in, his stance watchful, covering the two men who moved in behind him.

Straightening slowly, she did nothing to hide the weapon she was carrying.

"Timothy's spare weapon is missing," she whispered, knowing Dawg was aware of the hidden positions of the guns. "The backup he placed beneath the cabinet last year was still in place, but I was the only one here when he placed it."

Dawg nodded, his pale green eyes watching the dining room doorway carefully. "And he told you to keep it to yourself."

She licked her dry lips nervously, all too aware of the fact that Graham's eyes had flickered to the weapon she still held.

"Timothy, Mercedes, and Zoey aren't answering their cell phones," Natches stated softly. "Have you seen them? Heard anything?"

She shook her head. "There was no way to miss the fact that I arrived, though."

Dawg's gaze moved to her for a moment before turning back to the dining room entrance.

"Then you're the only one he'll expect," Dawg murmured.

"Timothy's security system has every room covered, except bedrooms," Graham stated softly, his gaze still locked on her. "They'll know we're here."

Dawg shook his head at that. "When I couldn't reach him, I instigated a fail-safe he has installed."

"Paranoid bastard," Natches muttered. "Especially since hooking up with Mercedes."

"Love does that to a man," Dawg growled, glancing back for a second, his expression hard, his gaze furious.

Graham remained silent.

"Zoey's not screaming," she whispered, moving closer to them. "You know Zoey, Dawg."

That terrified her. Zoey would rush hell with a bucket of water for their mother. And she would do it loudly. She may be a recluse, she may try every excuse in the world to avoid family, but she never avoided her mother, and now that her older sisters were no longer at the inn, she was there every morning and every evening to help Mercedes.

"I know Zoey," he agreed. "But she's not foolish, either."

"Let's get this taken care of," Graham ordered then, his own voice still below a whisper. "I have other things to do."

He had another flavor to find, no doubt.

Flicking him a contemptuous glance, Lyrica turned back to her brother, aware of Natches watching her carefully.

"If you ask me to leave, then I might shoot one of you." Her first choice wasn't family, either.

Dawg grunted at that. "Give things time, little girl. We have other interested parties moving into place. I'm just waiting for them to get ready." He touched his ear, revealing the small, almost invisible Bluetooth earbud he wore, which she knew was linked to a central radio.

They were moving through.

Natches moved slowly into the room and the door was closed silently before he and Dawg moved to either side of the door leading to the dining room. The dining room would be their warning, she thought as she watched them from the side. Anyone coming from the stairs would be within sight of the doorway leading to the foyer, directly across from the kitchen. Anyone coming from the hallway entrances to the guest suites had to pass by the dining room.

"Plan?" Natches murmured then.

Dawg's eyes narrowed. "We spread out and find them."

"Timothy would be in his office right now," Lyrica stated. "Mom should have been here in the kitchen with Zoey. If someone has them, then they'll be together upstairs."

Dawg nodded slowly as he said, "Did you get that?" His gaze narrowed. "Check it out."

Lyrica's eyes narrowed on Natches then. Shifting her weapon to a one-handed grip, she held out her other hand demandingly. She wanted her own link.

His gaze flickered icily, and a second later he gave a negative movement of his head.

They were going to push her out. The hard flash of pain that seared her chest was surprising. It shouldn't have been.

Before she could pull her hand back, Graham reached out and dropped one in her palm, the almost clear bud lying innocently in her hand as he glared down at her.

Natches's curse was a sibilant hiss as she curled her fist around the earbud, maneuvered it between her fingers, and tucked it in her ear. Once it was in place, she pressed the activation button at the end and waited.

"Angel can't get eyes in the office," Tracker stated softly through the link. "Rowdy, can you override the window darkening?"

"That's all internal," Rowdy answered soberly.

Lyrica tucked the Glock in the back of her pants, listening as Rowdy and Tracker discussed the best way they could possibly override the controls for the window darkening.

It wasn't possible, Lyrica knew that. Timothy had always felt that whatever trouble came inside the inn couldn't be as dangerous as what could be waiting outside the window of his office on any given day.

But there was another direct line of sight into the room that would afford a view of everything but the exact area where his desk sat. Should anything happen, Mercedes and her daughters knew they were to stay behind that line. If they came upon the office and the sliding doors that led to it from the hall and from the attached bedroom were open, then they were to get out of the house.

Fast.

"There's two other views in if there's trouble," Lyrica stated softly, quickly explaining the line of sight into the office.

"Checking." Hard, without emotion, a female voice came over the line.

"I have sight from the west," a male voice answered. "Sliding door retracted, no one in sight."

"Sight from the south," said the female long moments later. "Door retracted, no one home."

Lyrica shook her head.

The small area where it was possible to hide would have been large enough for Timothy, her mother, and Zoey. It would have been crowded, but very possible. Of course, no enemy would have much of a chance if they were that close to Tim.

She swallowed tightly.

Someone was there. Wherever her family was being held, they were no doubt being held. She knew it from the absence of the weapon normally hidden under the prep counter, the doors left open to create the view into his office, the utter silence in the house.

She waited.

Dawg, Natches, and Graham were too focused on the doorway at the moment.

"Options?" Tracker asked.

Graham's gaze shifted to Dawg's, Natches shook his head, and he blinked.

Lyrica moved quickly, rushing through the doorway into the dining room and sliding out of their reach.

"Wait!" she hissed when Graham moved to follow her.

He paused, but his expression assured her that only surprise had him pausing.

"They don't know you're here." She kept her voice at a breath of sound then tapped her ear. "You're with me. Cover me."

Graham was shaking his head.

"Can you do this, little sister?" Dawg asked somberly. "Are you sure?"

"No." Before Graham could pass through the doorway, both Dawg and Natches were blocking him.

"Back off," Natches hissed.

"Lyrica?" Dawg asked again.

"You two taught me," she whispered. "You taught me how to do this, just in case. Right?"

They'd taught her and her sisters how to help them protect or rescue them. Dawg, Natches, and Rowdy had also taught them how to play the decoy if they had to.

This was a have-to, she thought.

"No," Graham growled again as Dawg stared back at her for long, tense seconds.

If he didn't agree with it, then Natches would make sure it didn't happen.

"Did you think she was a little china doll we just wrapped up in cotton and sat on a shelf to look pretty, Graham?" Dawg asked then, his gaze still holding Lyrica's.

"No, I didn't," Graham snarled, furious. "She's not a soldier, either, nor is she a trained agent."

Turning to him slowly, she saw something in his expression that had her throat tightening. He was concerned, furious, worried. She might be more than a flavor, but still, she was far less than what she needed to be to him.

"It's not your choice," she whispered.

His jaw jumped in rage. "Get hurt, and it won't be your choice when I kill these two fuckers!"

Natches and Dawg glanced at each other, concern flickering across their expressions, urging her to move, warning her that they were no more than a second or two from changing their minds.

And didn't that make sense?

Why would Graham's threat bother them when he hadn't concerned them until now?

Turning, she moved quickly away from them and strode through the dining room and into the foyer.

"Mom? Tim?" she called out, as though confused. "I need to talk to you. Where are you? Zoey?"

Her sister. Her baby sister. Zoey had suffered the most at Chandler's hands, though none of them had ever understood why. She was the one he had struck at every opportunity. The one her mother had had to wait the longest to have returned to her when they were taken away. But Zoey was a fighter. She was the temperamental one, the one most likely to spit in the face of an assailant.

"Zoey? Dammit, where the hell are you?" she called out, anger covering the fear as she started up the stairs.

"Easy," Dawg murmured at her ear. Graham wasn't speaking.

Where was he? Had he left?

Would he desert her now?

"Lyrica," the voice announced as she reach the top of the stairs and Kevin Davis stepped from the family's private living room.

"Kevin." She forced herself to smile, to stare back at him as though pleasantly surprised. "Where is everyone?"

He frowned, scratching his head, his brown eyes giving a damned good impression of confusion. "I'll be damned if I know, Lyrica. I made it back early and wanted to surprise Carmina."

Propping his hands on his hard hips, he looked around, frowning. "No one's here."

"Did you check Tim's office?" She moved past him to stride up the hall, expecting him to stop her at any minute.

"I've been through every room, Lyrica," he announced from behind her. "Even the office. Do they usually leave the house unlocked when they leave?"

"Something's wrong," Natches muttered, whether to her or to the others, she wasn't certain.

The office was empty. "Did you open the other doors?" she asked, moving to the retractable door between Tim's office and the personal suite Tim and her mother shared.

"They were all closed." He sighed. "I left them open just in case there was a problem."

She turned to him slowly. "Did you expect problems?" she asked.

"The last time I was here there was a weapon hid in the living room and one in the dining room," he said. "They're not there now."

He didn't mention the kitchen.

"Mom's, Tim's, and Zoey's cars are outside," she said.

"Carmina's is parked in the back," he told her, his expression hard, suspicious. The type of look her brother or cousins got when they were concerned.

What was he up to?

She could hear Dawg and the others in the background, their voices hushed as they discussed the situation and Kevin's part in it. He was a damned good actor if nothing else, because if she didn't know better, she would swear he was innocent.

"Lyrica." He reached out for her then, causing her to jump back from him, her gaze going to his outstretched arm as he slowly pulled back.

His eyes narrowed on her.

"I know Tim's ex-DHS," he said so softly it was all she could do to hear him. "Something's wrong. He wouldn't leave his private office open otherwise."

"This is his home," she said warily. "Why shouldn't he?"

The look on his face and slow movement of his head from side to side was knowing, but there was a cold gleam to his eyes as well.

"Whatever you say. I just want to find Carmina. That's all that matters to me."

And she believed him.

"Careful, Lyrica," Natches warned her softly. "Angel detected movement in the basement. See if you can get him to head downstairs and we'll take over."

"Have you checked the basement?" Something was wrong here. She couldn't figure out what it was, but something was wrong.

He shook his head slowly, his head turning to look down the hall.

"I'll check it." And she prayed he would follow.

An exasperated curse sounded behind her.

"Dammit, this doesn't feel right," Kevin muttered. "What are you doing?"

"Looking for my mother, evidently," she muttered, starting down the stairs.

"Get the hell out of the way." Gently, but firmly, she was pushed aside as the much taller soldier, dressed in fatigues and a T-shirt, moved ahead of her.

Trailing behind him, knowing Dawg and Natches waited below, she was still shocked at how quickly it happened. Before she could blink, Graham had the other man against the wall at the bottom of the stairs, a wicked, too-sharp blade at his throat as Dawg and Natches moved behind him.

"Hello, Davis." Graham's voice was cold, hard, his expression savage. "You don't look near as dead as I heard you were."

Kevin's gaze moved to hers, slowly, deliberately as his hard lips quirked just a bit. "Very good, Ms. Mackay," he murmured. "Very, very good."

"Where's my family?" Lyrica kept her voice low, but there was no hiding the anger that filled it.

Frustration flashed in his eyes, savagery shadowing them as he stared back at Graham in sudden fury.

"Where's my fiancée?" he growled.

Where was his fiancée?

What the fuck was going on here?

Graham glanced up the stairs to where Lyrica stood, her gaze thoughtful, her body tense, prepared for whatever else may happen.

"Well, it appears the gang's all here." A new voice entered the fray, one that had Graham, Natches, and Dawg turning quickly to face a threat they had never expected.

Jimmy Dorne.

He was leaning against the doorway to the guest living room, cradling one of the short, thick-barreled automatic weapons used by the security company he once worked for.

"Come on now, Lyrica." He waved her down the stairs. "Come chat with us, before I kill your boyfriend in front of your eyes."

His blond hair was still cut short, so short he may as well have just shaved it and gotten it over with. Cold, pale blue eyes watched them with amused intent.

Thin lips tilted into a jeering smile as he sniffed in disdain, giving the thick, once-broken bridge of his nose a heavily flared appearance. With flat cheekbones and narrow eyes, he was a man Graham had never been able to trust.

From the corner of his eye Graham could see Lyrica coming down the stairs silently, eyes wide, her face brutally white as she met his gaze.

God help him.

He could feel the rage simmering inside him, building to a force he wasn't certain he could control. Every instinct, every fucking urge he harbored inside himself was screaming at him to do something, to do something now.

"Dorne," Davis growled, fury filling his voice as Lyrica came down the last step. "Where is Carmina?"

The question seemed to distract Dorne for the moment, allowing Lyrica to ease in between Graham and Dawg.

Dorne gave a low, jeering laugh before glancing to his side. "Carmina." He called her name softly.

She stepped from behind him, dressed in the black mission suit she'd worn on the lake. Graham recognized her figure now, and the black, snug suit minus the heavy vest that had disguised her breasts that day.

Graham glanced at Davis. The other man wasn't an idiot. There were no protestations, no disbelief.

"Why?" The question was simple and to the point. But the sound of his voice displayed the betrayal raging through him. A betrayal Graham was certain wasn't feigned.

Pouty red lips formed a little sneer as derision filled Carmina's brown eyes. "You were a means to an end," she said in answer. "I needed a reason to be here, and we needed someone to take the fall for little Lyrica's death. It was a simple enough plan until Graham decided to hide her away so effectively." She stared around the foyer, frowning.

"Why me?" Davis's question had her watching him for a long, thoughtful moment.

"Because you were the missing link to Betts." She shrugged. "I knew how easy it would be to make it appear you had killed Lyrica and her family in retaliation for my sister's death."

He was shaking his head as she spoke.

"What?" Her eyes narrowed at the smirk pulling at his lips.

"That wasn't going to happen," he told her softly.

"And why wouldn't it happen?" She snarled. "You're simply pissed I fooled you."

"That's true enough. I had no idea Betts even had a sister," he agreed. "But your plan wouldn't have worked because after Betts's death, the rumor of my death was begun so I could track him." He nodded toward Dorne. "I was part of army intelligence before Betts ever pulled me onto her team. Every time I've arrived here, I was on leave from my team and our search for Dorne."

"How interesting," she laughed. "But it doesn't matter either way. The proof of your intent will be found and no one will look further. There will be no one alive to question anyway."

Graham eased Lyrica slowly behind him as Natches and Dawg drew closer to help shelter her. She was too fragile, he thought helplessly. Too damned easy to hurt.

Too fucking easy to lose, and he hadn't even told her how imperative it was that he not lose her.

Lyrica couldn't fight them and she didn't dare risk it as she was slowly, firmly pushed behind the men. It gave her the chance she needed to slip the weapon from the back of her jeans and slide it into the back of Graham's.

He tensed at the feel of it, and then Kevin Davis was drawing her back as well, placing his body beside Graham's as the four men created a wall between her and the danger.

"So protective," Carmina murmured, flicking Dawg a look

that assured Lyrica the woman was seriously underestimating not just her brother and cousin but Graham as well. "Too bad you and your cousins are all but old men now. Not hardly in your prime any longer, are you, Dawg? And once we have the four of you nicely bound, you'll have to trust our tender mercy where she's concerned, I'm afraid." She shot Lyrica a mocking little wink.

"I ain't as good as I once was," Natches murmured, the line coming from a favorite country music song. "But I'm as good once as I ever was." Natches was fond of repeating the song's title line. He may not have the stamina, but he sure as hell had experience.

Carmina sniffed at the reference. "Get them with the others," she ordered Dorne, the order causing the tension in the air to rise that much further. "I'll make certain everything's ready up here, then we'll take care of them and leave."

"She orders you?" Graham said mockingly as a frown brewed on Carmina's smooth brow.

Lyrica could see the other woman's uncertainty, and her anger. She hadn't expected the men to arrive. She'd only expected Lyrica.

"Betts was head of the team before." Dorne chuckled, the lazy unconcern drawing another sharp look from Carmina. "Her sister's doing a damned fine job of taking her place."

Carmina was paying close attention to this part of the exchange.

"That's one way to do it." Graham nodded.

He was baiting Carmina. Lyrica watched the jealousy and anger filling the other woman's eyes and felt a frisson of alarm as Carmina looked up at Dorne.

"One way to do what?" Carmina snapped, the South American accent missing now.

"To bring back the dead," Graham stated softly as Lyrica

glimpsed the pitying look he gave the other woman as she watched his profile. "He was in love with Betts. Losing her had to hurt. You're nothing more than second best, Carmina. You don't look like a woman who accepts second place to me."

"Shut the fuck up, Graham," Dorne snapped before Carmina could speak, though the fury brewing in her eyes assured him he'd struck the right nerve. "Don't make me pull that little bitch of yours free of you right now. I don't have the time to hurt her properly. Yet."

A soft bit of static announced the link becoming active once again.

"Keep them distracted." Tracker's voice came across the line softly. "We're deactivating the basement security. Two of my men are at the door now."

God, they had to hurry. She couldn't let any of them take a bullet to save her. It would kill her as surely as being shot herself would.

She could feel the tension rising slowly, though, and she knew a critical point was arriving far faster than she was prepared for.

"Shut up?" Graham asked him as though surprised. "She doesn't know you were in love with Betts?"

"It doesn't matter what he felt for her," Carmina said angrily. "What he feels for me is much more. He's here with me, isn't he? For no other reason than to help me kill you for getting her killed."

Graham laughed. "Is that what he told you?" Crossing his arms over his chest to stop the two from watching him too closely, he directed an amusement-filled look Dorne's way. "Dorne doesn't want vengeance. He may have loved Betts, who the hell knows. What he needs you for is a convenient backup plan. He's here for what he thinks I took out of that desert, aren't you, Dorne?"

The soldier's lips thinned further as he shot Lyrica a hard, vengeful look. "Shut him up," he told her softly. "Or you and I will play serious later."

"Unfortunately, he doesn't listen to me," she told him. Thankfully, her voice wasn't nearly as weak as her knees were. "No matter what you may think."

No matter what she may have wished.

TWENTY-TWO

The tension between Dorne and Carmina was only thickening now. Anger filled her face, and icy contempt filled his as he glanced at her.

"What does he mean by that?" Carmina shifted, staring up at Dorne now, ignoring Lyrica.

Graham chuckled then.

"I mean, he's here for the two and a half million in stolen Taliban diamonds that disappeared when Betts was killed," Graham answered for him. "He's not here to gain vengeance for Betts, and he's not here for you."

"Where are they?" Dorne asked softly, a triumphant smile curling at the corners of his lips. "The only way to keep that pretty little thing behind you from being raped in front of your eyes is to tell me where they are."

Graham shook his head. "You know better than that, Dorne. Haven't you heard about my 'flavors' yet? Doing a friend a favor by protecting his baby sister doesn't mean I have a damned thing you can take from me."

Lyrica knew better, though. She knew he would give his life for her, just as he would for Zoey, Piper, or Eve. They were friends. She was more than a flavor—just not enough more.

The hiss of the link activated again.

"Basement door is open and we're taking them out," Tracker reported. "Give me two minutes and they'll be clear. I'll be in place with one of my men as you come down."

Two minutes.

"There were no diamonds." Carmina was watching Dorne suspiciously now. "Tell them, Jimmy. You weren't able to retrieve them."

"Is that what he told you?" Graham clucked his tongue at Dorne. "He got away with half of them. He thinks I have the other half. Two and a half mil. Don't tell me he's not sharing with you."

A tense, heavy silence emanated from the woman now. She wasn't looking happy at all.

"You said there were no diamonds retrieved," she reminded Dorne.

He flicked a hard look in her direction. "I was going to surprise you once I found the rest. How do you think we funded this little venture? It's not like you had any money to put into it."

"I think, when this is over, you and I will discuss this," she stated softly. "Until then, vengeance is what I came for."

She turned back to them, waving them toward the end of the foyer. "If you'll accompany us to the basement, we'll get you settled in with the others, then I'll get to the business of exacting my revenge." She smiled mockingly. "Unless you want to watch your whore die here, in the foyer." She flicked Lyrica a cold look before turning back to Graham. "Jimmy may believe she means nothing to you, but you forget, Betts was my sister. And there was much she did know of you, Graham. Did you think that getting my sister killed would go unpunished?"

Graham's expression was icy as he reached back as though reaching for Lyrica, but Lyrica glimpsed his fingers curling around the butt of the weapon. "I think Betts got herself killed. She was more concerned with her feelings for Dorne than she was for herself. She went chasing after him when that fuel truck went up in flames, believing he was dead. I didn't get her killed. Your lover did. And he did it deliberately."

Before they could react, before they could stop her, Carmina jumped back, her weapon aiming for Dorne as she read the satisfaction on his face correctly.

She wasn't fast enough though, and Dorne was evidently ready for her.

The report of his weapon sent several bullets slamming into her body, throwing her into the door frame before she bounced forward and toppled to the floor.

Before Graham, Dawg, Natches, or Kevin Davis could jump for him, Dorne had the weapon aimed in their direction once again.

Lyrica couldn't take her eyes off Carmina's body or the blood slowly pooling beneath her. Just like that, she thought, a sickening rush of realization roiling in her stomach. The man had killed his lover just that easily. Had used her just that cruelly.

And Carmina had paid the price for her need for vengeance. A price Lyrica was certain she hadn't expected.

"Now that we have all that nasty personal business out of the way," Dorne breathed out with a smile as he stared back at Lyrica. "Step out here, little girl, before I start putting bullets in all these brave bodies trying to shelter you."

"No." Graham did reach for her now. His fingers snapped around her wrist, holding her to him.

"It will only take a second to put a bullet through her, Graham," Dorne snapped. "Now let her go, before I start shooting."

Lyrica stared up at Graham, seeing the torment, the fury lashing at his eyes as the gold in them seemed to flame.

God, she loved him. So desperately.

Twisting her arm out of his grip, she moved away from him, pushing between Dawg and Natches as she stared at the bastard watching her with a mixture of triumph and evil intent.

She stopped just in front of Dawg, some sense, some warning halting her in her tracks as she felt Graham easing closer behind her.

Dorne tilted his head slowly. "Do you think he'll tell me where the diamonds are to save you?" he asked her curiously.

Lyrica swallowed tightly before shaking her head. "I don't mean enough to him for him to even consider remaining with me after this is over, so I doubt it."

His expression turned doubtful. "Really?"

"Why do you think I was here?" She couldn't stop the trembling of her voice. "I left when I found out my deadline was whenever I was dead or you were caught. So, yeah. Really."

He breathed out heavily, his gaze flickering to Dawg and Natches.

"Let's join the others in the basement." He gave Graham a hard look. "Then you'll tell me where the diamonds are, or you'll watch me hurt your little whore anyway. And then I'll finish what I started with that little girl down there. Maybe her brother can make you tell me. She does handle pain well, but her mother and stepfather aren't holding up so well watching it."

Terror gripped Lyrica, dragging a gasp from her lips at the thought of Zoey being hurt. Her little sister didn't handle pain well—she simply retreated further from the world whenever it was inflicted. And god help them all if Zoey retreated any further.

"You're dead." The tone in Dawg's voice sent a chill racing up

Lyrica's spine then. Even more frightening was the fact that Natches didn't say a damned word.

"Yeah, yeah, so little Zoey told me," Dorne laughed. "But as Carmina said, you're not so young anymore. And you're not armed. So I'm really not worried about you." He waved his hand toward the basement door. "Let's go now, before I have to put a bullet in her knee or something to make you hurry the fuck up. I'd like to get this little job done and head out for a beautiful beach with lots and lots of pretty girls."

"Like hell," Natches said then.

It was his tone that warned them.

It was the voice of the killer Dawg had described to her once, the one Natches had once been.

Chaos erupted suddenly.

The sound of glass shattering came at the same time that Dorne stepped into the foyer, freezing him in his tracks. His finger twitched on the trigger of his weapon, firing in a string of death as he went to the floor.

Lyrica was only barely aware of Graham throwing her to the ground as she watched the second death of the day.

Dorne went down, half of his face simply gone from the sniper's bullet that took him out. One side of his face was slack with surprise; the other side, just gone.

She blinked, the realization that it was over slamming into her senses like a sledgehammer.

"Stand down!" Natches was snapping into the link. "The shooter's mine. I repeat, the shooter's mine." He said it again, snarling, just to be certain he was heard. "I repeat, the shooter's mine. It was his shot, by god. Stand down."

The shooter was his? Since when did he have a shooter?

"Yours?" Dawg screamed. "Who the fuck is out there, Natches?"

Natches stared back at him, his expression filled with irritated self-disgust. "Well, it wasn't me. Who's the only fucking protégé I've ever had? The only man on the face of the earth that could have made that shot?"

No, it couldn't be Harley, she thought—Harley was gone. He'd been gone since the night Zoey's fragile heart had been broken.

Poor Zoey. She knew how her sister felt now.

Turning to Graham, the sense of unreality grew so strong inside her it was frightening. It soon became terrifying.

"No . . ." The word slipped past her lips as the arguments around her and through the link receded. "No. Please, god . . ."

She couldn't scream.

She wanted to scream, to wail, to release the building agony burning inside her.

"Graham . . ." She reached for him, realizing he had done exactly as she had been terrified he would.

He'd taken a bullet for her.

"Shhh." He reached up for her, his hand shaking, his face ghostly white as blood stained his shirt and the floor beneath him. A slow, oozing trail of blood. "It's okay, baby."

"No. No." Her gaze became blurry, tears falling from her eyes as she felt the sobs tearing from her chest. "Please, Graham . . ."

"Shhh." Her hand covered his, holding it to her cheek as Dawg and Natches were suddenly rushing to them. "Don't cry. Don't let Kye cry . . ."

"Don't you die on me!" Fury lashed at her now. "Damn you, Graham. You bastard! Don't you dare leave me like this where I can't even torture you for breaking my fucking heart!"

Sobs mixed with the fury pouring from her as she watched his eyes, watched the regret, watched emotion fill them.

"I want to tell you . . ."

"Dawg!" She was being pulled away from him, hard arms tearing her from him as her brother and cousin were suddenly hiding him from her. "Let me go!" She fought, clawed, kicked out at whoever, whatever was dragging her away from the man she loved.

"Stop it, Lyrica." Timothy was holding her, pulling her into his arms as she collapsed, sobbing, holding on to him as sirens could be heard screaming into the parking lot outside.

"I have to stay with him!" she cried, desperate to get back to him as the front door was flung open and EMTs rushed inside. "I have to stay . . ."

"Lyrica." The brutal, hoarse snap in his tone had her stilling, staring up at him, and seeing the tracks of tears staining his face.

"Tim?" she whispered his name, the agony lancing her, tearing ragged holes into her soul.

"Come on, Lyrica." He drew her to the door. "Let the EMTs take care of him. You can't be with him now."

"No, I can't leave him."

Tim was pulling at her, trying to pull her from the house.

"No!" The word was torn from her throat in a scream of rage as she broke from him, turning back to Graham as he was being loaded onto the gurney, the techs working frantically to stem the flow of blood.

"Come on!" Natches's arm went around her shoulder, his hands stained with Graham's blood, his expression dark with concern. "Let's get in the ambulance. You can ride with him."

"Natches . . ."

"It's bad, Lyrie," he whispered, his voice ragged, his eyes darkening as she shuddered, another sob ripping from her. "Come on, I'll get you in the ambulance with him, but just . . ." He swallowed tightly. "Come on," he repeated.

It was killing her.

She was dying inside as she realized what he was trying to tell her. Graham could die en route to the hospital, and she had to be prepared for it.

She couldn't survive losing him like that.

If she had to do without him . . . god, don't force her to do without him this way. Not like this. Not where she couldn't at least see him, at least know he was there.

She prayed.

She'd always tried hard not to pray for herself, and other than when she was in danger of dying, she'd kept that rule. But she prayed now, for Graham. For herself.

God help her, how was she supposed to survive if he was gone? If he was no longer a part of her life?

She couldn't survive.

If Graham died, she may breathe, she may walk, but Lyrica knew, inside where it counted, she, too, would die.

TWENTY-THREE

"I was shot." Graham sighed as he felt the presence
ease up to him and sit beside him.

He was in a white place, a bright place. This was a place he had
never been before, even those times Doogan had managed to get
him wounded.

"Yeah, son, you were shot."

He turned his head, resignation weighing heavily in his chest
as he stared back at his parents.

Garrett and Mary Brock looked as vibrant now as they had
the day they died, as they'd looked hours before they stepped onto
that doomed plane.

"Hell." Rubbing his hands over his face as he stared around
him, the total lack of anything but the pure white surroundings
and his parents convinced him as nothing else could—he was
dead.

His mother laughed, a sound as soft and loving as a breeze.

"You're not dead," she promised, easing down to sit on his other side.

He felt her arm slide around his waist.

"Then why am I here?"

"To help you decide if you're going to fight to live, or if you're going to give up," his father answered, that firm, commanding tone of his just as grating now as it had ever been.

He gave his father an irritated look. "There's days I'm convinced you're a Mackay."

It wasn't a compliment.

Garrett chuckled at the observation. "Rowdy, Dawg, Natches, and I were damned good friends at one time." He sighed. "But our lives were going in different directions." He looked around Graham and smiled at the wife who had died with him. "We needed different things at the time, I guess."

Propping an elbow on his knee and resting his chin in his hand, Graham stared into the white surroundings, wondering where the door was.

"Where do you want the door to be?" his mother asked.

"It's highly uncomfortable knowing you're doing that," he told her. The knowledge that she was hearing what he thought instead of what he said had him hoping he could control his thoughts.

"As a boy, you were always so serious," she said softly, a smile reflecting in her voice.

"I didn't grow out of that, Mom." He wondered if she had hoped he would.

"So I see," she murmured. "But what a fine man you've become, Graham. You've made more than enough sacrifices in your life, done more than enough to earn your chance at peace."

Damn, that wasn't what he wanted to hear.

"I don't think I'm ready for peace, Mom," he said warily. "I've still got some fight left in me."

"*Do you?*" *his father asked.* "*I haven't seen a lot of fight since you came back from Afghanistan. Even though the woman who died in your arms was a viper, still you let the memory of it hold you back from the place you know your heart belongs. That's not fighting, son.*"

Graham slid a slow look in his father's direction. "*It felt like a hell of a fight.*"

Garrett Brock chuckled at the comment. "*Love is sometimes the greatest battle a man can fight. You knew she wasn't like the woman who tried to be her in an attempt to deceive you. You've always known she was right there, waiting for you, loving you. Perhaps the question I should ask is, why did you fight it?*"

"*What does Lyrica have to do with this place?*" *The white peace was too encompassing. Too peaceful. And he didn't see a Mackay in sight.*

Life without Mackays would be boring, he thought morosely, realizing the part they'd played in his life for so long.

"*Those boys promised me the day you were born that they would always look out for you if I were to leave your life,*" *his father revealed.* "*They've done well. But it's not the Mackays in general you'd miss, is it, boy?*"

He hated it when his father called him boy. It meant he was disappointing him.

"*To return is to face her,*" *his mother said then, her voice gentle.* "*Having you with us would complete the circle we began in that life. But it would not complete the circle you were meant to build, Graham. Which choice will you make?*"

The whiteness slowly receded. It became a world washed in color, in sight and sound and scents that were incredibly sharp and focused.

He still sat. He was in the garden his father had created for the wife who so loved the sight and scent of flowers. He sat on one of the chair-size boulders, his position the same, chin resting in his palm as he watched the most incredible sight.

It was beautiful.

As he watched, the peace that suffused him was far greater than even that of the perfect white peace where his parents had come to him. It was soul deep. It was wonder and beauty; it was a perfection he'd never imagined existed.

"Mine?" he whispered, awed, so taken aback by what he was seeing that it was all he could do to contain his emotion.

"Yours," his mother whispered, her own voice thick with emotion now. "You knew it was happening. You've sensed it. Isn't it the most wondrous sight, Graham? Is this really what you want to leave? Is this what you want to continue to run from? If it is, then you can have that as well."

"No!" He jumped to his feet to hold on to the image, anger crashing through him at the knowledge that it was leaving, that it was being taken from him. "Make it stay!"

He turned to his parents, wild with the loss pouring through him, his heart racing as he'd never felt it before, a sense of pain clenching at his chest and arm.

"Only you can make it stay, son," Garrett said softly, somberly. "Only your choice can bring it back."

Turning, Graham willed it back, fought for it, snarled with furious determination as the white slowly morphed again, and the image returned.

Stepping closer, he felt tears fill his eyes.

Going to one knee, he reached out, touched her face, brushed his thumb over her lips as she slept.

Then his gaze returned to the children sleeping beside her.

A boy, his Mackay looks diffused with the strong, determined lines of his father's bloodlines.

The daughter, though, sweet heaven help them all. His daugh-

ter was pure Mackay in looks, already the image of her mother, with a hint of that bastard cousin of hers, Natches.

He couldn't help but grin.

"The son of a bitch is going to crow about that one," he whispered.

"Will you be there to hear it, though?" Garrett asked. "Or will Natches be the one to stand in for the father who couldn't fight hard enough to return to her?"

"We're losing him. Goddammit, we're losing him," Dr. Caine Branson yelled out to his surgical team, determination raging through him as he felt Graham slipping slowly away from him.

The EKG was quickly going to hell, BP was dropping.

"Like hell I'll let you go," he snarled softly. "I made that mad-assed father of yours a promise, Graham Brock, and I'll be damned if you'll see me break it."

A lot of men had owed Garrett Brock, and Caine was but one of them. But at this moment, Caine knew, he was the most important.

His surgical team worked like the well-oiled machine it was, as though the years of working beneath him had been solely for this moment.

For this young man.

The artery was repaired, but the bullet was far too close to the heart, and the other had clipped his liver before ripping out his back.

The surgeon repairing the damage below was one of the best protégés he'd ever had. Giana Worth was worth her weight in gold. She was working quickly, efficiently, refusing to allow the teams keeping his heart beating to distract her from her job.

"BP's coming up," Nurse Salyer announced, though Caine could feel it, sense it.

"Heart rate's coming back." The male nurse, Jeffers, called out numbers.

Caine kept working. The vein was repaired. The chips of bone were removed from their precarious location next to the heart. He was almost finished, the damage nearly repaired.

"Your dad made me promise if you ever made it onto my table that I'd make damned sure you were breathing when you came off it," he murmured.

He'd been talking to the boy since his gurney had been rushed into the ER.

"You make a liar out of me, boy, and when I reach the afterlife, I'm coming looking for you." He worked steadily, tirelessly.

"This isn't a good day to die," he muttered as Graham's heart rate fluctuated again. Garrett Brock had said that once, laughing as Caine warned him that his heroics were going to get him killed. "Buck up, boy. You're stronger than this."

Graham was indeed stronger.

Muttered comments and prayers slipped from the surgeon's lips as he worked, but he was prone to do that often, anyway.

Whatever it took, he often said. He'd always felt his patients could hear him, no matter how irrational that may seem.

"There's a girl out there crying for you, you know?" He kept the one-sided conversation moving. "Did you hear her crying your name when she came in with you? Really want to leave a Mackay sobbing, boy? Thought you knew better than that. Rowdy, Dawg, and Natches will strip your ass if they find you. Heaven or hell. It won't matter."

One of the techs chuckled, no doubt helplessly. They all knew the Mackays. Hell, sometimes Caine thought the whole world knew at least one Mackay, if not all of them.

"BP is strengthening," his nurse announced, calling out the numbers.

"Excellent." He breathed out in satisfaction. "That's it, son. Fight. Fight for her. She's worth it."

The commentary continued. Fierce and demanding when it needed to be, determined and encouraging as Graham responded with that fierce will to live.

He would live. Caine refused to allow him to do otherwise.

Lyrica was aware of her brother, her cousins, her sisters.

Her mother sat beside her, her lips split, one eye nearly swollen shut from where Dorne had struck her.

She hadn't realized Tim was limping at first. His leg was fractured. How he'd managed to walk like that amazed her. How he was still sitting in the waiting room, she hadn't figured out.

Even Zoey was there, her pale green eyes damp with tears, her broken arm casted, the deep bruising at the side of her face swelling her eye nearly closed.

Jimmy Dorne had been determined to force Tim, Mercedes, or Zoey to reveal where Lyrica was hiding.

They'd sworn they didn't know. Even Zoey, the one who feared pain the most, had fought him back, daring him to shoot her, sneering at him when he hit her. She'd declared she wouldn't tell him even if she did know. Her brother, she'd informed Dorne, had hidden Lyrica, and she'd dared him to try to force the information from Dawg.

They'd all suffered to keep Lyrica safe.

Curled in the corner of the hard plastic couch, she turned her head back to where she had rested it in her bent arm, and she continued to pray.

To wait.

She felt ragged inside.

Her soul felt shredded, destruction held back by the thinnest thread.

Graham.

Tears fell from her eyes again, pouring from her when there shouldn't have been tears left to shed.

She could live without him. If he was just alive. If he was just somewhere in the world finding happiness, even if it meant finding that happiness with another woman, then she would survive.

She would get up every morning, she would make herself go through each day, and she might even find a measure of peace.

Somewhere.

Without Graham . . .

What reason would there be to get up every morning?

Her mother rubbed at her shoulder and Eve and Piper sat close, trying to comfort her. But there was no comforting her.

He'd taken that bullet for her, knowing what he was doing. If he hadn't thrown himself in front of her then she would have been the one lying there in that operating room.

She would have much preferred it to be her.

"Hey, little sister." Natches's voice had her head lifting quickly, her gaze meeting his immediately as he squatted in front of her.

He and Rowdy both referred to her and her sisters as their own.

She looked around quickly. Neither the surgeon nor the doctor was standing there.

"He'll be okay," he said, the somber belief that gleamed in his eyes pulling a harsh sob from her chest.

Covering her trembling lips with her fingers, she fought to hold back the cries and was even mostly successful. The tears were another story.

"I love him," she whispered, her voice so hoarse she barely recognized it. "If he's just okay, then I can live without him, Natches. I can."

Reaching out, Natches tucked the long, mussed strands of her hair over her shoulder and thought he must really be getting old. Only one time in his life had he ever wanted to cry as much as he wanted to cry for this grown-up version of his precious Bliss.

"Did I tell you I used to know his parents really well?" he asked her gently.

Lyrica shook her head.

"Yeah." He grinned, a flash of the wicked sensualist she'd always heard he was gleaming for a second in his eyes. "There was a time, before Chaya returned to Somerset, that I wasn't the man I am today. Rowdy had married. Dawg and Christa were engaged, and I was a little lost," he stated, then grinned again. "Hell, I was a lot lost, I guess. I was skunk drunk, had just wrecked yet another motorcycle on some back road, was puking my guts up because my Chaya had just left town again, and I had no idea what the hell I was supposed to do." He winked with a flash of amusement. "Never occurred to me to just go get her. Right?"

Lyrica shook her head. Natches had never done things the easy way, she knew.

"Anyway." Rising, he sat beside her, and Lyrica didn't even question why she was turning to him, letting him draw her into his arms and against his chest.

He kissed the top of her head gently.

"So, here I am, about three days drunk, reeking of booze and probably my own b.o. My motorcycle was totaled, handlebars bent to hell and back, and this four-wheeler comes bouncing down that dirt track I was on. Seemed I'd done strayed onto Brock property, and Garrett Brock was real particular about having a Mackay around. He stared at me like I was scum, all distasteful and disgusted. And well, let's just say I was spewing more F-bombs than social niceties that night."

Someone gave a brief snort of laughter.

"So Garrett drags me to this pond, throws me in a time or two, laughing at all my Mackay rage, then drags me back out and pulls me back to his four-wheeler, where he starts pouring hot coffee down my throat. Seems he knew I was there before he started out from the house. Brought coffee, lots of it, a few sandwiches, and sat there with me till dawn while I poured out my itty-bitty heart." He rubbed at her shoulder. Her back. "Then he proceeds to tell me how butt stupid I was for letting my woman out of my life. And how he hoped his son wasn't too damned dumb to claim what was his when he finally met her. Then . . ." He paused, drew a deep breath, and lowered his voice. "Then, he made me swear on my honor, my life, my firstborn, and whatever else he could come up with that I might actually care anything about, that if his son did turn out that damned dumb, then I'd do what he was going to do. Put all my Mackay calculation and love of games into making sure his son smartened up and realized what he was losing. A week later, Chaya was back. He'd pulled a few strings, called some friends, and made sure I had another chance to make sure she never got away from me again."

"I knew what you were doing," she whispered when he paused. "I figured it out."

He grunted, then whispered low enough that no one else could hear. "Don't tell Zoey, 'kay? She's still a work in progress."

"He doesn't love me, Natches," she told him then.

This time, pure amused devilment filled the chuckle that sounded from him.

"Oh, Lyrica, sweetheart, that dumb-ass is so in love he doesn't know his ass from a hole in the ground and doesn't want to know the difference if it means losing you."

Lifting her head, Lyrica pulled back, staring back at him, knowing not to hope. Knowing she didn't dare hope.

"Now, whether or not he's smart enough to realize it, we'll see." He sighed. "But I'm going to tell you what his father told me to tell the woman he loved if he acted that stupid. A message he wanted me to give her."

"For me?" she whispered.

He nodded at that. "For you, sweetheart. Don't give up on him, he said. Graham will always be strong, always be stubborn, and letting go of himself enough to take what he needs above all things won't be easy. But if you have to, he said, tell him to remember what his mother told him before he left for the Marines."

"What did she tell him?" She frowned back at him.

"Hell if I know," he admitted with a grin. "But now, Mary was a smart one, don't think she wasn't. Knew what she wanted the first time she saw Garrett Brock, and even Mackay charm couldn't sway her. So whatever it was, remind him of it."

"If he wakes up," she whispered.

"He'll wake up," he promised her. "If he's Garrett Brock's son, and trust me, he is, then he'll wake up."

The operating room doors swung open and the surgeon, accompanied by Graham's doctor, stepped into the waiting room.

Lyrica came quickly to her feet, too afraid even to breathe as she felt Natches put his arm around her shoulder and her mother move beside her.

"Kyleene." The surgeon nodded to Kye as she came to her feet as well, Sam Bryce standing beside her as Graham's sister fought to stem her tears.

"He's out of surgery and everything looks promising," he announced. "It was touch-and-go a time or two, but he's strong, and he wants to live . . ."

Kye turned to Lyrica, her smile brimming with hope as her tear-drenched eyes overflowed once again.

"I told you," Kye whispered as she covered the short distance to give Lyrica a quick, hard hug. "I told you. He won't leave us. He'll not leave us."

He was alive, that was all that mattered, Lyrica promised herself as she returned Kye's hug and they stood together, listening to the surgeon as he described the injuries and Graham's recovery.

He was alive. She could live with it if he wasn't smart enough to love her. She could live with it if he loved another.

All that mattered was that he was alive.

TWENTY-FOUR

Four weeks later

The hard knock at the door of the inn's suite Lyrica had moved into surprised her.

It was close to midnight, and the rain-drenched Kentucky night was filled with steamy heat and a loneliness unlike anything Lyrica had ever known.

She'd gotten used to sleeping with Graham. She missed him, even now, a month later. She would awaken in the deepest part of the night reaching for him, realize he wasn't there, and lie until dawn, staring into the darkness.

Rising from the bed, she padded to the patio doors, pulled the curtain aside, and froze.

It couldn't be.

Fumbling, her fingers suddenly refusing to cooperate properly, she fought to unlock the door and pull it open.

"I'm going to spank your pretty little ass," Graham growled as he stalked into the bedroom, glaring at her, his expression filled with male irritation as he moved to the bed and sat down.

"What did I do this time?" Her hands went to her hips as she stared back at him, her gaze raking over him closely to make certain he was okay. "Aren't you supposed to be home resting? Kye said the doctor ordered no exertion. You're to stay in bed and rest until you're healed."

"Dammit, it's been a month. How much fucking healing do you think I need?" Irritation flashed in his eyes.

"However much the doctor prescribed," she snapped back, but once again, there was no heat.

"Undress."

The order had her blinking back at him in amazement.

"What did you say?" She couldn't have heard him correctly. Could she have?

He was unbuttoning his shirt, watching her broodingly until he shrugged it from his still-powerful shoulders while toeing off the leather sneakers he wore.

"I said, undress," he growled.

"And I should do that, why?" Joy erupted inside her like a sun exploding from the fiery heat it contained.

Oh god, she'd missed him so desperately.

"So I can fuck you until you're too damned exhausted to ever run from me again," he snarled, hunger, need, and so many other emotions she'd prayed to see in his eyes during the weeks she'd been confined at his home filling his eyes. "Until some of that damned Mackay stubbornness you obviously possess is tamed just a fraction."

"Won't happen." She was unbelting her robe, though, letting it slip from her shoulders before moving slowly to him.

Rising from the bed, he tore at the clasp of the khakis he wore, shedding them before she could reach him, his fingers curling around the stiff length of his cock.

"Probably not," he agreed. "But let's say I keep trying anyway."

"Let's say you do."

He reached out, pulled her to him, his lips covering hers as a needy, hungry moan left her lips. Her arms wrapped around his neck, her lips parting beneath his, taking his kiss and the power of his need and returning it. His hands moved over her back, her sides. Gripping the material of her gown, he released her lips only long enough to relieve her of it, then he was sipping from them again, hunger and heat building with rapacious intensity between them once again.

Turning, Graham had her on the bed in seconds, her legs spread as he moved between them, his lips pulling from hers as he guided the throbbing crest of his erection between her thighs.

Nudging at the entrance of her vagina, her slick heat flowing, coating the mushroomed head, he glared down at her.

"Run from me again and I'll paddle your ass."

She grinned back at him. "Are you trying to deter or convince me?"

His hips shifted. His cock impaled her until the heated width of the crest was lodged inside the snug, rippling tissue, causing devastating pleasure.

Lyrica cried out, pleasure so sharp it was almost pain tearing through her senses as she lifted to him.

"More," she cried out, her fingers fisting in the blankets beneath her. "Oh god, Graham, please."

He waited. He didn't move, the heavy throb of his cock head tormenting her as she ached, whimpered for a deeper thrust.

Staring up at him, she watched as he leaned back, his eyes locked with hers, his expression gentling.

"I love you, Lyrica," he whispered.

Her lips parted, shock, disbelief, pure happiness filling her where before only aching emptiness had existed.

"You love me?" she whispered.

Rocking against her, he tore another gasp from her lips as he pressed deeper, taking her slowly, raking across tender nerve endings and sending her senses flying.

"I love you, Lyrica," he groaned. "God help me. I love you."

There was no stopping either of them then. Pushing into her to the hilt, penetrating the slick, desperate depths of her pussy, Graham groaned in rising hunger, in a need that echoed clear to her soul.

Perspiration coated their skin and pleasure whipped around them, between them, tearing at the solitary moorings that once held them grounded and binding them together, mooring them to each other.

Deep, hungry kisses, whispered promises, pledges. He took her to the edge of rapture, pulled her back, and pushed her up once again.

His lips roamed to her breasts, suckling at sensitive nipples, sending slashing waves of heat and pleasure to race from the tender buds to the clenched depths of her vagina. His hands stroked, caressed. His body moved over her, inside her, until he tucked his head at the bend of her neck and began moving with hard, desperate thrusts, each thrust pushing her closer to a brink she raced for eagerly.

"Love me, Lyrica," he groaned, his voice hoarse, filled with all the desperate, hungry emotion that had ached inside her for so long. "Just love me."

Ecstasy ruptured inside her, blazing in such fiery eruptions of pleasure, joy, and melting bliss that she knew she would never, could never, be the same.

"I love you," she gasped, writhing with the extremity of the explosions racing through her, the pleasure and emotion surging free of the depths of her soul. "Oh god, Graham. I love you."

He stilled above her, groaning her name as she felt the heat and force of his release jetting hard and deep inside her, each pulse of semen another caress, another stroke of rapture racing across her nerve endings.

Until they were left, limp, ragged, exhausted. Weeks of lack of sleep, of searching separate beds for that single heartbeat, took their toll.

Rolling from her, Graham groaned at the weariness that poured through his body. He pulled her against his chest, tucked her close to him, then his hand moved to stroke and caress her still-slender belly.

"When were you going to tell me?" he asked then, his voice soft, curious.

She froze against him, almost holding her breath as he flattened his palm over their future children.

"What do you mean?"

He had to grin. He couldn't be angry. He'd be damned if he could blame her.

"When, my love, were you going to tell me you were pregnant?"

He let her go as she pulled from him and sat up, turning to stare down at him as he watched her with such a surfeit of emotion that she felt humbled by it.

"How did you know?" she whispered, those emerald green eyes wide, surprised. "I just found out myself. I haven't even told anyone."

"I've known for a while," he revealed, watching her face, seeing the fear that shadowed her eyes now. "Do you think I'm here because of it?" he growled. "Come on, Lyrica . . ."

"I just want to know how you knew." She slapped back the hand that would have stroked over her thigh.

Graham grinned at the move, staring up at her, god, loving her.

"I'll make a deal with you," he suggested.

Her eyes narrowed. "What kind of deal?"

"Marry me, and I'll tell you how I know we're going to have twins. A little boy with a blend of Brock and Mackay looks, and a little girl who's going to be the very image of her mother. If I have to listen to Natches crow over how much she looks like him, then I'm at least going to have a ring on your finger so he can't influence them too much."

She blinked.

Her lips parted, then closed.

"Twins?" She sounded as though she couldn't breathe.

"Twins," he promised. "Marry me, Lyrica. Don't make me sleep alone, without you, again. Don't let me go another day without you in my life."

Tears filled her eyes then. A smile filled her face.

"Tell me how you know it's twins."

He chuckled wickedly. "Not until you say 'I do' . . ."

To which she smiled back at him knowingly. "I'll say 'I do,' but only if you tell me what your mother told you before you left for the Marines."

For a second, surprise glittered in his gaze before it softened. He reached out to brush back the strands of hair that lay at the side of her face.

"How bad do you want to know?" he chuckled then.

"Just tell me," she groaned. "It's been driving me crazy."

His expression gentled then, fond memories reflecting in his eyes as he thought of his mother.

"She told me to make sure I came home safe, with my soul intact," he said softly. "Because without the soul, the heart can't survive. And if I didn't understand what that meant, then I would understand the first time I stared into the eyes of the woman who would hold my heart. And she was right. That first summer I met you, Lyrica. Standing on that dock at the marina, staring at me with equal parts innocence and a woman's knowledge, I felt you sink inside me like sunlight. But I knew even then, sweetheart, it wasn't time. Not for me. Not for you. When the time came, I was just too stubborn, and too damned terrified of how much you meant to me, to realize it."

"I always loved you, Graham," she whispered. "I always will."

"You're my life." And she saw it in his eyes, in his expression. "Without you, I'd never be complete."

He would be in a world without color, alone, staring into a void.

With her, he was all he was meant to be.

He was meant to be hers.

EPILOGUE

August - One month later

Zoey Mackay sat at the edge of the water as the small waves lapped at the bank, mere inches from her bare feet. With her legs bent, her arms wrapped around them, her chin resting atop her knees, she watched as the sun began to descend along the top of the mountains surrounding her brother Dawg's home.

She could hear the voices behind her, many raised in laughter as the Mackay family, relations, and friends came together. The family reunion grew every year. And it seemed to last longer every year as well.

Dawg's sprawling backyard was filled. Tables laid out with every food imaginable, the smell of hot dogs grilling, the sound of children playing in the pool rather than romping in the shallow water close to the bank, echoed around her.

The pool was safer for the kids, Dawg had remarked.

Not to mention a hell of a lot cleaner.

It was the usual sounds of the Mackay yearly get-together, and once again, Zoey found herself on the outside looking in.

She'd been on the outside looking in since they'd arrived in Somerset. Never quite comfortable. Never quite certain when her past would catch up with her, when it would destroy her life and hurt everyone she loved.

She'd tried, she thought. She'd tried to fix it, but the price had been far too high. She couldn't fix one betrayal by creating another, could she? She couldn't betray her brother, her cousins. Her sisters. That was the price of freedom, and realizing that she couldn't pay that price was destroying her.

"Hey, munchkin. What are you doing out here by yourself?" The question came as bare feet stepped up beside her, the ragged edge of a pair of men's jeans brushing against the sand.

"Nothing. Just watching the sun set." She moved to get up.

"Please don't, Zoey." Dawg touched her shoulder as he moved to sit next to her, his larger body dwarfing hers. "Here, have a beer."

He extended the chilled bottle as Zoey turned to him warily.

"Thank you." Accepting the bottle, she turned back to the lake and took a sip before sitting it on the sand next to the nearly full beer her cousin Natches had given her earlier. That bottle was sitting next to the soft drink Rowdy had brought her.

What was up with all the drinks anyway?

"You know," he sighed, long minutes later, "when you and your sisters first arrived at the marina, I had a second I wished Chandler was still breathing so I could kill him myself. Especially when I saw you. All that wariness and fear in your eyes . . ."

"Do we really need to go over this, Dawg?" She sighed. "We're here, we're safe. It's over."

That usually managed to get him to back off. At least for a few months.

"Yes we do, little girl, and by god, this time you can give me the courtesy of looking at me while I'm talking to you," he ordered, his tone lowering, darkening, causing her to jerk around and stare at him in surprise.

This was not the gentle giant she was used to. Dawg never spoke sharply to his sisters. Ever.

"What did I do?" She frowned back at him.

Dawg wiped his hand over his face before staring back at her, the firm, commanding look giving way to a loving exasperation that always made her feel as though she had no chance of measuring up.

"You didn't come to me," he answered then, and for a second she saw a flash of pain in his eyes. "Even your sisters come to me when they need me. But when it was important, you didn't do that, Zoey."

God, no. He couldn't know. There was no way he knew.

She jumped to her feet, aware that he was moving just as quickly. So quickly that as she moved to rush past him, he still managed to get to his feet and catch her by her arm. Gently.

"Let me go." Pushing the words past clenched teeth as she refused to look at him, Zoey fought back the anger, the betrayal she'd kept a handle on for four years now.

"Why didn't you come to me, Zoey?" he questioned her, the command in his tone once again. "Why didn't you tell me what was going on instead of hating us . . ."

"Is that what you think?" Jerking away, she turned on him, anger still a force that raged through her with such strength she had no idea how to contain it sometimes. "Do you think I hated you, that I blamed you somehow?"

Confusion flickered across his expression. "I would have helped . . ."

She laughed, a broken, bitter sound that caused her brother to flinch. "What would you have done, Dawg? What do you think you could have done?"

"Zoey, what have we done to you?" He gentled then. Reaching out, he pushed back a heavy fall of curls that trailed down the side of her face, until he could meet her gaze fully. "What have we done, baby sister, to make you think we'd not protect you?"

She trembled at the question. She couldn't stop the tears that filled her eyes or those that overflowed to run down her cheeks.

"I love all of you," she tried to reassure him. "You haven't done anything. Nothing is your fault."

"Why not tell him what you did, Zoey?"

Dawg jerked around, dragging her behind him as his big body blocked hers from the sight of the man stepping from the tree line.

Elegant. So handsome he made her heart break every time she saw him. The one man she'd prayed she could avoid just a little while longer.

The day of reckoning was here though. She couldn't hide from it any longer. She couldn't fight it any longer.

He may have betrayed her. He may have lied to her in the worst possible way, but it was her fault. She had no one else to blame.

"I'm so sorry," she whispered at Dawg's back, laying her forehead against him as a sob tore through her. "I'm so sorry, Dawg."

"Doogan, what the fuck are you doing here?" The sound of his voice was savage, like a predator determined to protect its offspring.

"Ask your sister, Dawg," Doogan's voice was quiet, intent. "Ask her why I'm here."

"Dawg, do we have a problem?" Natches asked the question.

"Doogan, this is a family party," Rowdy stated calmly. "You weren't invited."

"And you're sure as hell not family," Timothy, the man she often wished had been her father, stated with that razor edge of innate arrogance he always carried whenever he felt his family was being threatened in some way.

"Thank god," Doogan drawled then, the amusement in his tone causing her to shake. He was at his most dangerous now, his most cunning. "Why not tell them why I'm here, Zoey? Or are you going to force me to do it?"

"No." Pushing away from Dawg she forced herself out from behind him, trying to move in front of him, trying to stop the tide of destruction before it began. "Stop this," she demanded, anger raging through her now, shaking so hard now she wondered how she was still standing. "Don't do this, Doogan. Don't turn this into a war."

"Natches." Dawg's tone was the warning. Unfortunately, she wasn't fast enough.

Natches pulled her to him, against his side, holding her firmly as she struggled against him, staring back at Chatham Doogan, begging him silently, knowing it wouldn't do her a damned bit of good.

"Go to the house with Natches, Zoey," Dawg ordered firmly, never taking his eyes off Chatham. "We'll discuss this there."

"Where you can surround me with Mackay males and the agents you so carefully pulled away from me?" Chatham chuckled as though amused by them all. "That was an excellent move by the way, arranging to have my agents fall head over heels for the women they believed they couldn't have. What better bait than to make a man think he can't have a woman he desires? Ah Dawg, you're good. You, Rowdy, and Natches are really good . . ."

"Better than you know," Natches assured him as Zoey stopped struggling, shocked by her cousin's declaration. "Good enough to have already figured out exactly what you're doing here and why Zoey was terrified to come to us when she realized she was in trouble."

"Really?" Chatham drawled. "And why is that?"

Zoey shook her head slowly, holding his gaze, bitter, hollow rage destroying her from the inside out.

He was destroying her and he knew it. He would destroy her and her family and there was nothing she could do to stop it.

"Get the hell out of Somerset, Doogan," Tim demanded then. "Don't turn this into a fight. It's one you won't win and you know it. Not against me."

Chatham smiled. "Perhaps, perhaps not." His gaze never left hers.

"You know this is wrong." Helpless, desperate, she knew begging wouldn't help. Doogan would only see weakness in a plea. "We had a deal . . ."

"But you reneged on your side, sweetheart," he stepped forward slowly, his gaze pinning her, forcing her to remember, forcing her to make a choice.

"I didn't renege," she all but screamed back at him, hating him, hating herself more. "You lied to me, Doogan. You lied."

"Don't do it, Doogan," Dawg warned him softly. "You'll regret it."

Chatham only stared back at her mercilessly. "Zoey Mackay, you're under arrest for the murder of Harley Perdue . . ."

Then all hell broke loose.